TRAPPED

Other Eos Titles by
James Alan Gardner

EXPENDABLE
COMMITMENT HOUR
VIGILANT
HUNTED
ASCENDING

JAMES ALAN GARDNER

TRAPPED

An Imprint of HarperCollins*Publishers*

This is a work of fiction. Names, characters, places, and incidents are products of the author's imagination or are used fictitiously and are not to be construed as real. Any resemblance to actual events, locales, organizations, or persons, living or dead, is entirely coincidental.

EOS
An Imprint of HarperCollins*Publishers*
10 East 53rd Street
New York, New York 10022-5299

To the writers of the Wooden Whale

*And to friend and former roommate
Larry Hackman, who gave me the
gloomy tag-line*

And, looking back at what had promised to be our own unique, unpredictable, and dangerous adventure, all we find in the end is such a series of standard metamorphoses as men and women have undergone in every quarter of the world, in all recorded centuries, and under every odd disguise of civilization.

JOSEPH CAMPBELL, *The Hero with a Thousand Faces*

Were Niagara but a cataract of sand, would you travel your thousand miles to see it?

HERMAN MELVILLE, *Moby Dick*

(Yes, Mr. Melville, I would. A cataract of sand, especially one the size of Niagara Falls, would be mind-bogglingly cool.)

The best is the enemy of the good.

VOLTAIRE

Acknowledgments

Thanks to Khalid Shaukat for calculating the Islamic date. Thanks to A. A. Milne for Zunctweed. Thanks to Howard Gardner (no relation) for his theory of multiple intelligences, reflected here in aspects of the way psionic powers work. Thanks to John McMullen and Anton Kostechne for creative uses of nanotechnology. Thanks to Derwin Mak for winning the auction and dying so colorfully. Thanks to Linda Carson, Richard Curtis, and Jennifer Brehl for the usual editorial advice.

Death Hotel really exists, and I'm glad I got the chance to put it into a story. My only regret is that I couldn't work in one other tidbit about the Hotel: it sits close to a pioneer cemetery with a special gate designed to prevent witches from stealing corpses. Two hundred years ago, witches were supposedly incapable of turning sharp corners, so the gate forced people to turn sharply several times on their way in or out.

It must have been a great annoyance to pallbearers.

TRAPPED

1

THE POT OF GOLD

It began, as many things do, in a tavern: about eight o'clock on a Friday evening, in The Pot of Gold on Post-Hoc Lane in Simka. Contrary to its end-of-the-rainbow name, The Pot of Gold was a dreary blood-clot of a place—the sort of vomitous swill-hole where the lamps had to be locked in wire cages to prevent drunks from swigging the kerosene, where the tapman's only insurance policy was a trio of flintlock pistols worn on a grease-smudged bandoleer, and where the Steel Caryatid squashed a cockroach <BANG> with her tankard before asking, "Why would anyone go on a quest?"

"For glory," said Sir Pelinor.

"For God," said Sister Impervia.

"For kicks," said Myoko Namida.

"For Gretchen Kinnderboom," said I, "provided the task didn't take too much effort, and Gretchen promised to be extravagantly grateful."

The Caryatid slapped my foot (which was propped on the table beside her). "Be serious, Phil," she told me. "I'm talking about real, honest-to-goodness quests, not trotting down to Dover-on-Sea to fetch peach-scented soap."

I sat up straighter. "They've got a new supply of peach-scented soap?"

"Vanity, vanity," murmured Sister Impervia, whose own taste in soap could be described as "The more lye, the better."

1

"We're talking about quests," said the Caryatid, "and I don't understand why a sane person would go on one. Not that anyone at this table qualifies as sane."

Sir Pelinor sucked on his mustache, producing a wheezy, bubbling sound that was amusing the first time I heard it, irritating the next dozen times, totally maddening the three hundred times after that, and now a source of complete indifference. "Depends what you call a quest," he said. "Suppose a village hereabouts was having trouble with a largish animal—a bear, perhaps, or a cougar. I wouldn't call it insane to gather a few friends and go hunt down the beast."

"Especially," Myoko added, "if the villagers offered a reward."

"Or suppose," Sister Impervia said, "a gang of heathen bandits stole St. Judith's jawbone from the academy chapel. Wouldn't we be honorbound to organize a party and retrieve the saint's remains?"

The Caryatid made a face. "Those aren't quests, they're errands. You'd leave such business to the town watch . . . if Simka *had* a real town watch, instead of Whisky Jess and the Paunch That Walks Like a Man. I'm not talking about junkets to the countryside, I mean real live quests."

"What qualifies as a real live quest?" Myoko asked. "Finding the Holy Grail? Slaying the Jabberwock?"

"Saw a Jabberwock once," Sir Pelinor said with another mustache-suck. "Rusty mechanical thing in the remains of an OldTech amusement park. Four hundred years ago, parents paid for their kiddies to ride its back. No wonder OldTech society collapsed—if *I'd* seen that monster when I was a child, I wouldn't have slept again till I was twenty."

"I don't care about your Jabberwock," the Caryatid said. "I don't care about quests at all."

"Then why," Myoko asked, "do you keep talking about them?"

"Because," the Caryatid answered, staring moodily at the cockroach guts on the table, "this afternoon I had a sort of a prophecy kind of thing."

"Uh-oh," said the other four of us in unison . . . even Sister

Impervia, who's theologically obliged to treat prophecies as Precious Gifts From Heaven. We all knew the Caryatid had flashes of second sight; alas, her gift of prophecy only raised its head when something really ugly was about to happen.

I won't bother you with the full story of how the Caryatid got this way, but here's the gist: twenty years ago, when she still had a normal name and was doing her bachelor's in thaumaturgy, the Caryatid got shanghaied into a necromantic experiment run by a grad student. Like most sorcerous projects, this one required a long disgusting ritual . . . and partway through a procedure involving two tubs of lard and a hand-puppet, the grad student lost his nerve and ran shrieking from the room. Our friend Caryatid managed to slide off the pony and shut down the calliope before she could be incinerated by eldritch forces; but the experience gave her a serious sunburn and an incurable case of the premonitions.

Personally, I have nothing against premonitions if they provide useful information about the future . . . like whether your partner has a stopper in spades, or if Gretchen Kinnderboom will be in a forthcoming mood two weekends hence. But the Caryatid never foresaw anything helpful; she only perceived disasters, and then only when it was too late to avert them.

An illustrative example: at Feliss Academy's most recent staff party, all of us teachers had just finished dinner when a trout skeleton on the Caryatid's plate proclaimed, "You're sure going to regret eating me." The entire faculty rose as one, hied ourselves to the closest commode, and desperately stuck our fingers down our throats. Alas, to no avail—everyone from the chancellor down to the lowest lecturer in Latin literature succumbed to a dose of the trots.

If the Caryatid had received another vision of the future, the only sensible response was bowel-chilling dread. We therefore sat in clenched silence for at least a count of ten before anyone mustered the nerve to speak. Finally, it was Pelinor who ventured to ask the obvious: "So, er . . . what did this sort of a prophecy kind of thing say?"

"Well . . ." The Caryatid kept her gaze on the crushed cockroach rather than making eye contact with the rest of us. "I was in the lab cleaning up after Freshman Class 4A—"

"May they burn in hell for eternity," Sister Impervia said.

We looked at her curiously.

"It's book report week," she explained.

We all said, "Ahh!"

"I was cleaning up after Freshman 4A," the Caryatid resumed, "and I peeked into the crucible of Two-Jigger Volantés . . . you know him?"

We nodded. I had no direct acquaintance with the unfortunate Mr. Volantés, but word gets around. The Freshman collective unconscious had appointed Two-Jigger the Official Class Goat—the brunt of their jokes, the person nobody sat with at mealtimes, and the one whose underclothes were most often on display atop the school's flag pole.

"So what I found in the crucible," continued the Caryatid, "was what I call Goat Stew. Someone always convinces the Class Goat you can make an infallible love potion from eye of newt and toe of frog, wool of bat and tongue of dog . . . the whole Scottish formula. Let me tell you, that does *not* make a love potion."

"What does it make?" asked Pelinor.

"Blind newts, lame frogs, cold bats, and a cocker spaniel who makes god-awful sucking sounds when he's trying to drink from his dish. So I'm staring at this mess when suddenly the newt's eye turns my way. Then the dog's tongue says, *You're going on a quest.*"

"Do dogs have deep voices?" Pelinor asked. "I've always wondered. It stands to reason a Chihuahua would have a higher voice than a bloodhound, but if you got, say, a male Doberman and a female, would the male be a bass and the female an alto? Or would they both be baritones?"

"This particular dog was a tenor," said the Caryatid. "I don't know its breed or gender. So it told me—"

"Did it have an accent?" Pelinor asked.

"No," the Caryatid snapped. "And it had flawless diction, even though it didn't have lips or a larynx, all right? It told me, *You're going on a quest*. I said, *What kind of quest?* and it answered, *A dangerous one*. I asked, *Why on Earth would I go on a dangerous quest?* It said, *Hey, lady, I may be a talking dog tongue, but I'm no mindreader.*"

"Don't you just hate it," Myoko murmured, "when animal parts get uppity?"

"So," the Caryatid went on, "I say, *What's this quest about?* The tongue tells me, *Love, courage, meaning . . . the usual*. A lot of good that does me. *Details*, I say, *give me details!* The tongue wiggles around like a long strip of bacon, then finally gasps out, *Future cloudy: ask again later.*"

"That was the end?" Myoko asked.

"I thought so," the Caryatid said. "But as I set down the crucible, a piece of chalk flew into the air and scrawled on the blackboard, *Your friends have to go too.*"

Myoko and I groaned. Pelinor and Impervia exercised more restraint, but both showed noticeable bulges around their jaws as their teeth clenched. "Well," said Pelinor after a few moments' silence, "a quest, eh? What jolly fun."

We all glared at him. None of us truly believed his "knight of the realm" persona—rumor had it he was a retired corporal from the Feliss border patrol, and he'd faked both his résumé and his accent to get the cushy post of academy armsmaster. Still, he did his job well . . . and one had to admire the way he gamely kept up the facade of being a sword-sworn crusader. "Never fret," he told us, "a little adventure is just the thing to chase away our winter blues: battling monsters, righting wrongs . . ."

"Finding lost treasure . . ." Myoko added.

"Doing God's work . . ." Impervia put in.

"And perhaps impressing Gretchen Kinnderboom," I finished. "Won't that be ducky."

The Caryatid sighed. "If nothing else, maybe we'll be too busy slaying dragons to proctor final exams."

"I'll drink to that!" Myoko said, her face cheering up. "To our quest—may it get us out of promotion meetings."

All five of us clanked cups and tankards with exaggerated enthusiasm . . . trying to pretend we weren't terrified.

* * *

"Why are you so goddamned happy?" growled a voice from the door.

We turned. Three burly gentlemen had just entered, accompanied by the pungent odor of rancid fish—probably boat workers who'd docked at Dover-on-Sea and headed straight to Simka because of our higher quality night life (i.e., ladies of the evening who still looked female after they'd removed their clothes). These particular fishermen had already sampled copious liquid refreshment at other drinking holes, judging by the volume of their voices and the way they slurred their words.

"I'm afraid," said Myoko, "it's hard to explain the reason for our toast."

" 'It's hard to explain,' " the most voluble fisherman repeated, mimicking her voice and accent. "You come from that goddamned school, don't you?"

"We're teachers there, yes."

The talkative fisherman sneered. "So you sit around all day, kissing the arses of rich goddamned thumbsuckers who think they're too good for a normal school."

Sister Impervia pushed back her chair. "That is three times you've said 'goddamned.' The clergy occasionally debate whether such talk is truly blasphemous or simply vulgar, but they're universally agreed it's ignorant and rude."

"Are you calling me ignorant and rude?"

"Also drunk and smelly," Impervia said.

The tapman behind the bar removed a flintlock from his bandoleer and thumbed back the hammer. "Closing time," he announced.

"What the hell?" said the fisherman.

"The bar owner says to close this time every night."

"What time?"

"Thirty seconds before the fight." The tapman pointed his pistol at the newcomers. "We reopen thirty seconds after. Come back if you're still on your feet."

"*If!*" The head fisherman looked at the five of us, then emitted what would be called a Hearty Guffaw by anyone who didn't disdain words like Hearty. And Guffaw. "These pantywaists," the man said, "will fall down if I breathe on them."

"Quite possibly," Impervia replied. "On the other hand, we have little to fear from your fists."

"Out," said the tapman. "Now."

We complied, taking a roundabout route to the door so we didn't pass within arm's reach of the fishermen. In the doorway, Impervia turned back to the tapman. "Could you please make more tea while we're gone? We'll be back before it's cold."

The lead fisherman made a belligerent sound and blustered angrily after us.

The odds were five against three in our favor, so I strode out to Post-Hoc Lane without too much trepidation. Alas, the spring in my step turned to icy black winter as soon as I reached the cold cobblestones. By the light of the block's single streetlamp, I saw seven more fishermen weaving toward us: six of them human, one not.

The nonhuman was a half-height yellow alien, mostly hominid-shaped but with tangerinelike spheres on the top of his head in lieu of *Homo sapiens* ears. He belonged to one of the Divian subspecies, but I couldn't tell which—I've never been an expert on extraterrestrials. Suffice it to say, this fellow was yet another descendant of spacefarers who FTLed in to exploit our planet after OldTech civilization collapsed, and who got trapped here when the Spark Lords put Earth into lockdown. Since then, all aliens had come to be called "demons" . . . or more accurately, "slaves." The ET coming toward us was probably owned by one of the other fishermen, or perhaps by the captain of their boat; there were plenty of slave-aliens in the Dover fishing fleet, and many of them fit in so well they were allowed to go drinking with the rest of the crew.

So the Divian and his six buddies tottered drunkenly down the street. Add in the three from the tavern, and that made the odds ten-to-five against us. "I think we just got outnumbered," I said.

"Maybe," Myoko whispered, "that bunch are from a rival

fishing boat and they'll side with us against these other lollies."

"Hey, are you calling us lollies?" shouted a keen-eared someone at our backs.

"What's that?" yelled the Divian, clearly one of the boys even if he was a slave. "Something wrong there, Nathan?"

"Nothing wrong," replied the most outspoken man behind us. "We just got some eggheads to crack."

The new group roared their approval. "Goddamned time we found a fight in this town! They insult you, Nathan?"

"They sure did," answered the one called Nathan. "They didn't like the smell of fish."

"To be accurate," said Impervia, "I have nothing against the smell of fish. It was *your* odor I found objectionable."

Myoko sighed. "That line *Blessed are the peacemakers* went right over your head, didn't it, Impervia."

Before the good sister could answer, Nathan loosed a mighty bellow and charged straight at her.

Given that I haven't described Impervia, you might be picturing her as some elderly antique: the sort of wizened gray-haired woman who gravitates to the teaching profession for the love of smacking young knuckles with a ruler. Nothing could be further from the truth . . . except the part about smacking knuckles. Impervia was twenty-six and as lean as a bullwhip, with black skin and blacker hair shaved within a millimeter of her scalp. Between classes, she had a fondness for dropping behind her desk and doing one-armed push-ups until the next bell rang.

Impervia's Holy Order claimed to be spiritual descendants of the Shaolin monks, those soft-speaking folks who gave the world kung fu. I suspected this claim was false; for one thing, the Shaolins were Buddhist while Impervia was a Handmaid of the Magdalene. (Basically Christian, but with some exotic notions about Mary Magdalene being "purified" by Jesus and thereafter divine herself: the Trinity's *Spirita Sancta*.) More likely, the early Magdalenes thought the Shaolin name would give them added credibility, so they invented a fictitious lineage tracing their sect back to China. I judged this more probable than any genuine historical connection . . . but I never told Impervia I doubted her kung fu heritage. Whether she was true Shaolin or not, she could still kick a bull's testicles straight through its body and out the ring on its nose.

This explains why none of us tried to help the good sister as bull-like Nathan charged forward. In fact, we retreated to give Impervia more room. I planted my back against the door of a chandler's shop across the street and prepared to contribute to the fight by playing referee.

Impervia met the fisherman's charge in a businesslike kickboxing pose, fists up, chin down: no showy Crane-stance/Dragon-stance nonsense when she had real opponents to scuttle. She wore loose black clothing and black leather gloves—the gloves protected her against winter's cold, but also against getting her hands carved up in forceful collisions with an opponent's teeth. Nathan, in contrast, had no special fighting outfit, and attacked like a man who was

(a) drunk; and
(b) experienced only in fighting other drunks.

As a result, he took a single clumsy swipe at our friend: an ill-defined move that might have been a punch, a slap, or an attempt to grab her throat. Impervia sidestepped and smartly tossed a jab to the man's nose, a palm-heel to his floating ribs, and a full-force stomp on his foot. Not surprisingly, Nathan fell to the cobblestones, with nothing more than a grunting gulp. It was only two seconds later that he began howling obscenities.

"Why doesn't she ever try a good hard knee to the groin?" Myoko asked, slipping into the doorway beside me.

"She says it's overrated," I replied. "First, it's not the guaranteed man-dropper everyone believes—many men can shrug off the pain, especially under the influence of drink, dope, or adrenaline. Second, experienced bar brawlers often stuff their crotches with padding before they go to the pub; they *intend* to get into fights, so they protect the family jewels. Third, a groin attack is the only fighting maneuver a man can block instinctively. It takes practice to cope with a punch to one's face, but every male in the world has a built-in reflex to avoid getting kicked in the balls."

"What an education Impervia is," Myoko said admiringly.

At that moment, Impervia was educating the other two men who'd accompanied Nathan into the tavern. One of these men learned what it felt like to have an ax kick fracture his collarbone; the other came to a greater understanding of how a fist to the solar plexus can paralyze the nerves required for breathing. The kicked man staggered back cursing, but the recipient of the gut punch simply dropped to the pavement making surprised little wheezes.

Impervia's speed, skill, and strength also made an impression on the remaining seven fishermen—her flying fists looked like blurs. Then again, even a snail might have struck that group as blurry: all seven had reached the stumblebum stage of intoxication, and I think they knew it. No doubt they still felt obliged to help their friends, but none wanted to be first into the fray.

While those at the front of the fisherman pack hesitated, I caught sight of a metallic glint somewhere to the rear. The globe-eared Divian had pulled out a big fancy broadsword he must have had sheathed down his back. "Blade!" I shouted. "The alien's got a sword."

"On my way," Pelinor said.

Pelinor, of course, had a sword of his own. Pelinor also had armor, though he wasn't wearing it at the moment—one doesn't wander the back streets of Simka dressed up for a coronation. If, however, a coronation spontaneously broke out, Pelinor's room on the far side of town held enough arms and armor to equip a complete honor guard. In his decades of wandering as a knight errant (or more likely, impounding contraband on our province's border and keeping the best for himself), our school armsmaster had amassed an eclectic assortment of war-toys: everything from curare-tipped blow-darts to a slightly dented Sig-Sauer P-220 autoloader . . . sans bullets, alas, but still quite splendid for administering an effective pistol-whip.

Tonight, Pelinor carried a simple cutlass—heavy as a

meat cleaver but with a lot more reach . . . in case you wanted to chop pork from a distance. The pork in question (i.e., the Divian) shoved past his comrades and prepared to thrust his sword at Impervia; but before the blade could strike home, Pelinor's cutlass was there, slapping away the weapon with a loud metallic clank.

"A true swordsman doesn't attack an unarmed opponent," Pelinor said. "A true swordsman tests his mettle against an evenly matched foe."

The Divian just blinked at those words, his eyelids flicking from the bottom up instead of top down. Perhaps on his home-planet far across the galaxy, nature had never evolved the concept of "fair fight." His species might be more at home with the "leap from the shadows, stab in the back" school of combat. Still, the Divian collected himself with commendable speed and made a tentative stab in Pelinor's direction.

Even *I* could see it was a graceless attack; the alien held his weapon awkwardly, as if he'd never used it before. Perhaps he was hampered by the decorative fripperies on the sword's pommel—a profusion of braid and curlicues that must have interfered with getting a good grip. It looked more like a ceremonial weapon than a practical tool in rough-and-tumble situations. A cynic might even suspect the sword had been acquired under questionable circumstances, by mugging a wealthy merchant or drawing a hidden ace out of a shirt cuff. The weapon looked too ornate and expensive for an ET slave to own legitimately.

But no matter how the Divian got his sword, Pelinor parried the attack easily, exactly the way he did when facing a freshman who couldn't tell her quarte from her quinte. "Slant your blade slightly upward," our armsmaster said. "See how easily <CLANG> I can knock the sword down <WHANG> if you don't keep up the tip? <BANG> That's right, just a little tilt. No too much, though, or I can bap the blade back into your . . . <TWANG> Sorry, did I hit your nose?"

Pelinor had clearly ensured he *didn't* hit the alien's nose. He'd given his cutlass an extra twist so the Divian's weapon would turn and slap with the flat of the blade. This was, after all, a bar fight with drunks, and neither Impervia nor Pelinor wanted to dole out life-threatening injuries. Therefore, Pelinor used some quick flicking strikes to separate the sword-wielding extraterrestrial from the rest of his fellows, making it less likely the others would get accidentally nicked.

This left Impervia with nine opponents, three of whom were already nursing wounds while the remaining six wobbled half a beer short of passing out. It was now an even contest . . . barely. Six against one made for hefty odds, even when the six were staggery-sloppily stewed.

You must understand one crucial point: Impervia was undoubtedly faster and tougher than your average lager lout, but she was, in the end, just a schoolteacher. Not a professional fighter. Not an elite commando. Not even a third-order Magdalene, one of those select women within her sisterhood who were trained for "specialized" assignments. Impervia was only impressive when compared to untrained oafs—against topnotch champions, she was barely an also-ran.

There is, alas, a heartbreaking gap between the Good and the Best. As many of us have realized to our sorrow.

Even against drunken fishermen, Impervia was not a sure-fire winner. She almost never finished one of these Friday-night brawls without an eye swollen shut, a few cracked ribs, or a dislocated shoulder. Twice, she'd been battered unconscious before the rest of us could intervene. One had to wonder why she kept provoking these scuffles when she often got the worst of them; but she'd never opened up about her inner demons, and the rest of us didn't pry. We simply crossed our fingers and hoped she never truly got in over her head.

At the moment, it was the fishermen who believed they were out of their depth. The uninjured six stayed bunched together, blearily waiting for someone to make the first move. Finally the man on the ground, Nathan, shouted, "Get going, you fuckwits! The lot of you! Just pile onto her!"

The fisherfolk looked at each other, then shuffled reluctantly forward.

Impervia leapt to meet them. The man she reached first went down under a fast jab to the jaw followed by a teeth-cracking uppercut. In other circumstances, he would have toppled back; but his friends were behind him, still moving forward. Accidentally or intentionally, they shoved the man's semiconscious body toward the good sister, giving it a good hard push. She tried to dodge, but didn't quite get out of the way—the dazed man thudded into her shoulder like a dead-weight sack of flour and Impervia was spun half-sideways, ending with her back to three of the attackers.

She realized her danger and snapped out a low donkey kick: not even looking at the men behind her, just lifting her foot and driving it backward, hoping to discourage anyone from coming too close. One man groaned, "Shit!" and crumpled, clutching his leg . . . but the other two blundered forward, one cuffing the back of Impervia's head while the other seized her arm. She tried to wrench away from the man who'd grabbed her, throwing a distraction kick at his ankles to make him loosen his grip. By then, however, the men in front were attacking too—one with a punch to the face that she managed to diminish by jerking away her head, and one with a fist to the gut that she didn't diminish at all. The breath whooshed out of her as she was lifted off her feet by the blow. A second later, she flopped to the cobblestones.

"Myoko!" I shouted, "do something!" But Myoko, still in the doorway by my side, was already on the job: staring at Impervia with intense concentration, her hands clenched tight into fists.

Unlike Impervia, Myoko didn't look dangerous. Though she was almost thirty, she could pass for fifteen: barely four foot eight and slender, with waterfall-straight black hair that hung to her thighs, always pulled back from her face with two ox-bone barrettes. At the academy, outsiders mistook her for a student—perhaps the daughter of a minor daimyo, a quiet schoolgirl destined for flower arranging and calligraphy. But Myoko was neither quiet nor a schoolgirl . . . and if she ever wanted to arrange flowers, she could do it at a distance of twenty paces by sheer force of will.

Much as I wanted to keep my eye on Impervia—twisting and writhing across the cobblestones as the fishermen threw clumsy kicks at her—I couldn't help be distracted by the movement of Myoko's hair as her concentration increased.

Individual strands began to separate from the long straight whole, lifting up like puppet strings. In less than three seconds, all the ends splayed out from each other, fanning wide into the air. As a man of science, I assumed the effect came from static electricity; but the electrical charge was created by a source far more esoteric than the Van de Graaff generator we'd used to do the same trick back in college.

With a sudden lurch, Sister Impervia's body heaved off the ground and rose into the air. The tips of Myoko's hair lifted too, curling up like a counterbalance . . . and I told myself perhaps Myoko's brand of telekinesis *needed* the curling hair to produce counteracting leverage.

What, after all, did I know about the physics of psionics? Nothing. As a scientist, my only certainty was that psychic powers had been foisted on humankind by outer-space high-tech, courtesy of the ultra-advanced aliens known as the League of Peoples. Before the League visited Earth, psionics were a myth; after the League had passed through, ESP and suchlike abilities became undeniable fact, easily reproduced in the lab (and on the back streets of Simka). No one knew how or why the League had given one human in a thousand such a gift; all we could do was marvel at its effects . . . such as now, when Impervia soared aloft on Myoko's mental hoist, raised high above the mob's clamoring reach.

At first, the fishermen didn't grasp what was happening. One of them actually made a bumbling attempt to leap up and slap Impervia's legs, the way boys jump to tag dangling store signs as they walk down the street. The man missed and thumped heavily to the pavement . . . which seems to have been the moment at which he and his companions realized there was something less than ordinary about a woman levitating above their heads. They fell back open-mouthed, staring up at Impervia as if she were some new celestial object, a sweat-gleaming chunk of dark matter suspended in the night.

"Ahem. Gentlemen?"

The Steel Caryatid stepped from a doorway five paces down the street. She was pale in the lamplight, the sort of Nordic blonde who looks three-quarters albino . . . and like many a sorceress, she wore nothing but a skin-tight crimson body sheath. If that sounds seductive, you're too eager to be seduced. The Caryatid was a big-hipped woman of forty, broad, round, and motherly; ninety percent the kind of mother who bakes the best cookies in the neighborhood, and ten percent the kind who has to be locked in the attic and fed bouillon through a straw.

All the sorcerers I'd known had been that way: a little bit crazy. Or a lot. Maybe it was impossible to learn the craft unless you were slightly divorced from reality; or maybe the things sorcerers did were enough to make a sane person unbalanced. Incantations. Rituals. Attunements. I didn't believe that sorcery was truly supernatural—like psionics, sorcery started working only after the League of Peoples paid their visit to Earth, so "magic" was another type of high-tech in disguise—but even though I knew there had to be a scientific explanation, sorcery and its practitioners could be bone-chillingly creepy.

"Now that my friend is out of reach," the Caryatid told the fishermen, "it's time to say good night. And here's something to light you to bed."

She pulled a match from her sleeve and struck a light on the wall beside her. (The Caryatid possessed an inexhaustible supply of matches; I could almost believe a new box materialized in her pocket whenever an old box ran out.) The match flame flickered in the breeze of the laneway, but after a moment it stabilized.

"Do you like fire?" the Caryatid asked, as if she were speaking to children at storytime. "I don't mean the things fire can do. Do you like fire itself? The look of it. The feel of it." She swept her finger lazily through the flame, just fast enough to avoid getting burned.

None of the fishermen seemed to realize the match was lasting longer than it should. In fact, the men might have been so stupefied at seeing Impervia float overhead, their brains weren't questioning *anything*.

"I like fire," the Caryatid said. "I've always liked it. Some children talk to their dolls; when I was young, I talked to the hearth. It worried my parents . . . but fortunately, one of my schoolteachers realized I didn't have a problem, I had a gift. Something to remember: the right teacher can make *such* a difference."

Far from burning out, the match flame had begun to grow—roughly the size of a big candle now. Off down the street, Sir Pelinor knocked the broadsword from the Divian's hand and kicked the weapon down a storm sewer drain. "Listen to the lady," Pelinor told the alien.

"Fire loves those who love it back," the Caryatid said. "It's very warmhearted." She smiled. I usually liked her smile—it was the comfortable sort of smile you might get from a dowdy maiden aunt—but when the Caryatid had a flame in her hand, her smile could send prickles up my spine.

She swept her finger through the matchlight again. The flame curled like a cat responding to a caress. "Fire is a wild animal—not tame, but willing to befriend those who approach it the right way." One by one, she stuck her fingers into the flame and held them there for a full second; one by one, she removed each finger to show a dab of fire on the fingertip. She smiled girlishly at the fishermen. "They tickle," she said, wiggling the tiny flames. "They're furry."

Several fishermen whispered phrases Impervia would class as ignorant and rude. The words sounded more scared than angry.

"Would you like to meet my friends?" the Caryatid asked. Without waiting for an answer, she bent to the ground and lowered her burning hand as if she were setting down a pet mouse. Each of the flames hopped off a finger and onto the pavement—five small points of light. "Go say hello to the nice men," the Caryatid said.

For a moment, nothing happened. Then all five flames bounced into the air, coming down a pace closer to the fishermen. The Divian squealed and bolted. Pelinor stepped aside and waved good-bye as the alien sped past.

The flames leapt again, another pace closer. Each dot of fire was no bigger than a candle, but the fishermen staggered back, their eyes wide. Three more of them broke from the pack and dashed into the night.

"There's nothing to be afraid of," the Caryatid said. "My friends just want to meet you." The flames took another jump.

That was enough for the remaining fishermen. Clambering over each other, howling in fear, they took to their heels and thundered off down the street . . . all but one. Nathan, sprawled on the pavement, possibly unable to stand because of Impervia's stomp to his foot, screamed one last obscenity and drew a gun from his sleeve.

It was only a tiny pistol, some modern steelsmith's copy of an OldTech Derringer; half those things blew up in their owners' faces within the first ten shots. Still, this was no time for taking chances—Pelinor was way down the street, Myoko had to concentrate on keeping Impervia in the air, and the Caryatid's little flame friends were still several jumps from the fallen fisherman.

Gibbering with terror, Nathan lifted the gun and took shaky aim at the Caryatid.

Making it my turn to act.

My name is Philemon Abu Dhubhai—*Doctor* Dhubhai, thanks to my Ph.D. in mathematical physics. I shan't describe myself except to say I was thirty-five at the time and much too inclined to gloomy introspection. Amongst our band of tavern-teddies, Impervia had muscles, Pelinor had a sword, Myoko had brainpower, the Caryatid had sorcery, and I . . . I had a bulging money-purse. My family was stinking rich; even though I'd put an entire ocean between me and my relatives, they still sent regular pouches of gold so I'd never have to besmirch the Dhubhai name by darning my own socks. Therefore when my friends and I visited the drinking establishments of Simka, I always bought the first round of drinks, tipped the barmaid, and paid for broken windows. My role in bar fights wasn't as glamorous as my companions', but it still came in handy. When all else failed, I could throw money at the problem.

So I heaved my change-purse at the fisherman's head. It

was a big heavy purse, filled with several kilos of coins; I'd used it as a bludgeon more than once. It hit Nathan's face like a blackjack to the nose. The man's hand went limp and the gun clattered to the cobblestones.

I picked up my purse and gave it a fond little squeeze. As usual, the purse was utterly undamaged. It was made from some rubbery black material no one had ever been able to identify—not even back in college, when a chemist friend tried to analyze it. The best he could tell me was, "Airtight, watertight, impervious to all electromagnetic radiation: probably extraterrestrial in origin" . . . which didn't come as a surprise. I'd inherited the purse from my grandmother, who'd received it herself from the Spark Lords. Rumor said the Sparks got a lot of inexplicable trinkets from aliens in the upper echelons of the League of Peoples. For all I knew, the lining of my purse contained billions of fancy nano-devices for curing cancer, breaking the speed of light, and brewing a good cup of coffee. But if such devices existed, I had no idea how to activate them; so I used this wonder from beyond the stars for holding my spare change.

(Welcome to our modern world! Where OldTech computers serve as footstools, while the rusted remains of jumbo jets get converted to beer-halls and brothels.)

As I stuffed the purse back into my pocket, I checked that Fisherman Nathan was still breathing. He was. A trickle of blood seeped out of one nostril, but nothing too alarming. I arranged his unconscious body in the classic Recovery Position, designed to make sure drunks don't choke on their own vomit when they're sleeping off a bender.

"Thanks, Phil," the Caryatid said, coming up behind me. Her five tiny flames flickered excitedly, bouncing in a circle around Nathan's fallen pistol. "Now, now," she told them, "leave that nasty thing alone." She knelt on the pavement and held out her arms to the little fires. "Come here, darlings."

All five flames bounded back to her with the enthusiasm of four-year-olds who want a treat. They leapt into the Caryatid's hands, then bounced up higher, brushed past her face with happy little kisses, and vanished into her hair. The sight made me queasy—I once set my hair on fire in a university chem-lab and still had nightmares about it. But no fire would be so presumptuous as to singe the Caryatid.

"That woman is spooky," Myoko whispered to me.

I rolled my eyes. "Says the person who is holding up Impervia by willpower alone."

"Sorry. Forgot."

Myoko let Impervia drift feet first to the ground.

"Thank you, Myoko," Impervia said, adjusting her clothes with casual briskness . . . or at least attempting to. I couldn't help noticing the good sister winced as she moved; the fishermen had been too drunk to land any truly solid kicks, but there are inevitable cumulative effects of being used as a human soccer ball. Still, Impervia's voice was strong as she told the rest of us, "I found that most invigorating."

"The levitation or the fighting?" I asked.

"Are you suggesting I *enjoy* fighting?"

"I know better," I answered—and I *did* know better than to suggest Impervia enjoyed fighting . . . especially to Impervia's face. "It just seems odd," I said, "how often fights arise in a quiet little town like Simka."

"The Lord provides for his children," Impervia said. "Our Heavenly Father knows my skills would get rusty if they didn't receive constant polishing."

Without another word, she slapped open the door of the tavern and went back inside. As she passed the bar, the tapman handed her a cup of tea. "Longer than usual tonight," he said.

The holy sister sniffed with righteous indignation.

2

A NIGHT IN THE LONESOME ZUL-HIJJAH

My pocket watch said it was one o'clock. In the morning. Under cloudy black skies, I walked up the drive of Feliss Academy, gravel crunching beneath my boots. Alone, alone, all alone—my drinking companions boarded in rooms off campus, and didn't plan on returning to musty F.A. till the weekend was over. I, however, occupied a don's suite in the school's residence wing . . . which is why I was still on my feet, trudging a full kilometer past the town limits, when my friends were already snoring in their beds.

Let me list the pluses of don-ship: cleaning staff emptied my wastebaskets, washed my linen, and occasionally removed the dust coyotes that had long ago devoured the dust bunnies under my bed. Let me also list the minuses: long late liquorized limps from the pub, back to a place where I was required to serve as shepherd, mentor, and surrogate father to twenty teenaged boys, all either wealthy brats, wealthy wallflowers, or wealthy nice-kids whose eyes glazed over at the word "geometry."

The academy seemed peaceful as I approached. The calm was due to the season—in the official calendar of the Spark Lords, it was the Month of the Quill, but in the classic calendar still observed by my family, it was Zul-Hijjah: the ash-end of winter, leaving muddy clumps of snow mixed with snowy clumps of mud all over the school's campus. That night, the vernal equinox was a single day away . . . and while the weather was unlikely to change just because the almanac turned to a new page, I fondly looked forward to the moment I could shout, "Spring, spring, spring!"

Everyone I knew was sick of winter. The students had long ago lost interest in icy midnight frolics (diving naked into snow drifts or stealing trays from the refectory to go tobogganing down the greenhouse hill); every last kid in our dormitory was now a sweaty stick of dynamite, just waiting to explode in spring madness. One breath of warm wind and kaboom, the school grounds would be littered with teenaged bodies, wriggling under every bush, sprawled on the banks of our local creek, or snuggling in more imaginative trysting spots (up a tree, down a storm sewer, on top of the school roof) . . . but for now, it was still too cold, too muddy, and too much the middle of term. As summer approached—as holiday separations loomed, and, "Who knows if we'll both be back in the fall?"—the antics and romantics would sprout behind every bush, and I would . . .

I would . . .

I would seethe with envy at their feverish innocence.

Envy was an occupational hazard of teaching—envy and cynical disdain. Teachers affected by such feelings usually went one of two ways: either they acted like adolescents themselves, or else they viewed youth as a disease that must be cured by heaping doses of tedium. Our academy had plenty of both types in the faculty common room: middle-aged men and women dressed in frowzy imitations of youth fashion sitting cheek by jowl with other middle-aged men and women who ranted about "irresponsible immaturity" and devoted themselves to expunging every particle of teenage joy.

Was I becoming either of those? I fervently hoped not. I'd set my sights on becoming a font of inspiration, guiding young minds and spurring them on to heights of intellectual . . .

Damn. I wasn't drunk enough to believe my usual diatribe. Lately it had become my habit to wax eloquent about

the glories of my career as I tottered home after a session
of poisoning my liver. Some drunks weep about the girls
they left behind; others rage at the girls they didn't leave
behind; still others sing random verses of "The Maiden
and the Hungry Pigboy," or tell (for the fortieth time) about
the night they saw a Spark Lord battle a headless white
alien atop an OldTech skyscraper. When *I* was drunk, I
made speeches to myself: pedantic internal monologues
where I tried to find the perfect words to express why I
hadn't been wasting my life teaching the same classes,
year after year, to kids who'd forget every lesson the moment they graduated.

My goodness, what an important job teaching was! How
crucial for students to know someone like me, levelheaded
but possessed of a sense of fun, a man of science, a role
model! How especially vital it was to enlighten *these* children, the sons and daughters of privilege, the future leaders
of the world!

But I wasn't sufficiently soused tonight to believe my own
propaganda. The words I habitually recited to myself kept
getting confused with the truth: that I'd fallen into teaching
because I had nothing better to do, that I did an acceptable
job but not an extraordinary one, and that the whole student
body of Feliss Academy consisted of rich second-raters who
wouldn't recognize excellence if it bit them on the silk-
covered ass.

Take the Caryatid's Freshman 4A. All showed a modest
talent for sorcery, but none had the drive and obsession to
get into a genuine school of wizardry. Perhaps one among
them would surprise us; perhaps some formerly feckless
freshman would catch fire (so to speak) and go on to more
intense pursuits. The majority, however, would return un-
changed to their wealthy families, bearing with them a few
cheap parlor tricks, plus a handful of disconnected facts
that got lodged in their brains by accident and stayed behind like slivers under the skin. (A former student once
wrote me, asking for help on a question that was "driving
him wild": he could remember $F = ma$ because I'd harped

on it so much in class, but for the life of him, he couldn't recall what **F, m**, or **a** was.)

That was the type of student who came to Feliss . . . and
we teachers weren't much better. To return to Freshman 4A:
if the students were dullards, the Caryatid herself was only a
step above them on the ladder, a humble drudge compared to
any working sorcerer. She grasped the basic principles and
could present them in ways a teenager might understand; but
she was the first to admit she wasn't moon-mad enough to
practice magic for anyone more demanding than Two-Jigger
Volantés.

I wasn't moon-mad either. My curse was to have a docu-
mentedly high intelligence—back in college, I scored 168 on
an OldTech IQ test—but I was utterly devoid of genius. I
could get good grades in any academic subject, but apart
from answering exam questions, I hadn't a clue what to do
with myself.

Music? I could play, compose, and improvise on half a
dozen instruments . . . but I didn't yearn to fill the world with
glorious sound, I just futzed about writing funny songs, hoping I might someday impress a good-looking woman out of
her petticoats. Poetry? When depressed about the failure of
the aforesaid songs to woo the aforesaid women, I could ink
up the page with my woes . . . but they were such *humdrum*
woes: whiny pedestrian bitching, not deep outcries from a
passionate heart. (My immune system seems to produce
highly effective antibodies against angst.) And science? I
never got less than top marks in math, physics, or chemistry,
but when it came to original research, my mind went blank.
There was nothing I wanted to do, no realm of knowledge I
hungered to explore. I digested textbook after textbook, but
lacked the drive and vocation to aim my life toward any
thought-worthy goal.

Lots of brains but no special calling. All dressed up with
no place to go.

So after I got my Ph.D. (on a thesis topic suggested by my
tutor, regurgitating an OldTech treatise that applied pro-
jective geometry techniques to modeling the asymptotic be-

havior of relativistic space-times . . . in other words, sheer
mental masturbation), I fell into a job teaching at Feliss
Academy. Specifically, I was hired to teach the woefully elementary tidbits of science that were still relevant four hundred years after OldTech civilization had spluttered out, plus
a survey course on all the things we couldn't do anymore—
computers, rocketry, bioengineering, nuclear fusion, organ
transplants, mass production, heavier-than-air flight. Ye
Olde Wonders of Earth and Sky. Students approached the
subject as a not-very-interesting branch of mythology,
barely more credible than Gilgamesh, Sinbad, and the
Twelve Labors of Hercules. Thus I spoon-fed teenage
drudges the same material, term after term, year after year,
while visiting backstreet taverns each weekend in the hope
Impervia would start a fight and get my heart beating faster
for a minute or two.

As my willfully morose college roommate used to say,
"So it's come to this. And hasn't it been a long way down?"

The fastest way to the residence wing was a shortcut through
the school itself—the building was shaped like a four-storied
T, with classrooms forming the front crossbar and dormitories extending out the back. I used my pass key to unlock the
doors at the center of the T . . . and the moment I passed inside, I heard the sound of weeping. Quiet little sniffles,
welling up into tightly choked sobs. They echoed off the
walls and terrazzo floors so I couldn't tell where the whim-
pers came from.

Hmmm.

A corridor of classrooms ran left and right; a short passageway lay directly ahead, leading into the dorm wing. But
the whole area was pitch-black . . . no light except the spill
of starshine coming through the glass doors behind me.
Since I never carried a lantern on drinking nights (best not to
be holding breakable glass filled with flammable oil when
you expect to get into a brawl), there was no way to see who
was crying in the darkness.

Tentatively I moved forward, thinking the sounds must

come from the residence wing; this wouldn't be the first time some student crept out of bed and huddled forlornly in the hall, shedding tears over bad grades or love gone wrong. But as I advanced down the passageway, the sniffling grew fainter, fading to inaudibility. I backtracked, picked up the noise again, and was soon feeling my way past darkened classrooms—keeping one hand on the wall to maintain my bearings.

It's odd how the academy's smell changes at night. During the day, the aroma is young, young, young—dozens of different perfumes, lavishly applied by students who get their families to send the latest scents from Bangkok, Damascus, or São Paulo. After dark, though, the jasmine and ginger die away, to be replaced by fragrances much, much older: the dark varnished oak of the wainscoting; the mausoleum dryness of chalk dust; two centuries worth of oil paints from the art room, sweat from the gym, and book leather from the library.

At night, the school showed its age. Feliss didn't have the prestige of institutions that traced their lineage a full four hundred years back to OldTech times, but it was still venerable by conventional standards. There was good reason why we attracted students from important families all over the world—never the best, of course, never the talented eldest son or the brilliant youngest daughter, but the "tries-very-hard" middle children who needed decent schooling too. Feliss Academy provided such schooling, in an appropriately time-honored venue . . . and it was only at night that you could smell the decades of glum mediocrity accumulated within these walls: the psychic residue of generation after generation who subconsciously recognized they weren't destined for greatness.

No. I wasn't projecting my own thoughts *at all*.

The sounds of sorrow drew me on. The snuffles weren't loud—they seemed to recede as I moved forward—but they continued in quiet anguish, leading me to the Instrumental Music room at the end of the corridor. I stopped outside, peering through the small pane of glass in the room's wooden door. No sign of anyone within, even though an adequate amount of starlight trickled its way through windows on the far wall. Then again, my view of the room was restricted, showing the middle but not the shadowy edges.

When I tried the door, it was locked. That was mildly unusual; most rooms in the school are left open day and night. I got out my pass key again and slid it into the lock, making just enough noise that the weeper would know I was coming. No point in startling some heartbroken teenager who'd come all this way to keep others from hearing the sobs. Opening the door, I said, "Hello," in what I hoped was a comforting voice. "Is there some way I can help?"

No answer. The crying had stopped the moment I spoke. I looked around the room, but saw no one. "It's Dr. Dhubhai," I said. "Would you like to talk?"

Total silence . . . and I still couldn't see a soul. There were plenty of hiding places available—the big walk-in cupboard on my left where students stored instruments from alt-horns to zithers, plus a smaller one on my right where the teacher, Annah Khan, kept rosin, reeds, and sheet music. For that matter, a timid little freshman might be small enough to cower out of sight behind the tubas or the tympani. "It's all right," I said, "I'm not here to yell at you. Come out and let's talk."

No response.

I knew Annah kept an oil lamp on her desk. Groping through my pockets, I found my own matchbox and struck a light. The flame lasted less than a second before a sharp puff of wind blew it out. I tried another match; the same puff of wind gusted up in an otherwise still classroom, and I was back in darkness again.

Uh-oh.

Feliss Academy was not immune to drafts; however, such drafts seldom manifested themselves as well-timed, well-focused gusts that came from nowhere. I suspected something more than a chance breeze was making its presence known—especially in light of the Caryatid's sort of a prophecy kind of thing.

Just as the League of Peoples had given us psionics and sorcery, they'd introduced lots of other simulated mystical baggage from terrestrial folklore.

Like ghosts.

Something went <PLINK> in the darkness—a single note plucked on a string instrument. The pitch was high enough that I immediately thought, *Violin.* Then came a second note, lower, down in the cello range. Three more notes, low, medium, high . . . and I knew I was hearing the harp.

The school owned a splendid harp: a hellishly pricey thing all gold leaf and rosewood, donated by some doting father whose daughter was certain she'd become a world-famous harpist if only she could practice on a proper instrument. The girl's enthusiasm lasted an hour—the time it took her to realize she wasn't some prodigy who'd be playing Mozart her very first day. At the end of term, the girl departed and the harp stayed. Since then, a succession of other students had tried their hands at the instrument, some with modest success; but none ever came close to fulfilling the harp's true potential.

Now . . . plink, plink, plink. Single notes, played at random. Then one of the pedals creaked, and the strings began a slow, simple scale.

I'd never tried the harp myself, but I'd played enough other instruments to recognize the sound of a beginner: the hesitations between notes as the player reached to get the correct finger in place; the extra twang on strings that got plucked too hard, followed by soft almost-not-there notes when the player tried to go easier; the which-foot-do-I-use pause whenever it was necessary to use a pedal. The player in the dark never struck a wrong note, but I suspected the scale was an easy one . . . like C major on a piano, where you can't go wrong if you keep to the white keys.

The harp stood back in the corner of the room, behind the percussion section—not a good location for the harpist to be heard, but ideal if your first priority was making sure students didn't accidentally break the most valuable instrument in the music department. From where I stood, I couldn't see anyone sitting on the player's stool; but it was dark enough back there that I couldn't be sure the stool was empty.

Swallowing hard, I walked toward the sound . . . which is to say I began to clamber around the chairs, drums, and glockenspiels that separated me from the back corner.

Meanwhile, the music continued—a two-octave scale up and down, then repeated. The second time through was quicker and more even . . . as if the player had gained confidence after warming up. I, on the other hand, was losing confidence by the moment: the closer I got to the harp, the more clearly I could see that the instrument was playing itself. No one sat on the stool; if there were hands moving over the strings, those hands were invisible.

All right, I thought, *it is now time to leave*. This wouldn't be fleeing with my tail between my legs; I simply intended to seek advice from someone who understood pseudo-supernatural events better than I. The Caryatid and Myoko weren't close at hand, but surely some don in residence had occult experience. Chen Fai-Hung, for example: he was always boasting how he'd studied at Core Haven for three years, and made it to the second last round for Elemarch of Molybdenum. Fai-Hung might not know as much about uncanny phenomena as a sorcerer or psionic, but he must have learned more on the subject than I did in Differential Geometry 327.

Therefore I took a step backward, intending to scuttle from the room; but before I could retreat farther, a sob wrenched out of the harpist who wasn't there. A heartbroken, heartbreaking sound. At the same time the music shifted, from scales into a simple melody plucked one note at a time.

I didn't recognize the tune—something in Dorian mode, which always strikes me as bittersweet: close to a minor key but more melancholy, with just a tiny B natural of wistful hope. When the piece began, it had the same hesitations and unevenness as the first scale I'd heard, some strings plucked too loudly and others too soft. A few strings were also a shade out of tune . . . almost always the case with an instrument that spends much of its time unused.

But now, as the playing continued in the darkened room, the hesitations grew fewer and the music flowed more smoothly. Even the tuning got better—the melody never stopped, but I heard the low creak of tuning pegs, as if the harpist possessed a third hand for tuning while the other two hands played. Over the music, the weeping resumed . . . until gradually, the soft bleak sobs blended with the notes like someone humming through her tears.

Her tears. Yes: the humming sounded female. When I realized that, I couldn't help speaking again. "What's wrong? Are you hurt? Can I help?"

The music bloomed in response . . . losing all amateurish lack of control, the sound swelling in the blackness: melody, harmony, and counterpoint. A sorrowful song played by a virtuoso, something ancient and rare from an aching soul— as if I were hearing the distillation of all the music someone wished she could have played, a lifetime's worth of longing compressed into a single grieving requiem.

It ended with a minor chord that stretched the full range of the harp, a simultaneous clutch of notes that could never have been played with a mere ten fingers. Then, as the strings continued to echo, a single piercing shriek burst from the emptiness above the harpist's stool—a cry filled with pain and the anger of death. I hurried forward as if there were some way I could help the unseen woman . . . but when I reached out to where she should be, my hands passed through icy nothingness: a cold so fierce it wracked my fingers and chilblained my arms.

I jerked back quickly, shivering despite my winter coat. Shoving my bare hands into my armpits, I squeezed them tight, trying to force some heat into my flesh. As I did, I caught movement in the shadows beside me . . . and though it terrified me to look, I turned my gaze directly at the harp.

Slowly, very slowly, liquid trickled down a string. In the dark it looked black, but I knew it had to be red. Deep scarlet.

Blood. How else would a haunting end?

More beads of black crimson appeared out of nowhere, forming at the top of each string and dribbling down into shadow. Within seconds the whole harp was seeping, blood oozing from the air, flowing freely, pattering onto the floor. I felt a drip splash on the toe of my boot . . . and that's when I finally ran.

3

EATING HER CURDS-AND-WHEY

I stood outside Annah Khan's room, mustering the nerve to knock. Not that I was concerned about disturbing her at one in the morning—our musicmaster Annah was don of Ladies North 3, and in that capacity, she was obliged to accept crises during the wee hours. Heaven knows, *I* had people banging on my door after midnight several times a month: boys who wanted help with their lessons . . . boys who'd just had their first wet dream and were sure it was some horrid disease . . . boys who desperately needed to know if I believed in God (whichever particular God was weighing on their minds) . . . not to mention the future Duke Simon Westmarch who owned his own stethoscope and woke me at least once a week to listen to his heartbeat because this time he was *positive* it "had gone all funny." If *I* had to cope with such nonsense, why should any other don have it easy?

But Annah wasn't just any other don: she was a don who'd nursed a crush on me since we both arrived at the school ten years ago. A crush of operatic proportions, but conducted pianissimo. I'd catch her staring across the study hall with her huge brown eyes, wearing an expression so intense it seemed she might devour me . . . but when I talked to her, she barely answered. The few times I'd asked if she'd like to go for a walk—because she was certainly worth the attention, thirty-two years old and delicately lovely, like porcelain the color of coffee—she'd invented awkward excuses and practically fled the room. My psychic friend Myoko contended Annah didn't want me as a man at all; Annah wanted me as an object of Tragic Yearning, someone she could pine over from a distance while writing torrid sonatas for unaccompanied violin.

Therefore, knocking on Annah's door in the middle of the night was fraught with implications. In my then mental state (muddled with drink, and a touch hysterical over what I'd seen in the music room), I imagined she might react to my arrival in some extravagant way: screaming in terror perhaps . . . or shouting, "At long last, darling!" and throwing herself into my arms . . . or even letting the clothes drop from her body in naked surrender, a tear trickling down her cheek as she waited for me to slake my bestial appetites.

Or, I told myself, *she could react like a real human being instead of some drunk's sexual fantasy*—which meant she'd glare and say, "What the hell do you want at this hour?"

I knocked.

There was no noise within. All the rooms in the school's dormitories were moderately soundproof and the dons' suites deliberately more so—when a student and don had a heart-to-heart chat/sob/confession, it was best if such confidences weren't overheard by prying ears in the hall. The extra soundproofing was also useful when a don wanted to entertain company of a romantic nature without providing an audible show for snickering teenagers; and the teenagers liked the soundproofing too, since it meant they could sneak around after hours without the dons hearing. (Feliss Academy discreetly indulged interstudent liaisons. These were, after all, children of privilege; as education for later life, they were *expected* to dally with one another, provided they kept such affairs clandestine and Took Sensible Precautions.)

Ten seconds after I knocked, a light came to life on the other side of the door. I could see it through the peephole—not that the peephole was designed to let visitors see into the room, but I was standing in pitch blackness so it was easy to notice any illumination coming through the fish-eye lens.

Annah had lit a candle or lamp. I composed myself in front of the peephole, trying to look sober and respectable . . . but I gave that up as soon as I realized the hall was too dark for Annah to see me, no matter how much she peeped through the viewer. All she could do was open the door; and a few seconds later, that's what she did, holding a rose-glassed kerosene lamp in her hand.

She'd been sleeping in a long white nightgown—not excessively sheer, but modest white cotton simply isn't equipped to hide warm dark skin completely. Over the top of the nightie, she'd donned a thicker brown robe but hadn't bothered to tie the belt; no doubt she'd assumed the knock came from one of her girls, some fifteen-year-old with a sore throat or a broken heart. Why would Annah fret about modesty under such circumstances?

. When she saw it was me, she froze. Like a stage actor doing a double take: eyes going wide, body turning rigid. It almost made me laugh . . . but my nerves were so strained from the ghost-harp concerto, the laugh would have come out shrill. I swallowed the hysteria and simply said, "Annah."

My voice seemed to break the spell. Annah's hand flew to the lapel of her robe, ready to pull her clothes hastily shut; but then she let go, as if there was no point in covering up: as if some irredeemable damage had already been done. Instead, she moved the lamp toward my face, peering intently into my eyes. She said nothing. Just waiting.

"Annah," I said again. "I saw . . . I was coming back tonight and I heard . . . in the music room . . ."

Bollixed and tongue-tied. Wondering what thoughts were going through Annah's mind. She surely smelled the ale on my breath, not to mention on my coat and hair. I had the galling apprehension she saw me as a drunk turned amorous, on the prowl for some slap-and-tickle; I pictured her previous infatuation with me twisting into disdain, and though I'd been exasperated by her puppy-eyed glances, I didn't want to lose them this way. "Someone was playing the harp," I said. "A ghost. And there was blood. On my boot."

Stupidly, I held out my foot for her to examine. She never took her eyes off my face. My skin was turning clammy, my tongue stumbling over words. "I came here to ask if you knew about the ghost . . . or if there's someone in your classes, a girl who plays the harp, and maybe, if she died tonight, cared enough about the music that she'd play one final piece—"

Annah reached out and put her fingers to my mouth. Touching my lips, silencing me. Then she took my hand . . . drew me into the room . . . shut the door . . . set down the lamp . . . wrapped her arms around me and pulled my head into the curve of her shoulder where I blubbered into her hair.

Some time later, I pulled away. "Sorry," I said. I touched her hair where I'd pressed my face against it: the thick dark strands were damp with my ridiculous tears. "Sorry," I said again.

"Shock," she replied. A soft voice, but controlled. The Caryatid once told me Annah had trained as a singer, until some vocal coach informed her she'd never amount to much because she didn't have enough resonance in her head. Small sinuses or something. It tells you a lot about Annah that she took the coach's word and gave up immediately. It also tells you a lot that she turned straight to the violin instead . . . and to the oboe, the cello, the sitar, the celeste . . .

Music, one way or another. She'd known what she wanted to do with her life—what her calling was. I envied her.

Annah stepped back and studied me. For a moment, I worried she would revert to her habit of silent staring . . . but then she said, "Yes. Just shock. Delayed reaction. You think you saw a ghost?"

"I didn't see it; I heard it. In the music room."

She took another step back, then sat gracefully in a chair covered with a throw-cloth of red and yellow satin. Her eyes never left my face. "Tell me," Annah said.

I did . . . settling into a wooden rocking chair padded with a white wool quilt. It was positioned opposite Annah's seat—probably where girls from the dorm sat when pouring out their hearts. I felt sheepish being there. But she wasn't listening like a don forcing herself to endure the woes of a whiny adolescent; her eyes were bright and glistening, her whole body leaning forward to catch every word. And why not? A

ghost in her music room. A man who came babbling to her
door. A chance to embrace him and give silent comfort.
Deliriously operatic stuff. However soberly she sat, her face
shone.

"So," I finished a few minutes later, "I came to you. Because it's your music room. You'd know if there'd been
hauntings before. But I also wanted to ask who played the
harp. In your classes. If there's a girl so devoted to the instrument that when she died . . . that her ghost . . . not that I believe in ghosts . . . that some effect would make it look as if
her ghost had gone to play all the things she never had time to
learn . . ."

I stopped because Annah was nodding. "There is such a
girl. Who cares deeply. Who has a gift. When she arrived at
the school, she already played a number of instruments, so I
set her to learning the harp. It's such a lovely instrument; I
wanted to hear it played by someone who wouldn't just go by
rote. Rosalind's still just starting, but you can tell—"

"Rosalind?" I interrupted. "Rosalind Tzekich?"

"Yes. You know her?"

"She's in my Math C."

Rosalind Tzekich. Sixteen years old, very quiet, very intense. Perhaps the same sort of girl Musicmaster Annah had
been at that age, except that Rosalind had black hair cut in
bangs, a Mediterranean complexion, and a plumpish body
she hid under shapeless frayed-hem dresses. Compared to
the stylish fashion-plates who populated our school, Rosalind stood out like a sack of onions . . . though she could
probably buy and sell the entire families of many of our students.

Rosalind's mother, Elizabeth Tzekich—known also as
Elsbeth the Bloody, Our Lady of Shadows, or Knife-Hand
Liz—was the outlaw terror of Southern Europe . . . or at least
one of the terrors, since Hispania, Romana, Hellene, and the
Balkans all seemed to cultivate criminal organizations as
profusely as olives. (The Black Hand. The Hidden Cry. The
Circle of Friends. Each specializing in some form of ugli-
ness, from extortion to smuggling to kidnap.)

Mother Tzekich ran a band of thugs called the Ring of

Knives. They made their money through sleazy mod-and-aug operations in back alleys from Gibraltar to Jerusalem. Did you want a poison gland implanted in your tongue so you could murder someone with a single kiss? Did you want a winning smile and a constant halo of pheromones? Or maybe you just fantasized about looking younger, more svelte, better endowed. Your dreams could come true for a price: through surgery, through sorcery, through OldTech procedures that rewrote your genes. A number of patients died on the operating table, a number came out disfigured or blighted, and plenty emptied their purses for no results whatsoever; but a sufficient tally of customers got enough of what they wanted that the Ring of Knives grew and prospered.

Ambitious Mother Tzekich didn't rest on her laurels. After making a name in the slice'n'dice trade, the Ring branched into other realms of business: forcibly seizing enterprises run by other criminal clans. The resulting gang war shook the Mediterranean. Soon it escalated farther afield, as the Ring fought to expand east into Asia and west to the Americas. In skirmish after skirmish, the Ring never suffered a significant defeat—partly because Tzekich had a genius for choosing the right targets, and partly because the Ring decked out its people with subcutaneous armor, enhanced reflexes, and even (so the rumors went) genes spliced from nonhuman sources. Animals and aliens, plants and ETs.

So the Ring of Knives gashed its way around the planet. Rival gangs fought back without mercy: dons and capos and czars would stop at nothing to see Elizabeth Tzekich dead. All this time, Rosalind stayed with her mother; but after a close call with a bomb spraying OldTech neurotoxins, the girl had been sent away for her own protection, to a boarding school in Nankeen.

Then to Alice Springs.

Then Quito.

Then Brazzaville.

Then Port-au-Prince.

Now it was Feliss. Where the girl was expected to last another month or two before being hustled off in the dead of

night, moved to another school on another continent to keep
ahead of her mother's enemies. Rosalind's clothes were
worn and threadbare because she'd been living out of suit-
cases since she was thirteen; her soul was worn and threadbare for the same reason.

As far as I knew, Rosalind had never tried to make friends
at our school—why bother when she might be dragged away
at any moment? She did her homework as a way to keep
busy, but mostly she passed her time staring out the window.
In the middle of class I'd glance in Rosalind's direction and
she'd be gazing out at bare trees against the winter sky. Perhaps she was wondering if she'd stay long enough to see
leaves on those trees; or perhaps she didn't ask such questions anymore: she just disengaged her mind and let minutes
or hours roll by. I was glad to hear she had a passion for music . . . glad she cared about anything. Rosalind had struck
me as a girl who might do nothing but stare out the window
her entire life.

"We should check on her," I told Annah. "To see if she's
all right. Do you know which dorm she's in?"

"Mine," Annah answered. "I asked for her especially. Because she was so good in music. She's just down the hall."

Annah stood, reaching down the front of her nightgown
and pulling out a thin silver necklace. On the end was a pass
key, similar to the one in my pocket. (Similar, but not identical—for the sake of propriety, my pass key didn't work on
girls' rooms and Annah's didn't work on boys'.) I had to
smile at the notion a pass key was so valuable one had to
wear it on a chain close to one's heart . . . but that was just
like Annah, going the extra distance to imbue tiny things
with dramatic import.

She ducked her head and lifted off the necklace, squeezing
the chain in her fist as she stepped to the door. I rose to follow. Annah turned . . . and for a moment there was something in the air, something she was going to say or do; I could
see it pass through her mind, though I couldn't tell what it
was. Maybe she was just going to say she wanted to check on
Rosalind alone—to avoid embarrassment if the girl came to

the door in her underwear. Or maybe Annah was thinking something quite different. In the end, she simply picked up the rose-glassed lamp and said, "Let's go."

By the time we knocked on Rosalind's door, tousle-haired heads had appeared up and down the hall. I suppose they'd been wakened a few minutes earlier, by my babbling in Annah's doorway . . . or perhaps they possessed some instinct for sensing trouble. Whatever the explanation, all the girls on the floor had got up to see what was happening. Now they peered out of their rooms, holding their nighties closed and squinting blearily as if they needed glasses. Most of them did.
　　Without looking at anyone in particular, Annah announced, "Well-bred ladies do not pry into another lady's affairs." Her voice had a stern edge I'd never heard before; I hadn't suspected her capable of it. Full of surprises, our Annah—I mentally kicked myself and resolved to stop underestimating her. She was, after all, an experienced teacher . . . and a teacher needs many different ways to speak to students.
　　This particular way was effective. All along the corridor, doors closed immediately.
　　Rosalind didn't answer our first knock. Annah knocked again, more sharply. "Rosalind dear, it's Professor Khan. Sorry to wake you, but could we see you a moment?"
　　Not a sound from inside. No light through the peephole.
　　"Of course," Annah murmured, "the poor girl might be afraid to open the door. It's the middle of the night; how does she know we aren't enemies trying to kidnap her?"
　　"In that case," I said, "she may try to shoot us through the door."
　　Annah met my gaze. Firearms were technically forbidden in the dorms, but parents often went to great lengths to make sure their children had an ample supply of concealed weapons. Especially parents like Elizabeth Tzekich.
　　Quietly, Annah and I moved to either side of the doorway, out of the line of fire.
　　Seconds passed. Annah knocked a third time. "Rosalind, please, we're worried about you. If you don't answer, we'll have to come in."

Still no response. Annah clutched her pass key and gave me a look; I nodded. Staying off to one side, Annah slipped the key into the lock. The dead-bolt slid back with a solid thunk. Annah took a deep breath, then gave the door a light shove.

Neither she nor I tried to peek around the door frame—just in case Rosalind really *did* have a shotgun or some other violent reception for unwelcome visitors. Three seconds later, I knew we didn't have to look . . . because a terrible smell of meat and excrement oozed into my nostrils.

I hadn't seen death all that often—I wasn't a surgeon, soldier, or in any other profession that regularly produced cadavers—but I came from a family where generations lived and died together in the same house.

When I was very young, I clutched my mother's leg as she and my great-grandfather washed the wrinkled skin of his just-dead wife, carefully preparing the old woman for burial. Several years later, that same great-grandfather died right in front of me; he was withering away from a cancerous mass in his belly, and toward the end, everyone in the house took turns reading him the Koran, around the clock, twenty-four hours a day. (For some, it was the first time we'd read the Book: Great-Granddad was the only genuine Believer in our family. The generation after his had all become adamant atheists for reasons they never discussed, and those of us born later were brought up in bland secularity . . . idly curious about the old ways, but never to the point where we considered prostrating ourselves when the muezzin called.) I was waiting my turn to take over the reading from Aunt Rahel when the breath slipped out of the old man and the smell of his loosened bowels filled the room. (My aunt immediately turned to the Opening, Al-Fatiha, and read, "In the name of Most Merciful Compassionate God: Praise be to God, the Lord of all Being; All-Merciful, All-Compassionate, the Master of the day of judgment. Thee only do we worship and of thee do we beg assistance. Guide us in the straight path, the way of the blessed—not of those who have earned Your wrath or those who have wandered astray." Only then did she look

up and say, "He's gone.") And there were other deaths
through the years, great-uncles and elderly cousins, a maid
who drank poison (no one knew why), a gateman stabbed by
a thief, the thief himself brought down by guard dogs and
shot in cold blood by my grandma Khadija, a peasant boy
who'd climbed our wall and was found floating in the fish
pond (probably chased there by the dogs) . . . perhaps two or
three dozen dead in all. Not a lot of corpses by many people's
standards, but enough that I recognized the smell of a room
where life had vanished.

Rosalind's room had that smell.

I glanced across at Annah. Her expression showed that she
too recognized the odor of death. Even the oil lamp in her
hands seemed aware of the smell—the lamp's flame burned
brighter, fed by the gases of putrefaction.

Or perhaps I just imagined that.

It's hard to describe how I felt at that moment—not calm,
certainly, but neither was I falling apart. I'd already had my
breakdown. And the smell from Rosalind's room wasn't a
surprise . . . just the confirmation of something I'd suspected
ever since I heard that harp.

If I was worried about anything, it was Annah. Her hand
had begun to tremble; the lamp rattled in her grip, enough to
send our shadows veering across the wall. I reached out and
took the light from her. "Do you need to sit down?"

She didn't answer. Her other hand clutched the pass key so
tightly, the metal must have dug into her palm. I took a step
forward, opened my arms—intending to hold her the way she
held me. But she shrank away. "No," Annah said. "No.
Just . . . could you . . . you look. I'll be along. In a second."

"Are you sure?"

"Yes. I'll be all right. Please go."

I stared at her a moment longer—stupidly affronted she
wouldn't let me wrap her in my arms. But her body was
clenched so tightly she looked like she might scream if I
moved any closer. "All right," I said, "I'll go see what's happened. Call if you need me."

She gave the slightest hint of a nod. Not even looking in my direction.

With lamp in hand, I moved into the room. My first impression was how clean it looked—nothing strewn on the floor, no piles of books in the corner, not a single paper out on the desk. In my own section of the dorm, students kept their rooms more cluttered . . . even the boys who were taunted for being fastidious. Perhaps the difference was that my boys *lived* in their rooms; Rosalind Tzekich had simply been passing through. Beneath the window stood two modest carrying cases, as if the girl was packed and ready to go the instant her mother commanded. I could almost believe Rosalind locked her meager belongings in those cases every night, so there'd be no delay if she had to flee.

But now she was going nowhere.

Rosalind lay on her back in the bed: her plump body naked and spreadeagled, the sheets and blankets thrown open. I caught myself thinking, *She looks so cold*—splayed pale and exposed, as if she should be shivering in the dark chill. But she wasn't.

I crossed the room quickly, intending to cover the girl's corpse. Not just because she looked cold—it felt indecent for me to be seeing her breasts and bare pelvis, her lifeless legs spread obscenely wide. An unforgivable desecration. My hand was reaching for the blankets, my eyes locked on the girl's face to avoid looking at any other part of her . . .

. . . when I saw a gooey white nodule ooze from her left nostril.

My hand froze. I clenched my fingers. Drew the hand back without touching anything. Held the lamp closer to Rosalind's face.

The nodule reminded me of cottage cheese: a soft curdy nugget sodden with creamy white fluid. The same sort of fluid had run from her other nostril too—it glistened wetly on her upper lip. As I watched, another soft curd forced its way from her nose, like an insect egg being laid. The nugget balanced stickily for a moment, then slid off down her cheek. It left a damp trail on the girl's skin.

I retreated a step. Forced myself to be clinical as I ran my gaze over the naked corpse. No obvious cause of death: no bleeding, no bruises, no marks on the throat. There might be some wound I couldn't see, a stab or bullethole in her back, but I wasn't going to turn her over to check. I had the sudden suspicion it would be suicide to touch anything in this room. Certainly not poor Rosalind's body.

Reaching into my pocket, I pulled out one of the pencils I always carried with me. Back to the girl's face, holding the light close. I teased the point of the pencil between the girl's lips and levered it between her teeth. The jaw was slack—no rigor mortis yet. When this was over, I'd have to check my reference books to see how soon after death the rigor sets in; that could tell me how recently Rosalind had died. In the meantime, I worked the pencil until I'd pried open her jaw.

The dead girl's mouth was half full of curds. Cottage cheese goo. A mass of it clogged her throat, and the mass was growing. I could see it expand, inching up the girl's tongue. (The tongue was swollen a dark ugly red.) In a few minutes, the white infestation would spill out and slop down her chin.

I didn't want to be here when that happened. The sight would make me sick.

But there was one other thing to check before I got out of the room: the girl's eyes. Their surface had begun to flatten—internal fluids seeping away, unable to keep enough pressure for normal roundness—but it was easy to see tiny red dots in the whites. Pinpricks of blood I knew were called ocular petechiae. Typically seen in cases of smothering and strangulation. As the dying body struggles for air, as the eyes bulge wide, small blood vessels pop under the strain. The results were those scarlet specks.

Whatever the white substance was in her mouth and nose, Rosalind Tzekich had choked to death on it. Silently. Unable to scream.

The end of my pencil was damp with the stuff. I threw the pencil down and kicked it under the bed.

* * *

"Some sort of disease?"

Annah had come in quietly. Her face was composed into careful blankness—no tears, no expression. She leaned over Rosalind and pulled lightly on my hand to bring the lamp closer. Annah's fingers felt cold where they touched me. "I've heard diphtheria produces a growth in your throat. Something that suffocates you."

"This isn't diphtheria," I said. "Not a natural strain anyway. Diphtheria doesn't grow so rampantly it oozes out your nose. Besides, a normal disease takes time to develop. Fever. Pain. Days of being sick. Rosalind was in my math class this afternoon and she looked fine."

"Yes." Annah stared down at the dead girl. "I sat with her at dinner. We talked about music—a few simple pieces by Bach she might be ready to play. She had a healthy appetite; a little distracted but in quite a good mood."

Annah reached out as if she were going to touch the girl: pat her cheek, straighten her hair. I grabbed Annah's hand and pulled it back . . . maybe too roughly, but this was no time for delicacy. "Don't touch," I said. "We should get out of here fast. Before we catch something."

"You said it wasn't a disease."

"I said it wasn't a *natural* disease. Let's go."

I put my hand on her shoulder and tried to nudge her toward the door. Annah's body had gone rigid, eyes still on Rosalind. "You think it's sorcery?"

"Sorcery is extraterrestrial science; I think this stuff is homegrown. A plague made by OldTech bioengineers: very human, very deadly. Annah, please, let's leave."

I took her hand in mine. This time, she let herself be led away. I closed the door behind us and made sure she locked it.

Back to Annah's room. It wasn't until we got there that I realized I was still holding her hand; when I tried to let go, she kept a solid grip. "What is it?" she asked, refusing to release me.

"What is what?"

"Inside Rosalind. What was coming out of her nose?" When I didn't answer right away, she squeezed my fingers impatiently. "You think you know, don't you? Something OldTech. Tell me."

I sighed. "When OldTech civilization began its breakdown, certain governments thought there'd be war. A *big* war. They couldn't believe everything would just fall apart quietly—if their world was ending, there had to be an apocalypse. Nothing else would give *closure*. Never mind that there was no reason for anyone to fight: nothing to fight over, no enemy you could shoot to fix the world's problems. People thought there'd be war. So military scientists worked day and night to develop weapons worthy of Armageddon. Including bioweapons: ultra-lethal diseases; virulent molds and fungi; deadly internal parasites."

Annah looked as if she didn't believe me. "It's true," I said. "They created plagues. Some designed to stay latent a long time until they'd infected huge chunks of the populace; others intended to be deadly fast. The slow ones were for terrorism, the fast for actual war: spread quick-kill microbes on your enemy's army and within hours there'd be no one to fight you. Ideally, they wanted the effects of the disease to be horrifyingly repugnant . . . demoralizing for those who didn't actually catch the bug."

"And you think Rosalind died from a quick-kill germ?"

"You said she was perfectly healthy a few hours ago. Natural throat infections don't develop that fast."

Silence. For the first time, Annah seemed to realize she was holding my hand; she looked down, saw her fingers clasping mine, and let go. Flustered, she turned away. Her voice sounded muffled as she said, "Who did it? Enemies of the girl's mother?"

"Most likely. Some of the Ring's rivals go back centuries: the Omerta . . . the Sons of the Black Czar . . . the Third Hand of Allah . . . they all originated in OldTech times. Any of those groups could have pilfered bacteria from a germ warfare lab while OldTech civilization was crumbling. Toward the end, military security was practically nonexistent.

You must have heard about that group who stole an H-bomb and tried to blow up London."

"But they were stopped by the Spark Lords," Annah said. "That was the first time the Lords ever made an appearance. Then Spark Royal began the big purge—getting rid of the bombs, poison gas, everything. They eradicated mass weapons; that's one reason the Sparks claim they have a right to rule."

I shrugged. "There's a difference between finding huge nuclear missiles stuck in stationary silos and finding a single Petri dish containing a super-diphtheria. It's possible someone kept a germ culture alive all these years without Spark Royal knowing. Only using the germs for very special executions."

Annah shuddered. "I wish I didn't believe you—I wish I thought people couldn't be vicious enough to kill an innocent girl just to hurt her mother. But I know all too well . . ." She stopped herself, lowered her eyes, then crossed the floor and dropped into her chair. "It wouldn't have been hard to plant something in Rosalind's room. Probably tonight while we were at dinner; by then, most of the house staff had left for the weekend, so someone could sneak in without being seen."

"Right," I said. "An assassin would just have to rub some germs on the girl's toothbrush. The rim of her water glass. Any food she kept in the room. No difficulty at all; Feliss has never been a high-security institution."

"I used to think that was one of its charms." Annah let her head fall back against the chair. "Are we infected too?"

"Neither of us touched anything, and we didn't stay long in the room. We should be safe."

"We didn't inhale it from the air?"

I shook my head. "OldTech scientists weren't totally deranged—they didn't want to release something so impossible to contain that it might destroy the human race. An airborne germ would just be too risky; better to have a short-lived aerosol, or something thick and creamy that could be poured down on enemies like rain."

"The white stuff in Rosalind's nose."

I nodded. Now was not the time to mention that even a curds-and-cream disease was insanely dangerous. Fluids had a way of sinking into the water table . . . and water flowed into the sea. Furthermore, once you'd visited a disease on your enemies, those enemies could grow cultures of the same germ from infected cadavers. Next thing you knew, saboteurs would be dumping the stuff on *you*. OldTech scientists devoted a lot of ingenuity toward getting around that basic dilemma—making germs that couldn't live outside the human body, and germs that stopped reproducing within a few hours so they couldn't spread or be cultivated—but nothing was ever foolproof. Which is why (God is merciful) no OldTech nation ever attempted a large-scale deployment of bioweapons.

"There's another reason," I said, "why I doubt the disease is too virulent. If rivals of the Ring of Knives started an epidemic, the Sparks would declare total war. One hundred percent annihilation of those responsible for the plague—the killers, whoever hired them, all known associates, all associates of the associates, the seamstress who hemmed their trousers, and the boy who delivered their coal. The Spark Lords are ruthless, and when they call themselves Protectors of Humanity they mean it. Whatever criminal clan killed poor Rosalind, I can't imagine they're crazy enough to antagonize the Sparks over a sixteen-year-old girl."

Annah lifted her head, large brown eyes looking up at me. "You underestimate the craziness of criminals." She spoke in a low voice. "There are people who think they're so clever they can get away with anything, even if it's outwitting the Sparks . . . and others who don't care if they get caught, as long as they first have the pleasure of causing pain . . . and even a few who believe revenge is more important than life itself—an absolute necessity, a religious imperative, taking vengeance no matter the consequences to friends and family."

I wanted to ask how she knew such things—quiet intense Annah—but I couldn't think how to phrase the question. She even waited for me to speak . . . but when I didn't, she just got out of her chair. "I'm going to wash my hands. I didn't touch anything, but I'm going to wash."

She held out her hand to me. In retrospect, it was an odd thing to do if she thought she might have deadly microbes on her fingers; but at the time, her gesture seemed perfectly natural. I took the offered hand and we went into her small bathroom together.

We washed for a long time. Without saying a word. Perhaps we weren't soaping off germs, but death itself. The smell of it. The cruelty. The sight of a dead sixteen-year-old lying bare, cold, and cooling because she happened to have the wrong mother.

We washed and washed and washed. The more lye, the better.

4

TOBACCO SKYROAD

Annah checked her other girls. While she went from room to room making sleepy teenagers open their mouths and say, "Ahh!", I stuffed towels into the crack under Rosalind's door. However much I believed no microbes would ooze out, it was foolish to take chances. Eventually we'd have to incinerate Rosalind's entire room, preferably with the Caryatid supervising the flames . . . but that had to wait. If this was an OldTech bioweapon, we couldn't destroy the evidence until the Spark Lords had examined it.

We didn't want to upset the Sparks; they were a greater hazard to one's health than any disease. Besides, I truly didn't think the clotted-cream deposits in Rosalind's throat were overly contagious. Otherwise, I wouldn't have let Annah make the rounds of girls on her floor—I'd have locked us both into quarantine.

But I believed Annah and I were clean . . . thanks in part to the Caryatid's sort of a prophecy kind of thing. I was doomed to go questing—ergo, no illness would keep me home. In fact, the quest would almost certainly be a result of Rosalind's death; the only question was how that would come about.

I looked down the hall in Annah's direction. She was talking now to a seventeen-year-old named Fatima Nouri—a distant cousin of mine, though we'd never met before Fatima came to Feliss. (The Nouris controlled most of the power and money in Ka'aba province on the east side of the Red Sea, while my own family dominated Sheba on the west. Every generation, a diplomatic marriage was arranged between a Nouri and a Dhubhai as a gesture of goodwill . . . and as a way to plant spies in each other's camps.) I pushed the towels a little farther under Rosalind's door, then walked down to talk with my cousin.

Annah said nothing as I approached. Fatima grinned broadly, looking back and forth between Annah and me as if she was sure we were lovers—why else would we be together in the middle of the night? I could tell young Fatima was mentally composing a letter home: "Ooo, Cousin Philemon has a *girlfriend*. A dark and delicate houri." But let the girl gloat; let her flash her saucy grin as long as she could. She didn't know what had happened to Rosalind . . . and when my lascivious but decent-hearted cousin learned the truth, she would weep for days.

"Fatima," I said, "could you run an errand for me?"

"Now?" Her grin faltered. "Right now?"

"Right now. I'd like you to go into Simka and bring back the Steel Caryatid. Do you know where she lives?"

Fatima nodded. Her grin had returned in full—apparently she was tickled by the thought of sallying forth in the dead of night.

"Are you sure it's safe?" Annah asked. "A girl alone at this hour . . ."

"I'll take my sword," Fatima said. She turned back to me. "Can I take my sword?"

"As long as you don't stab the town watchmen. You'll recognize them; they're the ones asleep in the gutters."

Fatima laughed and whirled away—back into her room to get dressed. Annah looked at me reprovingly. "It's all right," I said. "Fatima can take care of herself." All the Nouri family, male and female, were trained from childhood in the Way of the Clever Blade. Fatima herself was Pelinor's prize pupil: fourth this year in the provincial fencing finals, better than any other academy student in the past two decades. She had nothing to fear from drunks, ruffians, or blob-eared aliens who couldn't hold their broadswords straight.

Annah continued her progress down the hall while I waited for my cousin. Third cousin? Fourth cousin twice removed? I'd never bothered to calculate the exact relationship; I'm sure Fatima hadn't either. We simply knew our families were connected, the same way we were connected with every other powerful clan from the Sahara to the Khyber Pass. Wherever people like us touched down in that region, we'd always have a great-aunt or nephew-in-law serving as deputy-something to the local governor . . . which explains why I fled to the other side of the planet as soon as I earned my doctorate.

Life wasn't so claustrophobic here. Fatima may have come to Feliss for the same reason, badgering her parents until they let her go to school on a strange foreign continent. When my cousin graduated at the end of the year, it wouldn't surprise me if she skipped going home and instead headed for Feliss City to join the governor's guard. Plenty of our relatives had done the same: third sons and fourth daughters who chafed under the omnipresence of family connections and ran off to new lands where they could breathe on their own.

Make your own mistakes. The story of my life.

Within minutes, Fatima emerged from her room in her version of street clothes (more slovenly than anything worn by the town's true poor). Her favorite scimitar hung in a sheath on her belt. The sword was an exquisitely functional weapon: no curlicues, no filigree, just a balanced blade in a solid grip. The Nouris always loved simple steel—simple *sharp* steel.

Fatima struck a pose, one hand resting oh-so-casually on the sword's pommel. "Do I pass, teacher?" she asked.

"Provided you don't go asking for trouble. Your job is to carry a message, not tangle with the thugs of Simka. Take the safest streets, straight to the Caryatid and back, all right?"

Fatima gave an indulgent smile, humoring a timid old fuddy-duddy. "What's the message?"

"Tell the Caryatid to come right away. To, uhh . . ." I considered where Annah and I would go after we'd finished here. "To the chancellor's suite," I said. "If not there, to Professor Khan's room."

"And if she asks why?"

Oh no, dear cousin, you don't get the juicy details that easily. Fatima must have realized something out of the ordinary was happening, but I could tell her thoughts ran to conventional scandals: a girl caught with a boy . . . or with liquor . . . or both. She was grinning too widely to suspect anything more sinister or tragic. "If the Caryatid asks what's going on," I said, "tell her the dog's tongue was speaking the truth."

"The dog's tongue?"

"The dog's tongue. Now get going."

Fatima hesitated a moment longer; then she favored me with one last grin and pounded a fist to her chest in a passable reproduction of my family's house salute. "Hail the Dhubhais!" she said, then giggled. She left at a gallop, scimitar bouncing against her side.

I'd said we'd be with the chancellor. When Annah completed her throat inspections, that's precisely where we went: to the penthouse atop the school's dormitory wing, the home of Chancellor Opal Quintelle.

Opal was the one person at the academy who knew as much science as I did; possibly *more* than I did, though she was too polite to make it obvious. From time to time, however, when we were discussing plate tectonics or the evolutionary effects of human emotions on other species (why do we find mammal babies appealing? perhaps because our hunter ancestors were more likely to kill animals that didn't engage our sympathies, so that, over the millennia, looking sweet and cute to humans became a useful survival trait) . . . from time to time, as Opal and I were conversing about such things, she would suddenly stop as if afraid of revealing too much and bite back whatever words she'd intended to say.

How did she know so much? I couldn't tell. She never talked about her past or her upbringing, and her accent didn't fit with anyplace I knew: as elegant as British nobility, but with different intonation on the long vowels. Her appearance gave no clue to her background; her face was unnaturally smooth and devoid of ethnic characteristics, with the waxy look of someone who's had extensive plastic surgery . . . either to remove signs of age (Opal claimed to be sixty-two, though she could have passed for much younger) or to correct some conspicuous disfigurement: scars or perhaps a birthmark.

As I was climbing the stairs to Opal's room, it occurred to me that plastic surgery was the stock and trade of Mother Tzekich's group, the Ring of Knives. Backstreet beautification. Was Opal a Ring of Knives customer? Or more than a customer? No one in the faculty lounge knew anything about Opal's life before she arrived in Feliss . . . so perhaps it wasn't mere chance that delivered Rosalind to our door. Perhaps some prior association had convinced Mother Tzekich that Opal could be trusted to keep her daughter safe. After all, there were plenty of schools like ours in the world, and a woman as shrewd as Knife-Hand Liz wouldn't pick one out of a hat. She'd want somebody in place to keep an eye on the girl; didn't that make sense?

Or was I inventing complications when we had enough *real* trouble to handle?

With such thoughts filling my mind, I knocked on the chancellor's door.

Opal answered the knock within seconds . . . and as always, she was turned out ready to meet royalty. Her silver hair hung loosely below her shoulders, but she was clad in an impeccable gown of subdued red suede. She must have kept the dress beside her bed, an outfit she could shimmy into without wasting time on buttons or hooks, so she could quickly and chicly present herself to whoever came calling at one-thirty in the morning. Perhaps in her youth, she'd belonged to some crack military unit that had to be ready at an instant's notice; or perhaps I was *really* letting my imagination run away with me.

When she saw who was calling, Opal raised an eyebrow. "Crisis?"

"Crisis."

"Serious?"

"Severe."

"Inside."

Opal beckoned us into her sitting room. It was a spacious place, decorated with the sort of bric-a-brac that accumulates in the chancellor's quarters of a school two centuries old: gifts from parents and grateful students. Jungle masks that were taller than me shared wall space with an ermine-covered cricket bat and several painted portraits where both subjects and artists had long ago faded from memory. On one table, five music boxes were stacked atop each other in diminishing order by size; the housemaids kept them free of dust, but no one bothered to polish the tarnished little plaques that told what tunes the boxes played. Another table held an assortment of plaster figurines, all of them kittens or puppies or chubby-cheeked children in dirndls and lederhosen. These trinkets were "the artistic heritage of the academy" passed from one chancellor to the next, like some pox nobody could cure. Opal sometimes talked about throwing everything out . . . but she never did. It seemed inevitable the next chancellor would inherit the same regrettable collection, plus whatever new "riches" would arrive during Opal's administration.

Annah and I sat ourselves on a "genuine-Inuit" couch upholstered in scratchy caribou hide. Our Esteemed Chancellor took a seat opposite us on a faux-Chippendale chair painted white with green vines twining up its legs and around its frame. She said nothing—Opal seldom wasted words—but she cocked her head to show she was ready to listen. Since Annah showed no sign of speaking, I took the lead. "Rosalind Tzekich is dead. In her room. Almost certainly murdered."

Opal's expression didn't change, but she shifted her gaze and murmured, "That's what 'expendable' means." When I stared at her in surprise, she focused back on me. "Sorry. Where I come from, that's a type of prayer for the dead."

She fell silent again. I waited a few seconds, then said, "There's more bad news. I think the killer used an OldTech bioweapon—the kind we should report to Spark Royal."

Opal looked up sharply. "Are you sure?"

I described what I'd seen: the white curds clogging the

girl's airways. I also told about the Caryatid's sort of a prophecy kind of thing, and the ghostly harp music that led me to Rosalind in the first place. Annah verified that Rosalind had been in perfect health at dinner, and that none of the other girls on the floor showed any signs of sickness . . . which argued against a natural disease, if any such argument was necessary.

Opal nodded as she listened, asking no questions, taking it all in. When I finished, she remained silent for several more heartbeats; then she settled back into her chair, lifting her gaze to a window that looked out on darkness. "So," she said, "here it is."

"Here *what* is?" I asked.

She didn't answer. Instead she rose and walked to the window, as if expecting to see something outside . . . but instead of looking down at the campus four floors below, her eyes were turned to the sky. "I'd hoped they were wrong," she said, facing the stars, "but of course they weren't. It sure is a bitch living in a universe where so many species are smarter than you."

I wanted to ask, "What are you talking about?" . . . but some inner voice said I didn't want to know. Despite all the horrors I'd experienced, I hadn't reached the true edge of the precipice until this moment: half-drunk, surrounded by ugly knickknacks, with our chancellor speaking in riddles. I'd been thinking my responsibilities would soon be over—that Opal would take charge of everything and absolve me from further decisions—but I suddenly realized with icy dread that Opal would offer no salvation.

In the end, it was Annah who spoke the words: "Opal . . . what do you know?"

"Can you keep a secret?" Opal asked.

I knew I should leave, but I didn't. I just nodded. Annah did too.

Opal turned back to look at us. "Promise?"

We nodded again.

"All right," Opal said. "All right." She paused, then muttered, "Where the fuck do I start?"

I'd never heard her use such strong language . . . and her

accent had grown more pronounced, as if she were slipping back into habits from some unladylike former life.

"Oh, what the hell," she said. "Once upon a time . . ."

Once upon a time, a baby girl was born far, far away. She grew up clever and strong, but not pretty; she was as far from pretty as you could get. So the people who decided such things told her she would be trained for special work in out-of-the-way places where her appearance wouldn't bother "decent folk."

[Annah shivered and drew a bit closer to me. I tried to guess which country Opal might come from . . . but my guesses were so utterly wrong, there's no point writing them down.]

In time, the little girl became an Explorer: a person sent to unknown places to see what was there. Sometimes the work she did was important; sometimes it was pointless; often it was hard to tell the difference. But she took great personal pride in her accomplishments, even on missions that achieved nothing useful . . . and her greatest pride was always coming back alive.

One day, her superiors assigned her to the service of a man named Chee: an aged and aging admiral full of whims. Some of his whims were inspired—his unconventional attitudes made Chee valuable on occasions when orthodoxy couldn't cope. Other Chee whims were just harmless or quaint, but occasionally . . . occasionally it was unlucky to be the subordinate of a man who was famed for caprice.

There came a time when Chee wanted pipe tobacco; and no tobacco would do except the very best leaf, fresh from the finest farms on Earth. So Chee commanded his flagship to set sail for an isle where tobacco grew most sweet and rich . . . but alas, due to old political enmities, Chee and his people were hated on that island. They couldn't land openly and purchase leaf in the market. Therefore Chee directed his ship to lie off at a distance, while the young woman Explorer landed under cover of darkness and stole as much as she could carry.

["Stole?" Annah asked. "You robbed some poor farmer?"

["Oh," said Opal, "each year, Chee had his Explorers leave a generous amount of gold as payment; but I don't know how many farmers dared to pocket it. There was a treaty in place that forbade all interaction between my people and the islanders. If the farmer kept the gold and was found out later . . . well, being robbed isn't half as bad as getting caught trading with the enemy."]

So in the deepest hour of night, the Explorer found herself in a field full of half-picked tobacco. At the edge of that field stood six tarpaper shacks—the curing kilns or "kills" where harvested leaves were baked until they were golden brown and ready for market. The plan was to check each kill to find one whose leaves were nearly finished curing. Those were the leaves Chee wanted, the ones the Explorer would steal.

But as the Explorer approached the kills, a man stepped out from the shadows between two of them. He was quite possibly the most handsome man she'd ever seen: young, virile, shirtless, barefoot, smiling as if he was about to greet a lover. The Explorer thought perhaps that's why he'd been waiting in the darkness; perhaps this man had planned a midnight rendezvous with another man's wife, or some sly-footed girl sneaking away from overprotective parents. He might have heard a noise and came out expecting to see his paramour . . . so what would he make of a stranger in odd foreign clothes?

The man smiled. "Good evening." Which the Explorer found surprising—on this island, the greeting should have been "Buenas tardes." But she didn't let herself dwell on that oddity. Instead, she reached (regretfully) toward a holster on her belt.

The Explorer carried a weapon, a pistol of sorts, which fired hypersonic waves on a range of frequencies that disrupted neural functioning. Her orders from Chee were explicit: shoot any witnesses immediately. One shot was sufficient to render an adult unconscious for six hours, but the effect left no permanent damage.

[That caught my attention; I'd never heard of such a weapon. The Spark Lords occasionally produced big bulky rifles with a "hypersonic stun" setting, but never anything as small and convenient as a pistol. The OldTechs had never used hypersonics either. If Opal's people had the technical expertise to create such weapons, it was something they'd learned on their own. Which suggested a flabbergasting degree of scientific sophistication.

[I've already said Opal knew more science than me; where could she have come from that was so much more advanced than the rest of the world? My alma mater, the Collegium Ismaili, was the finest university on Earth.

[On Earth.

[Another chill went through me. Opal had started with, "Once upon a time, a baby girl was born far, far away." How far was far?]

The Explorer raised her pistol. The man's smile never wavered; he made no move to duck or dodge, though in the darkness he couldn't possibly tell what kind of gun was aiming at his face. For all he knew, it was a normal flintlock, or even an OldTech weapon with enough power to stop an elephant. Yet the man continued to smile.

How odd.

The Explorer pulled the trigger. The pistol made a soft whir—an extra sound added to the gun's mechanism so the shooter would know it was working. (The hypersonics themselves were beyond the range of human hearing.)

Yet the man did not fall down. He whispered, "Surprise, Explorer. Your toy doesn't work on me."

Without conscious thought, the Explorer dived to one side, like a woman throwing herself from the path of a runaway horse. It was an automatic action, instilled by her training— whenever something caught her completely by surprise, combat reflexes took over. Dive, roll. As she landed, she crushed a dozen tobacco plants beneath her weight; but that barely registered on her consciousness. Her mind was occupied with more pressing concerns. How did the man know she was an Explorer? And how could he have been waiting for her?

She knew Chee had come to this place before—every year at this time, he sent one of his Explorers on a tobacco raid— but it was a big island, and Chee never targeted the same farm twice. How could this man be in exactly the right place at the right time to meet her? How could he resist the hypersonics? How could he know to call her "Explorer"?

From a few steps away, the man laughed. He was coming toward her through the tobacco, intentionally trampling plants as he passed. It wasn't easy—tobacco grows tall, with a tough thick stalk—but the man stamped hard, apparently from sheer spite. He seemed to relish the destruction.

The Explorer had rolled to her feet and was trying to put some distance between herself and the man; but the clothes she wore were bulky, and would slow her excessively if she tried to run . . .

[I had the vision of Opal in some kind of cumbersome spacesuit. Did that make sense? Yes. If she came from a world beyond our own, she might want to avoid exposure to our local microorganisms . . . and to prevent her own microbes from infecting Earth. Therefore she'd wear some airtight outfit like a perfectly sealed cocoon. It would be heavy and need its own oxygen supply—an unfortunate weight to bear if you wanted to flee from a threat.]

Meanwhile, the man just laughed and slashed through the tobacco after her. She tried to shoot him again, but the gun had no effect. Then he grabbed her and knocked the pistol out of her hand.

"What do you want?" she asked.

"Everything," he said. "Your weapon. Your equipment. You."

She tried to break free, but her clothes impeded her movement. The man held on. She stopped her struggles and asked, "How did you know I'd be coming here?"

He said, "Because I arranged it."

"That's not true."

"You're naïve. How did you find your landing site? You followed a beacon you sent ahead of time. What would happen if someone activated a much more powerful beacon? You'd land where he wanted you to land." The man laughed. "This is the time of year you always come. I've been waiting every night for a week . . . but in the end, I knew you'd come to me."

[I was frustrated at the details missing from Opal's account. How did she actually land on our planet? A small flying ship? Some means of teleportation, like the ones described in OldTech fantasy fiction? What kind of beacon would that involve? As a scientist, I wanted to know . . . but the gist of the story was clear, despite the lack of specifics. Opal had been decoyed from her intended landing site to the place where the man was waiting. I grudgingly admitted the precise mechanism didn't matter.]

"Why do you want my equipment?" the Explorer asked. "If you're smart enough to build a beacon to lure me, can't you build other things too?"

"This is a primitive place," the man said. "Advanced materials are hard to find. Attempting to produce or procure such materials can draw unwanted attention from the Spark Lords."

"And you're hiding from the Sparks?"

"Until I'm ready." He glanced at the stun-pistol lying in the dirt. "Spark armor can resist normal weapon fire; but that's not a normal weapon. It might give me an advantage— when the time comes."

"I don't want you shooting people with my gun." And the Explorer drove her knee into the man's testicles.

He didn't try to evade it. [No automatic reflex to avoid groin attacks.] *The Explorer's knee struck hard into flesh . . . and kept on going, like plunging into soft yielding sand. Immediately, she pulled back. Bits of the man's lower abdomen clung to the clothes around her knee. The scraps of flesh quivered for a moment, then shriveled into small dry grains reminiscent of gunpowder.*

The man said, "Full of surprises, aren't I?"

His hand shot forward . . . but it had ceased to look like a human appendage. It was black and crusted, each finger thinning to a spikelike tip. They stabbed through the Explorer's special uniform like rusty nails driven through paper; they pierced her shoulder, bringing a gush of blood and pain.

"What are you?" the Explorer whispered, trying to pull away but too deeply impaled.

"What do you think? An alien. A shapeshifter. Trapped on this insufferable planet, forced to flee from the Spark Lords, trying to stay one step ahead . . ."

"And failing miserably," said a new voice.

The Explorer and shapeshifter snapped their heads toward the voice. A woman stood among crushed tobacco plants, only a pace away. She wore armor of bright yellow plastic, a shell that covered her completely from head to toe; the visor of her helmet was a blank plate showing nothing of the face beneath. In one hand, she held a long sword. She tapped the pommel against her thigh and the blade shone forth with a buttery light.

"War-Lord Vanessa of Spark," she said. *"The introduction is for your benefit, Explorer. Your companion knows who I am. I've been chasing him a long time . . . and I finally caught up."* She chuckled. *"He gives off a stink that Spark Royal can smell—especially if he stays in one place for a while. Isn't that right, monster? I heard you say you've been waiting here every night for a week. Bad planning, BEM-brain. You should have stayed on the move."*

As a response, the alien twisted the talons still imbedded in the Explorer's shoulder. The Explorer winced in pain. *"If you come any closer,"* the alien told Vanessa, *"I'll kill this woman."*

"Feel free," the War-Lord answered. *"You'll save me the trouble later. And do it as messily as you can. We have to make an example of her . . . for any other intruders who think they can come here in defiance of the treaties."* Vanessa lifted her sword. *"Here's a plan: you keep ripping the crap out of that shoulder while I decapitate the bitch. Or maybe I'll chop off her hands—that's the traditional punishment for thieves, isn't it?"*

The alien growled in anger, or perhaps confusion at the War-Lord's response. In that moment, as the creature hesitated, Vanessa swung her weapon . . . but not at the Explorer. The glowing blade twisted at the last instant and bit deeply into the shapeshifter's neck. The trick maneuver didn't have as much strength as a full-motion swing, but it still came close to lopping off the creature's head. Furthermore, the

sword's yellow shine caused as much damage as the blade itself: while the blade severed flesh, the shine seemed to wither
surrounding tissues to the same black gunpowder the Explorer had seen after ramming the alien with her knee.

The force of Vanessa's blow threw the alien's head forward, nearly smashing it against the Explorer. The head lay
tilted for a moment; then it suddenly shot upward, wrenching
free from its body and hurtling several paces across the tobacco field. Before it landed, it had already sprouted legs
from its severed throat: black spider-limbs on which it began
scuttling for the shadows.

"Hold on to the body," Vanessa shouted to the Explorer;
then she ran off after the head. Almost immediately, the rest
of the alien began breaking into pieces too. Both legs and
arms detached themselves from the torso; one arm remained
stuck in the Explorer's shoulder, but the other parts fell to the
ground and extruded spider-limbs of their own. The Explorer
snatched up the alien's right leg before it could escape, and
threw herself down on her knees to pin the torso. However,
she had no way to stop the other leg and arm from scurrying
into the night.

The arm that was still dug deep into the Explorer's shoulder began to writhe, trying to break free . . . and perhaps
also trying to cause enough agony that she'd release her grip
on the leg or the torso. Too much more, and the Explorer
knew she'd pass out from pain; but before that could happen,
Vanessa returned.

Instead of a glowing sword, the War-Lord now carried a
small slim rod, as wide as a pinkie finger but three times as
long. She tapped a button on the end of the rod and suddenly
glitters of red and green light sparkled into life up and down
the rod's length. Quickly, she slapped the rod's tip onto the
arm that was speared into the Explorer's shoulder. The alien
limb vanished with a soft <BINK> : collapsing in on itself,
twisting and turning until it folded itself entirely out of this
plane of existence. Two more slaps on the torso and leg,
<BINK> , <BINK> . . . then all evidence of the alien was gone,
leaving nothing but a salad of trampled tobacco.

The Explorer remained on her knees, trying to keep from

vomiting. Vanessa crouched beside her. "You'll have to come to Spark Royal. That's the only place with facilities to clean your wound—it's sure to be infected with alien tissues."

"I thought you intended to kill me," the Explorer said. "For breaking the treaty."

Vanessa shrugged. "Usually we do kill outsiders . . . but your damned Admiral Chee has friends in high places. Very high. Each year the smug old bugger sends someone to steal tobacco, and each year he goes off thinking he caught Spark Royal with its pants down. It never occurs to the bastard we let him get away. Chee has no clue he's part of something larger—a long-term plan by forces far beyond him, or any other human."

"And you Sparks have to obey those forces?"

The War-Lord growled. "Sparks don't obey anyone. But we've come to an agreement with certain allies, and part of the deal is we don't kill Chee . . . or any other member of the Explorer Corps."

"So I'm safe," the Explorer said.

"No. You'll be dead in a week if I don't treat that wound. And don't get any stupid ideas about your own doctors dealing with it; that alien is way out of their league. Or League."

"What was that thing you killed?" the Explorer asked. "Was it really an alien? A shapeshifter?"

"Yes," Vanessa said. "I don't know the species's real name, but Spark Royal calls them Lucifers. Like a lot of advanced races, they're actually hive minds made up of millions of smaller units." She pointed to the gunpowder specks on the Explorer's knee. "Each one of those grains is a cellule, a separate organism . . . but it's in mental contact with almost every other Lucifer in the universe. Put a million cellules together and they can modify themselves to look like anything. Lucky for us, they don't reproduce quickly; it'll take years for those parts that got away to grow enough mass to impersonate humans again. But they're evil little shits who love to cause pain and death. I guarantee you've got at least one cellule still burrowed into your shoulder. It'll do its damnedest to kill you, just for spite . . . and as a shapeshifter, it's got a lot of nasty tricks at its disposal."

The Explorer tried to stand. Her legs were too weak to support her. Vanessa picked her up as easily as she would a child and started walking across the field.

"Chee expects me back," the Explorer said.

"Give him a radio call. Tell him you refuse to go home. The Explorer Corps treats you like shit and you've decided there must be better ways to spend your life."

"That's what I've decided, is it?"

"Yes," Vanessa said. She hugged the Explorer's body a little closer.

"And how will I spend my life in a place like this? I don't fit in; I don't know how people live here."

Vanessa chuckled. "Spark Royal will give you something to do. We're bastards that way. Once we save your life, you'll be in our debt and we'll exploit you shamelessly."

"How?"

"I'll have to think about that. If Explorers are as clever and resourceful as I've heard, there are lots of ways you can make yourself useful." Vanessa laughed. "Working for Spark Royal is just as dangerous as being an Explorer, but it's a hell of a lot more fun."

And the War-Lord was right. The Explorer felt no regrets at abandoning her former life. She radioed Chee and told him where he could put his missions and his tobacco; she returned to Spark Royal with Vanessa, where she received training, friendship, and a new face . . . this time an attractive one that didn't make "decent folk" avert their eyes; and she had many, many adventures with Vanessa all around the world.

In time she got too old for rough action; but Spark Royal had use for her, even in retirement. The Sparks controlled a network of spies in every part of the planet—not just placed at random, but in locations where trouble was expected. When Spark Royal told the Explorer she would become chancellor of an undistinguished school in Simka, she asked how such a place could possibly be considered a hot spot. "Haven't a clue," Vanessa answered, "but we've got it on good authority."

"What good authority?"

*"Some high hoity-toit in the League of Peoples . . . an ass-
hole who specializes in advance knowledge of where things
will go wrong." Vanessa sighed. "Just between you and me, I
hate the way aliens can predict the future. It's fucking
spooky."*

"How do they do it?"

*"According to them, superior brainpower. One of them
gave me this analogy: suppose you see a rock perched on the
edge of a cliff. You're smart enough to know the rock will fall
sooner or later; a wind will blow it over, rain will erode the
ground underneath, some kid will shove it off just for
kicks . . . however it happens, you have no doubt the rock will
plummet eventually. But lesser intelligences can't make that
connection—a dog or a cat or something similar just can't
see what's bound to happen."*

*"And these aliens compare us to dogs? We're surrounded
by rocks on the edges of cliffs and we're too stupid to recognize the inevitable?"*

*"Exactly," Vanessa said. "Also too stupid to recognize our
limitations. When someone else says, 'This is obvious,' we
don't believe it. We think it's a trick. We call it unfair or illog-
ical . . . when really, it's ridiculous to regard ourselves as the
ultimate judges of what intellect can do. Our brains are only
a few million years ahead of a dog's; and some alien races
evolved billions of years before we did. On the ladder of intelligence, we're barely off the ground—but it sure is a bitch
living in a universe where so many species are smarter than
you."*

*So the Explorer went where she was told. To the Feliss
Academy. She didn't believe anything important could happen in such a backwater . . . but one should never bet against
the Spark Lords.*

Opal spread her hands, then let them fall into her lap.
"And that's the end of my story. Or the beginning of someone
else's. Take your pick."

Annah and I didn't speak for several seconds after Opal finished. I was overwhelmed by the thought that this woman I
knew had come from outer space; but when I considered her

scientific knowledge—and those moments during past conversations when she'd catch her breath to correct me, then fall silent like someone afraid to reveal too much—I could believe she *had* been born on some world more advanced than Earth.

Even more boggling was the idea that she'd been assigned to our school in anticipation of some crisis. Five years ago, when Opal became chancellor, how could anyone foresee Rosalind's arrival and the use of a bioweapon? Could Spark Royal's alien allies really be that smart?

It was Annah who finally broke the silence. "It's an amazing story, chancellor," Annah said. "But I'm . . . it's . . . why did you tell us?"

Opal gave a humorless laugh. "Because I've been dying to tell someone for years. And because a sort of a prophecy kind of thing says Phil is going on a quest. I was an Explorer once; I don't like people heading into danger when they don't know all the facts. So I thought I should tell you what I could." She paused. "But remember, Phil; it's still secret. Don't go blabbing to those drinking buddies of yours."

"I'll keep it quiet," I said, "unless it really becomes necessary to tell my friends."

"Fair enough," Opal agreed. "And let's hope that never happens. Maybe your quest will go in some completely different direction."

"At the moment, we don't *have* a quest," I said. "What great deed needs doing? What sacred treasure has been lost?"

"I suppose we'll find out eventually." Opal shrugged. "Meanwhile, our next move is obvious."

"What is it?"

"Call the Sparks," she said. "Let *them* sort out this damned mess."

5

LOCAL BOYS

Opal had no direct way of contacting Spark Royal; she could only relay a message through Governor Niome in Feliss City. While Annah helped Opal write a note, I went to fetch the school's emergency courier—a seventeen-year-old with the unfortunate name of Wallace Wallace. He was a strapping local farm boy from a strapping local farm, the latest in a line of Wallace Wallaces stretching back two centuries to an ancestor with an unfortunate sense of humor. Like most of his predecessors, the newest Wallace Wallace swore he'd never burden his own son with such a ridiculous name . . . but considering how consistently his forefathers had surrendered to the weight of tradition, I wondered if our own Wallace-squared would stick to his resolve.

Perhaps he would. This Wallace had a distinction that set him apart from previous generations: a full scholarship at Feliss Academy. He'd earned his place through brains and discipline, not parental wealth. Each year the academy accepted a few exceptional teenagers from the Simka district, without charging a cent for tuition or board. Partly this was a ploy to placate people in the region by helping their best and brightest. Bringing in smart-and-hungry kids also increased energy levels in our classrooms, which otherwise would be populated by well-bred but second-rate plodders who'd grown accustomed to depending on family largesse rather than their own initiative. Added to that, our normal (i.e., rich) students benefited from having floormates who knew the seedier aspects of town—which tattooists used clean needles, which butcher shops sold the best lamb's-skin for condoms, which herbalists kept a supply of jinkweed hidden under the counter. Lastly, the school liked having a few spare hands who could be called upon to run errands in crises . . . like riding to Feliss City with a message for the governor. It was Wallace's turn to answer the call, which is why I fumbled my way through the pitch-dark corridors and tapped on his door.

He answered immediately . . . holding a candle and flashing a triumphant grin. The grin faltered instantly. "Dr. Dhubhai!" he said with a surprised yelp.

"Expecting someone else?" I asked.

"No, no," he answered in a transparent lie. "No, no," he said again, in case I missed his guilt the first time.

Considering the circumstances, I didn't have time to interrogate the boy . . . but my teacherly instincts couldn't help wondering which of our female students Wallace had expected to find knocking at his door. I couldn't remember seeing him with anyone in particular. Then again, the girl might want to keep their relationship secret; snooty elements of the student body considered kids like Wallace to be "peasant charity cases" and would mercilessly snub any high-born girl who sullied herself with a "barnyard beau." Plenty of girls would still fall for Wallace's charms—he was a smart, pleasant kid, good-looking in a fresh-from-the-cow-pen way—but the stigma of his "commoner" background might make a blue-blooded belle keep her feelings out of the public eye. The result: she'd sneak into Wallace's room at 2:00 A.M. rather than openly neck with him behind the stables. To be honest, I didn't much care if Wallace conducted a discreet cuddle session with some duchess/countess/heiress . . . but a horrid possibility crossed my mind.

"Just tell me," I said, "you weren't waiting for Rosalind Tzekich."

"Rosalind? Of course not. She's taken."

"Who took her?"

"Sebastian."

By which he could only mean Sebastian Shore, another

local boy: son of a successful metalsmith, prosperous by Simka standards but nowhere near the wealth of most students in our academy. Sebastian was a quiet sixteen-year-old who excelled in class but seldom socialized with his peers. He lived in his own head, having little contact with the world around him. When I thought about it, Sebastian might click perfectly with Rosalind Tzekich: both were self-isolated dreamers, staring out that classroom window.

"Doctor," said Wallace, "was there something you wanted?"

I shook off my reverie. "You're the courier on call, aren't you?"

He nodded, not looking happy about it.

"Then get dressed," I said. "You're going to Governor Niome, so wear something respectable. Something warm too—it's cold in the open wind. When you're ready, go to the kitchen and pack food for the trip. Then see the chancellor in her room. Got it?"

"Chancellor's room. Yes, sir." Wallace's face had brightened considerably; on the downside, he was going to miss his midnight tryst . . . but a jaunt to see the governor obviously struck him as acceptable compensation. He could take one of the school's best horses, see the famous Feliss Government House (home of the largest prison system in the world), and enjoy some time on his own. The city was a good ten hours' ride from Simka—maybe more, depending how snowy the roads were. Wallace would have a pleasant adventure to brag about to his friends when he got home.

"Get going," I told him. "The chancellor will expect you in . . . oh, twenty minutes." That would give Wallace time to get dressed and packed, plus (if he was smart) a few minutes to write a note apologizing to whichever girl he was standing up.

I've never liked ruining my students' love-lives.

I started back to the chancellor and Annah . . . then changed my mind and headed for the room of Sebastian Shore. If Sebastian had been close to Rosalind, perhaps he'd visited her earlier in the evening. Perhaps he'd seen something unusual in her room, some indication of an intruder. And perhaps (the thought made me shudder), he was lying dead in his bed with white curds dribbling from his nose. If Rosalind had been infected and Sebastian had kissed her good-night . . .

I didn't want another corpse on our hands.

Even if Sebastian *hadn't* been infected, the next few minutes wouldn't be pleasant. I'd have to tell the boy his sweetheart was dead. As a don, I wasn't a stranger to giving students bad news—over the years, there'd been several occasions where I'd had to sit down with someone and say, "We've received a letter from your home . . ."—but this was the first time I'd have to tell one of my charges about the death of a fellow student. For a moment, I hesitated outside Sebastian's door, trying to compose appropriate words of sympathy in my mind. I failed utterly. In the end, I took a deep breath and knocked before I slunk away like a coward.

Seconds passed. The boy didn't answer my knock.

I knocked again, louder. Still no answer. I told myself Sebastian was just sound asleep; heaven knows, some teenage boys can sleep through anything. But I couldn't help remembering poor Rosalind lying sprawled in her silent room. With my mouth dry, I gave one more knock . . . then got out my pass key.

There was no wretched smell when I opened Sebastian's door—just the usual fusty mix of unwashed laundry, cheap lamp oil, and apple cores rotting in an unseen wastebasket. "Sebastian?" I whispered. "It's Dr. Dhubhai."

I hadn't brought a lamp of my own and the room was inky dark, curtains drawn to shut out the tiniest glimmer of starshine. "Sebastian," I said more loudly, "sorry to disturb you . . ."

No response. When I held my breath, I couldn't hear a sound—definitely no snores or rustles from the bed. Feeling nausea grow in my stomach, I moved forward in the blackness, expecting any moment to trip over books or clothes or badminton rackets: the debris that boys perennially leave on the floor. But I found no obstacles until I bumped into the bed itself.

"Sebastian," I said. "Please wake up. Sebastian!"

Not a sound.

I reached into my pockets and found my matchbox. Another chill of *déjà vu* . . . but this time, when I lit a match, no ghostly breeze blew it out. The wavering light showed me an empty bed, neatly made, with a piece of paper lying on the pillow. The rest of the room appeared equally tidy—nothing tossed on the floor, every book put away, the desk clear of clutter. I stared around stupidly till the match burned down to the point where I had to shake it out. There was no dead Sebastian here; it looked as if the boy had cleaned up his room, then vanished.

Tonight of all nights, I doubted his departure was coincidence.

Feeling my way up the bed, I found the pillow and the paper lying on it. I could have lit another match to read the note . . . but I didn't. Instead, I took the page and hightailed it out of the room—locking the door behind me and scurrying posthaste to the chancellor's.

On the way, I couldn't help speculating why Sebastian had left. The least sinister scenario was that he'd learned Rosalind was dead. Perhaps the two had arranged a midnight assignation, like Wallace Wallace and his unknown lady love. Sebastian had gone to Rosalind's room; he'd discovered the girl's corpse; he'd run off in grief and horror. It might have been a shattering experience for the boy, but at least it was basically innocent.

There were so many other possibilities that weren't innocent at all.

By the time I reached the chancellor's room, the Caryatid had arrived . . . along with the rest of our drinking party, Myoko, Pelinor, and Impervia. When cousin Fatima delivered my message, the Caryatid had sent the girl to round up the rest of our group. "I wanted us all together," the Caryatid said. "For the quest, you know. So we can start right away." From the steely glint in the Caryatid's eye, I suspected she was really thinking, *If I get woken in the middle of the night, everybody else gets dragged out of bed too.* Motherly though she was, the Caryatid lived by the rule *I'm not going to suffer alone.* (Which, now that I think of it, is a very motherly attitude.)

While I talked with the Caryatid, Annah sat quietly on the couch, making no effort to converse with the others. She wasn't on bad terms with my tavern-touring cronies; she just didn't have much in common with them. They were all so extravagantly *loud* compared to Annah . . . yet Annah was the one who held my attention as she slid sideways on the couch, making room for me. When I sat beside her, she murmured, "You were gone a long time. I . . ."

She didn't finish her sentence. She didn't have to: as if the words *I was worried* jumped straight from her brain into mine.

"I had to check something," I said. Raising my voice, I announced to the whole room, "Wallace told me Rosalind had been spending time with Sebastian Shore . . . so I went to see the boy." I paused. "He's gone. Bed made, room tidied, note on the pillow."

"Uh-oh," said Myoko.

"Dear me," said Pelinor.

Impervia silently crossed herself.

I held out Sebastian's note to the chancellor, but Opal waved it away. "You read it," she said. "Aloud."

Reluctantly I unfolded the paper and looked at the message. Sebastian had scrawled it quickly in low-grade watery ink; still, the words were legible enough.

Dear Dr. Dhubhai:

If you don't know already, Rosalind Tzekich and I have eloped. We'll come back when we're ready, but we just want to be alone for a while. You'll see us again when we're married.

Tell our families not to worry. I know they'll disapprove to begin with, but when they see how much we love each other, they're sure to understand.

Sebastian

After I finished reading, there was a long silence . . . broken finally by Pelinor.

"Perhaps there's something I'm missing," he said, "but how can Sebastian think he's eloped with Rosalind when she's lying dead in her room?"

Impervia made an impatient gesture. "The boy must have written the note ahead of time. Most likely, he and Rosalind arranged to leave their dorms separately and meet off campus. Sebastian cleaned his room, wrote the note, then headed out. For all we know, he's still waiting at the agreed-upon rendezvous: shivering in the dark and crying bitter tears because he believes Rosalind has stood him up."

"Or," said Myoko, "he's blissfully run off with something that looks like Rosalind but isn't."

I spoke for us all when I said, "Ulp."

Though Chancellor Opal was a master of hiding her emotions, the look on her face was stricken. Her thoughts had to be similar to mine: thinking of the thing in the tobacco field. What War-Lord Vanessa had called a Lucifer.

Pelinor, however, hadn't heard the chancellor's tale. He gave his mustache a suck and said, "Come now, Myoko, that's a tad overimaginative. Impervia's version makes sense. Sebastian wrote the note . . . went off to meet Rosalind . . . didn't know she would never arrive. Plain and simple."

Myoko raised an eyebrow. "So it's just coincidence Rosalind died the night she planned to elope?"

Impervia gave a dismissive sniff. "Coincidences happen."

"So do doppelgängers," answered Myoko. She turned to the Caryatid and asked, "Aren't there spells that can make a person look like someone else?"

The Caryatid nodded reluctantly. "Some illusion spells can do the trick . . . but they're always flawed in some way. They mimic the face but not the rest of the body; or they duplicate the appearance but not the voice; or they do the whole job but last for only a few minutes; or the illusion simply can't be seen by some people—like Kaylan's Chameleon, which fools men but not women . . ."

"But it *is* possible," Myoko said. "That's the point. And sorcery is just one possibility." She turned eagerly toward me. "Didn't the OldTechs make androids that were perfect doubles of people?"

I shook my head. "The OldTechs never got that sophisticated. Most of their robots were just boxes on wheels, or big metal arms. The few that did appear human were no more than clockwork novelties: programmed with a set of simple gestures and a recorded speech track, but not enough to fool anyone more than a couple seconds."

"All right," Myoko said, "so the OldTechs couldn't make android duplicates—not during OldTech times, four hundred years ago. But since then, the people who abandoned Earth must have improved their technology. They might be able to make lifelike androids now."

I couldn't help glancing at Opal; her gaze was turned to the floor. Meanwhile, the Caryatid said, "Many things are possible, Myoko dear . . . but what would be the point? Why would one of our space cousins create a duplicate of Rosalind just to deceive a lovestruck teenager?"

Myoko didn't answer immediately—she was looking in my direction, but her eyes were distant. Finally, she gave herself a little shake and said, "Sebastian is more than a lovestruck teenager. He's special."

"How?" asked Impervia.

Myoko lowered her head. "Sebastian Shore is the most powerful psychic I've ever met."

Psionic folks always terrified me . . . even petite little Myoko. If her gift was strong enough to lift Impervia, it was also strong enough to reach into one's chest and squeeze one's heart to a standstill. Pinch one's carotid artery. Snap one's spinal nerves.

And that was just telekinesis. Other psychics had different psionic powers. Some were clairsentient, hearing or seeing things at remote distances. Others were telepathic, able to read the thoughts of those around them or (even worse) plant an idea into your brain as if you'd thought of it yourself. Some could artificially arouse emotions; some could induce hallucinations; some could strike you blind. Most, thank heavens, had to concentrate a considerable length of time before they used their power, and few had significant range. Still, they were spooky people . . . and after a prophecy, a haunting, and a bioweapon, I hated to find there was also a psychic in the mix.

"So," Pelinor said, "young Sebastian has psionic powers. Good for him. We need more psychics to . . . um . . . do whatever they do. Government work mostly, am I right? Spying and scrying, et cetera?"

Myoko shook her head. "Only a few work for governors: the empath who sits at Niome's right hand to tell her when people are lying; the telepaths who provide communications between provinces; clairvoyants who spy on a governor's enemies. But most psychics don't end up as provincial officials." She dropped her gaze to her hands. "Most psychics end up as slaves."

"Slaves?" Pelinor repeated the word in distaste.

Myoko nodded. "If they're lucky, they get a gilded cage: working for some rich merchant, a secret advantage in wheeling and dealing. Psychics like that are kept on a short leash, but at least they get some pampering. On the other hand, psychics who *aren't* so lucky . . ." She clenched her fists. "They can be kept in dungeons, half-starved and brutalized, because that's the way their owners keep freaks in line."

Myoko glared at us all, daring us to speak. No one did. Pelinor gave his mustache a self-abashed suck, but stopped immediately as it sounded in the silence.

Finally Myoko let her hostility drain away as she lowered her gaze. "I went to a school for psychics. A hidden place that developed our abilities. It was as secure as our mentors could make it . . . but a few students still went missing every year. Kidnapped. There are ruthless criminal bastards who'll do anything to get their hands on a first-rate psychic."

The Caryatid gave a shiver. "You think that might happen to Sebastian?"

"He's powerful," Myoko replied. "He wouldn't be easy to snatch outright. But if someone created a look-alike of his girlfriend and enticed him to run off somewhere . . . sooner or later, the look-alike could lead him into a trap, and then he'd be stuck for the rest of his life."

"But Myoko," Impervia said, "how would anyone know he was a psychic? You haven't told anyone, have you?" She gave Myoko a reproving look. "You didn't tell us, for example."

"No, I didn't. This academy can handle only weak little abilities—not powerful people like Sebastian. It was sheer accident he was accepted as a 'local outreach' student . . . and sheer accident I recognized the extent of his talents. For the boy's sake, I couldn't tell *anyone* how good he was."

"Then how did these hypothetical kidnappers find out?" Impervia asked.

Myoko didn't answer right away. Finally, with downcast eyes, she said, "I can think of one explanation. Rosalind."

The Caryatid's motherly eyes grew wide. "You mean he told Rosalind and Rosalind told . . ."

Her voice faded away. After a moment, Myoko sighed. "I made Sebastian promise to keep his powers a secret; but when kids fall in love, they hate hiding anything. If Sebastian confessed the truth to Rosalind, she might have reported it to her mother . . . and we all know what kind of woman Elizabeth Tzekich is."

Pelinor scowled in outrage. "You mean Rosalind *betrayed* him?"

Myoko shrugged. "I don't think she wrote her mom and said, 'I've met a guy you should enslave.' But she might have written, 'I've met a guy I love very much, and I know you'll let us get married because he's got these powers that are really special.'"

"But if that's so," Impervia said, "wouldn't the mother just tell the girl, 'You have my blessing, bring the boy for a visit?' Perhaps when Sebastian arrived at the Tzekich home, the mother would throw him in chains and tell Rosalind the wedding was off; but until then, there'd be no need to use force."

"Besides," put in the Caryatid, "the Ring of Knives might

kidnap Sebastian, but they wouldn't murder Rosalind at the same time. A mother would never kill her own daughter."

"I've heard that mothers kill their own children more often than they kill anyone else," Myoko said. "But maybe it's not Mother Tzekich at all. Maybe there's a spy in the Ring of Knives who learned Rosalind's secret. Maybe the spy told a rival criminal family, so the rivals killed Rosalind and kidnapped Sebastian."

"Or maybe," Impervia replied, "no one at all has been kidnapped and you're talking pure fantasy."

"Everyone calm down," Chancellor Opal said, holding up her hands to prevent further argument. "Let's gather more facts before we get lost in what-ifs. Myoko, Phil . . . search Sebastian's room."

"What are we looking for?" Myoko asked.

"Anything unusual. You two know the boy better than the rest of us."

Myoko turned to meet my eyes. I nodded. She'd been Sebastian's psionics mentor; I'd been his don. Between the two of us, we might notice if anything was amiss in the boy's room.

"We'll go," Myoko said.

Opal nodded, then shifted toward the Caryatid. "I'd like you to try a Seeking spell on Sebastian's note. See where the boy is."

"If he's a strong psychic," the Caryatid said, "I won't pick anything up. The more psionic power, the more resistant a person is to Seekings."

Opal gave a ladylike shrug. "Do what you can. As for the rest of you, start searching the neighborhood. Possible places Sebastian and Rosalind might meet. As Impervia says, the simplest scenario is that the boy is out in the dark somewhere, waiting for Rosalind to show up."

The others murmured agreement. Annah, still sitting beside me, glanced quickly my way. An egotistic voice in my head whispered she was sad I'd be going with Myoko instead of staying with her; a more sensible voice told me to stop being a self-centered jackass. Before my two mental voices could start arguing, Opal stood briskly and gestured toward the door. "Go. Be useful. Find something." She paused. "And nobody wander off alone. In case there *are* shapeshifters in the bushes."

6

BLADES AND SADDLES

Myoko and I headed for Sebastian's room. We walked in silence the whole way . . . and I could feel rage building up in her, a seething fury utterly unlike the cheerful drinking buddy I knew. I couldn't remember ever seeing her the least bit angry—not in the middle of bar brawls, not when complaining about the most idiotic of students. The worst I'd witnessed was when she'd walked past the mirror in our faculty lounge and noticed a gray hair on her head; as she yanked the offending strand, she'd embarked on a curse-laden diatribe bewailing the cruelty of a universe that made gray stand out so glaringly amidst "youthful black tresses." Only the initial burst of annoyance had been genuine: the ensuing tirade was comic relief, purely for the benefit for those of us watching.

That was the Myoko I knew. Funny. Fun. Playing off the disparity between her outward appearance (dainty, demure) and her joyfully wicked mind. She was one of those rare women who could truly be "one of the boys"—joking more crudely, swearing more colorfully, belching more forcefully, and always with exquisite timing. Best of all, she never went too far: everyone has seen women act more loutish than men, but only gentle-ladies with a feel for the game can make one laugh rather than wince. Myoko had made me laugh a lot; I'd felt comfortable with her from the first day we met.

But not now. Not with her walking tensely beside me,

arms crossed tight against her chest, her mouth a severe line. As if the two of us had just had a fight.

Maybe in her mind we had: the ongoing fight between psychics and everyone else. It wasn't something she ever discussed in public; but now that the subject had been broached, Myoko didn't suppress her long-simmering resentment. Though she'd told us how low-powered she was compared to "real" psychics, she must have lived her life in constant fear someone would decide she was worth enslaving.

Her fear was well-based. Naïve old Pelinor might have been surprised about psychics being treated as cattle; but that just proved he wasn't really a high-born knight. Those of us who'd truly been born under a famous coat of arms knew what powerful families did behind closed doors.

We Dhubhais had always equipped our houses with "resident psychics." They were treated with respect, fed well, dressed well, and provided with suitably eye-pleasing companions—but they were never allowed off the grounds, and one could often catch them staring into the distance, their expressions carefully blank. Other rich families in Sheba mocked us for our softhearted ways. Those neighbors ruled their "chattels" with an iron hand.

Was that what was waiting for Sebastian?

Myoko clearly thought so: that's why she'd concealed the truth about the boy, even from those of us who thought we were her friends. She'd wanted Sebastian safe; and what place was safer than Feliss Academy? No one expected a gifted psychic at a school like ours. If you truly wanted to conceal a person's talent—if you wanted to pretend your powers weren't worthy of attention—the academy was an excellent cover.

Which brought up the question of Myoko herself.

I'd always assumed she was like the rest of us—competent enough to teach students the basics, but an utter mediocrity compared to real professionals. Even a small chore like levitating Impervia seemed to require Myoko's full concentration, not to mention a plenitude of preliminary brow-furrowing. However: after tonight's squabble at The Pot of Gold, Myoko had chatted casually while holding Impervia aloft . . . and for a brief moment, it appeared as if Myoko wasn't exerting herself at all.

Could she be stronger than she pretended? Could she too be using the academy as camouflage?

Things to think about as we walked unspeaking through the halls.

I was carrying an oil lamp, borrowed from Chancellor Opal. When we got to Sebastian's door, I handed the light to Myoko while I got out my pass key. This broke some wordless barrier between us, because Myoko shuddered and said, "There's something in the air tonight, Phil. Something big."

"Is that a psychic premonition?"

She shook her head. "I don't do premonitions. Just TK. Sebastian, on the other hand . . ."

"He did premonitions?"

"He did everything," she said. "TK. Telepathy. Remote perception with all five senses. I've never seen anyone like him." She paused. "My teachers at psionics school would say it was impossible."

I gave a weak chuckle. "Imagine that! Teachers being wrong about something."

"Granted. But it's the nature of psionics that . . ." She broke off. "Phil, you've studied science. Do you know how psionics work?"

"I've heard many theories . . . but they're all hot air and hand-waving. The only thing scientists agree on is that psychic powers come from outside intervention. Alien hightech. And sorcery's the same. Someone a lot more advanced than *Homo sapiens* decided to get cute."

Myoko didn't look at me; she let herself lean back against the wall beside Sebastian's door. "You think the League of Peoples did something? To Earth? To humanity?"

"It's the only sensible conclusion. Maybe they thought it would be a good joke to make human myths come true. Or maybe they thought they were doing us a favor—fulfilling our oldest fantasies. Maybe they had some secret agenda we'll never figure out . . . but it's no coincidence everything changed at the exact moment they showed up."

Myoko didn't answer; she'd turned her gaze toward the oil lamp, watching the flame's soft glow. Finally, without looking at me, she said, "You know something, Phil? You're right."

I waited for her to go on. She didn't. Finally I asked, "What do you mean?"

"I mean . . . psychics *know*. The teachers who taught me—they know exactly what happened." She turned her eyes toward me. "It's a deep dark secret, but . . ." She shrugged. "Do you want to hear?"

Her voice was nearly inaudible. I said, "Do you want to tell me? If it's a deep dark secret?"

"Sure. Why not."

She was right about there being something in the air. A night for revelations. I fell silent as she began to talk.

"Do you know what nanites are, Phil? Nanotech? Microscopic machines the size of bacteria . . . or even smaller, viruses, single molecules. You've heard of such things?"

I nodded. OldTech fantasies had predicted nano would solve all the world's problems . . . provided the stuff didn't destroy the planet first. But before nanotech had progressed beyond a few rudimentary prototypes, OldTech civilization disintegrated to the point where we couldn't even make steam engines, let alone microscopic robots.

"This may surprise you," said Myoko, "but thirty percent of all microbes on Earth today—things that look like bacteria and viruses—are actually nanites in disguise."

"What?" My voice was suddenly shrill: loud enough to wake half the boys on my floor. I lowered it immediately. "What are you talking about?

"Outside intervention, just like you said. Someone covered our planet with nano: land, sea, and air. The nanites are designed to replace natural microorganisms, then work together to make sorcery and psionics possible."

A door opened behind me. The future Duke Simon Westmarch peered out to see who'd been shouting. He wore his stethoscope around his neck, like a medallion dangling over his pajamas. "Go back to bed," I told him. "Everything's under control."

He nodded without a word and shut the door—more proof that this was a night when miracles could happen. I turned back to Myoko. "How could anyone replace thirty percent of all microorganisms without scientists noticing? We still have microscopes; not fancy electron ones, but the best you can get with ordinary optics. When I was at Collegium Ismaili, the biology department examined bacteria every day, and I never heard them mention nanites."

"Two reasons for that," Myoko answered. "First, the nanites superficially resemble conventional microbes. Elementary camouflage. Second, the nanites are smart . . . at least some of them are. Some are like brain cells, coordinating other nano activity. If the brainy ones notice a biologist getting out a microscope, they tell their fellow nanites to clear out. If worse comes to worst, they send in nano-stormtroopers to crack the microscope lens."

"Nanites are strong enough to do that?"

Myoko put her hand on my arm. "Phil, they're strong enough to lift Impervia. That's how it works. My psionic powers are just a hotline to the local brain-nano. The brains summon other nano from the surrounding environment to act as microscopic sky-cranes . . . and up Impervia goes."

I tried to picture the physics of how that would work. If lifting Impervia was the action, where was the equal and opposite reaction? I couldn't figure it out and didn't want to display my ignorance, so I changed the subject. "So how did you get this psionic hotline?"

"There are nanites *everywhere*, Phil—in the food we eat, the water we drink, the air we breathe. They get inside us, the same way normal microbes do. Our lungs, our bloodstreams, everywhere. Some drift inside by accident; others deliberately target humans and work into specific areas of their bodies. Particularly into the wombs of pregnant women."

"That doesn't sound healthy."

"Consider it a mixed blessing," Myoko said. "Some types of nano—and there are thousands of different breeds, each designed to perform a specific function—some types target the brains of developing embryos. They embed themselves shortly after conception so they're incorporated into the child's gray matter."

I winced. "How many children are infected like that?"

"All of them, Phil. Every last child born on Earth for the past four centuries. Animals too—the nanites are everywhere, absolutely inescapable. You have them riddling every part of your brain; so do I; so does everybody."

For a moment, I thought I was going to throw up. "What are the damned things doing in there?"

"Mostly waiting. For instructions."

"From whom?"

"Psychics and sorcerers." She gave me a pallid smile. "Even I don't like to contemplate that fact too long. But how do you think telepaths read minds? It's not tricky once you realize everyone's brain is full of nanites that have been linked into your mental processes almost since conception. They know what you're thinking . . . and they transmit it to receivers in the telepath's brain. As simple as OldTech radio."

"Simple." I made a face. None of this was the least bit simple. Were all the nanites in my head taking up space that should have been used by brain cells? Did they actually *replace* brain cells, the same way they'd replaced thirty percent of the natural bacteria and viruses in our biosphere? Were all my thoughts partly running on alien-built nanites rather than regular neurons?

And how did they get enough energy to transmit radio waves? Only one way: they must tap into the body's energy, sucking nutrition from blood just like normal cells. Parasites. Extraterrestrial parasites in the brain. Though I'd lived with them all my life, I still felt close to vomiting. "If we all have these things in our heads," I asked, "why aren't we all psychics?"

"Ah," said Myoko, "there's the trick. The nanites most people have in their brains lie dormant till they receive an outside stimulus . . . but as I said, there are different types of nano. One particular type—extremely rare—also plants itself into people's brains; but this type has the ability to *initi-*

ate action. For example, it can tell the nanites in other people's brains to send it signals."

"And that's the difference between a telepath and everyone else? The telepath has one of these initiator nanites?"

"That's it. That's the whole secret." She gave a self-conscious laugh. "Of course, there are plenty of complications." Myoko lifted her gaze to meet my eyes. "Do you know what it feels like when I use my telekinesis?"

I shrugged. "I don't know . . . maybe like you've got a phantom arm?"

"An arm? Hell, I'd *kill* for an arm." She rolled her eyes. "You know what I've got, Phil? A phantom knee. My right knee, to be exact. When I picked up Impervia tonight, I visualized tucking my knee under her, then shoving her up, up, up . . . the feel of it, which muscles would move when, picturing everything exactly. Of course, I couldn't lift Impervia with my *real* knee—I can't keep a full-grown woman perfectly balanced with just my kneecap jammed against her back. My psychic knee can do things my physical knee could never pull off. But in the end, it's still just a knee; exasperatingly limited. When I think what I could do if I had a *hand*: the joys of manual dexterity, Phil, the joys of manual dexterity!"

I had to laugh. Myoko did too. "The thing is," she said, "it all depends where the initiator nanite plants itself in a psychic's brain . . . and how far outward it sends its pseudo-neural connections. My initiator landed in the part of my brain that controls my right knee. As simple as that. So when I focus my attention on my knee in a particular way, the initiator responds."

"Hmm." I thought for a moment. "And it responds by sending radio messages to nearby nanites in the air. It tells those nanites to get together and lift Impervia . . . or to do whatever else the initiator wants."

"Exactly!" Myoko gave my arm a squeeze. "A psychic's power is entirely determined by where the initiator settles in. If it lodges in your visual cortex, you'll be able to see psionically. Maybe you'll be clairvoyant: your initiator can link with nanites half a continent away and see what they see. Or maybe you'll perceive auras . . . which means your initiator communicates with nanites in other people and presents their emotional states as colors. You might even be able to project optical illusions; your initiator sends images from your visual imagination to receiving nanites in other people's brains. Voilà: they see what you want them to see. There are lots of variations—visual processing occupies great swaths of our brains, and you get different effects depending on where the initiator lands within those swaths."

"I suppose if the initiator lands in a hearing center, you can hear things happening far away . . . or project sound illusions, or maybe hear other people's thoughts, transmitted by their own mental nanites."

Myoko nodded. "That's the idea. Things get weird if the initiator plunks down in an exotic corner of your mind; there was one guy at school whose initiator lived in his primary pleasure center and he could transmit the most . . ." She suddenly stopped in embarrassment. "Figure it out yourself."

"Lucky guy," I said.

"No," she replied, "very *un*lucky. He disappeared one day when he left school grounds. Now he's probably chained in some brothel where he has to make sure the paying guests have a good time . . . or he's playing gigolo to someone like Elizabeth Tzekich, who'll beat him if he doesn't give her orgasms on demand."

Myoko's voice had suddenly filled with bitterness . . . and her hand on my arm was an eagle's claw, fingernails digging fiercely through my sleeve. "Come on . . ." I began; but she gave me a look that made me hold my tongue.

"Don't try to comfort me, Phil. If you do, I might ram you through the wall. It's . . ." Her voice trailed off for a moment. "The threat hangs over every psychic's head. Always. Forever. The only protection is being too weak to interest the sharks. In a lot of psychics, the initiator attaches itself only loosely to the brain. You get a small intermittent power that isn't much use . . . or a power that takes a lot of strength and effort to activate. People like that—like *me*—are usually safe: more trouble than they're worth. But if you have a good strong power . . ."

"Like Sebastian."

She nodded. "Like Sebastian. Then you'll be a target your entire life . . . until someone finally gets you." She glanced at Sebastian's door. Her grip on my arm eased and I thought she might be ending the conversation; but I still had more questions.

"How do you know all this?" I asked. "About the nanites. How do you know things that scientists don't?"

"Oh, that. Forty years ago, there was a psychic man named Yoquito—came from a five-hut village near the Amazon, never learned to read or write, died young from chronic tuberculosis . . . but he had a hellishly powerful initiator in some analytic center of his mind, and he was undoubtedly the greatest genius ever produced by *Homo sapiens*. He didn't just think with his own brain; he could use all the nano around him like extra neurons. Yoquito wasn't the first person to have a power like that, but he was far and away the strongest: he claimed he could draw upon the power of every brain-nanite in the whole damned rainforest."

"So he was smart enough to figure out how psionics worked."

"He didn't just figure it out, Phil; the nanites literally explained it to him. As if they'd been waiting centuries for someone to ask, and were thrilled they could finally spill the secret. They told him about psionics and sorcery—"

"Sorcery?" I interrupted. "He knew how that worked too?"

"Sure," Myoko said. "It operates through the same nanites . . . just invoked a different way. Sorcerers don't have initiators in their brains; they initiate effects through gestures and invocations. If you say certain words or enact certain rituals, it triggers the nano to do specific things. Picture the nanites as trained dogs: if you say, 'Sit!' in the right tone of voice, they'll do what you want."

"Or," I murmured, thinking it over, "picture them as library functions in an OldTech computer. You invoke the correct subroutine and the nanites behave in accordance with their programming."

"All right," Myoko said, "if you insist on getting technical. The nanites respond to people performing certain actions . . . and those actions are intentionally bizarre so the nanites aren't triggered by accident."

"You don't think the aliens just invented crazy rituals so they could laugh at stupid humans dancing naked around a goat's head?"

Myoko nodded. "Maybe that too . . . but weird magical rituals date back thousands of years, well before sorcery became real. The aliens may simply have designed sorcery to match existing Earth folklore."

She was right—lots of human cultures had developed mythologies about what sorcery should look like, long before nanites made magic a reality. Those myths could easily have inspired the nanite-designers when they were deciding how sorcery would work. "What about the way the Caryatid controls fire?" I asked. "She never performs any fancy rituals."

"She must have when she was younger. When you're starting, you need exactly the right rigmarole; otherwise, you can't catch the nanites' attention. After a while, though, they begin to follow you around and pay attention to smaller and smaller signals. Like a trained dog again: at first you have to say, 'Sit!' very clearly and firmly . . . but once the dog gets the idea, you don't have to be so formal. Dogs even read your body language and anticipate what you want. The nanites are the same way. Think of the Caryatid's premonitions—they didn't start happening to her until that ritual with the pony and the calliope. After that, the premonitions began to trigger themselves spontaneously."

"And hauntings?" I asked. "The harp in the music room was more nanite activity?"

"Right. Rosalind had nanites in her brain, just like everybody else. Under certain conditions, especially traumatic death, the brain nanites imprint some portion of the dying person's personality on nearby nanites in the air. It's not an accident—the aliens who set this whole thing up wanted to create ghosts, in accordance with human ghost stories. If

Rosalind suffered enough emotional turmoil when she died, her nanites were almost certain to create a ghostly manifestation. The ghost isn't the real Rosalind, of course. It's just an artificial reproduction of some part of the girl's psyche: deliberately manufactured for melodramatic effect."

I chewed on that a moment. What I'd seen in the music room had definitely been melodramatic—choreographed for heavy emotional impact. The soft weeping, the harp playing in an empty room, the blood . . . in a way, it was almost *too* faithful to the clichés of ghost stories. A real ghost (if there was such a thing) would probably be more original. Still . . . "These nanites are good at playing out scenes," I said. "Very smart."

Myoko shrugged. "What can I say? There are trillions of the little fuckers everywhere. And they were constructed by aliens who knew a lot more science than the OldTechs ever did. The nanites are smart and *very* powerful."

"Is there any limit to their power?"

"They're only present here on Earth, so you can't use them to travel off-planet. Apart from that, they seem to up for anything humans can imagine. Transmutation of lead into gold . . . teleportation . . . time travel . . ."

I gulped. "Time travel?"

"Think about it," Myoko said. "How can the Caryatid get accurate premonitions if the nanites don't play fast and loose with time? Information travels from the future back to us in the present. And Yoquito said the nanites could make physical objects do the same thing. I don't know of cases on record . . . but then, the records would have changed, wouldn't they?"

Ouch. Time travel always gives respectable physicists the screamie-weamies. Not that we're totally convinced it's impossible . . . but we know enough about the universe to realize just how much of the natural order time travel would screw up. The cliché of killing your grandfather isn't nearly as serious as killing the second law of thermodynamics. "I don't suppose," I said, "your analytic genius Yoquito ever mentioned how to avoid time paradoxes?"

Myoko shook her head. "Yoquito didn't live long enough. When the nanites explained all this stuff, he decided he had to tell someone . . . and the nanites directed him to a school that housed people with powers just like his. My old alma mater: the school for psychics. It took Yoquito years to make his way out of the jungle and reach the school. After that, he told what he knew, and died from his tuberculosis within a month. One of those cases where a man with a terminal illness keeps himself alive by sheer willpower until he accomplishes what he wants to do. Then he just lets go."

A short silence. After a while I had to ask, "If your school has known this for forty years, why haven't they told anyone else? Scientists would kill for this kind of information."

"That's the problem," Myoko said. "Some scientists *would* kill for it. At least we're afraid they might. In case you haven't noticed, we psychics don't trust outsiders. The school where I trained has no incentive to divulge the truth, and every reason to play things close to the vest. If scientists understood how psionics worked, maybe they could use that against us somehow. We didn't want to take that risk. Anyway," she said, her voice suddenly brisk, "scientists will find out soon enough. Every psychic who goes through the school is taught what's really happening; when that many people know something, it doesn't stay secret for long. I'm surprised it's lasted forty years."

"As you say, psychics don't confide in other people." I looked up and met her eyes. "Which makes me wonder why you're telling me."

She dropped her gaze quickly. "Because Sebastian is missing. Because he might be in trouble and I want to save him. You're a smart man, Phil, and who knows, maybe if you understand the truth you can use it to help."

"I'll try," I told her. "What did you say the boy's powers were?"

"Everything. As far as I can tell, he's got every damned power in the book. Clairvoyance, clairaudience, telekinesis, telepathy . . . some more powerful than others, but he's got it all."

"How can that be?" I asked. "Could he have initiators all through his brain?"

Myoko shook her head. "Yoquito said that was impossible. If a baby already has an initiator, other initiators stay away."

"Hmm. Did you ever ask Sebastian to describe what his powers felt like?"

She nodded. "Like the world was filled with happy puppies, eager to do tricks for him. If he wanted something, he asked the puppies and they fell all over themselves to help him out . . . whether it was lifting heavy objects, displaying pictures in front of his eyes, or telling him the answers on exams. They'd even act without being asked—like once, he almost got kicked by a horse; but the air between him and the horse's hoof suddenly turned into a solid wall and stopped the kick before it made contact."

"Okay," I said. "So the boy's happy puppies are actually nanites. And they want to do him favors: help him, protect him. Maybe the initiator landed in some part of his brain that deals with social relations. Friendships. Every bit of nano on the planet has become Sebastian's loyal pal." I pondered the idea a moment, then made a face. "No: that doesn't sound right. I'll have to think some more." I gave a sideways smile at Myoko. "Though it sure would be nice to have thirty percent of the entire world as my doting chum."

Myoko gave my arm a squeeze. "Sorry, Phil, you'll have to make do with me." Quickly she turned away, toward Sebastian's door. "Let's get this over with, shall we?"

When I'd entered the room in the dark, I'd thought the place had been cleaned up. Now that I had more light, I saw it was not so much "clean" as what the maids called "boy-tidy": clear in the middle of the floor, with clutter shoved against the wall and arranged in balanced stacks. This was still an improvement over the usual state of the room; Sebastian must have spent hours picking things up (or having his nanite friends do the work). That showed the boy hadn't run off on the spur of the moment—he'd put things in order first.

Myoko, standing in the doorway, surveyed the piles of oddments around the edge of the room. "What do we think we're looking for?"

"Clues to where he went," I said.

"Like what?"

"Coach schedules perhaps. Or a note from some priestess willing to marry two teenagers without parental consent."

"No one in Simka would perform such a wedding," Myoko said, "and if any kid asked, the church would inform the academy. Opal makes hefty donations to all the local chapels to keep them on our side." Myoko shook her head. "If I were eloping, I wouldn't make wedding arrangements ahead of time; I'd just hightail it to a big city, then look for someone bribable. Heaven knows, Rosalind has enough cash to smooth the way—I've heard kids talk about how much gold she carries. Almost as much as you do."

I thought about that. "It would be nice to know where Rosalind's gold is. Is it still in her room, or has it gone missing?"

"The only way to find out," Myoko said, "would be to search Rosalind's room for her money-belt."

"And entering Rosalind's room," I said, "is an unhealthy thing to do." I turned back to the jumble heaped around Sebastian's dorm. What *were* we looking for? The boy was too smart to leave obvious hints of where he was going. If we *did* find a coach schedule with a destination circled, it would likely be a red herring to send us in the wrong direction.

Still, we couldn't give up without looking. Maybe we'd be brilliant enough to deduce where he'd gone from the things he took with him. If, for example, he'd left behind all his warm clothes, we could assume he was heading for the sunnier south.

Either that, or he was a typical teenage boy who didn't think ahead when packing.

Myoko and I began to search: she rummaged through the closets and drawers, while I checked miscellaneous stacks of paper. Five minutes later I was scanning some barely legible history notes when Myoko called, "Phil, can you give me a hand?"

She was kneeling beside the boy's bed. Tucked underneath was a polished wooden case, half as long as the bed itself and thick enough that it just fit between the floor and the bed frame. The case had bright brass handles, gleaming in the lamplight; I grabbed one handle, Myoko took the other, and together we dragged the case out.

There were no markings on the exterior . . . and no lock either, just a small hook-and-eye to keep the box shut. Myoko slipped the hook and lifted the lid to reveal an interior lined with plush green silk. A light fencing foil lay in a pre-shaped cradle amidst the silk; beside it were three more cradles, empty but obviously intended to hold other swords. Judging by the size of the cradles and the indentations in the silk, I guessed the missing weapons were a saber, a rapier, and a broadsword.

"Pretty," Myoko said, looking at the foil. "Nice workmanship." She tapped her finger on the button at the end of the blade, the little nubbin that prevented the sword from impaling opponents during a friendly fencing match. "Odd that Sebastian would have such a good weapon. I thought his family was poor."

"Only in comparison to the rest of our student body. The Shores run a local metalworks . . . and they make good money catering to the lordlings of our academy. Custom weapons, repairs, that sort of thing." I gestured toward the case. "When Sebastian was accepted at our school, I'll bet his family gave him a set of their best blades. So he wouldn't feel outclassed by the other kids."

"Hmm." Myoko looked into the case again. "Where are the other three swords?"

"Good question." I ran my fingers over the empty silk cradles. "He probably took one with him—a reasonable precaution if you're wandering the countryside at night. Maybe he brought one for Rosalind too."

"Surely she had a sword of her own," Myoko replied. "People talk as if her mother armed the girl with every weapon under the sun."

"That was the *real* Rosalind. A false Rosalind might not have access to the real one's arsenal."

Myoko gave a grudging nod. "All right: one sword for Sebastian, possibly one for Rosalind. What happened to the third blade?"

I shrugged. "Maybe he hocked it. He often complained about needing cash to keep up with the other kids."

"He said the same to me," Myoko agreed. "That's why I thought he was poor. But he despised himself for feeling that way, and refused to go on spending sprees to impress what he called *those rich nobs*."

"But what if he needed money for something special?" I asked. "Like eloping with Rosalind."

"Yes," Myoko said slowly, "he might pawn the sword then. If he needed money to get away. And he'd want to pay for everything himself, without using Rosalind's gold."

I nodded. Sebastian might have been a psychic prodigy, but he was still a teenage boy. Romantic, proud, and stubborn—to prove he was a man, he'd want to finance the entire elopement by himself. So why wouldn't he decide to sell a sword or two?

Again I looked at the box's empty cradles: a saber, a broadsword, and a rapier. Sabers and rapiers were practical weapons, but broadswords were too heavy for anything but ceremonial combat. (Of course, the academy trained its charges in ceremonial combat as well as normal fencing—many of our students were destined for ceremonial lives.)

If I were Sebastian, I'd sell the broadsword first. But where? Not to another student: too much risk someone would blab to a teacher. Selling the sword to a store in Simka would also raise problems. People there knew the boy; if he tried to hock a high-class sword, word would get back to his family. Sebastian was smart enough to avoid such trouble. So where had he . . .

I smacked my head with my palm. "What?" Myoko asked.

"Those fishermen tonight," I said. "That Divian with the broadsword—he had no idea how to use it. As if he'd never had one in his hands before. And it was a fancy-looking weapon: more ornamental than practical."

"You think he got the sword from Sebastian?"

"Maybe."

I closed my eyes to think. The sword was easily worth enough to purchase passage for two on any fishing boat in the Dover fleet. The boat captain involved would demand payment in advance—*well* in advance—so Sebastian must have gone down to Dover immediately after classes ended in the afternoon. He'd just have time to go to the docks, hand over the sword to pay his fare, then return to the school for supper. Meanwhile . . . as soon as the boat captain got the sword as payment, he'd send away any crew members who wouldn't be needed for the trip. That would be about five o'clock: plenty of time for the fishermen we'd met to make their way to Simka and get rip-roaring drunk before they showed up at The Pot of Gold.

And why had the Divian been carrying the sword? My guess was that the captain wanted the little blob-eared swamp-rat to sell the blade in Simka—hock the weapon and turn it into cash. Either the Divian hadn't found a buyer, or he wanted to swagger around for a while with the sword in his hand before he had to part with it.

Yes. It all made sense . . . and the timing held together.

"Let's find Pelinor," I told Myoko. "He saw the weapon close up . . . and our noble knight knows about swords."

"Quite right," Pelinor said. "The sword was unquestionably from the Shore metalworks. Distinctive etching on the pommel: their top-of-the-line model." He sucked his mustache. "But *every* sword in Simka comes from Shore's. They're the only weaponsmiths from here to Feliss City."

We'd found him with Annah in the academy's vast stables. Following the chancellor's instructions, our armsmaster and musicmaster were searching for Sebastian . . . and naturally, Pelinor had wanted to check out the horses: "Just to see if one's missing."

Pelinor was a maniac about horses. He didn't own one himself—he told everyone he was "between mounts"—but when he wasn't drinking at The Pot of Gold or shouting at less-than-eager students not to let their foils droop, he was in the school stables badgering the grooms.

We had a *lot* of grooms. Every paying student at the school kept at least one horse, and most had more: a hunter, a traveler, a "steed" who looked pretty on official occasions, a war-charger, a pack-animal or two, and perhaps several others of varying colors, to make sure one always had a mount that matched one's clothing. At times, we had more than five hundred animals under the stable roofs, many of them high-strung, and all in need of pampering—heaven forbid if a single stallion showed the least little mange. Therefore we employed an army of stable-staff, all of whom gritted their teeth when they saw Pelinor coming.

Pelinor asked questions. Pelinor gave advice. Pelinor wondered if that roan in Stall 42 was favoring his right foreleg, and if they should add minced chestnuts to the fodder of that pregnant palomino. He was correct often enough that the stablemaster didn't lock the old boy out . . . and Pelinor was happy to shovel stalls or do other gruntwork, so workers didn't chase him away. Nevertheless, the hands paid for the help he gave; they paid by putting up with the old duffer's enthusiasm.

There were no grooms in sight at the moment: just hundreds of stalls filled with quiet horses. The nearest animals stared at us with equine curiosity—they seldom saw people in the middle of the night, especially people they didn't recognize. One beautiful chestnut gazed at me with particular soulfulness, no doubt hoping I was the sort of person who carried carrots in his pocket. Alas, I wasn't; I was the sort of person who had to investigate a murder.

"So," I said to Pelinor, "could the sword have been Sebastian's?"

"Perhaps. He owned one like that. But so do a dozen other people in town."

"Unlikely for a Divian slave to be one of them."

"Yesss," Pelinor said with another mustache suck, "it does seem strange. A broadsword decorated that much would be quite pricey . . . and impractical in a street fight. Better to buy a rapier or saber. Then again, the Divian may not have bought the blade himself. He might have stolen it. Or won it playing Beggar-My-Bum."

"I still think the sword was Sebastian's." I glanced at Myoko. "We'd better tell the chancellor."

"We'll come with you," Annah said softly. "We've discovered something too."

"What?"

She didn't answer. It was Pelinor who said, "Two of Rosalind's horses are missing. Her favorite mare and a nice quiet gelding. And Rosalind's saddle is gone from the tack room. Also the saddle Sebastian used in his riding classes."

Myoko made a face. "How can two kids walk off with a pair of horses in the middle of the night? Don't the stablehands keep watch?"

"The horses weren't taken in the middle of the night," Pelinor answered. "The head groom says Sebastian and Rosalind went riding this afternoon—the same time as every other student." That made sense to me; they probably went down to Dover to pay the captain for their boat trip. "With riders coming and going," Pelinor continued, "none of the grooms noticed that the two children never brought their horses back. On evening rounds, the hands saw the animals were missing; but someone had put notes on the empty stalls saying HORSES ON LOAN. The staff didn't know what that meant, but there was no reason to raise an alarm."

"So Rosalind and Sebastian might have disappeared this afternoon?" Myoko asked.

"No," I said, "they were both at dinner. In the afternoon, they must have taken the horses and tethered them somewhere. Sebastian's a local boy; he'd know hiding places where the horses would be safe. Then he and Rosalind walked back to put those notes on the stalls. That way, they wouldn't have to smuggle out their mounts later on."

"These kids planned ahead," Myoko muttered.

"So it seems," Pelinor said, "but there's one part that bothers me." He was looking toward the chestnut who'd been eyeing me earlier; he might well have been speaking to the horse rather than us humans. "If these students prepared so meticulously, why was Rosalind in bed?" He turned to me. "That's how you found her, correct? So why did the girl go to sleep instead of getting ready to elope?"

We thought about that in silence. Myoko finally said, "Rosalind was poisoned with curds-and-whey. Eventually, she'd start to feel sick . . . so maybe she decided to lie down. Hoping a rest would make her feel better."

"That doesn't quite fit," Annah said. "When we found her, Rosalind wasn't wearing clothes. Would she undress completely just to lie down? Especially when she planned to go out later?"

Myoko shrugged. "Maybe she wasn't thinking clearly. If the disease was making her delirious . . ." She stopped. "No, if the disease was making her delirious, Rosalind would just flop straight onto the bed. Too much trouble getting undressed. Unless she was burning up with fever and thought she could cool off . . ." Myoko shook her head. "That's not too convincing, is it?"

We nodded. Something about Rosalind's nudity didn't add up—one more out-of-place detail to confuse the picture.

"Let's go back to Opal," I said; and because the others didn't have any better suggestions, they followed me out of the stables.

7

HORSE HEROES

Half an hour later, we were back with the horses: watching disheveled grooms saddle six mounts so we could head off to Dover-on-Sea.

Five of the horses were for those of us who'd been present in The Pot of Gold: Myoko, Pelinor, Impervia, the Caryatid, and me. Chancellor Opal had decided if we were destined to go on a quest, that's what we should do—hie ourselves down to the docks and quest for Sebastian.

Hence, the five mounts. Plus one for Annah. Who hadn't been ordered to accompany us and hadn't said she wanted to go, but was following close enough on our heels that the stablehands assumed she belonged to our party. I couldn't tell if she'd truly intended to accompany us or was just letting herself be swept along—Annah had retreated to her usual shy passivity, silently lurking in the background while everyone else chattered. From time to time I tried to catch her eye . . . but she had far too much experience withdrawing from the world for me to dent her self-isolation.

It didn't help that the rest of our group were being their noisy selves, arguing over which horses they should take. Of the six of us, I was the only one who actually possessed a mount of my own: a sturdy white gelding named Ibn Al-Hahm. Despite his name, Ibn was not an Arabian—he was an Appaloosa I'd bought when I arrived on this continent. However, his characteristic Appaloosa splotches were small and

98

restricted to his hindquarters; when I was seated on him, he looked much like a purebred white stallion I used to ride on our family estate.

Everyone else in our party had to make do with animals owned by the school itself. Pelinor couldn't bear to buy a mount for himself unless it was absolutely perfect . . . and if there *is* such a thing as a perfect horse, it can't be purchased on a teacher's salary. Impervia, of course, had taken a vow of poverty; I wasn't clear on the specifics, but it certainly ruled out expensive possessions like horses. As for Myoko, she claimed she was too small to ride anything bigger than a pony; when asked why she didn't buy a pony, she gave an Impervia-style sniff and said ponies were beneath an adult woman's dignity.

Perhaps she just didn't like riding—that was certainly the Caryatid's excuse. The Caryatid, despite her roly-poly figure, displayed an obsession for walking: to her, horses were fine for pulling plows, but if you wanted to get somewhere, it was vastly more enjoyable to use your own two legs. The rest of us were hard-pressed to persuade her we shouldn't head for Dover on foot . . . but eventually, under the weight of "Time is of the essence," the Caryatid grudgingly agreed to ride.

At least we all *could* ride; our chancellor "strongly encouraged" every teacher to learn the basics. This policy was eminently practical—student groups went on numerous field trips throughout the year, whether to Feliss City (where Governor Niome would attempt to charm the brats with talk about "trade opportunities in our fair province") or around the countryside to see notable sights like Niagara Falls, the concrete ruins of Trawna, or just the color of the autumn leaves. These outings had to be supervised . . . and Opal didn't want any teacher avoiding the job with, "Oh, I can't ride."

Therefore, we all knew which end of a horse was the front, how to cinch a saddle, and when to let one's mount rest. We also rode regularly on the school's private horses to keep our thigh muscles in shape. (I don't know if any out-of-shape rider has actually died of stiffness the day after a long trip, but many have wished they could.) Even the Caryatid went for a canter several times a week; apparently, stints on horseback weren't immoral in themselves, you just weren't supposed to substitute them for walking. As for Myoko, she did look tiny, even on the school's smallest quarter horse, but she never had trouble controlling the animals she rode. If her size caused a problem, the only sticking point was her pride.

We received no formal send-off: everyone else was searching for Sebastian. Opal had rallied all available staff and faculty to scour the immediate neighborhood for signs of the boy. The grooms who saddled our horses were in a hurry to join the hunt—they hung around long enough to make sure we got mounted, then hastened into the night. Heaven knows why they were so eager to blunder through the muddy countryside; maybe they just wanted to get it over with, so they could then return to bed.

Whatever the explanation, we were left alone in the stable yard—dark except for the stars and a torch-sized flame sitting on the Caryatid's shoulder like a parrot. None of us believed this was just a quick trip to the lake. We were embarking on a quest; who knew when or *if* we'd return?

It was Pelinor who finally broke the silence. "There's no reason to be glum," he said. "We aren't heroes, are we?"

Impervia lifted an eyebrow. "What do you mean by that?"

"Well . . ." He gave his mustache a suck. "Quests go one of two ways: either the company dies off one by one until the hero is left to save the world single-handed; or everyone else survives and it's the hero who has to make a tragic sacrifice at the end." He looked around at our company. "Since nobody here shows heroic promise, perhaps we'll all come out of this with our skins intact."

"Unless," said Impervia, "God intends to demonstrate that *everyone* has the potential for heroism. In that case, each of us will be tested to the utmost . . . and we shall live or die accordingly."

"I'm a teacher," Myoko muttered. "I give tests, I don't take them."

Impervia attempted to blister Myoko with a haughty look.

In our holy sister's worldview, no one was immune to the occasional pop quiz administered by heaven.

"Of course," I said, "there's always the chance we won't be bound by the stereotypes of bedtime stories—that things will unfold, devoid of meaning, because we're living *in real life!*"

Annah, who'd slipped her horse beside mine, gave me the ghost of a smile . . . but the Caryatid gasped in shock. "Phil," she said, "this isn't real life. This is a quest."

I hoped she was joking; but I couldn't tell for sure.

The main road to Dover-on-Sea was an OldTech asphalt highway, cracked with age and lined with the shadowed hulks of collapsed buildings. Close to town, the buildings were mostly houses: shoddily constructed things, thrown up four hundred years ago when Simka was going through a period of overoptimistic expansion. Armies of aluminized clapboard had marched past the town limits into the countryside, wasting prime farmland; then a few years later, the people in those houses turned tail and ran . . . most of them heading for outer space, courtesy of the League of Peoples.

The subdivisions fell empty. The townhouses just fell.

I don't think it happened quickly—first the roofs sprang leaks, then the interior wood and plaster began to rot. Birds and mice and carpenter ants took turns nibbling holes for nests. Heavy winter snowfalls made the crossbeams sag; heavy spring rains undermined the foundations; heavy summer thunderstorms blew off shingles and siding; heavy autumn melancholy leached away whatever survival instincts the houses could muster as they slowly crumbled away.

A century of that, and Simka's version of suburbia was fit only for wrens and raccoons. Three centuries more and you could barely recognize the houses at all . . . but in places, one could still see concrete steps with rusty metal railings leading up to doors that weren't there, and netless basketball hoops standing on poles in the middle of tumble-down trash warrens.

Farther out in the country, the houses were mostly intact: farmers had occupied nearly every OldTech residence and they kept their homesteads in good repair. Admittedly, the houses didn't contain much of their original building materials—everything had been replaced over the past four centuries, except for hardy components like flagstones—but they were still standing in one piece, more or less on the sites where they were first constructed.

Therefore, if you saw a collapsed building in the country, it wasn't a house. It might be an OldTech diner with a paintless tin sign creaking rustily in the wind . . . or a country church with its spire toppled onto its briar-patch graveyard . . . perhaps an aluminum barn that once enclosed millions of snow-white mushrooms, still harboring mushroom descendants under heaps of debris.

These ruins were overrun with winter-shrunk weeds—mostly lemon verbena and mint-scented geraniums. The plants were escapees from some garden center four days' journey to the east; they'd been bioengineered for extreme hardiness, and when OldTech culture imploded, the plants had seeded themselves and spread from the greenhouses where they'd originally been developed. Native vegetation couldn't withstand the encroachment: thistles and milkweed and purple loosestrife gave ground before the onslaught. Much of Feliss province was now taken over, anywhere that wasn't kept clear by farmers or gardeners . . . and on hot summer nights, the tangled smells of lemon and mint would hang thick in the breezeless air.

We rode past it all in silence. There was nothing to say; or if there was, no one wanted to say it. Our horses clopped rhythmically along the age-degraded pavement, pausing now and then when a sound or a scent disturbed them. But nothing attacked us from the darkness—it was still cold enough that coyotes and lynx were mostly hunkered down in their dens, and the few that might be hunting stayed well away from the flame on the Caryatid's shoulder. The sky was a patchwork of clouds and stars with no threat on the horizon . . .

. . . until we were a minute away from Death Hotel.

* * *

Lovely name, isn't it? Death Hotel. It was a rural landmark halfway between Simka and Dover, one of the few OldTech buildings that was one hundred percent intact. The place was made of granite blocks, carefully chiseled and fitted together into a box-shaped edifice with a halfhearted attempt at a dome on the roof; if that doesn't give you enough of a picture, think, "Big, gray, and ugly." Add to that four centuries of passers-by slathering graffiti on the outside, mostly of the M. G. LOVES S. T. variety, and you've got the idea. At the very front, however, on the wall facing the road, some long-ago hand had painted DEATH HOTEL in big black letters; and over the years, local kids had repainted the inscription whenever it got too faint, in order to preserve the place's "charm."

Death Hotel had a story behind it. In fact, it had many stories, but only one I actually believed. Once upon a time, the place had been built as a mausoleum for some well-off family. Something went wrong—folklore suggested many possibilities, from believable problems like the family going broke, to extravagant hypotheses like a Romany curse or a prophetic vision warning of dire consequences if the tomb was ever used—but whatever happened, no corpse was ever interred within those thick gray walls. Instead, the place became a popular spot for transient workers to sleep while they waited to get hired in the local harvest. Those workers called the place Death Hotel . . . and eventually one of them painted the name on the outside.

For several years, the hotel grew in fame; on rainy nights, dozens of people took shelter inside, a few sleeping in the wall niches meant for coffins but most just lying on the floor. They never caused any trouble . . . and most Simka residents were amused by the idea of people sleeping in an empty mausoleum. Alas, a handful of loud-voiced fuddy-duddies called it a "desecration of sacred ground," especially since many of the transients had dark skins or foreign accents. In the end, the party-poopers prevailed upon authorities to brick up the entrances with cinder blocks; and the bricklayers had done such a good job, no one had got inside since.

That didn't end the hotel's popularity with visitors. Folks

continued to drop by and write their names on the walls. A few even claimed to see ghosts in the neighborhood. It didn't matter that the place had never contained a single corpse: a mausoleum is a mausoleum even without dead bodies, so why shouldn't people see phantoms there?

Before that night, I'd laughed at yokels who thought Death Hotel was haunted. But after my experience in the music room, I wasn't so ready to smirk . . . and the closer we got, the itchier I felt. What bothered me most was that we wouldn't be able to see the mausoleum until we were almost upon it—there were tall stands of spruce on both sides that shielded the site, even in winter. For all I knew, an entire undead orchestra could be planted on the snowy front lawn, just waiting for us to come into view before they struck up the funeral march from Beethoven's Third.

A hundred meters short of the hotel, I caught myself clutching at Ibn's mane, grabbing so hard the poor horse turned his head to look at me, wondering what I wanted him to do. "Sorry," I whispered, letting go and giving his neck what I hoped was a reassuring pat. Of course, there'd be no ghosts at the mausoleum—as a man of science, I could prove it by probability. The odds of seeing a single ghost must be a million to one, so the odds of seeing two in a single night were so immensely astronomical . . .

At that moment, something filmy and white streamed down from the sky.

It was a creamy tube of light, glinting with colors like the Aurora Borealis. Green. Gold. Purple. As it shimmered in the darkness, I could see the stars behind: the tube was like glowing milky smoke. It stretched so high it disappeared into the blackness as if it soared beyond our planet's atmosphere— but that was just as terrifying as if the thing were simply a ghost. A ghost could only go, "Boo!" Mysteries from outer space could cause *real* trouble.

I couldn't help thinking of Opal's story. A Spark Lord. A Lucifer. An Explorer from the galaxy at large.

The upper body of the tube flapped and fluttered like a banner in a stiff wind, but the bottom seemed rooted in place.

Though the trees blocked our view, I knew the spectral tube had attached itself to Death Hotel. I could imagine it like a phantom lamprey, mouth spread and locked onto the building's ugly dome; or perhaps the tube was a pipeline that fed ethereally into the sealed-up interior, and even as we watched, it was pumping down a horde of aliens. Or spirits. Or worse.

"Oh look," said Pelinor, pointing at the tube. "Isn't that pretty." Pause. "What is it?"

Nobody answered. The horses stopped one by one, either reined in by their riders or halting of their own accord as they saw the tube twinkling in the sky. The thing fluttered in silence—the whole world had hushed, as if even the horses were holding their breaths. Then, without a whisper, the ghostly tube snapped free of the mausoleum like a broken kite string, and in the blink of an eye it slithered up into the night.

Deep dark quiet. Then, beneath me, Ibn gave a snort that filled the cool air with horse steam. The other horses snorted too, perhaps trying to decide if they should worry or just shrug off what they'd seen. In front of me, Myoko cleared her throat . . . but before she could speak, an ear-shattering <BOOM> ripped the silence.

I had an instant to register that the noise came from the hotel: like a cannon being fired. Then there was no more time for thinking, as Ibn went wild with fear. He reared up whinnying, nearly bashing into Annah's mare, who was doing exactly the same thing. For several seconds, we were swept up in six-horse chaos, the animals trying to bolt, the humans trying not to get tossed off. My leg was slammed hard between Ibn and some other horse, but I couldn't tell whose—it was dark and confusing, voices yelling, "Whoa!" and "Easy!", horses neighing, Ibn lurching in panic as I tried to hang on.

Somehow Ibn got himself turned around and started galloping back toward Simka, his eyes bulging white. I had no choice but to let him run: if I tried to rein him in, he might rear and throw me off. The pounding of hooves behind me suggested the others were in the same situation, letting their horses run until the first burst of terror burned itself out.

Thirty seconds after he'd bolted, Ibn slowed a notch. He still had gallop left in him; but as I pulled lightly on the reins, he didn't resist completely. He didn't stop either: it took another half minute before he let himself be cajoled to a panting halt. Annah cantered past me, still working to slow her mount—she was always very tentative on horseback, just as in life. The other four, however, had got their animals under control; when I turned to look, they were stopped on the road behind me, bending over their mounts and murmuring, "It's all right, it's all right, it's all right."

The Caryatid was closest, only a few paces away. When she noticed me looking at her, she asked in a harsh whisper, "What the blazing hell was that?"

"How should I know?" Down the road, a cloud of dust or smoke drifted above the treetops: the remnants of whatever made that deafening bang. I couldn't see any light shining on the cloud from ground level; with luck, that meant the explosion hadn't started a fire in the surrounding forest.

The Caryatid was still staring at me, her face paler than usual in the glow of her shoulder-flame. "So," she whispered, "do we investigate the boom?"

"Of course we do!" That came from Impervia, riding up to join us. Her face was set in a grim smile, trying not to show too much enthusiasm. As always, she longed to charge straight into trouble, but did her best to hide it.

"We shouldn't get distracted," I said, knowing I sounded like a rationalizing coward. "Our first priority is Sebastian; is there a good reason to waste time on something that has nothing to do with him?"

Impervia made a scoffing noise. "It's got to be part of the same business, Phil. When was the last time we had mysterious deaths or strange things appearing from the sky? Never! And now they're all happening the same night. Everything's connected, and we have to find out how."

Without waiting for an answer, she turned her horse and kicked it into a trot back toward the mausoleum. Her mount, a gray gelding, showed no reluctance to head in that direction; perhaps the stupid beast had already forgotten the bang that made him panic.

The Caryatid gave me a look. "We can't let Impervia go alone, Phil." She tugged lightly on her horse's reins, and started up the road herself.

Sighing, I checked how Annah was doing. She'd got her mare under control and was coming back toward me. "Are you all right?" I asked.

"Fine," she said softly. "You?"

"Fine, fine, fine."

Pelinor and Myoko were fine too—they'd joined Impervia and were riding toward Death Hotel together. Annah's eyes met mine: a look that probably meant something, but in the darkness, I couldn't tell what. "We'd better keep them out of trouble," she murmured.

I nodded. Together we rode forward.

8

OPENING THE VAULTS

The air near the mausoleum reeked with a chemical stink, something acrid that made the back of my throat feel raspy. Our horses wouldn't go near it—we tied them to nearby trees and proceeded forward on foot. Needless to say, Pelinor went with cutlass drawn; Impervia kept her fists ready in a guard position, the Caryatid cradled a flame in her hands; Myoko's hair splayed out from her head like a huge black halo.

I would have pulled out my change-purse, but Annah might get the wrong idea.

Thinking of Annah, I turned toward her, intending to deliver some manly speech of reassurance like, "Stay close, I'll protect you." But when I looked around, she was nowhere in sight. Her horse was tethered with the others; I'd helped her dismount. But now . . .

Something touched my elbow. I consider it a triumph that I didn't squeal like a castrated piglet. Annah stood beside me in the darkness; but she'd put on a hooded black cloak that faded uncannily into the shadows. For a brief moment, I saw the white of her teeth under the hood as she smiled—a smile far more impish than one might expect from a quiet woman. Proud of herself for taking me by surprise. Then the smile vanished and Annah did too. Though I was staring straight at her, I could barely make her out in the silent blackness.

Surprise, surprise: our pretty musicmaster wasn't just a shy wallflower, she could literally fade into the background. I *had* to stop underestimating the woman—she was far far from helpless.

Our group moved wordlessly forward. The ground was muddy, but clear of snow; with the mausoleum and surrounding trees acting as windbreaks, the front lawn had been shielded all winter from the brunt of most blizzards. Whatever shallow snowdrifts may have built up over the past few months, they'd already melted in the spring thaw.

As we drew nearer the building, I could see rubble strewn on the far side. Impervia saw it too; she waved us in that direction and hurried her pace. The chemical smell grew stronger—not enough to choke us, but it made our eyes water. The stink reminded me of explosives my friends had made in Collegium Ismaili's chem lab . . . but I'd never paid enough attention to tell one incendiary chemical from another just by the after-blast odor.

Poor planning on my part.

When we rounded the building's front corner, we saw what the bang had done. Most of the mausoleum's side wall had blown out in a huge detonation, scattering stone and concrete like grapeshot. The spruce trees ten paces away had great ragged holes ripped through them; needles and branches had been pulverized by flying debris.

Much of that debris came from the cinder blocks bricking up the side entrance . . . but the blast had been powerful enough to loosen the building's granite as well. The entire edge of the roof was gone, exposing steel I-beams that had trussed up the weight of the dome. Here and there, the steel looked partly melted—the bottom lip of the I-beam sagged in places like softened candle wax.

Amidst the rubble, nothing moved. The mausoleum waited, filled with pitch-black shadow.

Pelinor stared at the hole. "Looks like something smashed its way out," he said in his usual hearty voice. I winced at the sound, piercingly loud in the silent night . . . but nothing attacked Pelinor or anyone else. If our luck was good, whatever had caused this wreckage was gone: stomped off to parts unknown while we were getting our horses under control.

Impervia moved toward the rupture in the wall, obviously intending to clamber inside. "Wait," said the Caryatid; she raised her arm and tossed her ball of flame through the breach with an overhand lob. Half a second too late, I wondered if there might be combustible gases inside . . . but the original explosion must have burned off anything capable of igniting. The Caryatid's flame ball landed tamely on the mausoleum's floor, merely lighting what there was to see.

To be precise: absolutely nothing.

One might expect the people who'd slept in the hotel to leave evidence of their stay—the usual litter and trash. If so, either it had been cleaned out before the place was sealed, or it had completely decomposed over the ensuing centuries. The floor showed dirt, nothing more. The walls bore splotches in shades of gray, as if they'd been covered with graffiti that had faded over time . . . but it might just as easily have been mold or lichen. The Simka region was perpetually damp, especially in comparison to the dryness of my birthplace; if there was anywhere on the planet that mold could survive four hundred years of complete darkness, it was here in Feliss province.

Impervia scrambled over broken stone and into the building. She stopped for a moment, looking ahead into the shadows; then she moved forward, with the little flame ball gliding half a step behind her like a curious dog. I watched as she walked the entire length of the crypt . . . but there was nothing to see, just the bare stone floor and tiers of shadowy casket-niches in the wall. Impervia checked each niche as she passed, but reported nothing: no caskets, no bones, no lurking horrors. From time to time, she even checked the ceiling; I don't know if she truly expected some monster to be clinging to the roof, but if she did, she was disappointed. Nothing above, below, anywhere.

When Impervia had searched her way to the far end of the

tomb, she came back quickly with a sour expression on her face. "Whatever it was, it's gone."

From behind my back, Myoko called, "I think it was a woman."

We turned. Myoko stood a stone's throw away, near the edge of the forest. She pointed down at the mud. "Footprints. A woman's boots. They look fresh."

I started forward, but she held up her hand. "Wait. You might trample the trail." Keeping her eyes on the ground, Myoko walked toward us, obviously following the tracks. She got halfway back when she stopped and peered about; she'd reached a spot where the rubble was fairly thick all the way to the mausoleum. At last, she shrugged and gestured toward the building. "Whoever it was must have stayed on top of the wreckage till she got to this point. Then she stepped into the mud. Her tracks are quite clear."

The rest of us hurried to see. When we looked where Myoko pointed, the footprints were easy to discern in the damp soil . . . and they definitely came from a woman's boots. Fancy, fashionable boots: the heel was a smallish triangle that dug deep into the earth, quite separate from the rest of the sole. It was the closest you could get to a high heel while staying within the bounds of practicality. Even so, such shoes would be better suited for walking down nice clean sidewalks than slogging through country mud. I glanced at the boots of my female companions; they all had much larger heels, choosing functionality over style.

One reason why I liked them.

The footsteps led away from the mausoleum. Impervia followed the trail a short distance, then turned to the rest of us. "You can see it's a straight line," she said, pointing back toward the building, then moving her finger to trace the path to the trees. "After the explosion, our mystery woman must have climbed out through the hole and headed directly for the forest."

"But how did she get inside the tomb?" Pelinor asked. "Hadn't it been closed for centuries?"

"Sealed solid as long as anyone can remember," I said.

"Either the woman was inside all along and that thing in the
sky woke her up . . . or else the thing we saw was a conduit
bringing her here from somewhere up above the clouds. It
funneled her into the interior, straight through solid granite.
Then she used a bomb to blow her way out."

"Phil," the Caryatid murmured, "I don't like either of your
possibilities."

"If you can think of another, I'm all ears."

She frowned but said, "You're right. Either the woman
was already inside the mausoleum, or she got put there by
that tube of smoke. Or was it ectoplasm? Milky, see-
through . . . it could have been ectoplasm." The Caryatid
shuddered. "Stupid. Why am I deliberately trying to scare
myself?"

Impervia laid her hand on the Caryatid's shoulder. "Fear
isn't stupid. Fear keeps you alert. But you can't let it stop you
from doing what's right." Impervia looked once more at the
bootprints and followed them with her eye to the edge of the
woods. "The woman's got only a short headstart. And she's
heading for Dover-on-Sea. If we follow her tracks, we might
catch her before she gets there."

"Then what?" Myoko asked. "Start a punching match
with someone who can blast her way through granite?"

"Only if necessary. We'll start by politely inquiring if this
woman knows what's going on." Impervia gave Myoko a
stern look. "I'm not completely deranged, you know."

"Sorry, Impervia," Myoko said. "I didn't mean—"

"Yes, you did," Impervia interrupted. "You all think I'm
too . . ." She paused, then smiled thinly. "Impulsive. Which
may be true. This time, though, I know we mustn't act
rashly." Her smile grew more fierce. "But we *must* act. We've
been *called*." She took a deep breath. "It's so desperately rare
that one receives a call, one must seize the moment with both
hands."

She spoke with quiet intensity, low but fervent—far from
the steely self-control she usually displayed. It was as if
she'd finally pulled off her nun's mask, the discipline, the
role . . . and none of us could meet her burning gaze.

"Look," Impervia said, "haven't we all been waiting for this? Something to *do*. Something that *matters*. A dozen times a day, I pray, 'God, God, call on me.' I don't care how often my Mother Superior says I *have* been called, that teaching is an honorable profession, that educating children is vital work . . . it's not enough. My confessor tells me I lack humility—who am I, a lowly handmaid, to think I deserve something more important? But still I've prayed, 'Choose me, God, *use* me. Just once in my life, let me do a great thing.'

"And can any of you say," she went on, "you haven't wished the same? Deep in your hearts, don't you long for a calling? A vocation so strong you can't doubt it? The voice of God crying from the whirlwind, 'Your destiny is at hand!' Not just passing the time and keeping yourself busy, but finally, *finally*, your true purpose. Isn't that what you want? An end to numb mediocrity?"

She glared, challenging any of us to deny it. No one did. How could we? After nights of drowning in bad ale, complaining, bemoaning the pettiness of our existence, how could we pretend we were happy with who we were? Even Annah, standing dark and silent beside me: I didn't know her nearly as well as I'd thought, but one thing I didn't question—she too had spent her life waiting, composing wistful music in empty rooms, waiting, waiting for pure sweet lightning to strike.

Passion. Meaning. Justification.

"All right," Impervia said, "let's not waste time. Get the horses; follow the trail; stay alert." Pause. "If any of you believes in God, this would be an excellent time to pray."

The good sister could obviously pray while walking; without a second's hesitation, she strode back toward our mounts. As for the rest of us . . .

The Caryatid said nothing; but she had a crazy joy in her eyes, a look I'd only seen once before, when she was cuddling a flame after two beers more than usual. Suddenly she'd started hugging the fire to her breast while her clothes smoldered. Rubbing it against her cheek, kissing it over and over: tears dribbling from her eyes and instantly turning to steam in the fire's heat, a heat so intense her cheeks were red and raw the next day. The only time I'd ever seen fire come *close* to burning the Caryatid. Now the same expression blazed across her face . . . and she followed after Impervia, walking, then running, then leaping—over rubble, over puddles, over nothing at all, just jumping for the sake of the thrill.

Pelinor watched the Caryatid leaping, jumping, skipping. For a moment his face was grim; then it softened into a grizzled smile. "Why not?" he said under his breath. "Why the hell not?" His eyes continued to follow the Caryatid as she caught up with Impervia and the two matched step. "There are worse things," he said. Then he smiled apologetically to the rest of us. "There are worse things," he said again. Then, not jumping or skipping, but walking with a quick firm pace, he followed the Caryatid's lead.

Myoko seemed to have been holding her breath; now she let it out and turned to me. "What do you think?"

I shrugged. Just a shrug but it felt strange, as if I were telling some kind of a lie. Feigning cool detachment.

"Yeah, well," Myoko said, turning away. "I always knew it would come." She was talking to herself now. "Sooner or later, it had to. Yeah." She drew in a sharp breath. "Only question was, who would start it: me or someone else? Might as well be me." She glanced back in my direction once more and gave a mirthless smile. "Here we go. Here we go." Then she headed for the horses, walking with her arms squeezed tight in front of her.

Just Annah and me left. When I looked at her, she'd thrown back the hood of her cloak; her eyes met mine.

How can eyes sometimes be so alive?

"Are you ready?" she asked.

"Sure," I answered, "someone has to keep them all out of trouble, so—"

She put her hand on my mouth. "Shhh." Her fingers stayed against my lips. "They're ready. I'm ready. Are *you* ready?" Her hand didn't move. "Don't make jokes or speeches. Are you ready?"

I was too proud to nod obediently; nor could I shake my head no. After a moment, I took her hand from my lips, then leaned in and kissed her on the mouth.

It felt like a good answer. Apparently, we were all ready.

9

WE MUST GO DOWN TO THE SEA AGAIN

The stand of spruce beyond Death Hotel wasn't big enough to be called a forest—it was just a thick windbreak separating the mausoleum from the farm fields beyond. Even so, the woman we pursued must have had trouble pushing through, thanks to snarls of undergrowth and drifts of unmelted snow. We couldn't take the horses into those woods; we had to go back to the road and trot to the far side while Impervia followed the tracks under the trees. She came out damp and disheveled, spruce needles clinging to her long black coat . . . but one look at the taut expression on her face, and none of us said a word.

"The tracks went straight through," she reported, pointing downward. The mystery woman's bootprints were visible in the mud at Impervia's feet. "And look at this."

She lifted the lamp she'd been using to follow the tracks. With the other hand, she held out a few scraggly threads of crimson, frayed on the ends. "I found these snagged on bushes."

The Caryatid shucked off one sleeve of her overcoat and laid her arm close to the fibers. The red of the threads matched perfectly with the Caryatid's crimson body sheath. When she looked up, we nodded in understanding. Centuries ago, the first Sorcery-Lord of Spark designated that particular shade of red as the "Heraldic Hue of the Burdensome Path" (i.e., the proprietary color of sorcery). There was no explicit law against others wearing that color, but nonsorcerers still avoided it. You shouldn't pretend to be something you're not; it's even worse when your presumption annoys people who can cast powerful spells.

"So our quarry is a sorcerer," said Pelinor. "Or rather a sorceress. And a powerful one, if she could blow out the side of that mausoleum." He glanced my direction. "You're the history buff, Phil; was there ever a major sorceress entombed hereabouts? You know the type—wickedly strong, diabolically evil, locked up for all time because not even the Sparks could kill her."

I made a face. "I haven't heard such stories, and wouldn't believe them if I did. The Sparks can kill *anyone* . . . and if by some miracle there *was* somebody they couldn't rip into constituent atoms, they wouldn't just leave her in an unguarded crypt. They'd bury her ten klicks underground, and surround her with the most god-awful traps they could devise, not to mention alarm systems, sentries, and heaven knows what else."

"Enough chat." This came from Impervia, who'd hopped back onto her horse while Pelinor and I were talking. "The trail goes this way. Let's move."

We moved: into the dark muddy field, the horses' hooves making soft sucking sounds through the wet.

The bootprints led in a straight line for fifty paces, then turned toward the road. Those fifty paces must have been how long it took the sorceress to admit that slogging through muck was a waste of strength—the winding road might not be as direct as trekking cross-country, but its OldTech asphalt made travel much faster. Once the sorceress reached the pavement, her footprints left a dirty trail for another twenty paces. After that, the mud had worn off her boots and there was nothing for us to follow.

At least we knew which direction she'd gone: toward the lake and Dover-on-Sea, the same way we'd been riding before we got sidetracked. We headed forward with all due haste . . . which wasn't too quick, given that the horses had to move carefully to avoid potholes in the road. It didn't help that we were traveling with minimal light to prevent the sorceress from seeing us; all we had were candle-sized flames tight to the ground, guided by the Caryatid at the speed of a shuffling walk.

In this manner we proceeded—silently peering into the darkness. Each time we rounded a bend my nerves would tighten, expecting to spy the sorceress ahead . . . but nary a sign did we see of her, ever. She too must be traveling in near darkness: walking fast, perhaps even jogging, and always keeping at least one bend farther in front.

Thus it continued all the way to Dover.

Dover-on-Sea is several hundred kilometers from the nearest ocean. The so-called "sea" is actually Lake Erie, entirely fresh water . . . for a sufficiently loose definition of the word "fresh." (Lake Erie is actually quite clean these days, now that it isn't being poisoned by run-off from OldTech megacities; but the people of Simka love to infuriate Doverites by pretending the lake is still a stinking cesspool. One of those regional rivalry things.)

Dover's harbor is the center of a thriving fishing industry and home to what the town council calls the largest inland fleet in the world. I view that claim with suspicion—the councilors have been known to invent spurious accolades ("Voted the prettiest village on the Great Lakes" or "Universally regarded as the best source of handicrafts in all Feliss"). The council then disseminates these accolades at genuine tourist attractions like Niagara Falls in an effort to attract gullible visitors to Dover's overpriced "country boutiques." Nevertheless, Dover's harbor *is* filled with a huge bevy of boats . . . many of which catch fish only one day in ten. The rest of the time, they devote themselves to grand-scale smuggling.

Dover-on-Sea is *definitely* the Smuggling Capital of Feliss province . . . though the town council never mentions that distinction in their advertising. Each time Governor Niome tries to stimulate the provincial economy by taxing imports, the benefits are first felt in the back streets of Dover: each new tax creates a new line of business for the smugglers. On any given night, so-called "fishing" boats drop anchor in shadowed inlets along the nearby shore, offloading contraband liquor and linen, not to mention all manner of illegal substances from narcotics to necromancy aids.

At least, that's the gossip I'd overheard in sordid places like The Pot of Gold. I had no actual *proof* of unlawful activity, or I would have been obliged to tell the proper authorities. Assuming I could find some customs agent who wasn't in the pay of the smuggling cartel. Also assuming I didn't care if I suffered some nasty retribution. The smugglers wouldn't try to break my legs, but I would never again be allowed to buy the extra-special "handicrafts" available to "favored customers" in the back rooms of Dover's aforementioned "country boutiques."

At the very least, no more peach-scented soap for Gretchen Kinnderboom.

Who, incidentally, lived in Dover-on-Sea. Gretchen owned a mansion on the lake (or rather on the bluffs overlooking the lake, with a canopied walkway down to the water) where she sponged off her family fortune and allowed me to visit when she had no one better to do. Our relationship was mutually nonexclusive; but like most people in an "open" arrangement, I tormented myself that she was laughing behind my back as she rutted like a maniac mink. I could picture her bedding a different lover every night, turning to me only when a scheduled beau was forced to cancel because he had to sail to Amsterdam to corner the market in diamonds . . . whereas I passed my nights getting drunk with platonic "chums" like Myoko, and inventing fantasies about women throwing themselves at me (including Annah and every other eligible female who passed within reach).

Admittedly, something was developing on the Annah front. Maybe. If I wasn't misconstruing the situation. And maybe the next time Gretchen sent me a peremptory message (TONIGHT, 10:00, AND FOR GOD'S SAKE, DON'T WEAR THAT

SWEATER), I'd have the backbone to answer, "Sorry, I'm busy with someone else."

All of which assumed I'd survive the next few hours. It'd be just my luck to get killed before I could brush off the exalted Fraulein Kinnderboom at least once.

By the time we entered Dover's minuscule "business district," even Impervia admitted we'd lost the sorceress. We'd never caught a glimpse of our quarry . . . and once she'd reached town, she could have gone any number of directions. To the docks, for example: either the "pretty" tourist docks, dotted with food stands, craft shops, and music halls, or the real docks with their omnipresent reek of small-mouth bass. Our sorceress might also have headed toward the palatial beach houses in Gretchen's neighborhood, or the more modest residences belonging to fisherfolk and shopkeepers. For that matter, she might have left Dover entirely, taking the lakeshore highway east or west to destinations unknown.

We therefore stopped at the town's main crossroads to discuss our next move . . . only to have the discussion cut off by Impervia saying, "Here's what you're going to do."

Dictatorship is so efficient.

Pelinor, Myoko, and Annah were dispatched to the fishing docks in search of anyone who'd seen Sebastian, the sorceress, or the Divian with the sword. Impervia, the Caryatid, and I would make inquiries at inns and taverns. No one liked that we were splitting up—Annah met my gaze with owlish regret and the Caryatid stared similarly at Pelinor (hmm!), while Myoko took me by the arm, squeezed my hand, and whispered, "Don't let Impervia get you into trouble"—but none of us had the nerve to argue, or could suggest better arrangements. With whispered good-byes and fervent last glances, our two trios went their separate ways.

Three-fifteen by my pocket watch—not the best time for visiting rum-holes, especially in Dover-on-Sea. All decent establishments were closed up tight as a tom-tom: nobody

awake except for whichever stablehand was stuck with the
midnight shift, watching for horse thieves. Surprisingly,
all such stablehands seemed to be avid readers of penny-
dreadfuls, the kind where no self-respecting hostler will
speak until given a handful of silver. I had plenty of cash
for such shakedowns . . . but with Impervia watching,
there was no point reaching for my coins. She didn't believe in paying for information when others should supply
it "out of the goodness of their hearts"; she did, however,
believe in the threat of violence, using fists or the Caryatid's candleflame. Her violence led precisely nowhere,
since none of the stablehands we browbeat had seen anything of relevance.

This left us to investigate establishments which were *not*
decent: hole-in-the-wall taverns and fleabag inns. Places fre-
quented by folks in murky professions where 3:15 is a regular working hour. Such people do not take kindly to
questions; and Impervia was incapable of being diplomatic.

Ergo, she barged into a dive called The Buxom Bull and
glowered at the patrons therein. She did not speak; perhaps
she was watching which patrons guiltily averted their gaze.
As for the assemblage of hard-bitten men and hard-biting
women, they showed no surprise to see a nun enter the premises. Either they were too jaded to care, or else Buxom Bull
patrons were used to "ladies" whose jobs occasionally required them to dress in nun's habit.

The inn's clientele were not so blasé about persons
dressed in sorcerer's red. Since the Caryatid wore a plain
black overcoat, her crimson body-sheath was not immediately visible; but the tavern was hot and stuffy, filled with
people who spent their days in hard physical labor on boats
reeking of fish, so the Caryatid shucked off her coat as soon
as she came through the door.

That caught everyone's attention.

Most of the tavern was dark—business would suffer if
customers could actually see what they were drinking. However, there were three bright oil lamps near the door to let
management give the once-over to whoever entered . . . in
case any newcomers were waving pistols, swords, or

badges. Therefore, everyone in the taproom could see the Caryatid's outfit as soon as she revealed it; and within seconds, every drink-slurred conversation faded to a strained silence.

Impervia gave an offended sniff that the onlookers could possibly be more impressed by a chubby little sorceress than a lean mean Magdalene. She recovered quickly and spoke to the crowd in her usual piercing tones. "Ladies and gentlemen . . . using the terms loosely . . ."

I gave her a warning nudge. "Be nice. We want answers, not bloodshed."

She glared at me, then returned to addressing the room. "We're teachers from Feliss Academy. One of our students has run off tonight—"

"She's upstairs blowing my brother!" a male voice shouted from the back corner. The crowd laughed.

"Very amusing," Impervia said. "However, the student we're looking for is a sixteen-year-old boy . . ."

"He's upstairs blowing my other brother!"

More laughter.

"How nice for your brothers," Impervia said. "It must be a pleasant change from paying you to do it."

"Oh yeah?" In the back corner, the man who'd been yelling witticisms jumped to his feet: a surprisingly handsome fellow of Chinese extraction, black hair, slight but sturdy. He wasn't especially imposing at first glance . . . but I'd seen enough fights to know that looks can be deceiving. Big burly types can sometimes crumple after a single punch, while slimmer middleweights can turn out to be as tough as terriers. The Caryatid, standing close by my shoulder, knew the same thing; in a low voice, she told Impervia, "Be careful."

"Don't worry," Impervia said. "I have a plan."

"What kind of plan?"

"I'll make a show of strength. To loosen the tongue of any patron who has useful information."

"Provided it doesn't loosen your teeth instead."

Impervia gave the Caryatid a withering look. Then she turned back to the man . . . who was attempting to barge through the crowd in an angry rush, but had trouble weaving between the tightly packed tables. Though he wanted to appear livid with outrage, I could see he was trying not to jostle people as he pushed past them. That boded well for Impervia. She wasn't facing a hot-tempered brawler; it was only a man who was *acting* hot-tempered, as if he wanted to impress the assembled spectators.

When the man finally reached Impervia, he stopped in front of her and opened his mouth to say something. I don't know what the words would have been. A threat? A demand for an apology? The truth will remain a mystery . . . because Impervia grabbed him by the lapels, swung him off his feet, and slammed him down on a nearby table top.

"Good evening," the good sister said. "My name is Impervia. What's yours?"

The man was slow to answer, maybe because his collision with the table had knocked the wind out of him. Impervia lifted him slightly, then slammed him down on the table again. "Your name?"

"Uhh . . . uhh . . . Dee-James. Dee-James Mak . . ."

"Well, Dee-James Mak, I've told you what I'm here for. A boy is missing from Feliss Academy. Have you seen him?"

Dee-James shook his head.

"Do you know anyone who might have seen him?"

Dee-James shook his head again.

"The boy might have booked passage on a boat. Do you know any boats that left harbor tonight?"

"N-no," said Dee-James.

"Who would know something like that?"

Dee-James didn't answer. Impervia thumped him against the table again. "Who would know?"

"Uhh . . . uhh . . . Hump."

"Who is Hump?"

"Me." The single word came from the table where Dee-James had been sitting, far in the shadowy corner. A chair scraped across the floor and thudded into the wall. A man rose slowly to his feet—an extremely large man. Because of the darkness, I couldn't see details . . . but size is size, and this man's size was intimidating.

Except, of course, to Impervia. "Yes," she said, "you certainly look like a Hump." She let go of Dee-James, who remained sprawled on the table. "Mr. Hump, would you care to tell us what we want to know?"

"Get fucked."

"I've taken a vow against that."

"Vows were meant to be broken," Hump said.

The good sister shook her head. "I may break your arms or your kneecaps, but never my vows."

"Impervia, shut up!" the Caryatid whispered.

"Don't worry," Impervia whispered back. "This is still my show of strength." She raised her voice. "Well, Mr. Hump?" She spoke in her best Intimidating Teacher tones. "Do you have any answers for me? Or is your mind a blank? Have your thoughts gone dry? Is that it? Are you a dry Hump?"

For a moment, the tavern went utterly silent. Then someone snickered. The noise was immediately stifled, but similar choked laughter sounded all around the room.

"Ah jeez," the Caryatid muttered. "That did it."

She was right. Growling obscenities, Hump kicked his chair over and began lumbering forward with murderous intent. He showed none of the qualms that Dee-James had about shoving people and furniture out of his way. Folks who got beer dumped in their laps only made soft damp gasps; they knew better than to complain. Considering that the ale-drenched people looked tough as nails themselves, the behemoth stomping our way must be the meanest ass-kicker in the bar.

With the possible exception of Sister Impervia. She turned to the Caryatid and me. "See? My plan is working."

I didn't feel much reassured. As Hump came closer to the light by the door, I could see he was no drunken fisher-lout, all blab and no balls—he virtually had ENFORCER branded on his forehead, not to mention tattooed on his knuckles and etched across his sharply filed teeth. He was a mean-eyed sneer-faced bruiser, dressed in leather that he probably ripped off the cow with his bare hands.

Considering how many Doverites took part in smuggling, it required someone special to keep them in line: someone so terrifying, nobody would dare skim the take or turn crown witness for the contraband cops. I conjectured that Hump was the man who cracked that whip . . . and for the sake of his bad-ass image, he couldn't let Impervia belittle him without reducing her to a bleeding pile of bones.

The good news was that he'd fight on his own; with his authority challenged by a single woman, he couldn't possibly accept help from anyone else. The bad news was he didn't *need* help: he measured a shaved head taller than Impervia and bulged twice as wide, but his bulk looked more muscle than fat. A man that big was apt to be slower than Impervia, but his extra reach, mass, and muscle-power made up for his lack of speed. Featherweight boxers are faster than heavyweights, but you don't see them taking on the big boys in title bouts.

So: Hump versus Sister Impervia for the championship of Dover. The Buxom Bull's tapman didn't say a word about taking the fight outside; the tapman, in fact, had abandoned his post, disappearing through a back door. A lot of patrons were bolting too, not even pausing to snatch up their tankards. The only exception was Dee-James, still lying on the table. Now he sat up and said with foolhardy but admirable courage, "Aww, c'mon, Hump, this is nothing. Let's just get out—"

Hump grabbed a tankard off a table he was passing and hurled it at Dee-James's head. The smaller man ducked and shut his mouth . . . but he stayed where he was.

That made Dee-James one of the only people who hadn't evacuated Impervia's vicinity. The others were the Caryatid and yours truly. The Caryatid held a candleflame in her cupped right hand, but looked reluctant to use it. If Impervia beat the enforcer in a fair fight, the crowd would show respect; if we stooped to sorcery, the bar patrons might attack en masse. Your average Dover sot bears the same enlightened attitude toward sorcery as the torch-waving peasants outside Castle Frankenstein.

As Hump passed the last table in his way, he picked up a chair and hurled it at Impervia's head—a traditional move, the redneck equivalent of a martial artist bowing to his opponent before a match. Impervia accepted the gesture in a similar spirit: she caught the chair in mid-flight and swung it straight back. If I may translate this body language into something more verbal, it went roughly as follows:

> HUMP: Good evening, sister. I believe we should consider chairs to be admissible weapons in our forthcoming contest.
> IMPERVIA: Very well, sir. I accept your proposal and will demonstrate my agreement in the most direct terms available.

Impervia had grabbed the chair by the legs . . . and it was a good solid chair of good solid wood, chunky enough to withstand the rigors of The Buxom Bull (e.g., lard-assed drunks unacquainted with treating furniture gently). However, when she slammed the chair into Hump using a hard downward swing, he barely noticed—he took it on one arm raised to protect his head, then simply drove forward, chair and all, straight into Impervia. She nearly got trapped between the chair and the wall behind her; but she threw herself sideways, just slipping clear before the chair struck the plaster with a chip-spraying whomp.

Hump tossed the chair behind him, presumably to keep such weapons out of Impervia's reach. Bare fists gave him an advantage. Then again, Impervia wasn't ready to get within punching range; instead, she lashed a kick at the enforcer's forward knee, barely missing as he jumped back.

They both had their hands up in guard position now, Impervia's hands open, Hump's hands closed. If I knew anything about martial arts, I could tell you what that said about their fighting techniques: "Ah yes, Impervia's open hands indicate the softer style of kung fu, while Hump's closed fists are more reminiscent of hard-style karate." But I don't know what I'm talking about, and anyway, there was no time for detailed analysis because Hump bulled his way forward, bellowing profanities.

He must have expected Impervia to retreat—no doubt he was used to folks running, the common response to a huge man yelling, "I'll rip your fucking head off!" and other such endearments. The good sister, however, subscribed to the easier-said-than-done philosophy of USE YOUR OPPO-NENT'S FORCE AGAINST HIM: if someone charged her, she charged forward too, so her strikes combined the speed of herself and the attacker. Of course, she didn't go straight head-to-head, but rather off at an angle: veering to eleven o'clock, and throwing a ridge-hand to Hump's nose as she went past.

I could hear the snap of gristle as the nose broke; but I could also hear a "Whoof!" from Impervia at almost the same instant. Hump had caught her with something as she sped by, an elbow or punch I hadn't seen. It connected somewhere on her torso: solar plexus, floating ribs, something like that. The hit wasn't enough to take her out, but it certainly didn't do her any good; she spun away fast, trying to retreat so she could catch her breath.

Hump had no intention of giving her a break. His eyes were watering from the crack on the nose, and his view of the world had to be blurred with tears; still, he knew where Impervia was because he barreled toward her, hollering the ever-popular, "Bitch! Bitch! Bitch!" Impervia heard him coming and straightened up fast . . . either through sheer force of will or because she wasn't quite as breathless as she seemed. (She sometimes faked injuries to put opponents off guard—a certain type of man turns careless if he thinks he's drawn blood.)

So Impervia was ready for the bleary-eyed enforcer. He popped a kick at her knee—not serious, just a distraction—then came down hard with his kicking foot, hoping to crush Impervia's toes. Simultaneously, his hand lashed out at her head, the punch timed to coincide with his toe-stomp. It looked like the kind of combination you'd practice in a gym, feint-kick to foot-slam with coordinated cross to the face.

Too bad for Hump that none of his strikes connected.

Impervia parried the first kick with her own leg, knocking Hump's kicking foot to one side. That meant Hump's stomp came down nowhere interesting: on bare floor instead of the good sister's instep. At the same time, she used a high block to deflect the punch over her head (a move made easier by the enforcer's height, since Impervia could slip under his shoulder). Finally, she delivered a strike of her own—a palm-heel driving hard under Hump's chin to snap his head back, then raking her fingertips down the man's face in a move she called the Tiger's Claw. This wasn't, as you might expect, a scratching maneuver intended to draw blood; Impervia kept her fingernails almost invisibly short, so she had nothing to scratch with. It was more a gouging action designed to wreak havoc on soft tissues like cheeks and eyes . . . not to mention Hump's nose, which had already taken one nasty hit. If the nose wasn't completely broken before, the Tiger's Claw finished the job, shifting the nasal position several centimeters to the left and rearranging all adjacent facial features.

Herewith, another translation from body language:

HUMP: Oh goodness gracious me!

Impervia was close to the enforcer's body, a dangerous place to be even when your opponent is half-blind and reeling with pain. I wondered if she'd risk staying there long enough to deliver a few more whacks or if she'd withdraw before she got cracked by the man's wild flailing. Impervia chose to disengage: not going backward but continuing forward, past Hump's back. As she went, she snapped a low kick behind her in the general direction of Hump's right leg. I couldn't tell whether she was trying to buckle the knee or to hit one of the femoral nerve points she swears will induce an instant charley horse if struck correctly. Either way, she missed . . . probably because she was distracted by a sudden ripping sound as Hump's leather jacket sleeves burst open from shoulders to wrist.

*   *   *

Impervia took cover, diving over a nearby table and kicking it behind her as a defensive wooden wall. I don't think she knew what had happened—she just wanted to get out of the way till she figured out what the ripping noise had been. A weapon hidden up Hump's sleeve? Some kind of concealed pistol? Hump was just the sort of man who'd carry extra "protection" to whip out when things didn't go his way. He'd already lost the fight; yes, he was still on his feet, but Impervia had hurt him enough that she could now whittle him down. Kick at his legs from a distance, try hitting him again with a chair . . . she had plenty of options, and with his damaged nose, he couldn't see well enough to fend off everything. From Hump's point of view, it was time to play his hidden cards.

In this case, said cards were razor-sharp spines growing out of his arms. Sharp enough to shred tough leather as they sprouted bloodily from his skin.

They reminded me of spikes on a sea urchin: organic white spurs, even if they were the size of the studs on a morning-star. Definitely not some strap-on weapon—these were part of the man himself, rooted in place by sorcery, surgery, gene splicing, or all three. The physiology that let the barbs extend and retract might be fascinating to study under more detached conditions; but at the moment, all I needed to know was that they were big, lethal, and heading for Impervia.

The good sister muttered something, possibly a quick prayer; but her words were drowned out by cries and curses from others in the room. Up till now, the patrons had been hiding in the shadows, staying out of the fight but watching keenly all the same—bar brawls no doubt passed for high entertainment in The Buxom Bull. However, a man with spikes running the length of his arms seemed more than the crowd could stomach. Amidst yells of panic, I caught words like "Demon!" and "Witchcraft!" . . . which brought to mind more images of peasants, torches, and Gothic castles after dark. Some night very soon, Hump might find himself waylaid by a mob who didn't like freaks in their midst.

But the mob wouldn't convene in time to help Impervia—
they were too busy scuttling for the exits. Meanwhile, Hump
treated us to his own show of strength by slamming his right
arm into a table. The spikes bit deep into the wood, spraying
splinters. When he lifted his arm, the table rose too, as if attached to the man by nails . . . but he clenched his fist and the
spines retracted, releasing the table and letting it fall with a
thump.

"Now you," Hump said to Impervia. His voice was low
and controlled—no screaming "Bitch!" now, just pure focused malice. Impervia's face was focused too: not the grim
smile she usually adopted for bar fights, but something more
somber. I don't think it was fear; it looked more like *finality*.

"As God wills," she said.

She was close to a chair, so she threw it. Just something to
keep Hump busy; in the time he took to knock it aside, she
was halfway toward the bar. The path was clear of by-
standers—people were stampeding out both doors, and even
through windows (smashing out the glass with hastily swung
tankards). Only Dee-James, the Caryatid, and I stayed where
we were . . . rooted to the spot like scared rabbits, hearts
pounding, barely able to breathe.

When Impervia reached the counter, she vaulted over with
gymnastic ease and grabbed two bottles of high-proof liquor.
One was cheap rum distilled in Feliss City; the other was
something colorless in clear glass, gin or vodka, maybe
schnapps. Both bottles were almost full. Impervia yanked the
corks with her teeth, one after the other, then threw them full
in Hump's face.

He hadn't been standing still through all this—he'd been
bashing his way toward the bar, kicking furniture out of his
way rather than going around. When the bottles came spinning his way, he swatted them aside with his hard-spiked
arms. The rum bottle was simply deflected (splashing rum as
it flew), but the clear bottle shattered against his bony spikes,
spraying glass shards and hooch in his face. Hump grimaced,
but didn't seem hurt. In fact, he was wearing an "Is that the
best you can do?" smile when Impervia reached for an oil
lamp sitting beside the beer taps.

It took Hump a moment to realize he was damp with flammable alcohol. He charged at the same instant Impervia grabbed the lamp and smashed its glass chimney on the bartop. Amazingly, the lamp flame didn't go out . . . but then, one should never be surprised by the behavior of flames when the Caryatid is close at hand. I don't know if our sorcery teacher really did keep the fire going by means of hocuspocus, but the lamp continued to burn, even as Impervia hurled it full in Hump's face.

The enforcer had no time to duck. His reflexes were good enough to shield his face with one arm, but that simply meant the lamp stuck sharp spikes instead of anything softer. Smash. The alcohol on his skin combined with flame and lamp oil to ignite with a gusty whoosh: a blue halo burst around his head and shoulders.

Beside me, the Caryatid murmured, "Pretty!"

Though the fire was searing hot, Hump didn't let it faze him. A man of blazing determination. Even Impervia was taken aback by his stubbornness—she stared in surprise a dangerous half-second, giving Hump time to get closer. Nothing separated the two of them now except the bar-top itself. Hump threw himself forward onto the counter, his hands streaked with fire, the spikes on his arms slanting toward Impervia as if they were hungry for blood. In the cramped space behind the bar, she didn't have room to dodge. Spikes and flames came straight for her. Nothing to do but tuck tight, arms in front of her head, the defensive tortoise position of a boxer who can't do anything but ride out a flurry of hits . . .

Then suddenly, everything stopped. The world froze as motionless as a painting. Hump in mid-lunge, spikes less than a hand's breadth from spearing their target. Flames around him snuffing out as if smothered. Impervia frozen too, like a bug in invisible amber. The Caryatid leaning forward, her mouth open slightly. Dee-James suspended a short distance off the floor—he'd been rolling off the table, preparing to run elsewhere. Even I was struck inert, not paralyzed but simply trapped, as if the air around me had turned rocksolid. It held me encased, no wiggle room at all. Breathing was like sucking wind through a woolen blanket.

Behind me, from The Buxom Bull's front door, somebody crooned, "Quiet now . . . everyone quiet. Hush-a, hush-a, all fall still."

It was a woman's voice, lilting softly as if singing a baby to sleep. I couldn't turn my head to look, but I guessed we'd found our mystery sorceress.

10

SUCH STUFF AS DREAMS
ARE MADE ON

She walked forward, <TIP>, <TIP>, <TIP>: as if she were up on her toes, trying to make as little noise as possible. The shy tread of a mousy person . . . but when she came into view, there was nothing shy or mousy about her.

She was the most beautiful woman I'd seen in my life.

I mean this literally—she was an exact double of my cousin Hafsah at age eighteen, and teenaged Hafsah was the most exquisite woman I've ever known. The last time I saw Hafsah she was still quite lovely, though approaching forty and uninterested in the draconian regimen required to preserve great beauty into middle age; but at eighteen, Hafsah was monumentally breathtaking . . . and I was a moonstruck ten-year-old whom she spent time with because my puppy love amused her. Sweet indulgent Hafsah was the pinnacle of feminine beauty and I would never meet anyone who could make my heart pound so fast.

We are all prisoners of our ten-year-old selves.

Now that I'd reached thirty-five, one could wonder why my tastes hadn't matured . . . especially since I knew eighteen-year-olds were not the amazingly sophisticated creatures I once believed them to be. But the woman tiptoeing into The Buxom Bull was living proof I hadn't outgrown my boyish infatuation; I saw her as Hafsah, the teenaged Hafsah, and that meant my beautiful cousin still had a smiling stranglehold on my psyche.

What am I talking about? Sorcery: a well-known spell called Kaylan's Chameleon of Craving. (Mage Kaylan was superb at research but a lowbrow hack when it came to naming his enchantments.) In scientific terms, the spell must have been caused by nanites in my brain stimulating whatever set of neurons encoded my ideal of feminine beauty. I saw what the nanites told me to see—the woman most guaranteed to arouse me.

Creating such an illusion had to be a complex neural process, but the result was utterly simple: when Kaylan's Chameleon was cast on a woman, every man viewed that woman as the embodiment of his personal lust. If a man was entranced by breasts, he saw mammaries of his favorite size, shape, and degree of gravitational impossibility. If he adored auburn hair hanging creamy smooth down to the ankles, that's what he saw . . . and what he felt too, if he ran his fingers through the tresses. If a man didn't pant after women, he saw another man . . . or a child, or a high-heeled shoe. And if a man dreamt of his cousin Hafsah (or his sister, his mother, or that nanny who used to spank him), Kaylan's Chameleon could be a real eye-opener.

Despite its vagaries, the Chameleon was one of the most popular spells in the world—a sure moneymaker for any sorcerer who endured the ritual to acquire it. Lots of rich women paid cartloads of gold to become artificially dazzling . . . including a number of girls at Feliss Academy. It was a popular first-menses gift from doting grandparents: the bestowal of Ultimate Beauty.

Or at least a hint thereof.

The extent of Kaylan's Chameleon depended on the power of the caster. When a bazaar-class sorcerer muddled through the spell, it might enchant only the woman's eyes, or her hands, or her navel. There was nothing wrong with a pair of eyes men couldn't stop pining for, but a mediocre mage had no control over which part of the subject's anatomy would become irresistible. A woman who paid her life's savings often felt cheated when all she got was a particularly winsome elbow. (Though I've heard of men who would crawl over hot coals to fondle such a thing.)

Even first-rate sorcerers had trouble enchanting a woman's whole body; they considered the spell a success if it charmed a meaningful subregion, like the face, torso, or legs. The Chameleon-bewitched girls at Feliss Academy almost all had this partial level of ensorcellment . . . and let me tell you, it had its drawbacks. I'm reminded of a warm lazy day outside the dorm when a blonde fifteen-year-old named Ilsa sunned herself in a meager bikini; it was most disconcerting to see the sharply marked "tan-line" at her waist where the pale Nordic skin of her upper body changed to the dark complexion of my cousin Hafsah, shapely brown down to the calves, then abruptly white again at the ankles. One boy who saw her ran screaming across the courtyard and vomited in the hollyhocks. Heaven knows what *he* saw.

But the woman in The Buxom Bull must have received her Chameleon from a stupendously powerful sorcerer—she was totally Hafsah from head to toe. And an exquisite head it was; a fine mouth-watering toe. Dark laughing eyes, demure yet kissable lips, softly rounded nose, chocolate brown hair that practically demanded you bury your face in it, and hips one could grab like a drowning man seizes a life preserver. She looked perfect and I knew she would *feel* perfect, whatever I kissed or nibbled.

That really pissed me off.

The *falseness* of her. Beneath her Chameleon glamour, she could be a scrawny twelve-year-old or a pock-marked crone of ninety; tall or short, dark or fair, and I'd never see the truth. I longed to ask the Caryatid what *she* saw—the Chameleon spell fooled only men, not women—but I couldn't speak a word with the air still solidified around me.

One last thing about the woman entering the room: she was dressed in an outfit Hafsah once wore to a formal family dinner (gold silk trousers of the style foreigners call "harem pants," a midriff-baring white shirt with a half-sleeved gold overjacket, assorted bangle-jangles and gold-mounted pearls), but in addition she wore something that clashed glaringly with the Hafsah persona: a billowing knee-length cape of crimson. *Sorcerer's* crimson. Hidden under the doppel-gänger of my cousin, there was indeed a sorceress.

The sorceress. Powerful enough to blast a hole through Death Hotel. Powerful enough to immobilize us all like bugs in a spider's web.

"Hello," she said with a baby-soft version of Hafsah's voice. "I'm called Dreamsinger: Sorcery-Lord of Spark."

Uh-oh. Even more powerful than I thought.

Dreamsinger continued a few more steps: TIP, TIP, TIP. She wasn't actually walking on her toes, but each time she placed a foot, she did so with gingerly caution, as if fearful of making too much noise. Not the spit-in-your-eye brashness one expects from a Spark Lord. In fact, she stopped in the middle of the room and looked around as if she had no idea what to do next. Lost and dismayed. At last her gaze settled on the Caryatid; her face brightened.

"Sister!" she cooed. The Sorcery-Lord tip-tapped to the Caryatid and air-kissed her cheek. This wasn't just an empty gesture, the way unctuous people pretend to kiss while avoiding actual contact—Dreamsinger's lips pushed as close as possible to the Caryatid's face, but a hand's breadth of so-lidified atmosphere blocked the way. The Spark Lord kissed the invisible barrier fervently, once, twice, three times. "Sister! Dear comrade on the Burdensome Path. Please tell me what's happening here."

The Caryatid remained motionless. Dreamsinger waited a moment . . . then a moment longer . . . then raised her hand to her mouth in the embarrassed horror of a little girl realizing she's done something rude. "You mean you can't just . . . but it's such a simple spell!" Dreamsinger leaned in close, her forehead pressed against the imprisoning air as she stared into the Caryatid's face. "All you have to do is shrug it off. A tiny trivial shrug. Not the *physical* sort, but you know when you focus your mind, then flip the magic away?"

No response. The Caryatid looked as if she was straining to shrug/focus/flip, but the only result was a flush of effort turning her cheeks pink. Dreamsinger watched a moment more, then dropped her gaze. "Well, ah, it can sometimes be difficult . . ."

Eyes still averted, the Spark Lord made a twiddly gesture with the last three fingers of her left hand. The Caryatid lurched forward, as if she'd suddenly regained her momentum from a minute before and was continuing her run toward Impervia. Dreamsinger waited politely (keeping her gaze elsewhere, pretending she didn't notice anything ungainly) until the Caryatid staggered to a halt. Then the Sorcery-Lord lifted her head and said, "So, dear sister, you were going to explain . . . ?"

The Caryatid curtsied low. My grandma Khadija (who'd been governor of Sheba for twenty-three years) had told me the Sparks hated people bowing or scraping—"They don't want deference, they want obedience." But Dreamsinger waited placidly as the Caryatid held the curtsy for a full five seconds. Then the Caryatid rose and said, "Milady, we . . . we're on a quest."

Dreamsinger's eyes grew wide. "Really? My brother says the only people who believe in quests are professors of literature. But he must have been teasing. My family likes to invent stories to see what I'll believe. They call me 'delightfully gullible.' "

She repeated the phrase in the singsong voice of a little girl who's heard the words frequently but doesn't quite understand them. Perhaps beneath her luscious exterior, Dreamsinger was far more child than woman. As I said, girls from affluent families often received Kaylan's Chameleon as a "Welcome to puberty" gift; take away the sorcerous glamour, and the real Dreamsinger might only be eleven, with scrapes on her knees and a first-figure bra. One might ask why her family let her leave Spark Royal without an adult chaperon . . . but her freeze-the-room spell showed she could take care of herself. Perhaps it was standard practice for the High Lord to send his children on the prowl: GO YE INTO ALL THE WORLD, AND INSTILL THE FEAR OF THE LORDS.

"I regret," Dreamsinger said, "I don't know much about Life. I have paid a great price to follow the Burdensome Path.

A grave and awful price." She looked to the Caryatid for sympathy. "Studying day and night, learning to reprogram the world. This is the first time I've been outside Spark Royal since . . . dear me, I don't remember. Sorcery has jumbled my brain."

She laughed: the artificial type of laugh one gives when feeling awkward, but not half so forced as the laugh the Caryatid gave in response. It's hard to sound jolly when a Spark has just confessed to being mentally unstable.

Dreamsinger let her laugh fade to an encouraging smile. "But you were talking about your quest. It must be lovely to see the world . . . meet people . . . make a difference instead of constantly performing horrid rituals. What is your quest about?"

"We don't know, milady. There was just this, uhh, sort of a prophecy kind of thing. It said we'd go on a quest. No hint of what we should do."

"Who gave you this sort of a prophecy kind of thing?"

The Caryatid cleared her throat. "A detached dog tongue, milady."

Dreamsinger didn't even blink. "And it didn't give instructions?"

"No, milady. But we're, uhh, we've run into things that demand attention. Earlier tonight, there was a haunting. At Feliss Academy. And a girl was killed with what my friend believes was an OldTech bioweapon."

Something changed in the Spark Lord's posture: a sudden stillness, an infusion of icy cold that wasn't quite hidden by the warm Hafsah illusion. "You say your friend believes this?" She looked at me, then Impervia. "One of these people?"

The Caryatid lifted her hand in my direction and opened her mouth to speak; but before a single word came out, Dreamsinger spun toward me, made the same three-finger gesture that unfroze the Caryatid, and caught me by the lapels as I suddenly fell free of my imprisonment.

"Your name?" she said.

"Philemon Abu Dhubhai." Short concise answers. Spark Lords like short concise answers.

"Clan Dhubhai, Sheba province?"

"Yes. The late Governor Khadija was my grandmother."

"Can you prove it?"

I thought for a moment, then reached into my pocket and pulled out my purse. "Spark Royal gave her this; I inherited it."

Dreamsinger examined the purse for a moment. Took it in her hand. Slapped it hard on a nearby table. Nothing but a jingle of coins from inside. She tossed the purse back to me.

"All right. What's your scientific background?"

"A doctorate from Collegium Ismaili. Phys-math."

Her eyes narrowed slightly. My assessment of bioweapons would have been more credible if I'd had a degree in biology or medicine . . . but at least she realized I wasn't a scientific illiterate. "Describe what you saw," she said.

"A disease or parasite, like cottage cheese growing in the girl's nose and throat. Death by suffocation. It developed very fast: at supper she showed no symptoms, by 1:00 A.M. she was dead. The girl was the daughter of Elizabeth Tzekich, leader of the Ring of Knives. We thought the mother's enemies might have—"

Dreamsinger shook me so fiercely my teeth clacked together. If she was an eleven-year-old girl, she was a stunningly strong one. "I see the obvious," she said. The Sorcery-Lord pulled me closer. "Are you certain the substance was like cottage cheese? It was white and wet, not dark and dry?"

"Very white and very wet."

Silently, I wondered what kind of bioweapon created dark and dry deposits, but I knew better than to ask. Dreamsinger had moved her face so close to mine I could feel her breath on my nose: the smell of cinnamon and mint, just like my cousin Hafsah. "Now, Philemon Abu Dhubhai," she said, "one last question and you must answer most truthfully. *Is the disease contained?*"

I swallowed hard. "To the best of my knowledge, yes. We believe the disease was planted in the girl's room; she caught it there and died without ever going out. Those who found the body didn't touch anything, and the room is now sealed. But, uhh . . . the girl had a boyfriend. He's missing, and we don't know if he visited her while she was contagious. We don't think he did, but we aren't sure. People are searching for him near the school, but we came down here because he might have—"

Dreamsinger tossed me aside. Literally. Not trying to hurt me, just removing me from her sight. Like a child who casts away a toy that bores her. She turned back to the Caryatid. "Dear sister, the dead girl's body is still at Feliss Academy?"

"Yes, milady."

The Sorcery-Lord reached up and tapped one of the pearl necklaces looped about her throat. At least that's what it looked like to me—someone not befuddled by Kaylan's Chameleon might have seen something different. The necklace made a soft whistle. "Spark Royal, attend," Dreamsinger said. "Give me Rashid. It's urgent."

The necklace whistled again. *Computer-controlled radio transmitter*, I thought. Frustrating that I couldn't see it because of the Hafsah illusion. Two seconds later, a male voice spoke from the same necklace. "Damn it, Dreamy, do you know what time it is?"

"No," she said. "I don't have a watch. My last one got broke." Dreamsinger's voice had acquired a layer of little-girl sulkiness. How old *was* she? "And even if I knew the time where *I* am, I wouldn't know what it is where *you* are. You could be anyplace from Gdansk to the Galápagos."

"You know where I hang out these days," the man answered. "Right now, it's three-thirty in the morning."

"*A Spark Lord is always on call.*" Primly reciting a lesson. "We've got a potential outbreak, Rashid. Supposedly a bioweapon."

"Says who?" asked Rashid—who had to be *Lord* Rashid, Science-Lord of Spark. He'd once visited Collegium Ismaili and spoken with several of my fellow students. (The *promising* ones. The ones with *goals*.)

Dreamsinger glanced at me. "The report comes from one of the Sheba Dhubhais. He claims he knows science."

"Hmph," Rashid said . . . as if he doubted the possibility of my knowing anything. "Which bioweapon is it?"

"Nothing I recognize. Cottage cheese in the nose and throat."

"Hmm. Cottage cheese. Not dark and dry?"

"Not according to this Dhubhai fellow."

Again, I wondered what threatening substance was dark and dry; but Rashid was speaking again. "All right, I'll check it out. Where?"

"Feliss Academy."

"Then I'm close already. Within a few hundred klicks. Meet you there?"

"No, I have other business." Dreamsinger glanced at me. "Tracking down a boy who may be infected."

"If there's somebody sick wandering in public—" Rashid began.

"I know," Dreamsinger interrupted. "First, you tell me if it's really a bioweapon, and if it's contagious. I'll handle the sterilization."

Rashid didn't reply immediately. Finally, he sighed. "You're first on the scene—it's your call. I'll radio back as soon as I check the academy."

The pearl necklace whistled once more. Dreamsinger turned straight to the Caryatid. "Dear sister, this boy who's missing . . . do you have some belonging of his so we can do a Seeking?"

The Caryatid shook her head, shame-faced. "I tried a Seeking but got nowhere. The boy's a powerful psychic. At least," she added hastily, "too powerful for *me* to find. So there was no point bringing his possessions with us. Besides, we thought Spark Royal would be annoyed if we removed anything of Sebastian's from the premises. That might be seen as tampering with evidence."

"True." Dreamsinger smiled: a sweet dimpled Hafsah smile. "This Sebastian is a powerful psychic? That's . . ." Her voice trailed off. Judging by the look on her face, I guessed some worrisome possibility had crossed her mind; but after a few seconds, she turned to the Caryatid and said, "Dear sister, you'd better tell me everything you know."

* * *

It didn't take long—we didn't know much. Several times the Caryatid looked to me for help, but Dreamsinger glared me into silence: only the Sorcery-Lord's "dear sister" was allowed to speak.

The Caryatid went through the facts (the dog tongue, the harp, the missing sword) and wisely omitted conjectures (the possibility of a doppelgänger Rosalind) until she reached the explosion at Death Hotel. I could see she was aching to ask if Dreamsinger had caused the kaboom, but didn't want to seem insolent. Therefore, the Caryatid tried leading statements such as, "The thread was sorcerer's crimson . . . like your cape," in the hope Dreamsinger would say, "That was me." No such luck. The Sorcery-Lord stayed silent to the very end of the tale.

And the silence continued long after the Caryatid said, "So that's everything." Five seconds. Ten. Thirty. Dreamsinger appeared lost in thought, eyes lowered, brow furrowed. The Caryatid met my gaze with a puzzled lift of her eyebrows, but one does not disturb a pensive Spark Lord . . . not even when she looks like a teenaged girl and a teacher's instinct is to ask such girls, "Would you like to talk about it?"

But I longed to know what was churning in Dreamsinger's brain. What did she know that we didn't? After all, she'd arrived in the neighborhood *before* she learned about the bioweapon . . . so she'd come here for some other reason. If this was a woman who got out so rarely she couldn't remember the last time she left Spark Royal, why had she suddenly left home to come to this turd of a village?

But I didn't dare ask. Grandma Khadija had drilled into our family the only way to deal with Spark Lords: never question, always obey. Anything else was suicide . . . or worse. And if you can't picture anything worse than dying, you don't know much about the Sparks.

With time on my hands, I stole a glance at Impervia. She'd been trapped in solidified air for several minutes; how well was she breathing? I remembered the sensation, like sucking air through a blanket . . . and Impervia had built up an unhealthy oxygen debt in her exertions during the fight. Now her eyes had an unfocused look, not turning to meet my gaze. She might have passed out inside her invisible cocoon—either that, or she'd deliberately forced herself to slide into some semimystic martial arts trance.

I hoped that was it. I hoped she hadn't completely suffocated.

Perhaps Dreamsinger saw me staring in Impervia's direction. With a sudden, "Aha!" the Sorcery-Lord snapped out of her reverie and strode toward the bar. Her goal, however, was not Impervia; she moved to the spike-armed Hump and clapped her hand in front of his mouth. "Speech only," she murmured. "Neck up, release."

Her words must have been a command to the nanites who held the enforcer in place. While Hump's body remained frozen, a breath exploded from his mouth followed by a great and grateful inhalation. Apparently the spell had let go of his head, allowing him to breathe freely. Dreamsinger gave him five seconds to guzzle oxygen, then squatted beside his shoulder. "Now," she said softly, "tell me about this town's Smuggler Chief. Name. Headquarters. Any defenses I might encounter on a visit."

Hump gave a snort he probably thought was a haughty laugh. "If you think I'll tell you shit, you're crazy."

"Oh, sadly," Dreamsinger said, "I *am* crazy. I walk the Burdensome Path." She glanced at the Caryatid with a *Dear sister, why must we suffer* expression. Then she returned to the enforcer. "But I am also a Sorcery-Lord of Spark. If you are not my loyal subject, you are an enemy of the human race."

"Ooo, I'm shivering," the man said. "You might scare these other lollies, but to me you're just a big-titty bitch. Someone taught you a pissy little trick, freezing the air . . . but as soon as I get loose, I'll show you some *real* magic, whore. I'll do you with my fist. Make you howl for mercy."

Uh-oh. Thanks to Kaylan's Chameleon, Hump must have seen Dreamsinger as some penny-a-poke prostitute . . . which told you something about the man, if that kind of woman most aroused his ardor. On seeing the image of his innermost lusts, his first inclination was to beat her up. What a world. Then again, maybe it was *good* the enforcer was an utter bastard—I wouldn't feel so bad when Dreamsinger chopped him to sashimi.

The Sorcery-Lord's face formed a gentle smile—a *fond* smile—and she patted Hump on the cheek. "Thank you, thank you, thank you, dear friend. Several people in my family say whenever I walk into a room, something bad in my head won't let me leave until I've killed at least one person. They tease me *mercilessly*; they say I'm compulsive. But you know what?" She leaned close to Hump's ear. "Whenever I walk into a room, I find there's always at least one person who *needs* killing."

Dreamsinger placed her hand lightly on the man's shaved head. He growled obscenities and tried to duck away . . . but she simply squeezed tighter, her gold-painted Hafsah fingernails digging into the man's scalp. With her other hand, she traced a complicated pattern in the air, as if spelling words in some arcane language. Soon she began to hum, a single tone that started in her throat, then moved without changing pitch: traveling into her nose, then opening up to get more lung-power and finally reverberating all the way to her diaphragm.

Wind rushed past my ears—as if invisible forces were answering a summons, gusting out of the night to do the Sorcery-Lord's will. *Nanites*, I thought. Nanites gathering by the billion for some hellacious spell.

The flame on the Caryatid's shoulder—burning all this time, even while the rest of us were frozen—disintegrated into a million tiny sparkles that flew in Dreamsinger's direction: nano-sized particles of magic, ripped from the Caryatid's weak power and drawn toward the Spark Lord's greater attraction. Every atom of enchantment in the room, every high-tech microscopic mite except the ones still holding Hump frozen, came in response to Dreamsinger's call. The unseen shell around Impervia evaporated; she gasped and crumpled out of sight behind the bar. I could hear her pant and wheeze, but didn't dare move to help her.

The expression on Dreamsinger's face had become beatific . . . and my friend Caryatid also seemed transformed.

Avid. *Hungry.* Like a music-lover who's spent too long listening to amateurs tweedle on tin flutes, then hears the full
glory of a great symphony orchestra: *Yes, I remember—this
is what it can be like.* The Caryatid possessed only modest
gifts of sorcery, but she knew the real thing when she felt it.

The real thing. Magic. Just how good good can be.

I saw it in the Caryatid's eyes—recognized it from my
own eyes twenty years past, when I was going to be *amazing.* When I was going to wield *power.* A world-shaking
physicist/mathematician/composer/philosopher/hero. Rev-
olutionizing society. Correcting the mistakes of previous
generations. Cutting through the crap and never getting
bogged down in distractions. Or self-pity. I'd stood on the
verge of an epic life, and was certain no great deed would
elude me.

Remember the feeling that anything was possible? How
we would ride Life like a wild stallion that only we could
tame?

I knew the Caryatid remembered as she watched Dreamsinger gather sizzles of magical force. My sorcerous friend
once told me she'd invented her guild name, the Steel Caryatid, when she was only thirteen years old: a name that would
look good in history books. Sorcery came so easily to her
compared with everyone else in her little school. Then she
went to the big-league sorcery department at her provincial
university . . .

You can fill in the rest yourself: shock, denial, bouts of
crazed studying, bouts of depression, bouts of self-sabotage
with men/drink/procrastination, finally leading to acceptance of a humbler destiny. But the Caryatid could still look
at Dreamsinger with sharp-edged memories of what it was
like to touch greatness. The power that might have been.

Hump sensed the power too. Sweat glistened on his
shaved head as he tried to slide out of Dreamsinger's grip.
She held on calmly, never once losing hold despite the man's
slick of perspiration. Her smile curled as tranquilly as the
Mona Lisa's . . . even as her hand began to glow a fierce
gold.

The enforcer must have noticed that fingershine—he

couldn't see the hand itself, but he couldn't miss a new source of light so close to his head. Especially one as bright as noon. He poured out a new round of curses, but I wasn't fooled by his bluster; panic underlay every syllable. As the light increased in intensity, he yelled, "What do you want, bitch?"

Dreamsinger didn't answer. Her one-note humming took on a tiny edge of pleasure.

"I'll kill you, bitch," the man wailed. "I'll fucking kill you." The bravado rang so hollow I would have ignored it . . . if I hadn't noticed Dreamsinger's lips move at the same time, mouthing the identical words. "Let me go, or I'll rip out your throat." The man spoke; Dreamsinger spoke with him. Her eyes blazed with inner amusement. When Hump jerked his head, trying to snap out of the Spark Lord's grasp, Dreamsinger's head moved too. Duplicating the motion in perfect unison.

That's when I noticed her own head had begun to glow: the same golden color as her hand, dim at first, but brightening quickly. Hump continued to curse; Dreamsinger continued to mimic his words and actions; the golden shine grew fierce.

I realized I was witness to a Twinning.

Twinning spells were legendary: sorcerers linked their thoughts to someone else as a way to pluck information from the target's brain. People talked about "copying brain waves," but I knew enough about cognition to realize it wasn't so simple. To clone thoughts from one brain to another required drastic restructuring in the receiver's mental architecture—not just writing a few chance thoughts onto the surface, but shuffling billions of neural connections. Our thoughts aren't superficial things; they're the conscious tips of unconscious icebergs, the end results of uncountable electric pulses channeled along complex chemical pathways. To duplicate the knowledge in someone else's head, you need the same chemical pathways: the same underlying linkages. Twinning wasn't just telepathic eavesdropping; it was gouging out your old brain, reconstructing every synapse to match someone else's blueprints, then seeing what useful information you could now recall.

Some people named it the Sorcerer's Suicide. Certainly, the spell could be used that way. Enchanters who hated their lives (the terrifying rituals, the fear and mistrust from "normal" folks) might grab someone who looked contented and perform a complete Twinning. Exit the sorcerer, enter a duplicate of a more cheerful person. Or rather, a would-be duplicate. Many a sorcerer had Twinned another man's happiness, only to discover the man was happy because he loved his wife, his children, his friends. The sorcerer now loved the same people . . . but they didn't love him back.

More misery. Much potential for disaster. Twinning never guaranteed "happily ever after."

It didn't even guarantee information. Consider Dreamsinger as she Twinned with Hump: presumably she wanted the name and whereabouts of Dover's smuggling boss. To get those facts, she had to absorb some significant quantity of her victim's mind—you can't pick and choose which memories you get first. Eventually, the spell would provide what Dreamsinger wanted . . . but by then, she might also have absorbed the enforcer's surly personality. She might, in fact, *be* the enforcer; maybe not a hundred percent, but enough to be unhealthy for those in the same room.

Yet she was doing it anyway—as if she believed her own personality sufficiently strong to resist being corrupted. If she was lucky, she'd discover the relevant information soon enough that she wouldn't change much: only a few of her own traits, memories, and perceptual matrices would get wiped out, replaced by ones copied from Hump. She could then halt the spell and walk away, only slightly damaged. If she was unlucky, however . . . we'd get two enforcers for the price of one.

The radiance around their two heads grew more brilliant by the second, a blazing gold so intense it was like staring into the sun. I had to look away . . . and as I did, I noticed a third golden blaze in the room. It came from Dee-James, still frozen in the act of rolling off the table. He burned with his own golden fire: a third sun orbiting at a distance from the other two.

I wondered how long he'd been glowing. With so much light from Dreamsinger and Hump, I hadn't noticed the third flare-up. For all I knew, he could have been ablaze for the past few minutes.

Even as I watched, his body unfroze; Dee-James fell to the ground with a dazed thump. The light surrounding him hurt to look at—I had to close my eyes. But why was he part of the Twinning? What did he have to do with . . .

Someone screamed. Ear-splitting. Then Dreamsinger croaked in a strangled voice: "Warwick Xavier, Nanticook House, four armed guards, and an antiscrying field. Three dogs patrolling the estate."

"That's all?"

The question came from Dee-James. Surprised, I opened my eyes to see Dreamsinger spit with rage toward him. The Sorcery-Lord shouted, "What the fuck else do you need, you little shit?"

"Nothing," Dee-James said, "and everything." He walked forward slowly, answering Dreamsinger's fury with a smile. "Dearest, dearest sister, you're so precious and lovely."

He threw his arms around Dreamsinger, squeezing her close and beginning a deep hot kiss. The man was good-looking but nothing compared to the Spark Lord's Hafsah beauty—his clothes were worn, his face a bit dirty—but in that split second, Dee-James seemed stronger and more self-possessed than the Sorcery-Lord. Venting some passion that was so demandingly *right*, it could overwhelm even a Spark.

But the kiss lasted only an instant. Then Dreamsinger lashed out with both hands, shoving Dee-James away so fiercely he slapped hard against a table. The impact must have hurt—his elbow thunked heavily on the table's edge, the sort of impact that sends pins-and-needles shooting through one's arm—but Dee-James only laughed. "Ooo, what a bully. Push me around some more."

Dreamsinger snarled and charged. She held her arms out from her body, an ungainly way to run . . . till I realized her brain must be so dominated by Hump's, she thought her arms were covered with razor-sharp spikes. When she reached Dee-James, the Spark Lord slammed her forearm toward the man's face—a vicious attack, even if you didn't have bone-spurs jutting from your body—but Dee-James, still chuck-ling, didn't flinch.

The instant Dreamsinger's blow made crunching contact, both the Lord and Dee-James were engulfed in gold light so searing I felt as if I'd been stabbed in the eyes. I snapped my head away, trying not to cry out. Eyes shut, I could still see an image scorched into my retinas—the Sorcery-Lord bringing down her arm, Dee-James smiling as he got his face clubbed, the burst of unbearable radiance.

Twenty seconds passed before the ache in my eye-sockets subsided. When I opened my eyes again, I could barely see through my blur of tears . . . and what I saw didn't make sense: Dee-James was back sprawled on the table, and Dreamsinger had pressed down on top of him, gasping through another fierce kiss.

I blinked. My vision cleared a bit, but the sight didn't change. A Spark Lord kissing a nobody. The nobody kissing back. The two of them almost convulsed with passion. I had time to blink once more; then Dreamsinger pushed away slightly, her face still close to Dee-James. "Your breath reeks."

"Awful me." The man's words were slurred; Dream-singer's blow half a minute before had split his lip. It might also have broken some teeth—blood dribbled from Dee-James's mouth. He lifted himself on one elbow and spit red onto the floor. "If my breath is so foul, perhaps I should kill myself."

"I could do it for you," Dreamsinger said.

"And rob me of my fun? Fuck you."

"If only there were time."

They both laughed and Dreamsinger stepped away, leav-ing Dee-James on the table. The man reached down toward his foot and drew out a bone-handled knife from an ankle sheath. Not a big blade, but practical. He rubbed his thumb on the blade to test it: not lightly across the metal edge, but hard down the length, slicing his skin clean open. "Sharp enough," he said, extending the bloody thumb for Dream-singer to see.

"I envy you," Dreamsinger said.

"Of course," Dee-James answered. "Here's what 'expendable' means."

He lay back comfortably on the table and planted the knife-tip just below his ribcage. With a strong upward jerk, he plunged the knife into his own heart.

Dreamsinger put one palm on the butt of the knife, then slapped hard with her other hand, driving the blood-drenched blade even farther into Dee-James's vitals. The gesture was unnecessary—the man had done an expert job of skewering himself, a quick and certain kill. Dreamsinger obviously didn't care; she wrapped her hands around the knife handle and tried to twist, as if the man still weren't satisfactorily dead. "Dear sister," she whispered. "Dearest, dearest sister."

She bent to give the dead man a last soft kiss . . . and finally I understood what she'd done.

Before Dreamsinger stole the enforcer's brain, she'd copied her own mind into Dee-James. A forced Twinning; it explained why Dee-James had been surrounded by golden light. The man's mind had been expunged, totally replaced by the Sorcery-Lord's. In effect, Dee-James *became* Dreamsinger . . . with all the sorcerous knowledge that entailed. Then Dreamsinger had proceeded to Twin with Hump, safe in the knowledge that her original personality was preserved elsewhere—"on backup," as OldTech computer programmers might say. Once the desired information had been obtained ("Warwick Xavier, Nanticook house . . ."), the Dee-James copy of Dreamsinger used another forced Twinning to restore the original Dreamsinger's brain.

The kiss between Dee-James and the Spark Lord had been Dreamsinger kissing herself.

Then Dee-James had rammed a knife into his own heart. Dreamsinger committing suicide. Why? Because she could die happy, leaving the horrors of existence to her other self?

As the duplicate died, the real Dreamsinger had said, "I envy you."

So much for the myth that Spark Lords revere life. And let's not forget Dreamsinger had wiped Dee-James's original mind as casually as borrowing a piece of paper to write down a note. The Sorcery-Lord needed a mental receptacle, and the man was close to hand.

Poor Dee-James. Martyred because he happened to be convenient.

And if he hadn't been there, would Dreamsinger have used someone else? Impervia? The Caryatid? Me?

I shivered.

"Dear friends," said the Spark Lord. "Shall we go to Nanticook House?"

Impervia, the Caryatid, and I nodded in cowed silence.

On our way out the door, Dreamsinger stopped with a dimpled smile. "Almost forgot." She turned back toward Hump, still frozen above the bar. "Boom," she said.

Hump went boom.

For weeks afterward, they'd be finding pieces of him caught in cracks of the walls.

11

BROKEN GLASS AND GOSSAMER

Nanticook House sat atop the bluffs east of town: the same pricey neighborhood as my on-again/off-again Gretchen. But "neighborhood" was the wrong word—people there didn't know what "neighborly" meant. The estates were big enough that you could see the house next door only with a telescope, assuming your telescope could pierce the high brick walls around each property. Nobody cared to view or visit the folks nearby. The only sense of community came from the packs of guard dogs who patrolled these grounds; some nights, the dogs on all the estates howled at the moon in unison.

The humans, however, avoided contact with each other. That's the difference between the small-town rich and their city counterparts. The urban upper crust enjoy getting together: they hold masquerades, go to the opera, and try to outdo each other with big weddings as they marry off their children in strategic alliances. There's always a whiff of arrogance (and often jaded decadence), but the aristocrats in cities are *sociable*. They have fun with each other; they talk.

The wealthy in Dover-on-Sea were different. They'd chosen privacy over personal contact; they had secrets to hide. My Gretchen, for example, entertained many a gentleman visitor from out of town, but never left her own property.

Nursing her secrets. And Warwick Xavier of Nanticook House apparently had secrets too . . . most notably, his position as Dover's Smuggler Supreme.

I'd passed his place often on my way to Gretchen's: his mansion was a two-story sprawl built around a big inner courtyard. From above it would look like a picture frame surrounding gardened greenery—a pleasant design for Mediterranean climates, but not very practical in Feliss winters. Every room was exposed to the elements on two walls, the outer and the courtyard side, so it must have been hell to keep the house heated. Most likely, Xavier walked around all winter in three layers of long-johns, looking like a wool-swaddled teddy bear. Then again, if he was Smuggler King, he could afford fireplaces in every room, plus warm-bodied companions who'd cuddle close whenever he felt a chill.

As we approached the estate, multiple chimneys were pouring out smoke. The wind blew toward us; soot had accumulated on the few piles of snow untouched by thaw. Though the wall blocked our view of the house, we could see lights shining up into the night. Warwick Xavier seemed to be awake, despite the late hour.

"Dear friends," Dreamsinger whispered, "leave your horses here. And please, *please* be quiet."

As I tied Ibn to a sapling outside the walls, I reflected how unnecessary it had been to ask us to shut up—we'd barely spoken a word since The Buxom Bull. I was the only one who knew where Nanticook House was, so I'd taken the lead; apart from the occasional "This way," we'd walked in complete silence. It would have been nice to speak to Impervia or the Caryatid, if only to ask what Dreamsinger looked like under the Hafsah illusion . . . but the most I could do was meet my friends' eyes and exchange plaintive looks.

Now the Sorcery-Lord moved to the front, making no sound as she led us forward. I wondered why she kept us with her. A Spark didn't need schoolteachers to protect her— if things turned messy, we were more likely to get in the way than provide assistance. Unless, of course, Dreamsinger needed us the way she'd needed Dee-James, as a holding tank for her mind.

But you don't walk out on a Spark, even when she's leading you into danger. So we all proceeded to Nanticook House's front gate.

The gate was wrought-iron, glossy black without a hint of rust. Sheets of wood had been fitted into the gaps between the iron bars, held in place by wires. The sheets were so thin, Impervia could have put her fist through them, but they weren't there as defense—just preventing gawkers from peering into the grounds.

Warwick Xavier must like his privacy.

Dreamsinger didn't bother to check if the gate was locked. She just made a gesture, her hands glowed red, and the wrought-iron frame flopped inward, as if its fittings had vaporized.

The gate didn't make much noise as it fell—with the gaps between bars filled in, it was like a sheet of light wood toppling over in a carpenter's shop, its descent slowed by air resistance. Nothing more than a breezy whump when it hit the ground. The sound still carried a short distance, but there was no one inside close enough to hear . . . no one anywhere along the gravel drive leading up to the house. No guard dogs either; with soot from the house's fireplaces filling the air, the dogs probably couldn't smell us, and by luck, they were all out of sight on the far side of the building.

The driveway was long and wide—over a hundred meters from the gate to the house and broad enough for two oversized carriages to pass each other comfortably. Xavier might be antisocial, but Nanticook House could accommodate guests if necessary. Perhaps I shouldn't have been surprised the Smuggler Chief had plenty of room for carts moving in and out; on occasion, the place might be as busy as a freight warehouse.

No carts were in evidence tonight, but something was definitely afoot. Every room on the ground floor showed lights, and not just a candle or two: the place beamed with lampfire, as if Xavier was hosting a dance-ball for everyone in Dover-on-Sea. No music played, however, and no gabble of conversation reached our ears as we drew near the house; I could see no movement through the windows.

Brightly lit houses are seldom so quiet. And when they are, it makes me nervous.

For a while, it looked like Dreamsinger would prance straight up to the front portico and tug on the bell. I think she considered it; she stopped on the stoop for a full count of ten—not, as far as I could see, listening for tell-tale sounds or using some sorcerous clairvoyance to peer through the door, but simply debating how brazenly she wanted to handle the situation.

While we waited, the Caryatid produced a flame from somewhere and began passing it back and forth nervously between her palms. Sister Impervia assumed what she called a "natural" stance—perfectly balanced, knees slightly bent, hands free at her sides—which is to say, a martial artist's attempt to look nonthreatening while still poised to dislodge your skull with a spinning hook kick. As for me, I'm sure I did something that showed my friends I was jittery as a June-bug, but I was *trying* to look nonchalant.

In the end, Dreamsinger was struck with an attack of discretion. She suddenly wheeled from the door and started to circle the house: moving quickly, peeking into every window we passed, but staying far enough out into the darkness that people inside couldn't see us.

We saw nobody in any of the front rooms; not a guard, not a servant, not even a parakeet. The decor looked costly but soulless—a lot of dark pine furniture and nondescript china on plate-rails. Each room (and there were a *lot* of rooms) held a single objet d'art: always a portrait painting, always undistinguished and always in murky colors, as if the painter had once seen a Rembrandt but could only remember it had dim lighting. None of the rooms showed any particular purpose; they were all generic parlors/drawing rooms/sitting rooms/lounges, rather than serving a recognizable function like a dining room, bedroom, or study. They were, in other words, strictly for show—the sort of rooms a real family would soon subvert with doll houses, billiard tables, and piles of Aunt Miriam's embroidery.

The side of the house was more promising than the front, with an honest-to-goodness kitchen and even two women at work. One woman was big, blonde, and bready, extracting the guts from a turkey. The other looked more decorative: young, slim, as dark as Impervia, and dressed in a short tight uniform designed for the pleasure of male viewers rather than the practical performance of scullery work. Still, she was diligently kneading a wad of dough, pushing it around the counter with experienced efficiency.

I wondered why these women were working at 3:45 in the morning . . . but maybe Xavier kept his whole household on smugglers' hours. Work at night, sleep by day.

We passed the kitchen silently, drawing no attention from either woman. Next door was a pantry and next to that, windows covered with cheap curtains—probably the servants' quarters, with the curtains put up by the servants themselves to frustrate peeping toms.

Since I couldn't see anything in those rooms, I turned my eyes to the stables that paralleled the house across a gravel yard. Two four-horse coaches were parked in the open drive-shed; I wondered if Xavier had company, or if he'd simply purchased two carriages because they were cheaper by the pair.

Finally, we reached the back of the house: the side overlooking the lake. There was little to see but a great crinkled blackness beyond the edge of the bluffs. At the mouth of the harbor below, a small lighthouse lit the water around its footings, casting a few meters of dappled dimness. Apart from that, the only hints of light on the lake were brief reflections of stars, caught for fleeting instants on vagrant ripples. The rest of the vista was dark and cold.

In contrast, the rear of Nanticook House blazed with more lamps and hearth fires—just as many here as on the side facing the road. Yet the dining room was empty, the table bare.

Beyond it was another drawing room, this one equipped with a bar: dozens of bottles on display, but no sign anyone ever drank from them. No hint that guests had ever pulled the chairs into a comfortable circle, or shoved furniture aside so there'd be room to throw darts.

I was beginning to think Warwick Xavier just didn't use the bottom floor of his house. Perhaps all life took place on the top story . . . yet there were no lights up there at all.

The next room looked equally ignorable. I was moving along when I nearly bumped into Dreamsinger—she'd stopped and was gazing inside, her eyes narrowed. Once more I glanced into the house but saw nothing of note; yet the Sorcery-Lord was staring as if enraptured.

I looked again at the house. Immediately my eyes shifted elsewhere: the lawn, the lake, the dark upper floor, *any place* but the room in front of me. Closing my eyes, I couldn't even picture what was in there—just that it was utterly uninteresting, not worth my attention.

Aha. This must be the "antiscrying field" Dreamsinger had mentioned while Twinned with Hump: an enchantment that made you believe the room was boring. Nanites inside my brain were playing games with my emotions and perceptions, perhaps raising my threshold of selective inattention whenever I looked in the room's direction—suppressing visual input so that it never reached my consciousness.

But Dreamsinger obviously could resist such trickery. She strode boldly forward, toward the room's windows. Assuming it *had* windows. Whenever I tried to look, my gaze slid off. It was better to watch the Sorcery-Lord herself, to train my eyes on her beautiful Hafsah derriere. That kept me moving ahead, despite a growing emotional force that pushed me away, crying, "Don't waste your time, there's nothing here!" Then I passed through some invisible boundary, the edge of the antiscrying field; and I could see Dreamsinger in front of me, reaching out, her hand touching window glass.

She whispered, "Boom."

*   *   *

The window exploded at Dreamsinger's touch, blasting shards of glass into the room. It was a big window; it had lots of glass.

The shards slashed like shrapnel into two brawny men who stood just inside. The men didn't have a chance: they went down under the barrage, blown off their feet, sliced by glass splinters. One man collided with a heavy chair, drove it forward half a meter, then toppled off sideways . . . striking the floor at an angle that shoved crystal daggers deeper into his flesh. Blood gushed from a severed artery—a fountain that lasted several seconds, then subsided to a pressureless drip.

The other man landed facedown on the carpet, slivers of glass protruding from his back like needles on a porcupine. He lifted his arm feebly, reaching blindly for nothing. Beneath his tattered clothes, bony spurs pushed weakly from the raised arm, then retracted again in defeat.

The spurs showed that Hump wasn't the only smuggler with pointy augmentation. Not that the spikes seemed to do much good. The man in front of us slumped unconscious and continued to bleed from a dozen lacerations.

Suddenly, I was grabbed from behind and thrown onto the muddy soil. "Idiot," Impervia whispered, pressing her body against my spine. I opened my mouth to protest but was drowned out by an eruption of gunfire from inside the house. Oops. I'd been so busy watching men die near the window, I'd never looked farther into the room. There must have been more guards inside, beyond the blast radius of the glass. Now they were shooting in our direction: shooting at Dreamsinger alone, since the Caryatid had hit the dirt beside Impervia and me.

The Sorcery-Lord made no effort to remove herself from the fire zone. As the shots continued, she stepped over the low windowsill and into the room itself. Bullets zinged through the air; a few passed through Dreamsinger's crimson cloak, tearing several holes in it before the cloak was ripped to rags . . . but the majority of shots were directly on target, plowing straight into Dreamsinger's body.

The bullets had no effect; they never quite made contact.

A violet glow had sprung up around the Spark Lord's outline, like a fringe of indigo fire. Each time a shot hit the glow, the bullet was met with violet flame—a blazing hot flame that dissolved the chunk of lead into spittles of molten metal. Stinking smoke filled the air as drops of liquefied lead fell to the floor . . . but none of it touched Dreamsinger. She just stood with a placid smile, waiting for the barrage to end.

Lying on top of me, Impervia whispered, "That glow around her . . . is it sorcery?"

"No," the Caryatid replied. "I've heard it called a force field. Projected by her armor."

"She's wearing armor?" I asked.

"What do you *think* she's wearing, idiot?" That was Impervia again.

"She's wearing Kaylan's Chameleon. Total coverage. I can't see a square millimeter of who she really is."

"Vanity, vanity," Impervia murmured. She shifted her body slightly against my back. "So, uhh, Phil . . . what *do* you see?"

I didn't answer.

The shooting dwindled to an anticlimax of prissy little clicks: firing pins hitting on empty chambers. A woman inside the house growled, "For God's sake, assholes, give it up. Xavier, will you please call off your dogs?"

A grunting sigh. "You heard her." An old man's gristly voice. "Stand down . . . but reload."

Both the man and the woman spoke with accents: something Central European. Teaching at the academy, I'd heard lots of accents from my students—but those accents were all upper class. The people in Nanticook House sounded rougher . . . more ragged and throaty.

"Warwick Xavier?" Dreamsinger asked.

"You know who I am," the man answered. A statement, not a question.

"She's a Spark," said the unknown woman inside. "She knows everyone." A pause. "Judging by the crimson armor, you're the female Sorcery-Lord. Serpent's Kiss."

"Serpent's Kiss was my predecessor. I'm Dreamsinger."

"Ach, such a fancy name," said Xavier. "Fine women, always so pretentious."

Impervia slid off me. On hands and knees she peered over the windowsill, into the room beyond. The Caryatid and I joined her—like the comic relief in a Shakespeare play, the three of us poking our noses up in the background while more important characters played the main action downstage.

Xavier stood beside the unknown woman at the far end of the room. He was white-haired, big-eared, stoop-shouldered, an imposing jowly man who might be as old as seventy, dressed in formal black-and-white; she was black-haired, fierce-eyed, sharp-boned, an imposing skeleton-thin woman in her early thirties, wearing gray silk pants and shirt, cut so loosely they seemed tailored for someone four inches taller and thirty pounds heavier. If Warwick Xavier was the Smuggler King, this woman might be his Queen or Crown Princess . . . either a wife half his age or his daughter. Maybe even granddaughter. Or perhaps she was his heir-apparent, ruthless in her own right and ready to take over as soon as the king showed weakness.

Before Dreamsinger's entrance, Xavier and the woman had been examining papers spread on a table—records, I assumed, of ill-gotten gains. Two gunsels stood nearby: big men who'd now holstered their pistols and stood with razor spikes bristling along their arms, ready to slash anyone who got too close. The sort of men who didn't know when they were out of their depth.

Dreamsinger ignored the enforcers. She gazed only at Xavier and the woman . . . smiling in what I thought might be recognition.

"You're a long way from home," Dreamsinger said.

It was the woman who replied. "I have many homes."

"And home is where the heart is," Dreamsinger observed. "Or within a few kilometers. Which came first, dear sister? This operation or Feliss Academy?"

"This operation, of course. I chose Feliss Academy only because I had an outpost nearby."

"Did your daughter know?"

The woman beside Xavier shook her head. "Rosalind is happier thinking she's not completely under my wing. But I don't send her to a school unless it's close to my holdings . . . and wherever she goes, I follow."

Dreamsinger smiled. "Dear sister, she's gone somewhere you *can't* follow. Your daughter died several hours ago."

The thin woman—Elizabeth Tzekich, Knife-Hand Liz—caught her breath. That was all. Then she clamped her jaw tight.

I saw no tears.

Where Elizabeth Tzekich was gaunt, Rosalind had been plump—possibly in rebellion, the daughter fattening herself to look as little like her mother as possible. Yet the mother's tight face, the way she suppressed all grief, reminded me of Rosalind concealing her own emotions: the careful hiding-behind-walls of a girl who'd given up making friends.

Like mother, like daughter. And the fierce woman in front of us must have been Rosalind's age when she gave birth to her child. How had that happened? A passionate elopement the way Rosalind had planned to run off with Sebastian? It wouldn't surprise me. Then pregnancy, and who knows? I couldn't imagine how a woman that young could create the Ring of Knives, but Elizabeth Tzekich had managed it. Not only spreading through Europe, but all around the world.

Rosalind had moved from school to school and Knife-Hand Liz had moved from one Ring outpost to another. I wondered who led whom. Was the mother following the daughter just to be close to her? Or was Elizabeth Tzekich touring her assets, inspecting her lieutenants, streamlining operations, spending a few months in every branch office . . . and whenever she moved on, forcing her daughter to move too, shunting the girl into any school that was handy at the next port of call?

Maybe a little of both.

But she *had* kept her daughter near her. When Rosalind came to Feliss Academy, Mother Tzekich must have moved in with Warwick Xavier—Xavier, who was district manager for the Ring, in charge of smuggling and miscellaneous skullduggery. Had Knife-Hand Liz crept near the academy from time to time in hope of catching sight of her daughter? Or had she stayed away, never trying to see the girl but staying close in case something happened?

In case the girl got in trouble. A mother wants to be there. But she hadn't been.

Tzekich asked, "How did Rosalind die?"

Dreamsinger shrugged. "Perhaps an OldTech bioweapon. My brother is investigating."

"But it was murder?"

"That seems likely."

"Who was responsible?"

Dreamsinger cocked her head to one side. "That's my question for *you*. Do any of your enemies have bioweapons hidden in their vaults?"

"Not that I know of—otherwise, I'd report the bastards for possessing banned substances. I'm a loyal subject of the Spark Protectorate."

Dreamsinger smiled. "Of course. Dear sister."

"So why are you here? Just to tell me my daughter's dead?"

"Oh no. That was an unexpected pleasure." Dreamsinger smiled again. Such a sweet smile. "I came to ask Mr. Xavier about a boy who's gone missing."

"I don't know any boy," Xavier said. His voice was tired; I suspected it wasn't Xavier's idea to be awake at this hour. Knife-Hand Liz had to be the one simmering with nervous energy, perusing papers long into the night.

"Who is this boy?" Tzekich asked. Her voice was sharp; she obviously had guessed this was connected to Rosalind's death.

"The boy intended to elope tonight. These people . . ." Dreamsinger waved toward the three of us at the window. "They believe he chartered a fishing boat to go somewhere. *I* believe the boat's crew would let you know what they were doing."

"Why would they?" Xavier asked. "It's no business of mine if some brat runs away."

Dreamsinger waggled a finger in his direction. "But it *is*

your business if a boat goes smuggling without permission. I'm sure you deal harshly with those who try to turn independent. To avoid such suspicions, any captain leaving port after dark likely sends you a note. *Gentle master, I'm just taking a passenger somewhere, so please don't break my knees when I get back.*"

Xavier looked surly, as if he wanted to deny Dreamsinger's words. Tzekich slapped him hard on the arm. "For God's sake, tell her anything you know!"

The old man's expression didn't change . . . but he turned his scowl on Tzekich. "In the old days, we didn't let outsiders deal with our problems. Your daughter is murdered? That's *our* business, not the Sparks."

Tzekich slapped him again. "Spark business is what they say it is."

Dreamsinger chuckled. "Despotism is nice that way."

"Besides," Tzekich continued to Xavier, "we can't deal with *anything* if a Spark kills us for being uncooperative. Stop stonewalling!"

Xavier paused another long moment, making sure no one missed his disgust. *A man of the old school,* I thought: responding to every obstacle with brute force, and if something didn't fall down, he'd just hit it harder. It explained why a man Xavier's age was still just a minor lieutenant, living in a backwater like Dover-on-Sea; he could be trusted to keep people in line and maintain a basic revenue stream, but he'd botch any job that called for finesse.

After one last glower, the old man turned and shuffled across the room to a grand piano shoved against the wall. The piano was placed wrong-side-out: if you opened the lid above the strings, the sound would be deflected into the wall rather than to the room at large. Perhaps Xavier had seen pianos in other people's houses and decided to buy the most expensive one he could find. Clearly he didn't care about music—the cover was closed over the keys, and stacked with piles of paper, mostly unopened envelopes. Xavier's filing system: toss incoming mail onto the piano, and deal with it whenever.

The message Dreamsinger wanted had just arrived that

night, so it must be on top of a pile. Xavier realized that we all would know that—otherwise, I could imagine him shuffling through papers with sullen slowness, while Tzekich grew more and more livid. But he found the note soon enough; then the only delay was the time he took unfolding the page and moving the paper back and forth until he established a distance where he could read the words.

"It's from Ian Nicoll of the *Hoosegow*," Xavier said. "Nice little boat, the *Hoosegow*. Ian gave it the name because he says it feels like a prison, but if you ask me—"

Tzekich snapped, "Just read the damned note!"

Xavier tried to hide a smile, clearly pleased he'd got under her skin. "All right, let me see. Let me see. Let me see." He squinted and shifted the paper a little closer to his eyes. Then a little farther away. Then back to its original position. *"Got some passengers tonight,"* he finally read. *"Two kids from that school in Simka. Eloping, the idiots. Going to Niagara Falls, to get married then fuck their brains out. Pathetic. But I get paid, so who cares? I'll be back in time for . . ."* Xavier stopped reading and folded the page. "The rest is just private."

Dreamsinger held out her hand for the note. Xavier only stared at her until Tzekich heaved an exasperated sigh. "Either you give it to her or she takes it from your cold dead fingers."

"If you want me to kill him, dear sister," Dreamsinger said, "just say the word."

Tzekich gave a humorless laugh. "No thanks, milady. That might sound as if I was giving an order to a Spark Lord . . . or asking for a favor, which is possibly more dangerous."

"Spoilsport," Dreamsinger pouted. She looked back at Xavier, her hand still held out for the message. With a grumpy look, he plodded across the room and gave her the page. Dreamsinger unfolded it and studied the message briefly. "What time did you receive this?"

Xavier said, "A few hours ago. From my man Ripsaw."

"When did Ripsaw receive it?"

"He walks around the port every night after supper. Between six and midnight."

"I want the exact time."

Xavier smiled as if he'd been hoping she'd say that. "Ask Ripsaw yourself." He pointed at one of the men who'd been standing too close to the windows when Dreamsinger blew them in—a man with more blood on his clothes than in his veins. Dreamsinger peered at the corpse with calculation in her eye; perhaps debating whether it was too late to try a Twinning, whether the brain was still intact or just soggy sweetmeats. After a moment, she sighed with regret.

"So," she said, "we don't know whether this note got written before or after passengers arrived at the *Hoosegow*. If it was before, the captain simply *expected* 'two kids from that school'—which doesn't tell how many really showed up. If it was after, and the captain was looking right at the two teenagers as he wrote his message . . . that would make things more interesting." She looked at Xavier. "Do you know if *Hoosegow* actually left port?"

The old man made a sour face. I suspected he did know, but disliked providing information that might actually be useful. Before he could vacillate on an answer, one of the two surviving enforcers spoke up. "I was on harbor watch tonight. *Hoosegow* left its slip at 11:05."

Xavier gave the man a dirty look; the enforcer ignored it, keeping his gaze on Tzekich. Obviously, the bully-boy had decided that pleasing the top boss helped one's career far more than humoring a surly deputy.

"So," Dreamsinger murmured, "the boat is on its way. No reason for that if it didn't have passengers; so Sebastian must have showed up and said, 'Let's go.' He wouldn't do that unless Rosalind was with him."

"Rosalind?" Knife-Hand Liz repeated. "I thought you said . . ." Her voice trailed off.

"Dear sister," Dreamsinger said, "one version of your daughter is dead. Another may be sailing to Niagara Falls; and now I'll have to follow." She shuddered. "Pity me, friends. Such a dreary place. So conventional and crowded. Why do people come from around the world to see water falling over a cliff? And all the hideous 'attractions'; they should be called *dis*tractions, built to prevent newlyweds from realizing the banality of what they've just done. I hate it all. Hate it, hate it, hate it. Hate it, hate it, hate it, hate it . . ." She stopped herself with an effort. "But, I suppose while I'm there, I can check—"

Her voice choked silent. Her face froze—as if some inner reflex held her expression immobile so we couldn't guess what was going through her mind. An instant later, she whirled to face the three of us at the window. "This Sebastian was a powerful psychic?"

We all nodded.

"What was his power?"

Impervia and the Caryatid looked at me to answer. I chose my words carefully. "Our psionics teacher says Sebastian can talk to the world: as if land, sea, and air are full of happy puppies, eager to fulfill the boy's tiniest wish. So his powers cover the whole spectrum."

"The boy talks directly to nanites? And he's headed for Niagara Falls?" Dreamsinger's voice had gone shrill. "With a creature that can make itself look like Rosalind?"

Mother Tzekich stirred at her daughter's name, but didn't have a chance to speak. Dreamsinger surged toward the window where Impervia, the Caryatid, and I still crouched. The Spark Lord grabbed me by the jacket and heaved me up as if I weighed no more than a rag doll. "Fool!" she whispered, so softly no one else could hear. "Those curds weren't a bioweapon. They were cast-off cellules from a Lucifer."

"But I thought . . ." Opal had said the flake-away bits of Lucifer were like grains of black gunpowder. Dark and dry. I suddenly remembered that both Dreamsinger and her brother had asked if I was sure the curds I'd seen were white and wet, not dark and dry. They both must have suspected there was a Lucifer in our neighborhood, but my talk of a bioweapon had made it seem like something else. "It looked like cottage cheese," I said. "Honestly . . ."

"The Lucifer mutated," Dreamsinger told me in another furious whisper. "It's been trying to do that for decades. It knows Spark Royal can track its life-signs . . . so the blasted thing finally managed to change its metabolism. And now it's going to Niagara Falls with a psychic?"

She tossed me aside in disgust. Pure luck let me grab a corner of the window frame and catch my balance; otherwise, I would have fallen onto the broken glass that littered the floor. Dreamsinger didn't care—she was already stepping over the sill, out onto the dark lawn. At the same time, she tapped her pearl necklace: the one that was actually a radio transmitter. "Spark Royal, attend," she snapped. "I need immediate pick-up, this location."

"Please activate anchor," a metallic voice said from the necklace.

"Give me ten seconds."

Dreamsinger reached toward her waist. To my eyes, she was grabbing at nothingness a short distance in front of her bare navel. *A belt pack*, I thought; her armor must have pouches and attachments that I couldn't see because of the Chameleon spell. A moment later, she pulled a small device from thin air—a black plastic box the size of a book, with four metallic gold horseshoes arranged in a diamond on its top face.

"Dearest sister," she called to the Caryatid, "could you come here, please?"

The Caryatid hurried forward.

"Do you see this switch?" Dreamsinger pointed to a toggle on the box's side. "When I'm gone, please push that; it turns the anchor off. Be careful not to turn it on again—just keep the anchor safe, and I'll come for it someday."

"Yes, milady."

"Good. Keep faith with me." Dreamsinger kissed the Caryatid lightly on the lips. Then she whirled and told the rest of us, "Only my sister on the Burdensome Path may touch the device. Everyone else stand clear."

Without waiting for an answer, she stepped away from the Caryatid, pushed the toggle-switch herself, and laid the box on the ground. "Spark Royal, attend," she said to empty air. "The anchor is active. Take me home."

A tube of creamy white lashed down from the sky: the same ectoplasmic smoke we'd seen at Death Hotel. It glinted with color, buffed gold, sea green, peacock blue . . . and again I tried to imagine what it might be. An energy beam projected from an orbiting satellite? Ionized particles like the Aurora Borealis, curled in a shimmering sleeve? Or perhaps a living creature, some ethereal worm hundreds of kilometers long, ready to lower its tail whenever a Spark commanded?

The thing stabbed down like a lightning bolt, straight for Dreamsinger's anchor. The device must have worked like a magnet, for the instant the smoke-tail made contact, its tip adhered to the box; then the tail's mouth spread wider, until its edges touched all four golden horseshoes on the anchor's top surface.

The tip was locked down and secure. But the rest of the smoke-tail flapped wildly, making no sound but whipping through the darkness in ghostly frenzy. A fluttering wraith reaching high out of sight.

Beyond the house, dogs began to bark—Xavier's guard pack, finally noticing something was amiss. Why hadn't they come running when Dreamsinger made the windows explode? Idiotic beasts. Then I realized the explosion had taken place inside the antiscrying shield; since the dogs were outside, the antiscrying sorcery would make them ignore the din of smashing glass. They wouldn't react till something became visible on their side of the shield.

Something like a big smoky tube sprouting from the lawn to the stratosphere.

Three German Shepherds dashed snarling into view; then they stopped in a doggy double-take. They paid no attention to those of us still within the antiscrying shield: all they saw was a pillar of ghost-smoke flicking around the yard, sweeping past the bare-branched trees, occasionally billowing out over the bluffs before whisking back to the house again. The tube's random swooping soon took it in the dogs' direction . . . and they backed off, whining in their throats. The smoke didn't touch them—it didn't touch anything, not the house, not the trees, not a single blade of winter-parched grass—but it came within a hair of grazing everything in sight, skimming past my face, darting at the Caryatid's feet, even looping once around Impervia's neck before uncoiling again and careening off. As if it were stalking each of us in turn, trying to make us flinch.

Flinch we did . . . and the smoke-tail wagged itself happily, heading off to scare the dogs again.

The metallic voice spoke from Dreamsinger's necklace. "Anchor established. Ready for transport to Spark Royal."

"Dear sister, I must go," Dreamsinger told the Caryatid. "Turn off the switch when I'm gone."

The Caryatid nodded. Dreamsinger smiled back, then squatted beside the anchor box. She slid one finger under the tethered end of the smoke-tail, slipping her fingertip into the mouth of the tube . . . and suddenly her whole body was sucked inside, her bones, her flesh turning as malleable as clay. It looked like something from a comic drawing, a woman's body pulled thin as a garter snake, then rammed into an aperture no bigger than a mouse hole; but there was no humor in seeing such grisly distortion for real. The whole thing lasted less than a second, and made no sound except a soft swish of air—otherwise, I might have been sick on the spot.

The Caryatid, looking equally queasy, forced herself to press the anchor's toggle-switch. Click. Immediately, the smoke-tail slipped free, jerking loose from its tether and bounding high into the sky like a taut rope suddenly cut. It soared halfway to the clouds, dropped down once more to the treetops, then flew straight up out of sight.

Mission accomplished. The tube had removed Dreamsinger to Spark Royal—whence, presumably, she'd ride a similar tube to Niagara Falls. There'd have to be an anchor device somewhere in the Niagara area, ready to catch hold of the tube's tail end . . . but I suspected there were anchors all over the world, planted in out-of-the-way corners, waiting for the day a Spark Lord needed to get somewhere in a hurry.

There'd been one in Death Hotel—a place the small device could lie undisturbed for centuries. It was probably radio-controlled, ready to activate itself when a signal came . . .

My train of thought was interrupted by someone behind

me seizing my arm. I looked around. Elizabeth Tzekich was there. "The Spark Lord's run off," she said. "Leaving you to my tender mercies." Her eyes flashed. "Now you're going to tell me what's going on."

12

DEMON, DEMON, LOVER

Tzekich pulled me across the parquet littered with glass. I tried not to tread in the blood of the dead . . . but Knife-Hand Liz walked straight through. When she reached a clean section of floor, she left sticky scarlet slipperprints.

Back at the windowsill, the Caryatid and Impervia climbed inside. Staying loyally with me, even though they could have run off into the night. My friends.

Meanwhile, the surviving bully-boys from the Ring unholstered their pistols. Behind the enforcers, Xavier broke into a wolfish leer—he must have regarded us all as human punching bags, here to help him forget the humiliation of submitting to a Spark Lord. Lucky for us, Tzekich outranked the old bastard . . . and she was so irked by Xavier's stupid intransigence, she treated Impervia, the Caryatid, and me with utmost gentility. She obviously wanted to annoy her deputy as much as he'd annoyed her.

"Please sit," Tzekich said, gesturing toward a black leather couch. "Tell me everything you know."

We sat, we talked. The facts, but no interpretation. I didn't recount Chancellor Opal's encounter with the Lucifer, nor did I mention what Dreamsinger whispered to me before she left. I'd have to ponder her words some time soon, but not with Elizabeth Tzekich and two armed guards hovering over me. For now, I just stuck to the bioweapon version of the tale;

171

suddenly changing my story might antagonize Knife-Hand Liz to the point of violence.

She was angry enough as it was—during my recitation, Xavier made a constant nuisance of himself with pointless intrusive questions, aggravating Tzekich to the verge of fury. I couldn't understand why she didn't toss him from the room . . . or borrow a gun from an enforcer and create a new opening in her organization. But she tolerated Xavier's petty interference with clenched teeth, only once giving him a lethal glare and saying, "I am *trying* to find out about my daughter."

Of course, Tzekich asked questions of her own—and from their tone, I realized she didn't want to believe her daughter was dead. If there were two copies of the girl, why couldn't the one still alive be the real Rosalind? Perhaps an enemy had created a sorcerous duplicate of her daughter as a way to infiltrate the Ring of Knives. But Rosalind had defeated the double by using the impersonator's own cottage cheese bacteria; then the girl had run off with "that Sebastian boy" to escape before more enemies arrived. Elopement was so utterly ridiculous at Rosalind's age, it must be a ruse to throw off pursuers.

That made sense, didn't it?

No one wanted to argue—not even spiteful Xavier. There are some things it's not safe to say when a mother is being willfully blind.

Tzekich rose from her chair and snapped her fingers toward her men. "We're leaving now. Let's go."

Xavier grunted. "Just like that, we're off?"

"To Niagara Falls. Get your fastest boat."

"Ach . . . it won't be as fast as that Spark Lord."

"No," Tzekich said, "but it might be fast enough to catch the *Hoosegow*."

Xavier shook his head. "They got a good wind, a long headstart, and the Falls are only ten, twelve hours away. *Hoosegow* will beat us."

"We'll still be close behind." Tzekich headed for the door. "I refuse to sit here while my daughter's in danger."

Xavier's expression was easy to read: *The girl's not in*

danger; she's dead. But he simply pointed a thumb at Impervia, the Caryatid, and me. "What do we do with *them*?"

Tzekich stopped in the doorway. She turned back to consider us. Impervia and I tensed, ready to put up a fight . . . but the Caryatid simply toyed with the anchor device Dreamsinger had left in her keeping, idly tracing one finger along the inlaid gold horseshoes. Did Tzekich want to mess with a Spark Lord's "dear sister"?

A tense silence. Then Tzekich said, "Forget them." She glared in our direction. "Get the hell out."

We didn't need to be told twice. Before Tzekich vanished from the doorway, before Xavier could have us roughed up behind his boss's back, we three teachers were out the window and scurrying into the darkness.

The guard dogs raised a ruckus on our way off the property; but with the Caryatid waving flames in the dogs' faces and Impervia swinging a fallen tree branch as a club, the animals soon decided their duty lay in snarling from a distance rather than outright attack. They saw us to the gate, yapping all the while and continuing long after we were gone. Dogs on other estates took up the barking, making an awful racket . . . and I cringed at the noise until I realized it was harmless.

We'd survived.

After running afoul of a spike-armed enforcer, a Sorcery-Lord, and the Ring of Knives, my friends and I had survived. We were also cut loose from our burdens: the Sparks were on the case, and didn't need help from mere schoolteachers. We'd even told Knife-Hand Liz her daughter was dead . . . and once you've informed the authorities and the parents, what more must a teacher do?

Quest over. Home to bed.

But even as these thoughts passed through my head, Impervia asked, "So how do *we* get to Niagara Falls?"

I groaned.

Arguing with Impervia was futile. Besides, my heart wasn't in it—though part of me wanted to run back to Simka, another part oozed with guilt at abandoning Sebastian. If I could believe Dreamsinger, it seemed certain the boy was now in the clutches of a Lucifer. Furthermore, the Sorcery-Lord was in hot pursuit of the couple; even if she saved Sebastian from the shapeshifting alien, I doubted that she'd treat the boy kindly. A lunatic like her would probably consider Sebastian the Lucifer's partner-in-crime.

Boom.

Besides, if we went home now, we might never learn what was going on . . . and despite my past deficiencies in scientific curiosity, this time I wanted to know *everything*. Therefore, when Impervia began preaching about our divine calling to see this business through, I put up only a token protest: I just pointed out that Dreamsinger and the Ring might both slit our gizzards if we meddled, and that by the time we got to Niagara Falls, all the excitement would likely be over.

Impervia admitted the risk of gizzard-slitting but not that we might be too late to affect the final outcome. We'd been called; therefore we had a part to play. God and the Magdalene had summoned us, and if we stayed true we would end up where we were supposed to be. Holy foot-soldiers in a divine battle plan.

I had no answer to such rock-hard faith. My own sense of religion had never developed one way or the other: I was too embarrassed to say I believed in God, but not angry enough to say I didn't. Neither hot nor cold. I'd always longed to receive a clear vocation ("Philemon Dhubhai, this is your purpose!") but mistrusted anything so pat. When Impervia said we'd finally been called, all I could do was dither.

"Yes, but . . ."

"No, but . . ."

"I see that, but . . ."

"I know that, but . . ."

I was saved by the arrival of Myoko, Pelinor, and Annah.

They'd been down on the docks when they saw the milky tube descend from the sky. Hard to miss on a dark silent night. So they'd left their fruitless questions about Sebas-

tian—in a port full of smugglers, no one would divulge anything—and they hurried up the cliff-road to the mansions of
the rich. Dreamsinger's travel-tube had vanished by the time
they arrived; instead, they followed the howling of dogs and
found us at the epicenter.

Myoko shook her head ruefully as she approached. "What
did you do *this* time, Impervia?"

Impervia only sniffed.

Tales were quickly told. Myoko said she envied us for finding so much excitement. The Caryatid suggested where she
could put that excitement . . . and much crude-mouthed ban-
ter ensued.

Annah, of course, did not take part—not quiet, doe-eyed
Annah. She merely listened with a polite smile, glancing my
way from time to time. I couldn't tell if those glances meant
she was glad I'd survived or if she was having second
thoughts about me, my friends, and this whole crisis-prone
outing. Before I could draw her aside and ask, Impervia's
voice cut through the chatter.

"Enough! We have to find a boat for Niagara Falls. A *fast*
boat. Did you see any possibilities in the harbor?"

"Not among the fishing boats," Pelinor answered. "For
speed, you'd want the marina; the expensive pleasure yachts
that rich people keep here over winter."

"I'll bet," Myoko said, "we could find a yacht that wasn't
securely locked up . . ."

"Don't even think it," Impervia growled.

Myoko pretended to be surprised. "We can't commandeer
a boat in the service of God?"

Impervia only glared.

"I know people in town," Pelinor said. "Horse breeders
with money. They probably own boats."

"If we're thinking of people with money," said the Caryatid, "there's always Gretchen Kinnderboom . . ."

Everyone turned toward me—even Annah, who I'd
hoped might not have heard any gossip about me and
Gretchen.

I sighed. "Yes, Gretchen has a boat—and she claims it's

the fastest in Dover. That's likely just idle boasting, the way she always . . ." I stopped myself. "Gretchen has a boat. It's supposedly fast. Come on."

Silently, I led the way forward.

Kinnderboom Cottage was thirty times the size of any cottage on Earth; but Gretchen reveled in twee diminutives, like calling her thoroughbred stallion "Prancy Pony" and the three-century oak in her side yard "Iddle-Widdle Acorn." (Gretchen had a habit of lapsing into baby talk at the least provocation. She was that kind of woman . . . and beautiful enough that I often didn't care.)

Like all houses in this part of Dover, the Kinnderboom mansion squatted in the midst of a pointlessly large estate overlooking the lake. The building itself was an up-and-down thing, equipped with so many gables it seemed more like a depot where carpenters stored their inventory than someplace people actually lived. Wherever you looked, there was an architectural *feature*. Each window had a curlicued metal railing; each door had a portico, an arch, or an assemblage of Corinthian columns. And everything changed on a regular basis: an army of construction crews, landscapers, and interior decorators passed through each year, ripping out the old, slapping up the new. I don't think Gretchen really cared what any of the workers did—she just hired them so she could have more underlings to boss around.

The workers were always men.

The grounds of Kinnderboom Cottage were surrounded by a wall; but I had a key to the gate, plus a good deal of practice sneaking in under cover of darkness. I let my friends enter, locked the gate behind us, then motioned everyone to stand still. Ten seconds . . . twenty . . . thirty . . . whereupon an unearthly creature appeared from the shadows, his stomach pincers clicking as he walked.

"Ahh," he said. "Baron Dhubhai."

Myoko turned toward me and mouthed the word *Baron?* I shrugged. I had no title in my native Sheba—no one did, except a few old men, indulgently allowed to call themselves princes—but Gretchen knew how rich my family was, and she fervently believed such money would make me at least a baron in any "civilized" province. Therefore, her household slaves were obliged to address me in that fashion.

As for this particular slave, he was the size of a full-grown bull but built like a lobster. Eight legs. Fan tail. Chitinous carapace—colored cherry red, though it looked nearly black in the darkness. His body angled up centaur-style to the height of a human, so his head was a hand's breadth higher than mine. He always had a light smell of vinegar, faint here in the open air but still quite noticeable. His face: flat and wide with dangling whiskers and a spike-nosed snout. His arms: two spindly ones almost always folded across his chest and two nasty pincer claws at waist level, jutting forward at just the right height to disembowel an adult human. He was still clicking those claws idly as he looked us up and down.

From past visits, I knew this alien's name was Oberon. He served on guard duty every night; Oberon was one of Gretchen's most trusted "demons."

All of Gretchen's staff were extraterrestrials. In fact, the Kinnderboom fortune came from "demonmongery": breeding and selling alien slaves. Gretchen didn't dirty her hands in the family business—she didn't dirty her hands with *any* sort of work—but she kept more than a dozen ETs in her household "for the sake of appearances." Foremost among those ETs were Oberon and his family, who came from some species with human-level intelligence but an antlike predisposition to follow the commands of a queen. Even though Gretchen couldn't have resembled the queens of Oberon's race, she still filled that role in his eyes. After all, Oberon had never seen a queen . . . and he'd been raised from the egg by Gretchen herself, brought up to obey her every whim.

There in the yard, lobsterlike Oberon was obviously trying to decide how Gretchen's whims would run tonight. If I'd been alone, he would have let me proceed to the house immediately; Gretchen's standing orders were to let me pass, and she'd decide for herself whether to admit me to her glorious presence. But I'd come with five strangers in tow, and Oberon wasn't eager to let them close to his exalted mistress.

He belonged to his species' warrior caste, and his first instinct was to keep his queen safe from outsiders.

He clicked his pincers softly. "We weren't expecting guests tonight, baron."

"I know. But we need to see Gretchen immediately."

"The question is, does *she* need to see *you*?"

"Excellent point, good fellow," said Pelinor. Our noble knight liked aliens almost as much as he liked horses; he'd been gazing in admiration at Oberon ever since the big ET had appeared from the darkness. And just as he had a feel for horse psychology, Pelinor could guess what was on Oberon's mind. "How about this," he told the demon. "You keep us here while, uhh, Baron Dhubhai goes for a private chat with Ms. Kinnderboom. No problem with that, is there?"

Oberon nodded immediately and waved me toward the house. I gave my friends one last glance (attempting a soulful meeting-of-the-eyes with Annah, then a warning glare at Impervia, who was gazing at Oberon with the thoughtful look of someone considering where to punch a lobster for maximum effect); then I hurried up the gravel drive.

The front of Kinnderboom Cottage was dark: no lights in any of the rooms, just a single oil lamp above the main entrance. Still, I was certain Gretchen would be awake; for the past five years, she'd slept days instead of nights. If anyone asked why, she'd say, "I'm a vampire now, darling, didn't you get my note?" . . . but in fact, she was just a woman on the high side of forty, trying to deny she might ever show her age. Daylight was too unforgiving, especially since the cottage had mirrors in every room. Gretchen preferred to see herself by candleshine, or when she was greatly daring, by the muted glow of sun through curtains. Her bedroom had curtains in three different colors—red, gold, and dusky brown— plus meters of thick white lace, so she could make love in the afternoon and tint the lighting to whatever shade made her feel sexy.

She never went outside. Ever. Sometimes after a night together, she would nudge me out of bed at dawn and get me to open the doors to the balcony outside her window. She would

ask me to pull the thinnest lace curtains across the opening,
like a sheer white veil; then she would make me get back into
bed, and she would go alone to the doorway, standing naked
in the sunrise, inhaling the morning and the breeze that fluttered the curtains around her.

But she never threw the curtains wide open. Never took
that last step onto the balcony to feel the sun on her skin. She
always stayed behind the thin lace barrier. Sometimes I wondered if this was all just a performance, so I could see her
body backlit by dawn and imagine the breeze licking her nipples, the sheer curtains swishing against her stomach and
thighs . . . but at other times, I was sure I could sense an ache
inside her, a yearning to be truly outdoors instead of a single
step shy. She would stand there for minutes, closing her eyes
and taking deep silent breaths; then she would come back
wordlessly to bed and either cling to me like a little girl or
throw herself into ravenous love-making, driving, driving,
driving until we were both obliterated.

Those moments were what made me keep coming back to
Kinnderboom Cottage—not for the sex itself, but for the
woman who used sex to run from herself. Lonely, silly, ex-
ploitive Gretchen. She made me feel needed . . . which is not
the same as being loved or appreciated, but it can still be ad-
dictive if you don't ask yourself too many questions.

The door opened as I walked up the front steps. Oberon's
mate Titania stood in the entrance, bowing low in greeting.
Like her husband, she was built on lobstery lines, but
smaller and colored a deep earthy brown. Instead of pincers,
Titania had a second pair of arms: nimble and strong despite
their thinness. She served as Gretchen's majordomo, keeping the other slaves organized. If Titania were human, she
might easily have become total mistress of the estate, since
Gretchen had neither the shrewdness nor the discipline to
resist. Gretchen could have become a pampered prisoner
with Titania controlling the staff and the purse-strings. But
Titania was not human; she was an alien lobster whose instincts to follow a queen were just as strong as Oberon's.
Though Titania ran the cottage far better than Gretchen ever

could, Titania would never dream of usurping ultimate command.

"Good evening, baron," Titania said. "It's provident you came. Mistress Gretchen could use some company just now."

"I'm afraid that's not why I'm here. I need Gretchen's help."

Titania stared at me a moment, the tips of her whiskers lifting. I'd come to recognize that as her species' look of disapproval: Queen Gretchen was apparently in some black mood and Titania wanted me to make things brighter, not bring new problems of my own. On the other hand, it was not a courtier's place to shield her queen from making decisions; in Titania's mind I was behaving with commendable sense, approaching Queen Gretchen with a humble petition for aid. That's what loyal subjects *did* . . . and loyal retainers didn't stand in the way.

"All right," Titania said, making an effort to relax her whiskers, "I'll present you. But take off your boots—they're filthy."

We walked up to Gretchen's room in silence: Titania in front and me behind, because she was too big for us to walk side by side through corridors built to normal human scale. She held a kerosene lamp in one hand, but its shine was blocked by her body; climbing the stairs, I was almost completely in the dark.

Then again, I didn't need any light—I'd gone up and down this stairway so often in blackness, I knew exactly how many steps there were and which were likely to creak under my weight. Heaven knows why Gretchen and I were so furtive when there was nobody else in the house except slaves, and the slaves were aliens with precious little interest in human sexual affairs . . . but we always conducted our meetings like an adulterous couple sneaking around while their spouses slept nearby.

Stupid habit. But that's what Gretchen and I had: just an ongoing habit.

Titania tapped on the door of Gretchen's suite, then went inside without waiting. I followed into the so-called Sitting

Room: a place seldom used but often redecorated, with its appearance changing from season to season (sometimes month to month, or week to week). At the moment, it was designed to fight the dourness of winter with warm/hot colors—wallpaper of ferocious carmine red accented with a black and gold border around the top. The furniture (couch, rocking chair, ottoman) matched the color scheme with appropriate upholstery or afghan throw-covers draped neatly over bare wood. The neatness of the afghans proved Gretchen truly was in a bad way. When she was feeling good, she sprawled wherever she wanted with no regard for how the afghans might slip; when she was in a mood, she needed everything just so, and could spend hours fussing to get proper tucks and folds.

Titania crossed the room as quickly as her eight legs would go—I think she deliberately avoided seeing how fastidiously everything was arranged—and she knocked at the door to the bedroom. "Mistress Gretchen," she murmured, "Baron Dhubhai has come to visit." Titania looked my direction as if daring me to say otherwise; then she turned back to the closed door and asked, "May I let him in?"

If any answer came, it was too quiet for me to hear. Nevertheless, Titania turned the knob and pushed the door open. "The mistress will see you now."

I nodded. Titania bowed once more, then silently brushed past me as she headed downstairs.

I'd never seen the bedroom so brilliantly lit: every flat surface held two or three shine-stones, beaming dollops of quartz I assumed had been enchanted by sorcerers working for Papa Kinnderboom in Feliss City. Usually Gretchen only kept one or two stones out in the open, and she often draped those with squares of thin cotton to mute the gleam; but tonight there were dozens all over the place, standing uncovered on the vanity, the dressers, the night stands, even scattered on the floor. My eyes ached from the brightness—I had to shield my gaze with my hand as I searched for Gretchen herself.

Despite the incessant remodeling in other parts of the

house, Gretchen's bedroom hadn't changed in years—except for the darkening curtains, the place was always white, white, white, the walls, the bedding, the carpet. For variation, the furniture was painted in a range of bleached grays. There were also accents of color where Gretchen had thrown a sapphire blue dress over a chair, and left a crimson bra pooled on the floor; but the overall impression was still that eye-glaring white, illuminated now by several dozen shine-stones.

Quite bright enough to show that Gretchen was missing.

She'd recently been in the bed: the covers were thrown back and the sheets rumpled. The sight made me think of dead Rosalind, her covers wide open too. But Gretchen was not lying sprawled across the mattress . . . nor was she sitting at the vanity or lounging in the giant bathtub against the far wall. I peeked into the walk-in closet, but saw no sign of her. I didn't get down to look under the bed, but I glanced in that direction while staying on my feet, and decided it was unlikely Gretchen had managed to crawl out of sight. Since there was nowhere else she could hide (short of scrunching into a cedar chest or one of the trunks in the closet), I was on the verge of leaving; then a puff of breeze swirled the curtains in front of the balcony doors.

The doors were open. Despite the chill of the not-yet-spring night.

The hairs on the back of my neck bristled as I walked across the room. If she'd finally taken that last step into the open air . . . I kept picturing her throwing herself off the balcony in some fit of despondence. Or bid for attention. We were only one story up, so she'd almost certainly survive; but I didn't want to look over the railing and see Gretchen lying below. I had to force myself to push through the curtains, into the cold night breeze . . .

. . . where Gretchen stood quite alive, naked and hugging herself, rapidly puckering into one gigantic goose-pimple.

"Hi," I said.

"Hi yourself." Her teeth chattered. "Could you, uhh . . ." She lifted one arm to gesture back into the room, then quickly went back to hugging herself. It took me a moment to realize what she wanted.

"The lights?" I said.

"Please."

I hurried back into the bedroom and collected shine-stones, dropping them into the thick velvet sack where Gretchen usually kept them. As I worked, I couldn't help chuckling—imagining Gretchen as she heard the knock at her door. She must have realized she was surrounded by more light than a summer afternoon . . . so she scuttled to the balcony to keep me from seeing her in the unforgiving glare. All those times I'd tried to get her outdoors, I'd been using the wrong tactics.

I laughed again.

Soon I was carrying a bag full of shine: all the stones except one. I'd left that one on the night stand and covered it with a scarf of turquoise gossamer that had been balled up on the vanity. The resulting light tinted the room either sickly green or sea-mist blue, depending on your tolerance for turquoise . . . but it seemed to satisfy Gretchen, for she immediately came back inside, and closed the doors behind her. For a count of three she tried to bluff out the moment, letting her arms fall to her sides and striking a pose of regal nudity, pretending to be unfazed by cold. Then the shivers hit her and she stumbled forward, ripping a comforter off the bed and wrapping herself as her body shook.

I took her into my arms. She was a tall woman, almost exactly my height, long-legged and lean . . . but at that moment she seemed much smaller, shrinking into me as she opened the comforter and wrapped it around the two of us. Her bare body pressed against my clothes. Milky skin, green eyes, russet hair—all of which seemed entirely natural, but when a woman's daddy has sorcerers on his payroll, one can never tell how much cosmetic help she had in her formative years.

Kaylan's Chameleon isn't the only beauty spell cast on developing girls—sorcerers have plenty of "tuck 'n' tweak" enchantments, making eye color more vivid, hair more lush, and adolescent body development more in keeping with local fashion. There was a reason my cousin Hafsah had such memorable loveliness: my grandma the governor paid for it. For the same reason, Gretchen's creamy complexion showed no hint of the usual freckles, moles, and other punctuations that flesh is normally heir to.

Yet sorcery has its limitations—it can correct imperfections, but it can't stop time. Removing a mole just means banishing pigments from a specific area of tissue; removing a wrinkle from a forty-ish woman's face means fighting the whole course of physical development, all the ongoing changes that lead to dry skin, slowing hormones and declining glands. Aging isn't one thing, it's *everything* . . . and neither science nor sorcery has identified all the body's clocks, let alone figured out how to turn them back in unison. There are too many proteins and enzymes and secretions that have to be balanced: if you stop the formation of crow's feet by changing the quantity of a particular body chemical, other body chemicals shift too. *Lots* of chemicals. Next thing you know, there might be a rash, or sores, or an epileptic fit.

Aging isn't an aberration that can be set back on track . . . it's the track itself.

I looked at the woman in my arms, and despite the dimness of the light, I could see everything she didn't admit was there: the wrinkles, the crinkles, the lines. A puffiness around the jaw; lapses in the sleekness of her neck. All very subtle, what most of us would consider insignificant—anyone standing back a few steps would see a woman at the peak of her beauty. But that wasn't enough for Gretchen. When she invited a man to her boudoir, she had no intention of keeping him at arm's length.

"I'm glad you're here," she whispered. Her breath caressed my neck; a moment later, her lips did too.

"Gretchen," I said, "I can't stay."

"Don't be a silly billy." She kissed my neck again. "You just got here."

"I have some friends outside. There's been trouble at the school, and we need to borrow your boat."

"What?" She blinked as if I'd just pinched her.

"One of our students has run off. People are after him—

dangerous people. We need a fast boat so we can find him before they do."

"You're just here to take my boat?" Her voice had an edge of outrage.

"It's important, Gretchen. A girl is dead. Murdered. And other people are dead too, thanks to a Spark Lord who—"

"A Spark Lord? Which Spark Lord?"

"The female Sorcery-Lord. Called Dreamsinger. She showed up at a tavern and—"

"You met a Spark Lord? When?"

"Tonight," I said. "Just a while ago. Now she's gone to Niagara Falls, and we need your boat to—"

"So this Sorcery-Lord is in Niagara Falls?"

"That's where she said she was going."

"And you want my boat to go there too?"

"Yes."

She drew away from me—not abruptly, but in typical Gretchen fashion: a squeeze of mock affection, then an ooze of regretful detachment, and finally a playful flash of her naked body before she closed the comforter around herself. "All right," she said, "we'll head for Niagara Falls."

"We?"

"Yes: *we*." She threw off the comforter and began to get dressed.

She'd probably claim that she dressed in a hurry . . . and she *did* abbreviate her usual routine of trying on half her wardrobe before deciding what suited her mood. But Gretchen was not one of those heroines from fiction who can switch instantly from pampered beauty to rugged adventurer. If her bedroom caught fire, she wouldn't leave until she'd tried on half a dozen outfits to see which matched the flames. As for being seen in public without rouge, mascara, perfume, et cetera—silly billy, what *are* you thinking?

So I sat on the bed and waited as patiently as I could. Trying to rush Gretchen was worse than useless—if you annoyed her, she slowed down to punish you. The woman had a knack for petty vindictiveness: entirely unconscious too. She'd be genuinely shocked if you suggested she was deliberately taking longer than necessary to redden her lips, pluck her eyebrows, and choose which garters went with which stockings inside which boots to wear on a muddy night in late thaw; and then she'd slow down even more.

Gretchen could drive a man mad in so many ways.

"Now tell me," she called as she rummaged through boxes in her closet, "what did this Dreamsinger look like?"

"Don't know," I answered. "She was hidden in Kaylan's Chameleon."

Gretchen stuck her head out of the closet. "Now I *really* want to know what she looked like. Me perhaps?"

"If you were my ideal sexual object, do you think I'd admit it?"

She laughed and disappeared back into the closet—no doubt convinced I couldn't possibly desire any woman besides herself.

I said, "You realize this trip might get dangerous? We aren't the only ones going to Niagara. Have you heard of the Ring of Knives?"

"God, those people? I swear, that dreadful Warwick Xavier spies on me with a telescope."

"He's a smuggler; he watches the lake for customs agents."

"He watches my windows for a glimpse of my booboos."

"Do you ever give him one?"

Gretchen laughed. "Of course. Every girl needs someone to torture."

"In addition to herself."

Gretchen didn't dignify that with an answer. For a while, the only sound from the closet was the squeal of metal hangers scraping sharply along clothes-rods.

"So," I finally said, "why so many shine-stones tonight?"

"Nothing, darling, just a whim."

"What kind of whim?"

"An idle one."

Since she couldn't see me, I rolled my eyes. "You weren't, for example, afraid of the dark and wanted as much light as possible? Or feeling so depressed, you thought the light would cheer you up?"

"Don't be ridiculous. I feel fine."

"Really? Titania was worried about you."

"What did she say?"

"She didn't say anything. But she has a way of twitching her whiskers . . ."

"Titania should keep her whiskers to herself." Gretchen stuck her head out of the closet again. For some reason, she was wearing a green felt hat shaped like an iguana. The rest of her was still naked. "Really, darling, I'm fine. Honestly."

"Good."

"Good."

She vanished once more into the closet. I could hear boxes being shoved around . . . or possibly being kicked. Under all that racket, she murmured something so softly I couldn't make it out.

"Beg pardon?" I said.

Gretchen didn't answer right away. Then she spoke in a manner intended to sound airy and offhanded. "I suppose Titania thought I was upset because the Earl of Brant canceled his visit yesterday. But why should that bother me? He's a busy man; he said he had pressing affairs of state."

I winced. For centuries, the phrase "affairs of state" has meant hopping into bed with some trollop. The expression is so universally associated with sex that people in government avoid it when referring to legitimate activities—if you truly spend your time on official duties, you don't say you're dealing with affairs of state. That only makes folks snicker.

Besides, I *knew* the Earl of Brant: a rake in his mid-twenties, far too good-looking and rich. Brought up by a doting aunt whose only means of discipline was telling the boy how much better he was than anyone else. "So don't you think you should act better too?" I couldn't picture the earl spending a nanosecond on real administrative chores; if he'd wriggled out of a date with Gretchen, it was only because he'd found someone younger, prettier, and/or double-jointed.

Gretchen must have known that too: she was blind about many things, but astute in detecting the lies of unfaithful lovers—she had extensive knowledge of such lies, having used them all herself. No callow pup like the Earl of Brant could deceive Gretchen Kinnderboom, especially with such a transparent excuse. Affairs of state indeed! The earl was thumbing his nose at her, as if she wasn't worth inventing a better story.

I knew it. Gretchen knew it.

Gretchen must also have known I'd see through the earl's lie . . . yet she told me anyway. Almost as if she were *confiding* in me. As close as she could come to sharing her pain. My eyes stung with tears, and guilt. If Gretchen had ever reached out to me before this, rather than toying with me, dangling me on the hook, never admitting she might need me for anything more than scratching a sexual itch—if she'd ever acknowledged the slightest crack in her armor—perhaps I would have been thinking, *I hope Gretchen doesn't get jealous over Annah.* But I was thinking, *I hope Annah doesn't get jealous over Gretchen.*

That was the way things were. I cared what Annah thought, but all I had left for Gretchen was pity: that the earl's cruel brush-off had shaken her so badly she was finally seeking an emotional connection with me.

Just a few hours too late.

"So you must have been bored," I said, trying to keep my voice light, "sitting here without company. Why didn't you send me a note?"

"Don't be ridiculous. I wasn't bored." The rummaging in the closet had gone silent. "Besides, what would you think if I *had* invited you? The gentleman must petition the lady, never the other way around. Otherwise, it looks like she's groveling."

"No. It looks like she needs a friend."

"A *friend*?" She must have realized her voice had gone shrill, because she broke off and forced out a laugh. "If I need a friend, I'll buy a spaniel. What I can't buy is a *man*."

"True." Though she'd tried to buy men on many occasions. "So why are you interested in this Spark Lord?"

The rummaging sounds resumed, plus the clatter of hangers and the opening/closing of the drawers built into the closet. "I've never met a Spark," Gretchen said as she rifled through her wardrobe. "It's one of my lifelong dreams." She faked another laugh. "You know what a horrid social-climber I am."

"This Spark isn't social, she's a socio*path*. The type who bursts people into bloody giblets just so she can make a dramatic exit."

"But she won't do that to *me*," Gretchen said. "It wouldn't make sense."

"I don't think Dreamsinger cares whether her actions make sense. She's a few candles short of a black mass, if you catch my meaning. Either that, or she just *acts* like a crazy woman to intimidate us lesser mortals. I'll admit that's a possibility. All Sparks act unbalanced: sometimes benevolent, sometimes homicidal. Ruling by both love and fear—Machiavelli would approve."

Gretchen stuck her head out of the closet again. Still naked from the neck down, she had on a black suede cowboy hat and long diamond earrings. "You talk as if you know all about the Sparks," she said.

"No one knows all about the Sparks; but my governor grandma studied them as best she could. Asking other governors for information . . . gathering reports on where particular Spark Lords had been seen . . . what they did . . . whom they associated with . . ."

"It's a wonder the Sparks didn't kill your grandmother for snooping."

I shrugged. "They expect such behavior from governors; they even approve. The more a governor learns about Spark Royal's capabilities, the less that governor is likely to cause trouble."

"Because the Sparks are unpredictable and have outrageously powerful technology?"

"Exactly."

Gretchen disappeared back into the closet. "Rumor has it they're backed by extraterrestrials."

"Yes," I agreed, "rumor has it."

"High-up races in the League of Peoples."

"Supposedly."

"You don't believe it?"

"The League claims to oppose the murder of sentient creatures. It's supposed to be their most fundamental law—not to take life deliberately or through willful negligence. So why would they support a bunch of killers like the Sparks?"

"Mmm." Something went <SNAP> in the closet: an elastic waistband, a garter belt, some kind of fastener. Gretchen said, "Maybe the League needs the Sparks for special services."

"What special services?"

"I don't know—necessary work that's beneath the League's dignity. Emptying chamberpots . . . slitting throats . . . going to bed with crazy Uncle Hans so he won't bother anyone else."

I laughed. "The League of Peoples has a crazy Uncle Hans?"

"*Everyone* has a crazy Uncle Hans." Her voice was muffled, presumably by a garment being pulled over her head. "Seriously, darling, everyone has a kleptomaniac aunt, or a cousin who plays with his peepee in front of guests. Perhaps Spark Royal looks after the League's embarrassments. In exchange, the Sparks get fancy weapons and armor and gadgets to keep those embarrassments under control."

"So Earth is a prison planet and the Sparks are the guards?"

"Not guards, darling. Baby-sitters."

Gretchen came out of the closet, a traveling case in one hand and her clothes swirling. The greatest swirl came from her dress: a warmth of forest green that stretched with eye-fetching cling from throat to waist, then flared out below to eddy around her ankles. For tramping outdoors, the hem was almost too low: one wouldn't want it dragging through the mud. But Gretchen had also donned knee-high buckskin boots with platform soles, not ridiculously high but enough to keep her gown clear of the muck. Another swirl above her waist came from a woolen shawl the color of burgundy, pinned at the neck with a silver ankh. She'd abandoned silly hats in favor of a thick green band that held her red hair back and wrapped warmly around her ears . . . all in all, a more practical outfit for traipsing through slush than I would have expected.

"Well?" Gretchen asked, flashing her dimples.

"Ravishing as always. I didn't know you had outfits for leaving the house."

"Silly billy. I have outfits for *everything*."

"But you don't go out, do you?" I tried to meet her eyes, but she pretended to be busy, picking nonexistent lint off her sleeve. "Why now, Gretchen? What do you want with Dreamsinger?"

"I told you, darling, I'm such a flighty social-climber—"

"Don't lie," I interrupted. "If you have some harebrained idea you can get something out of a Spark Lord—if you think you can charm or outwit her—you don't know who you're dealing with. Dreamsinger is nowhere near sane. If you make her angry, Gretchen, she'll kill you. Maybe the rest of us too."

"Darling," Gretchen said, "I don't make people angry. I don't make *you* angry, do I? I'm just curious to meet someone truly important."

She swirled from the room without letting me answer. Without even pausing to freshen her makeup one last time.

Uneasily, I followed her out.

13

A NIGHT FOR REVELATIONS

Titania said nothing as she held the front door, but she did something odd with her whiskers: a diagonal weave, right-side-up/left-side-down, then vice versa, back and forth several times. I had no idea what it meant in her species . . . maybe surprise, maybe a smirk, maybe some lobsterish emotion with no human equivalent.

Gretchen ignored it completely—she linked her right elbow in my left, wrapped her free hand around my arm, then surged off into the darkness. (I, of course, was carrying her traveling case. It wasn't light.) The way she pressed her body against mine could easily be mistaken for passion. Few people would have recognized the effort of a housebound woman driving herself outdoors by sheer momentum, clutching me for moral support. I could feel her shiver, though she was thoroughly wrapped against the cold.

It would have been cruel to push her away, but I still considered it as we approached the gate. I hated the thought of my friends seeing Gretchen barnacled to my side. They'd met her once, when she threw a special soiree for them ("Phil, introduce me to all your widdle chums!"), and it had been every bit the nightmare you'd expect. Gretchen played La Grande Hostesse, determined to flaunt her wealth and pedigree; Pelinor and the Caryatid had embarrassed themselves by trying to act "sophisticated"; and Myoko and Impervia had radiated such pure contempt all evening, it was a wonder they hadn't blistered the paint off the walls.

As for Annah, I cringed to think of her seeing Gretchen cling to me. Gretchen groping my sleeve. Gretchen talking her baby talk, or gushing about some party she'd held for the Duke of This and the Viscount of That.

Unquestionably, Gretchen *would* gush. She'd gush and twitter and fondle my arm in front of everyone. And I'd have to bear it. Not only did we need Gretchen's boat, but I found myself in that state of endure-anything politeness that descends like a portcullis when you've separated yourself mentally from an old flame but haven't yet told her you're leaving. You'll suffer any cloying demand for affection, you'll be punctiliously attentive, because it's your penance for what you soon intend to do.

I wondered what Annah would think when she saw Gretchen all over me. I just hoped she wouldn't burst into tears of betrayal.

Annah laughed. Loudly. White teeth appearing in her dark face, lips opening, a surprisingly throaty chuckle. She covered her mouth quickly, but I could still hear giggles behind her hand. By the light of the Caryatid's flame, I could also see Annah exchanging looks with Myoko. For a moment, I had no idea what was going on; then I realized Myoko must have predicted Gretchen and I would appear in exactly this way, Gretchen pawing me possessively. It was always the same whenever Gretchen met my female friends—she'd immediately make a big show of fawning over me, as if to say, *This man is mine.*

"You took long enough," Impervia declared. She probably thought Gretchen and I had stopped for a brief romp between the sheets; to Impervia, the world was a hotbed of fornication, always just beyond her sight. "We've already taken the horses to Ms. Kinnderboom's stables," she said. "And rubbed them down. And listened to Pelinor fight with the hostler about what kind of fodder they need."

"Please forgive us," Gretchen oozed. "The delay was my fault." She was using her charm-the-peasants voice—a tone

of creamy condescension that was never as false as it
seemed. Though she sounded phony, Gretchen *liked* people:
almost everyone she met. Her mistake was thinking she
could make them like her in return. "I had to get dressed,"
Gretchen said. "Your mission sounds so important, I'm coming too. To help any way I can."

Out of Gretchen's sight, Myoko rolled her eyes. Pelinor,
however, clapped Gretchen on the shoulder. "Good for
you—that's the spirit. I assume your vessel is large enough to
hold us all?"

"Of course. Shall we go?"

"Oh yes, do let's," said Myoko, making her voice as low
and satiny as Gretchen's. She slipped Gretchen's traveling
case out of my hand and tossed it to Oberon (who caught it in
one of his pincers). Then Myoko took my right arm in exactly the same grip as Gretchen held my left, and batted her
eyelashes outrageously.

Behind my back, Annah broke into another bout of giggles.

I crossed the grounds of Kinnderboom Cottage with women
clutched to my arms. Gretchen spent the time quizzing
everyone on their impressions of the Sorcery-Lord, but got
little information in response. The Caryatid answered every
question as if the Sparks might be listening: never speaking a
negative word, praising Dreamsinger's power and "force of
personality." Impervia, who usually loved detailing the character flaws of people, chose to be contrary this time and told
Gretchen nothing.

The only new data I gleaned from conversation was a description of Dreamsinger's armor: a body shell made from
glossy plastic, colored sorcerer's crimson, and shaped to
mimic the contours of a female body. The helmet had no
holes for eyes or mouth . . . just a plate of smoked glass that
offered no glimpse of the woman inside. The several times
Dreamsinger had kissed someone—Dee-James, the Caryatid—she hadn't removed the helmet, so no one had seen
her face. She could still be anything from a bandy-legged
twelve-year-old to a gray-haired grandam.

When we reached the bluffs, Myoko and Gretchen were forced to release their grip on my arms—the stairway down was only one person wide. I made sure Gretchen had a firm hold on the banister, then took the lead downward.

The canopy that usually covered the stairs had been removed for the winter. Therefore, we had a clear view of the lake stretching off to the horizon, glimmering with catches of starlight. On either side of the steps, tangles of thistle and burdock grew despite the looseness of the soil. The weeds had gone brittle in the winter's cold, but plenty of life remained in their roots: they always sprang back when the weather warmed, and I expected Oberon would soon be down here using his pincers to prune any vegetation that encroached on the stairs.

Thinking of Oberon, I glanced back over my shoulder and saw him making his ponderous way down the stairs. The big lobster refused to leave his queen unprotected among strangers . . . though at the moment, the greatest threat to Gretchen was that Oberon would miss his footing and become a bull-sized avalanche plummeting down upon us.

But Oberon was sure-footed despite his ungainly size: eight legs bestowed remarkable stability. We descended the steps without incident and found ourselves on Gretchen's private pier, facing the good ship *Dainty Dinghy*.

It was not, of course, a dinghy . . . nor was it close to dainty. Gretchen's boat was a full-fledged frigate, a former ship-of-war in the Rustland navy and decommissioned in its prime under dubious circumstances.

Specifically: in Gretchen's youth, when she was wild and adventurous and unafraid of open sunlight, Gretchen had wanted a ship. She voiced this desire to a Rustland admiral over whom she exercised undue influence. The admiral somehow arranged for the frigate to be declared "obsolete and supernumerary," whereupon Gretchen purchased it at a rigged auction for vastly less than its true worth. Later, the admiral had been court-martialed, and it was now ill-advised for either Gretchen or the *Dinghy* to venture into Rustland

waters; but lucky for us, the lake's north shore from Dover to
the Niagara river was Feliss territory. We were entirely safe
from Rustland's old grudge.

Unless we were blown off course. Which I didn't want to
think about. Our streak of bad luck had to end sometime,
right?

"Ahoy, the ship!" Pelinor shouted. Good thing he'd taken the
initiative. If we'd left the job to Gretchen, she'd have stood
on the dock who-knows-how-long, genteelly clearing her
throat until somebody noticed us.

Two seconds later, a head poked into view above the
ship's railing. It was not a human head; since the light from
the Caryatid's shoulderflame didn't carry far, I couldn't see
the face distinctly, but I knew it lacked eyes, nose, and
mouth. This was Captain Zunctweed, an alien I'd met several times. He belonged to a race that demonmongers called
Patatas: Spanish for potatoes, so-called because his people
had pock-marks all over their bodies like the "eyes" of a po-
tato. Some of Zunctweed's pock-marks *were* eyes, randomly
arranged from head to toe. Other pocks were breathing ori-
fices, others were for eating, a few were for smelling or hearing . . . and the rest had yet to be understood by what we
laughingly called Science on post-Tech Earth.

All we knew about Patatas, one could learn from a brief
inspection of any member of the race:

(a) They were human-shaped with two arms, two legs,
and a head. However, they had practically no torso—
their legs came up almost to their armpits, giving them
a gangling gawky appearance but truly astonishing
speed when they chose to run.
(b) Despite their sprinting prowess, Patatas never ran
when they could walk, and never walked when they
could lie in a hammock, bawling out orders.
(c) It took bitter cold or heat before Patatas would
wear clothing. Quite simply, they liked showing off
their unclad bodies. And no two members of their race
had anything close to the same skin coloration—I'd

seen one covered with swirls of lurid red and orange, another who was eye-watering turquoise with zebra stripes of mauve, and a third whom I might describe as "reverse cheetah": dark brown with flaming yellow spots.

Captain Zunctweed was mostly white with smears of soft green on his elbows, knees, and other major joints. Oberon claimed that Zunctweed "enhanced" his true coloration by rubbing himself with grass . . . but given the time of year, he hadn't had access to green grass for several months, so at the moment he was *au naturel.*

Zunctweed folded his hands resignedly on the deck-rail in front of him and looked down on us like a dignified grandfather interrupted by noisy brats. This was quite a trick, considering that he had no facial features to give this impression. Still, the collection of flecks and divots on his cranium radiated aggrieved forbearance. "Yes?"

The alien's voice was a chorus of whispers—his multiple mouths talking simultaneously, saying the same words. I theorized that each breathing orifice on his body had its own small-scale lungs; no single mouth could draw enough air to achieve significant speech volume, but acting together, they could make themselves heard. I'd always had a modest desire to dissect Zunctweed and see if my theory was correct . . . but like my other vague notions for Scientific Research, nothing had ever come of it.

"Good evening, captain," Gretchen said. "We're here to go for a sail."

"A sail?" Zunctweed repeated the words as if he'd never heard them before. "A sail. A *sail.* No one informed us of any sail." He gravely turned to speak with someone behind him on deck. "Have we received any memoranda concerning a sail?"

He was answered by a high-pitched chitter. That had to come from a member of *Dinghy*'s crew—aliens called NikNiks, like rhesus monkeys but as smart as human five-year-olds. They understood English, but didn't speak it; their mouths couldn't shape the words. Instead, they talked in high-pitched squirrellike tirades. Zunctweed claimed to understand them perfectly . . . and since nobody else could comprehend a syllable, he'd become captain: the only slave in Gretchen's possession who could converse with both humans and the crew.

"Zunctweed," Gretchen said, "you haven't heard about this trip because I just decided on the spur of the moment. Wild and spontaneous . . . that's how I am."

She smiled prettily. With dimples. Gretchen could make her dimples appear at will.

"Ah," replied Zunctweed. "Wild and spontaneous. I see. Gaiety. Song-and-dance. Here we go round the mulberry bush. Eat, drink, and be merry, for tomorrow we die. All very well for *some* people—those who can afford to leap before they look. Still, at your age, one might expect such thoughtless frivolity would have begun to taper off."

Gretchen gasped in outrage. Oberon clacked his pincers. "Zunctweed! You're talking to our mistress."

"*Our* mistress?" Zunctweed repeated. "Our *mistress? You* may have the pleasure of such a relationship, Oberon, but Ms. Kinnderboom is not my mistress, she is merely my owner. A subtle distinction, but there it is. Whatever gratification you find in being a slave, I am only kept here by sorcery."

"Captain Zunctweed," Gretchen said sharply, "I'm aware you dislike your position in my household. But you work for me and you'll take my orders. I've decided to sail to Niagara Falls; that's all you need to know."

"That's it, is it? All I need to know. Well." Zunctweed spoke with half his mouths while the other mouths heaved ostentatious sighs. "Then I don't need to know how long it takes to make a boat shipshape after long periods of disuse? Years when you were too busy with parties and fine food and umty-tiddly to care about basic nautical maintenance? And that's not to mention the winter just past. It's a good thing I don't need to know how hard winter is on a ship. When the lake freezes and ice crushes against the hull—"

"Captain," Gretchen interrupted, "the boat was *not* locked in by ice. You took it into the middle of the lake where the water doesn't freeze, and you sailed around doing God knows what for most of the winter. Probably smuggling and piracy."

"Smuggling and piracy? I see. I'm a smuggler and a pirate. Yo-ho-ho and a bottle of contraband rum. Dancing the hornpipe on a dead man's chest." Zunctweed made a pathetic attempt at capering, waving his arms ponderously. "Tra-la-la, I'm a jolly buccaneer."

"The point *is*," Gretchen said, "you've been using the *Dinghy* for months. I'm sure it's perfectly ready to sail."

"And in all those months, could it be we used no provisions? Yes, that must be it: we weren't supposed to eat. And now you think our larders are brimming with venison and lark's tongue, not to mention mangoes and kiwis and amusingly shaped rutabagas . . ."

"Quiet!" Gretchen snapped. "We're going to Niagara Falls! A mere ten hours away. Neither you nor your crew will starve in that time, even if you *have* run out of food, which I strongly doubt. And if we *do* find ourselves maddened by hunger, I know whom we'll kill and eat first."

"Oh. So it's come down to threats. The owner/slave relationship laid bare. Well. There it is. Never mind that one of my hearts is shutting down. I'm supposed to soldier on obediently, even if I'm too blinded by pain to navigate and we all end up on the rocks. Being wild and spontaneous is so much more important than responsible maritime practice . . ."

Beside me, Impervia moved. I'd expected it sooner than this, but perhaps she'd needed time to figure how to board the ship. The *Dinghy* was a sizable vessel, not a modest yacht or pleasure craft. Its deck was two stories above us; its hull was a solid wood wall along the side of the pier, and there was no gangplank to welcome guests. There were no rope ladders either, nor chains, nor any other accoutrements someone might scurry up. Even the ropes securing the boat to the dock had big wooden funnels clamped around them, mouths facing toward us: obviously the funnels were attached to prevent anyone from clambering up to the deck. I wondered if these were normal precautions, or if Zunctweed had some special reason for sealing off the ship.

Impervia was going to find out. She crossed the dock and

whispered into Myoko's ear. Myoko nodded. Pelinor and the Caryatid stepped back to give more room—they knew what was coming. While Gretchen and Zunctweed continued their verbal fencing, Myoko's hair rose . . . and a moment later, Impervia rose too, lifted by telekinesis for the second time that night.

Zunctweed didn't notice until she was level with the deck. The captain only had time to say, "Bother!" Then Impervia was over the railing and landing with a thunk.

"Good evening, sinner."

Zunctweed ran. It was futile, considering he was stuck on a ship with nowhere to go . . . but he gave it his best, fleeing from Impervia with the inhuman speed of his overlength legs. Impervia chased him anyway, both of them disappearing from view, their footsteps echoing across the timbers. I could track the sound as they raced below decks, then a door slammed: probably Zunctweed locking himself inside the captain's cabin. Five seconds later came another slam, which I took to be Impervia kicking the door off its hinges. Squeals ensued, then bumps and thumps.

A fight. Impervia had got into a fight. How astonishing.

"Perhaps," said Pelinor, drawing his cutlass, "I'd better go up there too. Myoko, if you'd please . . ."

With a running start, he leapt energetically toward the deck. It was the old knight's way of being helpful—the few times he'd needed a telekinetic pick-me-up during street fights, Pelinor always made an effort to jump so Myoko didn't have to lift him as far. She'd given up trying to explain he was just making things more difficult: forcing her to snatch a moving target. On occasion, she just hadn't caught him, whether because she wasn't ready or because she wanted to teach him a lesson; once or twice, he'd landed amidst a flurry of fists, taking punches till Myoko deigned to spirit him away. This time, however, Pelinor stood to suffer more than bruises: he'd hurled himself toward the boat at top speed. If Myoko didn't nab him, he'd whack against the *Dinghy*'s side, then fall into the narrow gap between ship and pier—down into cold winter water, dredged deep enough to float a frigate. Prime potential for drowning. Not to mention the rocking of the waves might crush him between the boat and the dock's pilings.

I had a split-second to glance at Myoko. Her hair had returned to normal since lifting Impervia—no static-electric spread, just a little residual puffiness. She growled in exasperation, "Pelinor!" Then the knight soared upward, over the *Dinghy*'s side-rail, and onto the deck's solid planks.

Myoko's hair didn't move at all.

Pelinor disappeared in the direction Zunctweed and Impervia had gone. I ignored him. Instead I stared at Myoko. "You just lifted Pelinor, but your hair didn't—"

"Shush! Just shush." She glanced furtively at the others. The Caryatid, Gretchen, and Oberon were busy trying to see up to the deck; Annah stood apart from them, hidden in her cloak, almost invisible in the dark. I didn't know if fading into the background was just a reflex for her or if Annah was deliberately making herself inconspicuous.

Myoko looked at them all for a few moments, then turned back to me with a scowl. The scowl lasted a long ten seconds . . . then faded into a sigh. In the cold night air, the sigh billowed clouds of steam.

"What's on your mind, Phil?" Myoko asked.

"Your hair," I murmured. "You use your TK to lift it, don't you? You lift your hair whenever you lift anything else. To make a big show, so people will think you're *safe*; they don't have to worry about you pulling some sneaky TK trick because the hair always gives you away. But you do the hair deliberately. And you flipped Pelinor onto the deck without even wrinkling your brow. All that hard concentration you usually do is just another show."

Myoko said nothing. Her eyes were lost in darkness.

"You're hiding," I said. "Pretending to be a low-talent nothing, useless for anything but teaching in a mediocre school like Feliss. When really—"

She put her hand to my lips. "Yes. When really."

When really it was a clever ruse to protect herself from people who enslaved psychics. After all, if Myoko's powers were what she pretended, how could she be used to someone's devious benefit? She supposedly couldn't do her tricks quickly; she couldn't work without people noticing the levitating hair; and she demonstrated only modest lifting strength, about the same as a muscular man. So why would anyone kidnap her? There was nothing she could do psionically that couldn't be done more simply by a common laborer.

"So," I whispered, "bad guys leave you alone and you can have a real life."

"No. If I had a real life, I wouldn't lie in bed every night making a mental list: the few people I couldn't bring myself to kill if they ever learned the truth."

Silence. A chill went through me. Myoko turned away. "Relax, Phil—you're on the list."

She walked stiffly back toward the others . . . as if I'd somehow injured her deeply and she was pretending the wound didn't hurt.

Annah's hand slid softly into mine. "She's in love with you," Annah murmured. "Myoko. The way she looks at you when you aren't watching—in the faculty lounge, or when she 'accidentally' passes your classroom while you're teaching—Myoko's loved you for years." Annah shrugged. "I used to ask myself why she didn't tell you. Why she went out of her way to convince you she was 'just one of the guys.' What fear was holding her back?" Annah squeezed my hand. "It's certainly a night for revelations."

I couldn't answer. I'd gone speechless.

Sometime in the past few minutes, the *Dinghy* had fallen silent: no more fighting, no noise of any kind. Now, a thump, thump, thump came from the ship, accompanied by footsteps and grunting. The sound was moving upward: someone carrying something heavy up a flight of steps. By the time the thumping moved onto the deck, the Caryatid had sent her flame to the height of the railing. "Hello," she called, "who's there?"

Pelinor's head appeared over the rail. "Not to worry.

We're all in one piece." He paused. "Some of us more than others."

"What does that mean?"

"Give me a minute."

Pelinor disappeared. Part of the railing opened like a gate and a gangplank slid down to the dock. Oberon scrambled up at once, his mass making the plank bend and creak . . . but the plank's reinforced wood was designed to hold rum barrels and other heavy cargo being rolled aboard, so Oberon made it to the deck without mishap. Myoko and the Caryatid hurried close behind; Gretchen followed at a more sedate pace, but she was clearly eager to see what was happening.

I was not quick to join the procession: my brain had slipped a gear, detached from the world. (Annah thought Myoko loved me. My good-time pal Myoko. Who had hidden her feelings because . . . because she was protecting her secret, and wouldn't allow herself to get close to me. How do these things happen? I could have sworn I was just Myoko's drinking buddy . . . and Gretchen's sexual fallback, Annah's excuse for melodrama. A stick man to them all: a *convenience*. Now, all three women had somehow changed into *involvements*. How do these things happen?)

Annah nudged me toward the gangplank. My feet responded but my head didn't; she had to prod, drag, and coddle me before my wits rallied and I moved of my own volition. She gave me a wry look . . . then she released my hand and went up the gangplank unburdened.

On deck, the others stood in a circle around a white lump the size of a backpack. Myoko poked the thing lightly with her toe as Pelinor said, "So when I came through the door, Zunctweed caught one glimpse of my cutlass and he collapsed. Literally. Dropped to the floor and folded into this tight little bundle." Pelinor pointed at the lump. "You wouldn't think you could tuck a whole person into something that small."

"Oh, demons," Gretchen said with a dismissive gesture. "They all have a few silly tricks."

Oberon tapped the whitish bundle with his forefoot. "This is obviously a defense posture. The top's quite bony." He pressed down harder. "And strong. The whole skeleton must be hinged to form a protective dome over the vital organs." Oberon glanced at me. "Knowing you, baron, you must be consumed with scientific curiosity to dissect the body and see how the anatomy is constructed."

A groan came from the bony white bundle.

"No one's dissecting anyone," the Caryatid said in a Children-must-not-misbehave voice. "I don't know why you brought Zunctweed up here at all," she told Pelinor.

"Because Impervia didn't want him staying with her."

"Where *is* Impervia?" Myoko asked. "What's she doing?"

"Standing guard," Pelinor said.

"Over what?"

"Over what Zunctweed didn't want us to see." He waved toward a companionway that led below. "Take a look for yourselves. I'll watch the captain."

Gretchen didn't have to be told twice—she headed immediately toward the stairs. Oberon, the ever-faithful body-guard, raced to go down ahead of her . . . only to find he couldn't fit through the companionway's narrow opening. He stood there squinching his whiskers in agitation until Gretchen rapped on his shell: "Move, slave. You're in my way."

"Mistress Gretchen, you don't know what's down there. You don't know whether it's safe."

"Oh, it's safe," called Pelinor. "I think. Yes. I'd definitely say it's almost certainly safe."

This didn't reassure the big red lobster . . . but Gretchen wouldn't tolerate slaves telling her no. She banged again on Oberon's shell. "Move. Now. That's an order."

"Don't worry, dear," the Caryatid told Oberon. "We'll look after her."

Still reluctant, Oberon shuffled away from the opening. Gretchen went down without hesitation, though she did it in the landlubber way: facing the steps and holding the iron banisters, like climbing down a ladder. The rest of us followed close after. (Just for the record, the Caryatid descended à-la-landlubber too; Myoko slid down like an old salt, back to the steps, face out, feet barely touching the treads; I attempted to do the same, though without much grace; and Annah almost seemed to teleport—one second she was at the top of the companionway, then her cloak billowed and she was standing beside me. Making me feel ridiculous for having poised myself at the bottom, arms out and ready to catch her if she needed help getting down. I really had to stop underestimating that woman.)

The corridor below-decks was short, but had four doors leading off: one forward, one back, one each side. Chittering came softly from behind the closed side doors. The NikNiks must have gone into hiding when Impervia chased Zunctweed—the little monkey-things had fled into the crew quarters till the furor died down. NikNiks didn't like other people squabbling; it distressed them mightily, not from fear but embarrassment. They ran at the first hint of confrontation and would stay out of sight for days if necessary.

The forward door was open and lamps burned within. Though the room was appallingly small, it was clearly the captain's quarters—it had a real bed (narrow but mattressed) and a small table whose legs were secured to the floorboards. Gretchen, the Caryatid, and Myoko stood before the table, blocking my view of whatever lay on top . . . but it had to be something of interest, because one of the women had just gasped in surprise.

Annah and I squeezed into the room. Impervia was off in the corner, dour as usual and surreptitiously pressing her hand against the side of her chest. She always held herself that way when she'd cracked a rib but wanted to pretend it didn't hurt. Obviously, Zunctweed wasn't a total pushover when it came to fighting. I sidled toward the good sister, ready to tape her up—I carried first-aid supplies for just such contingencies—but Gretchen thought I was trying to get close to the table, so she made room for me.

That's when I saw what Zunctweed had been hiding: a

helmet of bright orange plastic. Featureless, except for a smoked glass plate in front of the eyes. It might as well have had PROPERTY OF SPARK ROYAL printed all over it.

Gretchen let out her breath. "That's Spark armor, isn't it?"

The Caryatid nodded. "It's the same style as Dream-singer's."

Annah glanced at me, as if I could confirm what Dream-singer's outfit looked like. I only shrugged. Still, the helmet on the table was undoubtedly of recent manufacture—it had none of the scratches or weathering you see on plastic from OldTech trash heaps—and these days, the Sparks were the only people who could mold plastic so flawlessly. This helmet had to come from them.

"Orange," Gretchen said, still gazing at the helmet. "Orange is for Mind-Lords."

Everyone in the room turned toward Myoko. Mind-Lords were masters of psionic power . . . and they spent their spare time getting to know other psychics. Especially psychics of first-class strength. Just as the Science-Lord had visited the best students at my university (completely ignoring *me*), a Mind-Lord must have visited Myoko's school occasionally to chat with those who stood out.

Like Myoko?

She said nothing—just stared at the helmet. After a while, the Caryatid touched her on the arm. "Are you okay?"

"They called him Priest," Myoko whispered. "He never gave any other name. Mind-Lord Priest. The saddest man I ever met."

She lifted her head, accidentally caught my gaze, and immediately lowered her eyes again. "He was constantly talking about religion. All religions. New ones, old ones, bizarre ones. He wanted to believe in something, but he was too, oh, *inhibited* to make a leap of faith. The sort of man who reads books full of prayers but never says a single one; who could describe fifteen different meditation techniques, but had never sat down and closed his eyes. I think he was afraid of being disappointed. The saddest man I ever met."

Myoko reached out as if intending to touch the helmet. A

few centimeters short, she let her hand drop limply to the table. "He came to our school several times a year. Spent a day with each class: exactly from dawn to dawn. I don't know when he slept. Maybe he didn't need to. He'd just talk, let us ask questions. But he didn't give direct answers; more like sermons on whatever came to mind. We loved him deeply. I suppose we couldn't help that because of his power, but still . . ."

"What was his power?" Gretchen asked.

"You felt what he felt. Whatever made him angry made you furious; whatever made him happy filled you with joy. It seemed like you'd touched his soul and fully comprehended the wisdom of his opinions. Whatever he thought was right—whatever he considered *necessary*—you believed the same, as if everything in your life had led you to that conclusion." She shook her head. "As if you understood exactly who Priest was, and saw that he was *holy*."

Myoko suddenly clenched her fist. "I've told myself it was all just fake. He was a Spark, right? You can never take Sparks at face value. Wouldn't a Spark Lord enjoy people thinking he was sweet and sad and poignant? He could wrap us around his fingers. But Priest never tried to exploit us . . . though, God knows, we were ripe for it. Young, idealistic, infatuated. Every last one of us would have walked through fire just to ease his terrible sorrow . . ."

Her voice trailed off. The rest of us didn't speak. Finally, Impervia broke the silence: her words brisk, trying to dispel the deep melancholy that had gripped us. "I don't know why we're jumping to conclusions. Yes, this looks like a Spark helmet; yes, orange stands for Mind-Lords. But there can be more than one Mind-Lord at a time; why think this belonged to your Priest?"

"It's his," Myoko said. "I can feel it."

"No, you can't. You're not the sort of psychic who feels things."

"With this I can." Myoko reached out again and this time touched the helmet with her fingertips. "That was Priest's power: making people *feel*. I can feel his essence, and I know something happened to him. Something deadly."

"You're being ridiculous—" Impervia began, but Myoko cut her off.

"It's his *helmet*! It couldn't just fall off. I've seen Priest's armor, and everything locked securely . . ."

Myoko picked up the helmet as if she was going to show us whatever mechanisms kept it attached to the rest of the suit. But the moment she lifted it off the table, something fell from the helmet's neckhole, plopping softly onto the table-top.

Gooey white nuggets like curds of cottage cheese. Spilling from the Spark Lord's helmet.

14

SHIPS THAT PASS IN THE NIGHT

"Eww," Gretchen said. "What's that?"

Nobody answered. Myoko set down the helmet, carefully covering the curds that had fallen onto the table. She stepped back quickly, bumping into the wall behind her.

The rest of us did the same—even Gretchen, who hadn't heard the details of Rosalind's death. There was something about those moist white nuggets that made you shy away.

"I think," Myoko said, "we should ask Zunctweed where he got the helmet."

Nods all around. We tried not to leave the cabin in an undignified stampede.

Up on deck, Oberon and Pelinor stood on either side of Zunctweed. The captain was still folded into a peeled-potato lump, headless, legless, armless. Impervia crouched beside the alien's origamied body and rapped on his bony hide. "Open up! Now!"

A muffled voice answered, "Shan't."

"*Shall*," Impervia told him. "Otherwise, we'll tie a rope around you and toss you into the lake. Tucked in like this, you'll sink like a stone . . . and the lake water here was ice a week ago. We'll leave you until you start drowning, then we'll drag you out. We'll keep doing that again and again, leaving

you under a bit longer each time till you're ready to cooper-
ate."

Annah gazed admiringly at Impervia. "You have such a
gift for teaching."

Impervia almost broke into a smile . . . but her face went
blank again quickly. Impervia hated to seem too human.

We never got to see how Zunctweed responded to ice-water.
Impervia trussed him up with a rope Pelinor found—I hoped
the rope hadn't been attached to something important—and
Myoko lifted the alien over the side by sheer force of will.
We could have done the lifting by hand, but we thought
Zunctweed would loosen up more if we went beyond the
mundane: so Myoko put on an impressive show, furrowing
her brow with fierce concentration, spreading her hair into a
great intimidating sphere (hip-long tresses stretching to
arm's length in all directions), then shakily levitating
Zunctweed off the deck, banging him against the rail as he
went over the edge, bumping him repeatedly against the hull
on the way down . . . at which point he moaned, "I know it
won't help if I beg for mercy; but consider how bad you
might feel about this if someday you acquire a conscience."

Myoko stopped his descent. Impervia called down to the
hovering alien, "I have a conscience; what I don't have is information. Where did you get the orange helmet."

"Is that all you want to know? And you couldn't ask before this? No, I don't suppose you could. It's more fun tormenting a slave than asking direct questions. What if I
answered them willingly? Then you'd have no excuse for entertainment."

Oberon, standing by the rail, gestured impatiently with his
pincers. "Shut up and start talking."

"You self-righteous claw-thing," Zunctweed muttered.
"Go back to licking your mistress's boots."

"Stop whining," Gretchen said. "Are you going to tell us
what we want?"

"Didn't I say I would?"

"No."

"Lift me up and I shall disclose the whole story."

"We'll get better answers," Impervia said, "if you stay where you are. Provided"—she turned to Myoko—"you can hold him?"

"For a little while," Myoko answered in a strained voice. "I'll manage if he speaks quickly." She winked at us all; we'd seen Myoko hold a human in the air for more than five minutes. But she let Zunctweed wobble a bit, just to center his thoughts on cooperation.

"I said I'd tell!" he protested.

And he did.

Dainty Dinghy had spent the winter offshore: far out in the lake where the water didn't freeze. Zunctweed wasn't the only captain to anchor in that neighborhood—he was part of a small contingent, nine boats this year, that spent the cold months afloat rather than going into dry dock or risking the ice in the harbor. With the first snowfall, *Dinghy* and the other ships offloaded all but a skeleton crew, filled their larders with provisions to last till spring, and sailed out to meet each other at a spot reputed to be the best winter fishing ground on the lake. The boats were lashed together in a cozy floating village, then the crews passed the season amicably: fishing with hook and line, playing endless games of Deuces High, and getting sozzled on whatever rotgut they'd stowed in their holds.

Thus the flotilla passed winter's short days and long nights: taking a holiday from smuggling rum and netting small-mouth bass. Gossip was shared over the card table, including critiques of the Ring of Knives—everyone loved to expound on Warwick Xavier's stupidity—but it was understood such opinions would never be repeated back home. The winter anchorage was a time apart . . . a season outside the real world, when you could tell your greatest secrets and know they would never come back to haunt you.

There was one secret that never came out amidst all the drunken confessions. Most of the company believed Zunctweed and a bevy of NikNiks were the only aliens among them; but Zunctweed knew differently. To Zunctweed's inhuman eyes, a captain named Josh Jode was clearly not native to

Earth. Humans saw Jode as the perfect skipper: a grizzled vet-eran, sunburned so thoroughly from years on the lake that his skin was parched clay and his hair bleached to dirty white. But Zunctweed's alien retinas perceived far outside the spec-trum visible to humans; he saw down into infrared and up to ultraviolet, at which frequencies Josh Jode bore no resem-blance to *Homo sapiens*.

Zunctweed had no words for the IR and UV colors that gleamed from Jode's flesh. He could only say Jode's skin must have evolved on a very different world than Earth: a world where a different atmosphere filtered different wave-lengths from the light of a different sun. Zunctweed instantly recognized a fellow extraterrestrial . . . but he never revealed what he knew, to Jode or to anyone else.

Zunctweed was an infuriating curmudgeon, but he wasn't stupid.

So Jode never realized Zunctweed knew his secret—which is why Zunctweed was still among the living and why the winter anchorage passed uneventfully until five nights earlier.

In the darkest hour before dawn—when the candles had gut-tered to blackness and the only lamp still burning was close to running dry . . . when even those who'd lost at cards were too tired to say, "One more hand, just one more" . . . when the men and women of the winter anchorage had returned to their own ships, and were standing on deck for one last sniff of the wind, telling themselves the thaw had finally come—the only warning was a flurry of turbulence at the center of the flotilla, a roiling and bubbling as if some trapped gas pocket on the lake-bottom had suddenly broken open. It lasted just long enough for heads to turn in its direction; then a figure in orange plastic burst from the surface, riding a plume of rocket smoke pouring from the soles of its boots.

The armored figure shot upward, high over the gathered boats. In night's last blackness, the armor glowed: sur-rounded by a dim violet radiance, like the aura of a saint in a Renaissance fresco. That aura allowed watchers to follow the figure as it flew above each ship in turn—not that there *were* many watchers, for those with a sense of self-preservation fled below-decks as fast as they could. On the *Dinghy* every NikNik vanished, leaving Zunctweed alone on the forecastle; on other vessels, only those too drunk to be afraid remained gawking at the sky.

Josh Jode was one of those who fled out of sight—not that it helped him. The armored figure flew over Jode's ship just as it had with the others . . . then it dropped down to land, thumping onto Jode's deck and dashing below to where Jode was hiding.

Zunctweed couldn't say what happened in the following minute. Sounds from Jode's ship were muffled: voices speaking an unknown language . . . some scuffling, but not a major fight . . . a silence, then thuds, then more silence. All around the anchorage, those watching from their decks exchanged glances—asking each other what was going on. No one spoke; no one made any move to get involved. One drunken fisherman drew a flintlock pistol, then couldn't decide where to point it. The man kept swiveling his head, staring first at Jode's vessel, then abruptly looking back over his shoulder as if something might be sneaking up from behind. Drunk as he was, he might soon have shot himself by accident; but before that could happen, the Mind-Lord burst through the deck of Jode's ship.

Deck planks are solid: thick lumber, nailed down securely and braced with cross-beams. Yet the Spark broke through like a cannonball, smashing up from the captain's cabin into the open, scattering hunks of wood and splinters into the rigging.

He came out headfirst, and the impact should have killed him; armor or not, the jolt of having your cranium slammed through a wooden floor should snap your neck. But the armor was surrounded by that violet glow of unnatural fire. It had flared to blinding intensity as the Mind-Lord crashed into view—so fierce, Zunctweed thought it might have incinerated the wood in its path a millisecond before the Spark Lord hurtled upward. Like a battering ram of flame, it hit so hard and hot that it vaporized a section of decking before the armor actually made contact with the timbers.

Whatever saved him, the Mind-Lord was still alive as he soared into black sky. He writhed like a snake with a nail through its belly, rocketing haphazardly as if his suit was out of control. Now and then, the boot-jets misfired, cutting out for a second of sputtering . . . and in those moments of silence, one could hear muted gagging inside the armor. The sounds of a man choking to death. Then the suit's engines would gust back to life, spewing steam into the cold night air and drowning out the strangled noises within.

High overhead the Spark Lord flew, tracing a zigzag path. When his jets fizzled out, he would plunge toward the water; when they caught fire again, he would aim himself upward, as if height might offer salvation. No telling why he didn't head for shore . . . but he remained above the anchorage, glowing in the darkness, a bright purple star—

, —until he exploded.

A sunburst of light and hot flame. Perhaps deliberate destruction; perhaps some disastrous malfunction, a tiny electrical discharge igniting the tanks that fueled the suit's rockets. Whatever the cause, it was ferocious: a ripping blast that boomed through the night, scattering orange armor in all directions. The man inside plummeted, hair on fire. A human match-stick, falling through blackness . . . until he smacked the surface of the water with an ear-cracking slap. The flames on his head were doused out. One nearby fisherman caught a glimpse of charred flesh and a face with its eyelids burned off; then the blackened remains sank into the lake's embrace.

Bits of armor rained down on the ships. Zunctweed claimed he was almost brained by a falling glove—an orange plastic gauntlet that struck the *Dinghy* hard enough to chip the deck. The plank beneath the glove caught fire, smoke curling up between the fingers until Zunctweed grabbed a water bucket and dumped it over the blaze. (A hiss of steam. The smell of wet ash.)

Zunctweed nudged the gauntlet with his foot. The motion dislodged a nodule of gooey white from the wrist of the glove—something that must have been clinging to the Spark

Lord's hand when the armor exploded. Gingerly, Zunctweed
picked up the glove and shook it; more curds plopped onto
the deck. Zunctweed stared at them, then backed away. Later,
he would order the NikNiks to swab the little white nuggets
into the lake.

But for now, he kept his distance and turned back to look
at Jode's ship. Jode had come up on deck . . . if it really *was*
Jode. To Zunctweed's eyes, the creature returning from the
captain's quarters was the same color Jode had been in the IR
and UV parts of the spectrum. To everyone else, it must have
looked different—a beast wearing Jode's clothing but no
longer close to human.

It was oozing and puffy, its skin resembling white sponge
toffee covered in syrup. Milky fluid dripped on the deck and
sloshed as the creature walked. Jode's head was a lump of
wet bread dough, unmarked by hair or facial features. The
hands showed no fingers now—just bulging stumps, as if all
traces of human physiology had been kneaded into undiffer-
entiated protoplasm. Slowly the creature moved to the railing; then it spoke in a gargling version of Jode's voice.

"I should kill you all."

The words carried eerily over the water; the only other
noise came from waves lapping against boat hulls. "I should
kill you all, but that goddamned Spark may have sent a may-
day before he died. If reinforcements are coming, I can't
waste time silencing you."

The creature made a fierce chittering sound. Jode's crew,
a group of NikNiks purchased from Papa Kinnderboom
when Jode first arrived in Dover, scurried up from below and
began to weigh anchor. "Now pay attention," the monster
called to the people on other boats. "Keep your fucking
mouths shut, or I'll come back and kill you. Trust me on
this. If you talk, you'll die. I can look like anyone—your
mother, your wife, your very best friend—and you won't
know it's me till your throat is slit. So not a word! To anyone!"

The thing slapped its hand on the railing . . . a heavy wet
sound. "Sooner or later, more Sparks will show up—asking

what happened to their precious brother." Jode pointed to where the Mind-Lord's body had sunk. "Not a word, you hear me? Or you'll regret it."

Jode spat over the railing—a clot of maggoty white. Then the creature turned to his NikNiks and shouted more orders at them in their ratty tongue. Preparations for departure didn't take long; Jode must have kept the boat ready to leave at a moment's notice. Within minutes, the ship drew away from the anchorage, heading farther out into the lake . . . and in all that time, no one else uttered a word.

Next dawn, the anchorage dispersed. Few people spoke to their neighbors; those who did, mumbled they were leaving because the thaw had finally come.

Zunctweed traded away the gauntlet that had fallen onto his deck—the human glove didn't fit Zunctweed's alien hand. In exchange, he got the helmet. The woman who'd pulled the helmet out of her rigging was glad to get rid of it; she said it gave her the creeps because it always seemed to be watching her.

Jode's ship ran aground on nearby Long Point two days later. No one was aboard. The bodies of three drowned NikNiks washed up on a little-used beach the following night. The rest hadn't yet been found.

The Mind-Lord's body hadn't been found either. I doubted it would ever turn up. Fish must be ravenously hungry after a long cold winter.

When Zunctweed had finished his tale, the rest of us said nothing for a long while. Finally, Myoko broke the silence. "Now we know why Dreamsinger came to Dover. Looking for her brother."

Impervia sniffed disapprovingly. "If this Mind-Lord Priest disappeared five days ago, why did it take Spark Royal so long to investigate?"

"Busy elsewhere," I said. "Nobody knows how many Lords there are at any one time, but it's probably less than a dozen . . . and they have to police the entire planet. A crisis or two, and there's no one left for other things. Besides,

Sparks can take care of themselves; and they're given a lot of autonomy. The High Lord certainly doesn't organize a search party if one of the kids misses dinner."

Pelinor sucked his mustache. "So this Mind-Lord runs afoul of Jode . . . and eventually Dreamsinger comes to check her brother's last known location."

"But what *was* Jode?" Gretchen asked. "I've never heard of a demon who could look human."

"I have," I said.

I told them our chancellor's tale of stealing tobacco . . . and of the creature the Sparks called a Lucifer, waiting there in ambush. Annah helped with parts of the story, for which I was grateful; if Annah hadn't been there, Impervia might have thrown me over the side to keep Zunctweed company. As it was, she simply glowered like a thunderhead. When I finished, Impervia said, "You couldn't have mentioned this sooner?"

"Opal wanted it kept secret," I answered. "She made Annah and me promise we wouldn't tell anyone else unless it became absolutely necessary."

Impervia glared . . . but she couldn't very well say we should have broken our promise. Meanwhile, the Caryatid (ever a peacemaker) said, "What's past is past. The point is, now we know what's happening."

"Do we?" Pelinor asked. "Oh good. What's happening?"

Myoko growled in exasperation. "There's a shapeshifter thing called a Lucifer. It pretended to be a man named Josh Jode. It killed a Spark Lord, leaving behind little white nuggets. Rosalind died the same way . . . so she must have been killed by a Lucifer too."

I remembered Dreamsinger grabbing me in Nanticook House, calling me a fool for thinking the curds had been a bioweapon. All along, it had been the Lucifer. Probably the same Lucifer. But Dreamsinger said it had mutated. Somehow it changed itself so its metabolism no longer matched its former profile.

Did that explain what happened to Mind-Lord Priest? He must have had some kind of detection equipment that regis-

tered Josh Jode as alien . . . but thanks to the Lucifer's mutation, the equipment couldn't identify what kind of alien Jode
was. The Mind-Lord hadn't suspected he was dealing with a
Lucifer; therefore, he'd been taken by surprise.

But why did Priest come after Jode in the first place? Had
Jode done something to attract attention? Or had . . .

Wait. Opal told us she was stationed in Feliss because the
Sparks believed something bad would happen in the neighborhood. Given that kind of advance information, the Sparks
would take the precaution of sweeping the area now and then
for anything unusual. Priest had shown up a few days ago; he'd
set his detection gear to search for alien life-forms; and he'd
got a reading on a species his equipment didn't recognize.

The Mind-Lord had confronted Jode. But Priest hadn't
been careful enough.

"And now," Myoko said, finishing her summary for Pelinor's benefit, "the shapeshifting Mr. Jode is pretending to be
Rosalind Tzekich. Heading for Niagara Falls with Sebastian."

"Oh," said Pelinor. "And Sebastian doesn't know? I
thought he was a top-notch psychic."

"He is. But his powers don't usually activate unless he
tells them to. What are the odds he's explicitly going to check
if his girlfriend is an alien in disguise?"

"I've wanted to check that with some of my boyfriends,"
Gretchen said.

Everyone ignored her.

"Zunctweed," the Caryatid called. "How long has Jode been
in Dover?"

"Five years," came a voice from just above the waterline.
"A long, long time. When one compares five years to the
short period I've been suspended above this lake, I know I
shouldn't complain. Still, there you are. They say one's experience of time is relative to one's mental suffering . . . and I
discover it to be true. Isn't that interesting? Perhaps Dr.
Dhubhai would like to write a scientific paper."

Myoko, who'd been holding Zunctweed all this while
(and who'd been so distracted by my tale of Opal and the Lu-

cifer that she'd let her hair fall back to normal), made a dis-
gusted face and flipped the Patata captain back onto the deck.
Meanwhile, the Caryatid said, "If Jode was here five full
years, you have to wonder why."

"Sebastian," Impervia answered immediately. "Jode was
watching Sebastian."

"You think so?"

Impervia nodded. "You saw how Dreamsinger reacted
when she realized a Lucifer was taking the boy to Niagara
Falls. She squealed like a stuck pig. Obviously, Dreamsinger
had a suspicion Jode would use Sebastian for something horrible."

"Like what?" Pelinor asked.

"Damned near anything," Myoko told him. "From Opal's
story, these Lucifers hate Spark Royal. There must be something Sebastian can do in Niagara Falls that will drive the
Sparks wild."

"Like what?" Pelinor asked again.

"We don't know," Myoko said. "But Jode's been watching
Sebastian for five years. Perhaps waiting for the boy's powers to mature. Sebastian has always been gifted, but it's taken
him time to gain control."

"Also," Impervia said with disgust, "Jode may have been
waiting for Sebastian to discover the opposite sex. This Lucifer is clearly a vile creature; from the first, it must have intended to control Sebastian through seduction, so it had to
wait until the boy was old enough to be seduced. It could easily check on Sebastian from time to time—a shapeshifter
would have no problem disguising itself as someone else and
spying to its heart's content. When it got back from the winter anchorage, it learned Sebastian had finally fallen in love.
Jode eliminated Rosalind and took her place."

"But how did Jode know about Sebastian's powers?" I
asked. "Weren't they a secret?"

"I'd hoped so," Myoko said. "But I told you there were incidents when Sebastian was young . . . like that time the
horse tried to kick him. I was always afraid word might leak
out. Silly me, I was only worried about slavers; I didn't even
think of shapeshifting aliens."

"So let me get this straight," Gretchen said. "There's a horrible gooey alien who's already killed several people including a Spark Lord. This alien intends to trick some hideously strong adolescent psychic into doing something awful. There's a homicidal Sorcery-Lord who's on her way to stop them . . . and that lecherous old Warwick Xavier is tied into this too, plus the entire Ring of Knives. All these dangerous people are racing to Niagara Falls for some unknown cataclysmic smash-up, and you want my boat so you can be at ground zero when the shit hits the fan?"

Silence. I said, "Yes, Gretchen, that pretty well sums it up."

She smiled radiantly. "Then what are we waiting for? Let's go."

15

EAST WITH THE NIGHT

According to my pocket watch, we set sail at 4:35. NikNiks yammered in the rigging; Zunctweed grumbled at the wheel. The rest of us turned in to grab as much rest as we could.

I can't say I slept much. In a spirit of adventure, Gretchen issued us all with hammocks to be slung in the *Dinghy*'s bunkrooms: bunkrooms stinking of NikNik, a wet furry smell that was much like any other wet furry smell, but more pungent. NikNiks practice basic hygiene and sanitation, but they still produced a junglelike stench of suffocating proportion—fierce farts and pheromones, not to mention the aromas of mating and childbirth.

Gretchen took the captain's cabin and gave me a long lingering leer that suggested we should share the bed. I turned my eyes elsewhere, drawing on the full awesome power of my Y chromosome to feign obliviousness. (*What hints? I didn't see any hints. Why don't women just come out and say what they're thinking?*) Now was not the time to provoke a Gretchen/Annah furor . . . or even worse, Gretchen/Annah/Myoko. Let confessions wait until we'd faced whatever lurked in Niagara Falls.

So I headed for the bunkroom with everyone else—even Impervia, who'd been loath to leave Zunctweed unsupervised. She suspected our captain would head for the hills if someone didn't watch him . . . though Gretchen swore the

221

Kinnderboom family sorcerers always enchanted their slaves with spells to prevent escape or disobedience. If Zunctweed tried any tricks, his muscles would seize and he'd fall over in an epileptic fit. Most slaves made the attempt only once; after that, they resigned themselves to servitude.

But that didn't satisfy Impervia: she would have stayed on deck all night if Oberon hadn't insisted *he'd* be the one to watch Zunctweed. Our holy sister gave the big red lobster an appraising look, and apparently liked what she saw. After a moment, she patted Oberon's shell and headed below.

So we bedded down in the hammocks. I shan't describe the inadequacies of such sleeping contraptions—more eloquent writers than I have expounded at length on the sensation of being webbed in, the saggy discomfort of no back support, the disturbing sway as the ship rolls—nor shall I grouse about occupying such cramped quarters with so many other sleepers. Pelinor didn't snore, but one of the women did . . . and in the darkness, I couldn't tell which it was. I crossed my fingers it wasn't Annah.

Or perhaps Myoko.

Even without the snoring, I wouldn't have fallen asleep easily—too many thoughts churned in my head. Especially about Niagara Falls.

I'd seen the Falls once while chaperoning a field trip from the academy. Despite its reputation as a wonder of the world, I wouldn't have gone to Niagara on my own free time; I didn't expect to be impressed by water obeying the law of gravity. But when I got there, the Falls were truly impressive, with their roar, their mist, and their fury . . . not to mention the spectacular gorge they've cut over the eons, kilometers long, slowly eaten backward by the plummeting water. One look at that gorge and I *knew* the world was ancient. That in itself justified the trip.

I was also grudgingly impressed by the area immediately surrounding the Falls. Several city blocks were remarkably preserved from OldTech times. Twenty-story buildings (hotels and casinos) still scraped their fingernails against the sky, their decor hardly changed since the twenty-first century . . . including the electricity running the lights and elevators.

Yes, electricity. For five centuries, a portion of the Falls' plunging water had been diverted through sluices, hurtling down millraces and directed over turbines to generate hydro power. Niagara was a major energy center in the OldTech era, and tourist guides claimed the facilities had remained in operation ever since, tended by a monastic order called the Keepers of Holy Lightning. The Keepers were typical crack-pots, believing that OldTech days represented the peak of spiritual enlightenment. By contrast, the world of the present was a cesspool of Vanity and Sin, an affront to everything sa-cred, blah, blah, blah. Therefore, the Keepers disdained mod-ern ways (sorcery, psionics, associating with aliens) and applied themselves to Living In The Past. They kept Ni-agara's turbines turning, repaired any breakdowns in the power grid within three kilometers of their generating sta-tion, and even hand-crafted lightbulbs so their electricity would have some useful function to perform.

You can find similar orders in other parts of the world. In Sheba, a group of ultra-conservative Sufis still operated the facilities at Aswan . . . sponsored (said my grandmother) by the Sparks, who had no interest in Sufism or electricity but wanted technologically competent people to care for the whole facility. Spark Royal didn't want a dam break that sent a wall of water careening down the Nile valley. That was the sort of thing Sparks were sworn to prevent—disasters on the grand scale.

Such thoughts made me wonder if the Sparks also sup-ported the Holy Lightning in Niagara Falls. Possibly. Proba-bly. It doesn't take sophisticated equipment to produce electricity from falling water, but it's hard to make every-thing you need with just a small cadre of true believers. Even simple copper wire requires ore, a refining furnace, and wire-pulling equipment . . . all of which added up to a hefty wad of cash. Did the electricity business really produce that much income when the power was being used only to dazzle tourists?

The more I thought about it, the more I was certain the Niagara hydro station survived through Spark backing: money, materials, and more. (If some tooled-tungsten chunk of OldTech machinery broke down, where could the Keepers get a replacement *except* Spark Royal?) So why did the Sparks do it? Unlike Aswan, Niagara had no dam; if the generators broke and the power went out, it would put a damper on tourist business but wouldn't endanger lives.

Why would the Sparks care about the Falls?

Unless they were using the electricity for something themselves.

Unless there was some life-or-death need to keep the turbines running.

Unless there was some secret something, a deadly threat known only to the Sparks; and all hell would break loose if the machines ever fell silent.

In which case . . . in which case . . .

I couldn't finish the thought. I couldn't even imagine what the threat might be.

But Jode was taking Sebastian to Niagara. A Lucifer had gained influence over a powerful psychic who could do almost anything.

I could see why Dreamsinger flew into a tizzy when she realized what Jode planned. The possibilities tizzied me too.

Dawn came and went. In the bunkroom, the morning was scarcely noticeable—the *Dinghy* was a nice tight ship with few chinks the sunshine could penetrate. Still, light oozed in photon by photon. The night's pitch blackness yielded to something less Stygian, enough that my dark-adjusted eyes could make out the hammocks around me.

Waves rocked the boat like a cradle. I dozed off and on, drifting into dreams and back again. At some point, I must have slipped into a deeper sleep; when I finally awoke (with a clear head and no hangover, praise God), the bunkroom was empty. Heaven knows how the others got out of their hammocks without waking me—I had a hell of a time fighting my way free, nearly dropping facefirst to the floor. Good thing my friends weren't around to laugh. I pulled myself to-

gether, straightened my clothes as much as a wrinkling
night's sleep would allow, and headed up to the deck.

Bright sun, wispy clouds, brisk breeze. The first person I
saw was the Caryatid, her cheeks as red as her clothing. She
huddled with her back to the wind, baking a withered apple
in a flame that sprouted from her fingertips. (Trust the Caryatid to heat her apples rather than eating them raw—she leapt
at any excuse to light a fire and nuzzle it like a pet mouse.)
When she saw me, she smiled in her motherly way. "Good
afternoon, sleepy-head. You missed breakfast. And lunch."

"Zunctweed lied about the ship being out of provisions?"

"Of course." She reached into a small basket beside her
feet and tossed me a hunk of cheese. "Eat fast. We're almost
there."

As I munched, I looked over the railing. The *Dinghy* was
too far out for me to see the shore clearly . . . but beyond the
narrow sand beach, I could discern open areas (fields), low
trees (orchards), and thick forests (wood-lots and windbreaks). Local farmers must be out today, checking which
fences needed mending, or gazing at morasses of mud and
judging how soon the soil would be dry enough to plow. Perhaps the cattle had been let out to pasture, hoof-deep in muck
but glad in their bovine way to be munching on sere yellow
grass rather than stale fodder.

Even as I watched, the ship angled toward land. Up ahead,
a small harbor housed fishing boats—far fewer than the fleet
in Dover-on-Sea, but enough to show the presence of an active port. The Caryatid said, "That's Crystal Bay. We'll put in
there. Zunctweed says there's no point going as far as the Niagara River, because it isn't navigable for a ship our size."

"What about the canal?" The Welland Canal had been dug
in OldTech times to circumvent the Falls. Back then, the
canal's lift-locks were controlled electronically; but locks
can function perfectly well without fancy automation, and
they'd continued on pure gravity feed long after the electric
pumps had become useless. As far as I knew, the canal was
still a working part of the Great Lakes seaway.

"The canal isn't open," the Caryatid told me. "They close
it every winter once ice shuts down shipping."

"But the ice has melted."

"Doesn't matter. Zunctweed says the schedule was cast in stone years ago by government fiat. The canal won't reopen until it's supposed to."

"But if the ice is gone, we could just sail through."

The Caryatid shook her head. "Every lock is completely shut down. No way past. Zunctweed says Crystal Bay is the closest the *Dinghy* can get to the Falls."

"And we believe Zunctweed?"

"We believe Zunctweed when Impervia has a firm grip on his throat."

Impervia wasn't actively engaged in strangling the captain, but she stood within arm's reach as Zunctweed chittered orders to prepare for landfall. Pelinor was also close to the action, not to help Impervia, but because the old knight had developed a sudden enthusiasm for seamanship. In the same way that he badgered stablehands about horses, he hung at Zunctweed's side in pursuit of nautical lore. "What does 'belay' mean?" "How do you do something 'handsomely'?" "Which is 'abaft' and 'abeam'?"

Not far away, Oberon clung to the rail looking miserable. He wasn't actually seasick—Lake Erie's waves were minuscule compared to an ocean's, especially on such a pleasant day—but the big lobster clearly had acquired a loathing of surfaces that moved beneath him. Each time the boat dipped down a wave crest, Oberon fought not to slide in the same direction . . . and after hours of constant exertion, grappling the rail with his pincers, he must have been counting the seconds before we put into port.

The rest of our group was nowhere in sight. The Caryatid told me our missing companions were all in the captain's cabin. "Looking at maps. Arguing about the fastest way to the Falls." She rolled her eyes. "As far as I'm concerned, we should just talk to people in Crystal Bay. They'll know what's best. If we let Gretchen choose our route, we'll gallop ten kilometers up some road, discover a bridge has collapsed during the winter, and have to come all the way back again."

The Caryatid was right: no sense relying on maps when

we could get more up-to-date information with a few simple questions. And from what I could see of the town, Crystal Bay looked big enough to justify a stagecoach stop . . . maybe even a dispatching depot. Better to hop a stage than rent horses and strike off on our own.

Still, I felt a niggling urge to peek at a map, just to get the lay of the land—I'd feel better if I had a picture of where we were going. Accordingly, I headed to the captain's quarters with a blithe and jaunty step, nothing in my brain except cartographic curiosity . . . but that evaporated instantly when I bounced into the cabin and realized who was there.

Three heads turned my way when I entered. Three pretty faces. Gretchen, Annah, and Myoko: all my complications in one cramped little room.

Gretchen was mostly naked: wearing nothing but a crimson bra like the one I'd seen on the floor of her bedroom, and a pair of matching panties that were surprisingly demure by Gretchen's standards—no lace or frills or cut-outs. She looked up at me as I came through the door, but gave only a distracted smile. If I'd been some other man, she would have felt obliged to do something flirtatious (flash her cleavage, wiggle her hips, pretend she had to cover up to protect her "modesty"), but with me, she didn't bother. I considered that a compliment.

As soon as Gretchen had deigned to recognize my existence, she turned back to Myoko and said, "Well?"

Myoko took longer to collect herself—she looked flustered and even blushed slightly at my arrival. My rough-and-ready "Platonic" friend was betraying a hitherto unsuspected bashfulness . . . as if I were her husband and had caught her *in flagrante delicto* with a nearly nude woman. Not that anything salacious was going on; Myoko herself was fully clothed, and from what I could see, she was simply trying to unknot the lacings on the back of a red knit gown. No doubt the gown was Gretchen's, taken from that traveling case she'd packed the night before. Perhaps Myoko was merely embarrassed to be seen playing Gretchen's dressmaid. But it was a small cabin, and Myoko had no room to keep her distance from Gretchen's bare skin. As I watched, she surreptitiously tried to squeeze a little farther away, dropping her gaze to the knots she was trying to untie. "Don't rush me," she mumbled to Gretchen.

The blush burned more brightly in Myoko's cheeks.

Annah was behind the other two, higher than both because she was standing on the captain's bed. Like Gretchen she gave me only a distracted smile; then she went back to arranging Gretchen's hair. In the dim confined quarters, I couldn't see much of what Annah was doing, but I assumed she was making a braid. Annah had a reputation for braids: at the academy, girls sometimes tried to transfer to Annah's floor solely so she'd do their hair. Personally, I've never understood the female fascination with braids—braids always remind me of the ugly leather bumps on a crocodile's back—but I learned long ago to keep quiet on the subject.

Gretchen soon grew bored watching Myoko worry at the gown's knots, so she turned back to me. (Behind her, Annah made an exasperated sigh and tried to hold Gretchen's head still.) "So, Phil, *darling*," Gretchen said, "aren't you just *amazed*?"

I almost said, "By what?" The part of my brain devoted to self-preservation vetoed that initial response and frantically searched for some source of amazement I'd overlooked. Gretchen's body? Always delicious, but I couldn't see anything different from last night (except the absence of goose-pimples). The fact that Myoko and Gretchen weren't sniping at each other? Yes, that was amazing, but probably not what Gretchen meant. I looked around the room, knowing I was taking too long to answer, but unable to see anything but the three women . . . Gretchen in her underwear . . . the crimson gown . . .

Crimson? *Sorcerer's* crimson?

Gretchen's lingerie was the same color. And I'd seen a crimson bra in her bedroom the night before.

I blurted, "You're pretending to be a sorceress?"

Gretchen's eyes flashed. "No, silly billy—I *am* a sorceress. Do you think I *buy* all those shine-stones?"

* * *

My mouth hung open for an undignified length of time . . .
but meanwhile facts were sorting themselves out in my brain.

Gretchen had grown up with sorcerers: her father employed quite a few to cast obedience spells on demons. Most
children of wealthy families also received training in sorcerous fundamentals, partly to prepare them for managing spell-
caster underlings, and partly to see if they themselves had
any aptitude for enchantments. It wasn't necessarily good
news to find you had a knack for magic—considering the nature of most arcane rituals, sorcery wasn't a respectable profession—but just as the well-to-do are allowed to draw and
paint as long as they don't become *artists*, they're allowed to
cast spells as long as they don't get too *mystical*. All of which
argued it was possible that Gretchen had received substantial
arcane tutoring from mages on her father's staff.

Then I remembered how Gretchen had suddenly been so
interested when she heard I'd encountered a Sorcery-Lord.
She'd immediately announced she'd accompany us to Niagara, where Dreamsinger was going to be. And now
Gretchen was putting on crimson, the first time I'd seen her
wear the color. Why? So Dreamsinger would recognize her
as another dear sister on the Burdensome Path?

"Gretchen," I said, "seriously, *seriously*, Gretchen: this is
a bad idea."

"What do you mean? A sorceress can wear crimson whenever she wants."

"Yes, but—"

"You don't think I'm real, is that it? I'm just some deluded
brat? *Oh that Gretchen, she might know a few tricks, but
she's nothing special.* Is that what you think?"

"What I think is that Dreamsinger is an unpredictable lunatic. Anyone who wants to meet her is suicidal."

"Well, maybe I *am* suicidal." Gretchen stormed forward
the three steps it took to cross the room. The partly woven
braid was yanked out of Annah's hands and flopped forward
along the side of Gretchen's head. Gretchen ignored it; she
gave me a fierce push, her hands hitting my shoulders, her
eyes glaring into mine. "Have you looked at me lately, Phil?"

I was looking at her now. The braid hanging down by her

ear had begun to unravel. "You aren't suicidal, Gretchen. It's not in your nature."

"Maybe not. But desperation is." She dropped her gaze; she glanced quickly back at Myoko and Annah as if trying to decide whether to talk in front of them. Then she took a deep breath and returned to me. "I'm good, Phil. I'm good at sorcery. I think." She gave a twittering laugh. "But I don't know for real, do I, darling? I've just . . . I've done nothing with it. Instead, I lived off my father's money. Slept with a lot of pretty men. Kept my sorcery to myself because I didn't want someone saying, *Gretchen, the spells you're so proud of are really quite trivial . . .* "

Her hands were still on my shoulders. She let her head slump against my chest. "Whenever I wanted to convince myself I was good, I'd whip up another shine-stone. The spell's actually quite complicated . . . at least I think it is. Then again, what the hell do I know?"

I thought about all the shine-stones in her room the previous night. Dozens of them. Made to reassure herself she was *somebody.*

"And Dreamsinger?" I asked. "What do you want with her?"

Gretchen sighed. She kissed the front of my shirt, then straightened up and gave her head a little shake. The last of her braid unwound. "I can't put it into words, Phil. It's just . . . she's a Sorcery-Lord. If there's anyone who could look at me and say, *You've got potential . . .* "

She gave another twittering laugh—a choked sad sound. "Here's where you tell me it's ridiculous to talk about my *potential* when I've never made an effort to use it. If I had an ounce of *real* potential, I'd get off my dumdum and *do* something. Go to school . . . buy an apprenticeship . . . or just start incanting on my own. *Something.* Instead, I'm squandering my existence. On parties and fine food and umty-tiddly, as Zunctweed says. Doing nothing, day by day."

She suddenly turned to Myoko and Annah. "Do you know what it's like to have dropped out of life? To have had a hundred chances to be special, but you avoided them all? Or just botched them up because you were a horrible coward, afraid of letting yourself change. You clutch your comfortable excuses, saying, *Someday I'll be brave, it won't take a lot, just give me one more chance and this time I'll grab it.* But chances come and go. It would be easy to do something, but you don't. You just don't. Do you know what that's like?"

Myoko and Annah nodded. Their faces were both so sad.

Gretchen nodded too. "So here we are. Here I am. A woman of . . . a woman who's no longer young . . . who got her feelings hurt by some stupid young earl and found herself looking in the mirror under bright, bright light . . ." She turned back and gave me a small rueful smile. "I suddenly thought, maybe it's time. This time it's *time*. To see if I'm somebody or just a middle-aged slut who lies to herself about being gifted. Next thing I know, my one true friend comes along . . ." She held out her hand to me; I took it, feeling awkward and guilty but fond. ". . . and he tells me there's a way to meet a Sorcery-Lord."

She gave my hand a squeeze before letting it go. "So it's really my chance. To talk to this Dreamsinger and find out once and for all. To find my place. That's all I want: to find my place. You three have done that already. Right? You must be happy being teachers. I know Phil is. A font of inspiration, guiding young minds and spurring them on to heights of intellectual achievement. That's what you say, darling, and it's wonderful. You've found your place. All of you."

If she'd looked my way at that instant, I couldn't have met her eye. Myoko and Annah couldn't either. But Gretchen didn't seem to notice. She moved back and plucked the crimson gown from Myoko's hands. "I can dress myself," Gretchen said. There might have been tears in her eyes. "We'll be coming into port soon. Why don't you all go watch the landing?"

Annah looked at me, then asked Gretchen, "Are you sure you don't want anyone to stay?"

"No, no, all of you, go ahead." Gretchen tried to smile. "I can't have you learning the deep dark secrets of how I put on my makeup."

Annah gave Gretchen's shoulder a pat before stepping down from the bed and moving toward the door. Myoko reached out to do the same, stopped herself for a split-second (probably a spasm of shyness, touching a near-naked woman), then continued on to press her fingers lightly against Gretchen's cheek. "We'll see you when you're ready," Myoko said.

Annah, Myoko, and I left quietly, almost on tiptoe. We closed the door behind us and said nothing as we climbed up on deck.

Dainty Dinghy didn't try to put in at the docks: we dropped anchor well out from shore. When Pelinor asked why, Zunctweed said he didn't know the depth of the harbor—he had no detailed charts of Crystal Bay and wouldn't trust them if he did. Our frigate drew a lot more water than fishing boats; if we wanted to avoid running aground, we had to stay out a goodly distance.

At least, so Zunctweed claimed. Quite possibly, the rotten Patata was just being spiteful: forcing us to row in by jolly-boat rather than giving us an easier option. But none of us had enough sailing experience to know if Zunctweed was lying. Impervia and Oberon both tried their best piercing stares, but Zunctweed wouldn't back down. Eventually, they had to yield to our captain's nautical "expertise."

As the NikNiks lowered the jolly-boat over the side, I examined Crystal Bay: both the harbor and the town. This close, I could see the fishing boats were aswarm with activity. Crew members toyed with ropes or dangled over the sides to examine the hulls; others banged away with hammers or swabbed hot pitch around holes that needed to be sealed; still more mended rips in fishing nets or dabbed bright red paint on the nipples of lurid figureheads. It was a furor of spring renovation, getting boats shipshape after winter's long languishing.

People lifted their heads to look at the *Dinghy,* but did so only briefly—this was the first sunny day after thaw, and no one had time to waste. Besides, our ship was the sort used by Feliss customs agents to track down smugglers; and while Dover-on-Sea was Lake Erie's smuggling capital, Crystal Bay surely had its own share of midnight runners. When the locals saw what they thought was a customs ship docking in their harbor, people kept their heads down and looked industrious.

On shore, the same attitude prevailed: folks were ostentatiously busy at various jobs, mostly refurbishing the docks. Like docks everywhere, these were lined with automobile tires serving as rubbery bumpers; and it says something about OldTech times that after four centuries, you could still find plenty such tires. You didn't even have to visit a garbage dump—go to any crumbling subdivision and beside the collapsed townhouses you'd find the rusted hulks of cars. Generations of kids would have pried off the most interesting bits, the mirrors, chrome, and hood ornaments . . . yet the tires would still be in place, weathered but adequate for nailing to the side of a pier.

Beyond the tire-strung piers were the usual dockside attractions—a ship-chandler's shop, a salting house, and half a dozen shrines to whatever saints or spirits the local sailors appeased before setting out each morning. I didn't see a tavern, but I wasn't surprised; these fisherfolk weren't itinerants who hung around the waterfront, they all had houses in the main part of the village. *That's* where the taverns would be: in the center of town, where you could go after supper, drink a few liters, and have only a short distance to stumble home.

Thoughts of taverns turned my mind to the previous night—The Buxom Bull and its aftermath. With a start, I remembered that Knife-Hand Liz had headed for this same area shortly before we did. Had she landed in Crystal Bay? I looked around once more, but saw only fishing boats. Perhaps the Ring of Knives chose some other harbor for their landing (Zunctweed had admitted there were several ports that were equally good for traveling to Niagara); perhaps the Ring's boat had been slow enough for *Dinghy* to pass in the night; or perhaps a fast ship owned by smugglers looked the same as an ordinary fishing jack, especially to a landlubber like me. Tzekich and Xavier might be watching us, hidden among the other ships . . . and all of a sudden I felt dangerously exposed.

I turned to say something to Annah beside me . . . but she

was already scanning nearby boats with a wary eye. So was Myoko, a few steps away. And Impervia paced back and forth along the rail, like a guard dog who expects trouble. Oberon lifted his head high, sniffing for odd smells on the breeze. Pelinor had quit asking nautical questions and was simply watching the harbor. Even the Caryatid had stopped fussing with her pet flame; she'd gone still, holding a single unlit match.

I gazed out on peaceful boats in a peaceful port. I saw no sign of danger; but that didn't comfort me.

The NikNiks released the jolly-boat. It dropped the last few centimeters into the water, splashing lightly. Pelinor had already tethered a rope ladder to the railing; now he slung the ladder over the side and clambered down. The jolly-boat scarcely rocked as he stepped into it—solid and seaworthy. It could hold eight people: three pairs of rowers, plus someone in the rear to hold the tiller and an authority figure in front to shout orders (the boat swain or coxswain or whatever one calls the tinpot tyrant of such a tiny craft). The boat would admirably hold our somber band . . .

. . . except Oberon. He'd barely fit in the boat on his own, let alone with us sharing the space. I had no idea how he'd get to shore—though he *looked* like a lobster, I didn't know if he could *swim* like one. Nevertheless, one thing was certain: if Gretchen came with us, Oberon would never stay behind on the ship.

Speaking of Gretchen, she still hadn't shown up on deck. If I wanted to be cynical, I'd say she was just avoiding the sunlight . . . and perhaps making everyone else wait for her. But that was the old, manipulative Gretchen; the new, vulnerable Gretchen wasn't so easy to characterize.

"I'd better get our hostess," I said.

Beside me, Annah nodded and squeezed my hand.

"I've been waiting for you," Gretchen said.

She stood in the cabin doorway, dressed in her crimson gown: as stylish and form-fitting as all her other clothes, cut to keep a man's eyes glued to her body. She had a matching jacket and cape, plus dyed suede boots and a broad-rimmed sunhat, all in crimson. I wondered how long ago she'd had the outfit made—how many years she'd kept it in her closet, having it catch her eye whenever she rummaged for something to wear.

"So you're really a sorceress?" I asked.

"That's the question, isn't it?"

The only light came from above us, sun shining down the companionway. The cabin behind her was dark—all lamps blown out, all shine-stones put away. Her sunhat cast shadows that hid her face.

"Do you know," she asked, "what kind of spells I'm good at?"

"Besides shine-stones?"

"Besides them. What would I specialize in, Phil? You can probably guess."

"I'm not sure I want to."

"I don't suppose you do." She gave a humorless laugh. "Love and beauty, darling. I specialize in love and beauty."

"They say there's no such thing as a true love spell."

"Of course they *say* that." This time her laugh was a bit more real. "It depends how choosy you are. The purest truest love may be impossible to impose artificially, but there are some truly diverting facsimiles. Ways to make a cold night hot."

She waited for me to speak. I refused to ask the obvious— if she'd ever cast a spell on me. Never ask a question when you don't want to hear the answer.

"Anyway," she said after a moment, "there's more to love spells than just making some pretty man pant for you. There are spells to find out if a pretty man loves you—or someone else." She paused. "I wasn't sleepy when the rest of you went to bed last night . . . so silly, silly me, I thought I'd start my renewed career as a sorceress by casting a few spells. Ones I'd avoided before."

She tilted her head back slightly; her eyes glimmered wetly in the shadows beneath her hat brim. "How long have you loved Annah, Phil?"

*   *   *

I considered denying it. Something must have shown on my face, because Gretchen said, "Hush," and put her hand to my lips. "Don't you dare cast aspersions on the awesome insights of my witchcraft."

"Gretchen—"

"No," she interrupted. "Just don't. It's not like I thought we'd grow old together. Although I have, a bit. Grown old. With you." She forced her voice brighter. "But I'm starting a new life as a sorceress, aren't I? It's good not to have entanglements. Or illusions. Or—"

I bent forward and kissed her. Her arms came up to pull me nearer; for the briefest instant, I thought she would squeeze me with all the lonely desperation of a middle-aged woman afraid to let go. But she returned the kiss with nothing but tenderness: soft and gentle . . . almost motherly.

When our lips parted, she whispered, "The last kiss should always be sweet." She reached up to her head; her crimson hat had a veil attached, thrown back all this while. Now she lowered it to cover her face . . . so the brightest sun could never reveal her wrinkles, her age, or her tears.

"These things happen, darling," she said. "They happen all the time. I of all people know that." Then she took my arm and let me help her ascend into sunlight.

Most of our group had already climbed down to the jolly-boat; only Myoko and Oberon were still on deck. Oberon bowed low to Gretchen. "Are you ready to go, sweet mistress?"

"Absolutely. What a bright delightful day!" She went to the railing and waved gaily to the people below her. Pelinor waved back just as enthusiastically; Annah and the Caryatid returned the wave with more restraint, while Impervia just glared.

"But Oberon," Gretchen said, "there's no room for *you* in the boat."

"Don't worry, sweet mistress. I shall swim."

"You can swim? Well, of course you can, you're a lobster." She studied him a moment. "Do you have gills?"

"Not that I'm aware of, mistress . . . but thank you for asking. I can swim quite adequately, however—I've done so many times in the lake near Kinnderboom Cottage. On a hot day, the experience is most refreshing."

"It'll be more than refreshing today," I told him. "The water is only a few degrees away from ice."

"My species is less susceptible to cold than yours," Oberon answered. Despite his "perfect butler" demeanor, his voice had an edge of smugness—I'd never seen him wear clothes, even on the coldest days of winter. His armored carapace obviously provided abundant insulation, but I still decided to keep an eye on him as we boated to shore. Oberon was just the type to keep plugging away without complaint until he passed out from hypothermia.

While Oberon and I were talking, Gretchen had been eyeing the rope ladder to the jolly-boat. Climbing down in her long crimson gown would be difficult enough . . . but before she could even try, she had to find some way up and over the rail. I could see she had no clue how to manage it—she'd led such a pampered life that when faced with the problem of climbing over a barrier slightly higher than her waist, her mind simply drew a blank. I was ready to volunteer my help, when Myoko murmured, "My treat."

Myoko's hair didn't lift a millimeter, but suddenly Gretchen soared into the air. She gave a shriek of terror. It wasn't that Myoko was handling her roughly—I think Myoko intended this as a friendly joke, showing Gretchen she'd been accepted as "one of the gang" by subjecting her to impromptu rowdiness. But Gretchen wasn't ready for such antics; she might be a worldly woman in the bedroom, but otherwise she'd led a sheltered existence. In genteel circles, well-bred persons did not get slung around by unseen forces: darling, it just wasn't *done*.

By the time Gretchen landed (feather-light) in the jolly-boat, her body was rigid with shock. Utterly frozen. It was an open question whether she was still breathing.

Myoko still had a half-smile on her face . . . as if she realized she'd gone too far, but apologizing would make it all right. Oberon, however, was not smiling in the least. His whiskers had splayed wide like a cat with its hackles up, and his waist-pincers twitched ominously. Even more alarming, a thick smell of wood smoke poured off him—so heady it made my eyes burn. The only scent I'd ever smelled from Oberon was his perennial tang of vinegar. This new aroma caught me off guard, but I knew enough biology to realize it was likely a chemical signal: a pheromone communicating to others of Oberon's kind that he was on the warpath. Something had grabbed his sweet mistress, thrown her into the air, and paralyzed her with panic. Such an insult must be avenged. The only thing preventing Oberon from snipping Myoko into fish-food was that he hadn't figured out she was responsible.

Any moment now, he'd realize the truth—he'd seen Myoko use her powers the previous night when she'd lifted Impervia and Pelinor onto the *Dinghy*. I had to divert him before he put two and two together.

"Quick," I said, "someone's used sorcery on Gretchen. Maybe the Ring of Knives. We're sitting ducks out here on the water—we have to get to shore fast. You go secure the beach."

He didn't hesitate a nanosecond: Oberon might have spent his life as a butler, but deep in his genes, he was one hundred percent warrior. He'd been longing for the day he could secure a beach for his queen. With a roar he charged forward, not even breaking stride as he struck the ship's rail; the wood snapped like tinder under his weight, and he continued in an airborne parabola till he struck the lake like thunder.

A perfect cannonball belly-flop: the slap of his bulk on the surface splashed spray in all directions. Those in the jolly-boat got drenched head to foot with water nearly as cold as ice. Even Impervia gasped; the Caryatid sputtered curses in some language I didn't understand, Pelinor did the same in a language I understood all too well, and Annah . . . Annah's jaw dropped and her eyes opened wide but she never made a sound. As if she'd trained herself to keep silent when taken by surprise. For a long moment, she remained unmoving, water streaming off her hair and down her dark face; then she began laughing, covering her mouth but unable to stop the giggles that bubbled between her fingers.

The others stared dumbly for a count of three; then Gretchen began laughing too. The frigid splash must have roused her from shock . . . and I suppose she'd seen everyone else soaked to the bone, and felt immensely better at the sight. A bonding experience: covered in dripping wet clothes and watching lake water stream from your hems. Pelinor joined the laughter as he wrung out his doublet. The Caryatid, who'd been holding another unlit match, now made a mock-tragic show of tossing the soggy match-stick over the side of the boat. Even Impervia couldn't help cracking a smile: it was a startling look for her but rather becoming, as she good-naturedly brushed her hand across her close-cut hair and swept water onto the boat's decking.

As for Oberon, he never looked back. He had to secure the beachhead: swimming slowly with powerful sweeps of his tail. His red body lumbered through blue waves dappled with sunlight . . . and for a moment, it was a glorious, bright, simple day in spring.

The Caryatid took the rudder while Gretchen took the bow— just like the buxom figurehead on a fishing boat, except Gretchen was clothed and had a damp crimson veil plastered against her face. The rest of us grabbed the oars: Annah paired with me at the front, Pelinor paired with Myoko amidships, and Impervia (ever the overachiever) handled the rear oars by herself.

Zunctweed remained aboard the *Dinghy*. He'd mumbled, "If I must," when Gretchen ordered him to stay in Crystal Bay till she returned, but after that he hadn't deigned to recognize our existence. No good-byes or salutes. As our boat pulled away from the ship, I couldn't see Zunctweed at all. Perhaps he'd gone to his cabin to air out every vestige of Gretchen's perfume.

Gretchen herself had bounced back from her momentary panic and was now in high spirits. She kept praising how well the rest of us rowed: it was her way of contributing and probably more helpful than if she'd actually taken an oar. Gretchen wouldn't have been good with oars. And no one looked disgruntled about her idleness, not even Impervia—you don't blame a lapdog for not being able to hunt.

We quickly established a rhythm to our stroke. I didn't realize how fast we were going until we passed Oberon, still working his ponderous way toward the beach. He shouted at us to stop until he secured the landing site, but Gretchen only laughed. "Silly billy, don't worry."

Beside me, Annah muttered, "Maybe we *should* slow down."

She was still wet, her hair drooping, her clothes puckered against her body—not a bad look, especially with steam trickling off the parts most warmed by the sun. "What's wrong?" I asked.

"Oh, just superstition: I hate it when someone says don't worry."

I glanced over my shoulder toward the shore. We were sitting backward in the boat, facing away from the front because Impervia claimed that was the correct way to row. Backing blindly into unknown territory. "Slow down," I told the others. "Let Oberon land first."

"We don't have time," Impervia said. "Every second we waste puts Sebastian at risk."

"Slow down!" I repeated, my nerves starting to jangle. "Gretchen, keep a watch on shore."

"What am I watching for?"

"Whatever you see."

"Since you ask so nicely, how can I refuse?"

Gretchen shifted in her seat; she'd been facing our way to give us encouragement, but now she turned front, peering at the docks. Out the corner of my eye, I could see her rise off the seat, leaning forward with her hands on the gunwales. She stayed there only a few seconds, then muttered, "To hell with this. I can't see a thing."

I thought she was giving up; but she just took off her hat and veil. They must have been blocking her view. Now, either she'd steeled herself to being seen in sunlight, or she'd decided if she was facing away from us we wouldn't notice

her crow's feet. Maybe she was just sick of wet lace sticking
to her nose. She pulled off the headgear and shook out her
hair, open to the sun at last.

"This is nice," she said. Then a rifle cracked on shore, and
Gretchen's blood splattered like surf crashing over the boat.

16

WE SHALL FIGHT ON THE BEACHES . . .

"Hold on!" Myoko yelled from the stern.

I barely had time to grab a gunwale when the front of the boat lifted clean from the water—as if the boat's nose had been hoisted on a crane. The rifle cracked again . . . but now the boat was tilted up at a forty-five-degree angle, forming a thick wooden barrier in front of us. The bullet thunked into the hull but didn't get through; then Gretchen's limp body slid down the slanted decking and slumped against my back.

Switching my grip on the gunwale, I turned to see if there was any chance to save her. No. None. The bullet had gone in cleanly through her forehead and out messily through the rear of her skull. Bone chips and brain matter snarled in her hair. I tried to tell myself, "At least she didn't suffer," but the words didn't mean a damned thing as her blood gushed onto my shoulder.

Another shot. This one missed the boat and whizzed into the water. It might have been aimed at Oberon. At any rate, the giant lobster decided it was time to stop being a bright red slow-moving target—he plunged out of sight beneath the waves. Oberon swam a few strokes underwater, then rose just high enough to stick his snout above the surface . . . nothing showing except his nose-spike and nostrils. I could hear him take a deep breath; then he submerged once more and struck toward the beach as fast as he could go.

More bullets sliced the lake in his vicinity, but I don't think the shooter knew where Oberon was. Sunlight dappled the surface; I soon lost sight of the big lobster myself. Even if a chance shot found its target, Oberon's armor would probably stop a bullet that had already been slowed by water. He'd be safe till he reached the shallows. After that . . . his shell was better than no protection at all, but I doubted it could stand up to high-power slugs.

Then again, maybe the slugs *weren't* high-power. When the shooter realized Oberon was just a waste of ammunition, the barrage turned back to the upraised jolly-boat . . . and bullet after bullet struck the hull without getting through. Thank heaven for solid oak timber.

Meanwhile we continued shoreward, propelled by Myoko's mind plus strenuous rowing from Pelinor and Impervia. They'd moved to the stern of the boat, the only part still in contact with the lake. Fighting the oarlocks (which weren't designed to function when the boat was two-thirds upright), Pelinor and Impervia heaved us ahead, skating the jolly-boat toward shore as if it were riding an invisible wave.

Beside me, Annah produced a mirror from some hidden pocket in her cloak. Though it looked like an ordinary face mirror, it had a long telescoping handle: useful for looking around corners if you practiced a profession where looking around corners was useful. Impervia might carry such a mirror for spying on students . . . but Annah? I'd ask her about it later. In the meantime, she extended it deftly around the edge of the boat and tilted it to scan the shore.

"See anything?" I asked.

She shook her head. Drops of Gretchen's blood darkened Annah's right cheek. I reached up to brush the gore away, then realized my hand was even bloodier. Gretchen's corpse still slumped against me, but she'd stopped sliding downward: one of her legs had got wedged under the wooden thwart where I'd been sitting to row. Blood streamed from her head wound, soaking into the crimson gown.

She'd have been horrified by the way her dress was ruined.

I laid my hand across hers (my fingers sticky with blood, her fingers clean and warm but lifeless). Under my breath, I whispered words I remembered from long ago. "In the name of Most Merciful Compassionate God: Praise be to God, the Lord of all Being . . ."

Another bullet chunked into the boat. "Yes!" Annah murmured, still using her mirror. "I saw the muzzle flash. He's behind one of the shrines."

"Which shrine?" Impervia snapped. "Describe it."

"Bright white—all the others are colored. An hourglass shape, maybe two and a half meters tall. The shooter's taken a position where the hourglass curves inward; steadying the gun against the shrine itself."

Impervia growled. "If people in Crystal Bay had any true righteousness, they'd charge the shooter to stop him defiling their altar."

"Maybe they will," the Caryatid said, "when the gun runs out of bullets."

No locals were rushing to get themselves shot. We were well inside the harbor by now, passing fishing boats at anchor; not a soul was visible, despite the number of people who'd been working here minutes before. At the first sign of trouble, they must have dived for cover—into the holds where they stored their fish, or straight over the sides of their boats. These folks had no urge to get involved in our troubles. They might have risked their lives for fellow villagers, but not for strangers who'd just arrived in an imposing military vessel. As far as these people knew, we were either soldiers or customs officers; facing criminals was our job. Therefore the people of Crystal Bay would lie low until the shooting had stopped . . . and only then would they poke up their heads to ask, "What was that all about?"

So we were on our own. Desperate, but not devoid of resources. When we got close enough, perhaps the Caryatid could send a pack of flame-buddies to set the shooter's clothes on fire. Even easier, Myoko could knock the rifle away and hold the shooter helpless till Impervia and Pelinor subdued him.

Assuming Myoko had any strength left by the time we got to shore. She was sitting on the thwart just below me, her body rigid with concentration and her face deathly pale. I'd seen the same color on people so sick they were ready to pass out. The Caryatid must have noticed the same thing, for she'd clambered up from the rudder seat to perch at Myoko's side: wrapping motherly arms around Myoko's small frame and holding her, helping keep her balanced and warm despite the strain.

Myoko began to shiver. She was supporting the weight of seven people plus the jolly-boat, which was several hundred kilos in itself; and on top of holding us up, she was driving the boat toward the beach. A fierce sustained effort after years of not using her full power. Like someone who'd spent a decade never lifting anything heavier than a glass of ale suddenly hoisting a loaded hay-wagon . . . and keeping it up for ten seconds, twenty seconds, thirty . . .

"How close are we?" I asked Annah.

"Almost to the beach."

"And from there to the shooter?"

"Twenty meters."

Twenty meters: two or three seconds of sprinting, even for someone as fast as Impervia. And running on sand would slow her down. The shooter would have plenty of time to aim and fire. Even if we all charged en masse, he'd get at least two of us before we crossed the gap.

"Any cover we can use?" I asked Annah.

"No. The people of Crystal Bay obviously like an unobstructed view of their shrines when they're out on the lake."

"Damn."

I tried to picture how far twenty meters really was. A reasonable stone's throw, but too far to hurl a knife with any accuracy. An easy shot for an arrow, but none of us had a bow. Besides, if we could draw a bead on the gunman, he could draw a bead on us. For the past ten seconds, he hadn't fired a single round. Probably reloading . . . or at least conserving ammunition. It would be nice to think he'd used all his bullets, but I didn't believe we were that lucky.

Sand crunched beneath the jolly-boat's keel. We were still

in the water, but we'd bottomed out in the shallows. "Ten meters from here to the beach," Annah said. Impervia and Pelinor dug their oars into the sand, trying to pole us forward like punters . . . but the only result was a harsh rasping sound as the keel buried itself deeper. We'd run aground and pushing would only make it worse.

Myoko took a shuddering breath. The Caryatid squeezed her: "Hang on, hang on . . ." If Myoko dropped us now, our prow would fall forward, leaving us exposed to gunfire at close range. We'd have to flatten ourselves on the bottom of the boat; the hull would protect us, but we'd be pinned down for as long as the shooter wanted to toy with us.

Suddenly, the boat soared upward: hurtling out of the water as if propelled from a catapult, flying in an arc that ended with a brutal collision as the boat snapped up to the vertical and slammed its flat stern onto solid land. We almost tipped over, our balance precarious—the boat was now completely upright, nose pointing to the sky. If we hadn't been holding tight already, we would have spilled into the line of fire. Pelinor and Impervia jammed their oars out into the sand on either side, making diagonal struts to keep us from wobbling left or right . . . but it was Myoko who saved us, giving the boat one last shove downward, driving the stern a full hand's breadth into the sand. Planted deep and solid. Then Myoko went limp, blood gushing from her nose and mouth.

The shooter blasted another bullet into the jolly-boat's hull. It didn't go through—we were still safe. If "safe" is a valid word when you're stuck on an open beach, and your only protection is an upright rowboat. It was as if we'd taken cover in a tiny privy-shack while a murderer waited outside.

"Phil," Impervia whispered, "how much money are you carrying? Enough to buy our way out of here?"

"Yes and no," I told her. "I have enough cash to pay a healthy bribe . . . but if we tell the shooter that, he'll just have more incentive to kill us. Once we're dead, he can get rich looting our bodies."

"Let's skip the bribery," Pelinor said. "We'll try Plan B. We do have a Plan B, don't we?"

Impervia scowled. "Bribery *was* Plan B. Plan A was having Myoko jam the rifle down the shooter's throat."

We all looked at Myoko where she lay ashen and unconscious in the Caryatid's arms. The bleeding from her mouth and nose had slowed to a seeping ooze; I hoped that was a good sign.

A moment's silence; then Impervia said, "Flames," in a cold hard voice. "Caryatid, can you set fire to this man who wants to kill us?"

"I don't know." The Caryatid continued to gaze down at Myoko: rocking the limp body, the way one might rock a sleeping child.

"Can you do it?" Impervia said more sharply. "There's no way to help Myoko right now; first we have to deal with the gunman. If you aren't up to the job, just say so and we'll try something else."

The Caryatid forced herself to look up from Myoko and meet Impervia's gaze. "I don't have much range on making flames obey me. And I can't control them at all if they're out of sight."

Without a word, Annah handed her the mirror.

"All right," the Caryatid said. "I'll try."

The Caryatid's ready supply of matches had got soaked when Oberon did his belly-flop. She had to find more matches in her pack, then search for a dry place to strike a light, but at last she had a single flame balanced on her fingertip.

(All this while, the shooter stayed silent. *Everything* was still—the town, the docks, the fishing boats. Oberon had to be somewhere, but I couldn't see him. I assumed he was lurking in the water, just deep enough to stay hidden: snout breaking the surface now and then to breathe, biding his time for a chance to rush the shore.)

The tiny flame leapt from the Caryatid's finger and skittered across the sand like a blazing insect-sized crab. As it rounded the edge of the jolly-boat, it flickered in a wash of breeze . . . but it held itself together and slipped out of sight. Only the Caryatid, watching with the mirror, could keep an eye on its progress.

"I see the shrine," she murmured. "And I see the shooter. I think . . . yes, it's Warwick Xavier."

"Not much of a surprise," I said. Nobody but the Ring would shoot us on sight; and nobody but the Ring had the connections and incentive to acquire first-rate firearms in this part of the world. Knife-Hand Liz must have landed in Crystal Bay and left Xavier here to stop anyone who might be following. Either that or she was so sick of Xavier's surly attitude, she ordered him to stay behind just to get him out of her hair.

Xavier must have started shooting as soon as we came into range. But why did he kill Gretchen first? He knew her by sight; he'd spied on her back in Dover. Why waste his first shot—his one chance at surprise—on a woman so utterly harmless? Impervia and Pelinor were far more dangerous threats; you could tell that just by looking at them. But Xavier had taken aim on Gretchen's skull and killed her with a sniper's deliberation. Why?

A bullet cracked at close range. Sand sprayed as the shot hit the beach. "Damn!" the Caryatid said. "He got my flame."

"I saw that once in a carnival," Pelinor said. "Fellow shot a flame off a candlewick."

"Xavier's not that good. He didn't hit my flame dead on, but the sand he kicked up did the job."

"So light another flame," Impervia said. "And move it faster so Xavier can't hit the moving target."

The Caryatid shook her head. "Any quicker and the flame will go out. There's too much wind."

She was right. A spring breeze played around the beach at random, darting in off the lake, then whisking the other direction or swirling crossways. It wasn't strong, but it could easily blow out a candleflame. As if to emphasize that, a gust puffed in my face, carrying with it a mixture of fragrances— fresh tar for patching fishing boats, the scent of last season's catch, a piercing smell of wood smoke . . .

Familiar wood smoke: the pheromone that poured off Oberon when he thought Gretchen was in danger. Its smell stood out amidst all the other odors of the port. I'd been wrong when I thought Oberon was hiding in the lake—he must have circled around underwater and come up somewhere out of sight. Now he was sneaking back, close enough that the quirky wind brought his whiff to my nose.

"We've just been handed Plan C," I told the others. "Oberon is nearby: probably creeping up on Xavier."

"How do you know?" Impervia asked.

"I can smell him." I turned to the Caryatid. "Whip up another flame—if you can distract Xavier, it'll give Oberon a chance. Maybe. It's hard to believe Xavier won't notice a giant red lobster sneaking up on him, but let's do what we can."

"We'd better get ready to attack too," Impervia said. "Whether Oberon makes it or not, we'll never have a better chance to take Xavier down."

Pelinor nodded. The Caryatid was concentrating on lighting another match. Until she got it going, we needed something else to draw Xavier's attention away from Oberon. "Hey!" I shouted. "Xavier! Can't we talk this over?"

"Nothing to talk about," a gravelly voice answered. "Unless maybe you come out and let me end things fast."

"You mean shoot us in cold blood?"

"Blood is always warm, boy. Or boiling hot."

"I'll show him hot," the Caryatid muttered. She'd finally got her match lit. The flame jumped to the ground and scampered across the sand. As soon as it rounded the corner of the boat, a shot rang out. The Caryatid, watching her thimble-sized blaze in Annah's mirror, said, "Hah! Missed, you bastard."

"Going to waste ammo on miniature fires?" I called to Xavier.

"I have dozens of rounds," he laughed. "The Ring just smuggled a big shipment from Rustland."

"Bet we have more matches than you have bullets."

"I'll take that bet," Xavier said. "And the price of the wager is your life, you stupid—heh?"

A sudden roar. Oberon's voice. "Assassin!"

"Rush him!" Impervia yelled.
My feet hit the sand as a rifle shot fired.

Impervia and Pelinor moved faster than me; they were already racing up the sand as I rounded the edge of the jolly-boat for my first glimpse of the situation.

Oberon had got within ten meters of Xavier: coming in from the left, taking cover behind the dockside salting house. I don't know whether Oberon had already begun his final charge when Xavier saw him, or if Xavier caught sight of Oberon first and the big lobster had no choice but to race in headlong; either way, both sides must have acted almost simultaneously. As Xavier brought round his rifle, Oberon must have shouted, "Assassin!" in the hope that a lobster-demon's bellow would make the gunman miss.

Oberon's strategy worked. Xavier fired but the bullet went wild, zinging into the salting house wall. Before Xavier could correct his aim, Oberon had crossed the gap: claws set at a perfect level to disembowel his target. A normal man wouldn't have dodged in time . . . but Xavier was the sort who'd been brawling since boyhood, and despite his seventy years, he was still fast and slippery. As Oberon galloped forward, Xavier feinted one way, then leapt the other. The big lobster couldn't adjust quickly enough; he plowed into the hourglass shrine, knocking it off its supports with a thunderous crash.

Xavier swung his rifle around for another shot. Oberon had plenty of fight left, despite hitting the shrine like a battering ram; but the demon's pincers had stabbed deep into the shrine's pine timbers, and he couldn't pull them out.

Stuck. Trapped.

Xavier laughed as he took half a second to draw a bead on Oberon's face. Pelinor, running fast in front of me but nowhere near fighting range, hurled his cutlass at Xavier, end over end like an unwieldy throwing knife. He couldn't have expected it to do damage—just ruin the gun's aim. No good: Xavier evaded the sword with a casual sidestep. Staring straight into Oberon's eyes, he tightened his finger on the trigger . . . at exactly the same instant Oberon thrust his head in Xavier's direction.

Leading with the spike on his nose.

I doubt if Oberon intended to hit the rifle muzzle. Instead, I think Xavier realized the danger of that nose-spike coming toward him, and he tried to block the spike with his gun. His trigger finger was still squeezing, even as the spike and rifle made contact: exactly as the point of the spike caught the barrel's mouth and jammed its way into the hole.

Back in OldTech times, guns rarely exploded. Nowadays though, when firearms are built from OldTech blueprints but without OldTech metallurgy—no fancy alloys, no computerized quality control, just a single steelsmith muddling away with hammer and anvil to get something that sort of maybe looks right—these days, a rifle barrel with its end plugged tight by a nose-spike is the next best thing to a pipe-bomb.

As Dreamsinger would say, "Boom."

The rifle barrel blew itself apart in a shower of shrapnel. Oberon was thrown back, his face a lacerated mess. Chestnut-brown fluid spurted from gashes where steel fragments had sliced through his carapace into the tender flesh beneath. The brown fluid must have been blood; there was a devastating amount of it.

Xavier's blood was red, but it flowed just as freely. The explosion had slashed the right side of his face where he'd been sighting up the shot . . . but it had also blown wads of debris into the upper part of his torso, perforating the old man's leather jacket in a dozen places. The damage was far more extensive than one would expect from a single bullet; the initial charge must have detonated the rest of the gun's ammunition, blasting apart the breech where Xavier had it nestled under his arm. Slivers of wood and steel stabbed straight into the man's chest cavity . . . not to mention flaying his hands to bloody pulps.

When Impervia reached the scene, she kicked the rifle's shattered remains out of Xavier's blood-smeared grip . . . but it was an empty gesture. The gun would never fire again, nor

would Xavier pull another trigger. He was wheezing with untold damage to his lungs, and the right half of his face looked
like chopped meat. Still, he managed a vicious smile with the
half of a face he had left.

"Went out fighting," he whispered. Impervia crouched beside him, not to offer help but to pat him down for weapons.
Xavier went on talking as she roughly pulled a knife from a
sheath at his ankle. "And I killed a Spark Lord," he whispered. "That must be worth something, yes? Tell everyone . . ." Cough. "I killed a Spark Lord."

"Which Spark Lord?" Pelinor asked.

"That Dreamsinger." Another cough, this one bringing up
blood. Xavier spat it out and turned proudly toward Pelinor.
"Shot her clean between the eyes. You saw, yes?"

Pelinor stared back confused; so did I. Impervia stopped
searching for weapons and leaned into Xavier's face. "Fool.
The person you shot wasn't Dreamsinger—it was Gretchen
Kinnderboom. A vain woman, but harmless. Killing her was
no great victory."

"Gretchen?" Xavier's face puckered with confusion. "I
wouldn't kill Gretchen. She's . . . beautiful . . ."

I groaned, understanding at last. When Xavier had seen
Dreamsinger last night, she'd been disguised with Kaylan's
Chameleon; so what had the Spark Lord looked like in his
eyes? What sort of woman did he lust for?

One like Gretchen. Whom he'd spied on with his telescope. He fantasized about Gretchen, and when he looked at
Dreamsinger, that's who he saw. Maybe not an exact look-
alike—maybe overlaid with features from other women he'd
known over the years. But close enough if you were looking
at someone a good distance offshore. And when he saw
Gretchen wearing sorcerer's crimson . . .

He'd jumped to the wrong conclusion. And my clothes
were now spattered with the blood and brains of a woman I
once (might have) loved.

Bending over, I snarled into Xavier's face, "You didn't kill
Dreamsinger, you killed the real Gretchen. How does that
make you feel?"

I never got an answer. I hope he lived long enough to realize he wasn't some great Spark killer: just a stupid man who'd murdered a woman he found beautiful. But I'll never know if my message got through. By the time I'd got out my last word, Xavier was dead.

Oberon was dead too. Pelinor tried to help the big lobster . . . but there was no way to staunch the bleeding or repair the damage from metal shards gouging Oberon's brain. His pincers clutched convulsively, clack-clack, clack-clack, in some kind of postmortem reflex; Pelinor had to keep back for fear of getting sliced in two. But Oberon had already stopped breathing, unable to draw air through the mutilated mess of his mouth.

After a minute, the brown blood stopped flowing. It began to cake. The claw-twitching continued but with longer gaps between each clench.

Clack . . . clack.

Clack.

Clack.

Pelinor looked away, brushing his eyes with his hand. Impervia stepped over Xavier's corpse and went to kneel beside Oberon. "In nomine Patris, et Filii, et Spiritae Sanctae . . ."

If she'd prayed like that when Gretchen died, I hadn't heard it. Possibly Impervia had been too busy rowing the jolly-boat; or possibly, Magdalenes didn't pray for rich idle women who were caught in the wrong place at the wrong time. They *would* pray, however, for anyone—even an alien—who died in righteous battle.

We all have standards for who is worthy of our prayer. I wondered if anyone would ever pray for Warwick Xavier.

17

BEACHHEAD

I made my way back to the jolly-boat. People peered surreptitiously from nearby fishing jacks: peeping over railings or around the corners of deckhouses, wondering if the shooting had stopped. A few slipped out of sight when they saw I'd noticed them—the folk of Crystal Bay had no intention of getting involved with whatever death and lunacy we'd brought to their town.

Inside the jolly-boat, Myoko was still unconscious in the Caryatid's arms. Blood had dried on Myoko's upper lip; I don't know why the Caryatid didn't wipe it away.

Annah had blood on her face too. Gretchen's blood. Annah laid Gretchen's corpse on the sand and began fussing with the arrangement of limbs, clothes, etc. She looked up as I approached.

"Oberon?" Annah asked.

"Dead. Xavier too."

"And he was the only Ring man here?"

"The only one we've seen." I glanced up the beach toward the center of the village. An empty street led from the docks to a muddy square where several horses stood at hitching posts. No people in sight. "We'll keep our eyes open for bully-boys," I said, "but if I were Elizabeth Tzekich, I wouldn't deplete my forces by leaving people in places like this. She knows she might run into Dreamsinger; she'll need all the troops she can get. Probably she dumped Xavier here because he was getting on her nerves."

Annah nodded. She spent a moment trying to arrange Gretchen's hands in the classic "Death is peaceful" pose: folded serenely across her chest. The hands were too limp to stay put; they kept slumping onto the sand. After several attempts, Annah gave up. "So what now?" she asked softly . . . as if she didn't want anyone else to hear. "Do we keep going on?"

"Sebastian is still out there. Do we leave him to Dreamsinger? Or the Ring of Knives? Or Jode?"

"If the boy's such a powerful psychic, maybe he can take care of himself."

I looked at her in surprise. "Are you suggesting we abandon him?"

She didn't answer; she was still gazing at Gretchen's body. Gretchen's corpse. Finally she said, "It's not about Sebastian, Phil. You know that. He's just the excuse we're using."

"What do you mean?"

"Impervia thinks this is a holy mission. She's received a heavenly calling and doesn't give a damn what it's about; all she cares is that God has finally given her a job. Pelinor's the same, but without the divine overtones. He didn't start pretending he was a knight just because he wanted to teach at the academy—to him, knighthood was a romantic ideal. A way to use his sword for more than forcing people to pay some pointless border tax. Pelinor's been hungering for a knightly quest the way Impervia's been hungering for a sacred vocation: to be lifted out of a humdrum existence and into something *worthy*."

After a moment, I nodded; Annah must have thought this all through back on *Dainty Dinghy*. I could imagine her waking early, before those of us who'd stayed up late drinking in The Pot of Gold. She might have gone quietly up to the deck, leaned against the rail, and watched the shoreline drift past as she asked herself why we'd let ourselves come this far. "Go on," I said.

"The Caryatid's here because Pelinor is. She loves him, you know; she'd never let him run off alone."

I tried not to gape. "She loves him?"

Annah laughed. Softly. "Not Romeo and Juliet love—not teenagers who'll die if they can't hurl themselves into bed immediately. The Caryatid and Pelinor have something more courtly: fondness rather than passion. Quite possibly they *do* share a bed from time to time . . . but it's not their most urgent priority. They're comfortable, not torrid; but they're still in love, and wherever Pelinor goes, the Caryatid will follow." Annah paused. "Much like Myoko following you."

"Don't say that." I looked over at Myoko. The Caryatid had laid her flat on the sand, feet elevated by propping them on the jolly-boat's rear thwart. Standard first-aid for clinical shock—slant the body to send blood into the heart and brain.

But Myoko's face was paler than ever.

"It's not your fault," Annah said. "She would have come, even without you—she wouldn't let Impervia and Pelinor go off on their own. Myoko always has to prove herself." Annah paused. "You've noticed she's not as weak as she pretends?"

I didn't want to betray Myoko's private confession to me. "I noticed she dragged seven people and a jolly-boat several hundred meters at top speed."

Annah nodded. "She's strong, Phil—as strong as any psychic I've ever heard about. But she pretends otherwise. I think maybe she came on this trip for the chance to cut loose. To use every drop of her power in a meaningful cause."

"And perhaps to impress me?"

"Perhaps. Or to remind herself what she's capable of. Pushing the boat across the bay . . . it hurt her, Phil, but she kept on going. Maybe it felt good to stop pretending."

"Even if she dies from the strain? I've heard of psychics dropping from brain hemorrhage if they push too much."

Annah dropped her gaze. "We all might die, Phil. We know that, but we're still here."

"What about you?" I asked. "Please don't say you're following me too."

She gave a little smile. "Heavens, I'd never do anything foolish just for a *man*. Women don't do that, do they?" Annah lifted her eyes to mine. "You tell me why you keep going and I'll tell you why I do."

I thought about it. She was right—this wasn't really about rescuing Sebastian. I wanted to do that, of course; but that was just the job, not my reason for doing it. I'd still have come this far, even if we were chasing a complete stranger.

So why was I here? Why did I intend to pick myself up and keep going to the bitter end?

Loyalty to my friends.

Curiosity about what lay in Niagara Falls.

Anger at the monster that killed Rosalind and a hope we could make it pay for its crime.

The desire not to act like a coward in front of Annah. (How much of everything done in the world is an attempt to impress the opposite sex?)

But above all else . . . the feeling that I was finally *doing* something. No longer waiting for life to begin. Like Impervia and Pelinor, I'd always had a secret belief I was destined for something more important than marking tests and trying to keep my students awake until lunch. It was a ridiculous, dangerous fantasy: an adolescent delusion that God would single me out as special. Blame it on my privileged background, my vanity, or a simple lack of common sense; but I'd always assumed I would someday hear the Call to Adventure like some mythological hero.

Trials and tribulations. Physical ordeals. The love of beautiful women. Tragedy and betrayal. Victory and vindication. Heroic joy, heroic pain, heroic life, heroic death.

"I'm here," I told Annah, "because I'm an ass. There's a dead woman at my feet, killed in an ugly ignoble way . . . and I'm still not as afraid of dying as I am of being ordinary."

She took my hand—my blood-smeared hand—and pressed it to her lips. "Me too," she whispered. "No more being ordinary. *I will drink life to the lees.*" She paused. "Alfred, Lord Tennyson. 'Ulysses.'" She paused again. "I've been a teacher *way* too long."

Impervia and Pelinor set off toward the central square, supposedly to scout the town and make sure there were no more Ring thugs waiting in ambush. In truth, Impervia was just too keyed up to stay in one place; Myoko couldn't be moved in her current condition and Impervia couldn't bear watching helplessly while our friend looked so pallid and frail. There was nothing anyone could do except keep Myoko warm and hope her blood would soon start circulating normally. That wasn't enough for Impervia: she went off on the prowl, and Pelinor tagged along to keep her out of trouble.

I too was feeling keyed up. I trotted down to the lake to fill a canteen so we could splash Myoko's face . . . then I couldn't decide if splashing would help or just add to the level of shock. Every teacher at the academy had been trained in first-aid; but our textbooks had been OldTech ones. That meant we learned the best temporizing techniques OldTech experts knew, but most of the write-ups ended with OBTAIN PROFESSIONAL MEDICAL HELP AS SOON AS POSSIBLE.

We were four hundred years too late for that.

"She's waking up," the Caryatid said. Annah and I knelt beside her; we all saw Myoko's eyelids flicker. As soon as her eyes opened they closed again, squinting against the sun. We'd laid her in the brightest spot we could find in an effort to keep her warm.

"How are you feeling?" I asked.

"Like shit." Her voice was a thready whisper. "Who's . . ." She couldn't finish the question.

The Caryatid said, "Oberon died but took Xavier with him. Everyone else is alive—thanks to you."

"Okay . . . good . . ."

"Rest," Annah said. "Don't waste your strength."

"Too late," Myoko whispered. "Way too late."

"Don't say that!" the Caryatid told her. "You'll be fine."

"I *am* fine," Myoko said. "Did my bit. What I was . . . here for . . ."

"Myoko!" The Caryatid's voice had gone steely. "God-damn it, don't you *dare* surrender. It's *stupid*. People don't just die when it suits them. Don't give up. Myoko! Myoko!"

The Caryatid shook Myoko by the shoulders. Myoko's head flopped limply in response. A little more blood trickled from her mouth. Then a bit from one ear.

When the Caryatid let go, Myoko slumped to the sand. Bright sun. A spring breeze. And death.

Impervia and Pelinor returned. With them came a wagon driven by two sullen teenagers: one boy, one girl, both about sixteen, both with flaming red hair and freckles, both glaring resentfully at Impervia. The wagon held a single coffin.

"I found an undertaker," Impervia announced, jogging up ahead of the cart. "It was—"

"You only brought one coffin," the Caryatid said. Her voice was flat and lifeless.

"For Gretchen," Impervia said. "There was nothing big enough for Oberon, and Xavier can lie where he is. Let the crows pick at his . . ."

She stopped. She'd seen Myoko.

"We need another coffin," the Caryatid said.

Impervia closed her eyes and let out a shuddering breath. When she knelt beside Myoko, she needed almost a full minute before she could speak the first words of a prayer.

The grumpy teenagers were named Vickie and Victor: twin children of the local undertaker. Pelinor prattled on about the whole family having bright red hair, mother, father, all the children who'd been hanging about the shop. No one listened to what he was saying, least of all Pelinor himself—he was just filling the silence, trying not to break down in tears.

Myoko was dead. Gretchen was dead. Oberon was dead.

Only ten minutes had passed since we left *Dainty Dinghy*.

The red-haired teenagers lumpishly hauled the coffin off the wagon and dragged it to the jolly-boat. They set down the coffin beside Gretchen; I suppose they thought Gretchen looked more dead than Myoko. Impervia immediately broke off her prayers. "This one," she said, pointing at Myoko. "This one first. Then the other."

"You want them in the same casket?" Victor asked.

"Of course not!"

"We only got the one casket," Vickie said. "Either we double up or somebody goes without."

"You'll get another casket." Impervia's voice was the hissing fuse on a bomb. "You'll put this woman in the casket you have and you'll get another casket for that woman there. You'll be quick about it and you'll handle them with respect."

"Here," I said, stepping forward. I had my trusty purse out and enough cash in hand that I hoped Vickie and Victor would shut their mouths. "This will cover your expenses. Just do what needs doing."

Vickie and Victor stared at the money a moment, then both reached to grab it. They had a three-second shoving match over which of them would take possession of the gold.

Under other circumstances, it might have been funny.

Impervia stomped away to the edge of the lake and stared out over the water. She kept her back turned as the teenagers picked up Myoko's body.

Pelinor drew me aside. "While Impervia was speaking with the undertaker," he said, "I arranged for a coach to Niagara Falls. There's no regular run scheduled, so, uhh, we'll have to pay extra."

I nodded; whatever the price was, I could cover it. Didn't I always pay for everything? I could afford the coach and the coffins as easily as I bought the first round of drinks whenever we went to a tavern.

(It occurred to me, we'd probably never go bar-crawling again. With Myoko gone, we couldn't bear the hollowness. We might even start avoiding each other.

(Nothing would ever be the same.)

Annah went with Vickie and Victor back to their wagon. She spoke with them quietly for several minutes. When she returned, she said, "The undertaker will hold all the bodies while we're in Niagara."

"And if we don't come back?"

"If we don't return in three days, they'll take the corpses to Gretchen's ship."

At which point, Zunctweed might throw Gretchen into the

lake—or worse. The spells that made slaves obey their owners didn't apply once the owner was dead . . . and I'd seen
slaves commit gross atrocities on their late owners' bodies.
Even slaves who seemed resigned to their lot might take
posthumous vengeance for years of indignity. Kicking, muti-
lating, attacking the corpse with any weapon they could find.
Then, after the savagery was over, they'd docilely report to
their owner's heir. Slavery spells didn't end with one owner's
death; they just took a brief holiday, then reasserted themselves with a new master.

I wondered whom Zunctweed would go to once he
learned Gretchen was dead. Maybe me. Sometimes when
Gretchen got into a huff, she'd threaten to leave me
Zunctweed in her will.

As if I didn't have enough problems.

18

BING BANG BOOM

We left Vickie and Victor moping over the impossibility of lifting Oberon's body into their cart. With all of us heaving, we might have been able to move his massive weight, but Impervia refused to let us try. She was furious with the world, and the undertaker's children were the most immediate targets for her wrath. "I saw how much Phil paid them," she told the others. "They can deal with this on their own."

Perhaps she just wanted to get moving again. Away from the beach and the corpses. With seething glares, she forced us to gather our gear and depart.

Leaving our dead friends in the less than capable hands of Vickie and Victor.

As we walked up the street into town, Pelinor gamely tried to fill the silence with overhearty remarks about our surroundings—"Pretty little sign on that store there, what's it supposed to be, a hammer do you think?"—but no one else responded to his efforts at conversation. That didn't stop him: Pelinor was the sort who handled his grief by talking trivialities.

I didn't mind his babble; it was better than empty quiet. No one else tried to shut him up either—not even Impervia. She was putting up a good front of being in control, but underneath . . . underneath, she was a deeply emotional woman who thought most emotions were sinful. Someday that inner conflict might rip her apart.

262

But not yet. Not yet.

So we trudged through Crystal Bay's central square. Along the way, we passed numerous tethered horses, all of whom received a "Good day," from Pelinor and comments on their hocks and withers. Local residents who saw us coming ducked into stores or side streets until we were gone. Considering Impervia's mood, I'd say people were smart to hide . . . but it was still unnerving to see our presence turn the place into a ghost town.

Therefore I was glad when we finally reached the stagecoach company. If you could dignify it with the name "company." Its meager excuse for an office was nothing more than a windowless shack in front of a stable. The stable was not much fancier—room for only one coach, and perhaps eight horses if they doubled up two to a stall.

Not what you'd call a big operation. Quite possibly, the stage ran only once a week, doing a circuit of nearby villages, then ending back at Crystal Bay. The rest of the time, the coach driver apparently served as the local blacksmith; a shed beside the stables had its door open to reveal an anvil and a furnace, neither of which were currently in use. In fact, there was no one in sight at all. The only promising sign was that the coach had been trundled out of its shed and hitched to a team of four, all of whom looked adequately strong and healthy.

Pelinor went off to talk to the horses while Impervia stuck her head into the office shack. "Empty," she reported. The glowering look on her face suggested dark suspicions—that the driver had absconded with our down payment, that he was hiding and ready to ambush us, or perhaps that he'd been murdered by Ring agents—so it must have come as a letdown when a man emerged from a privy at the back of the yard, his trousers still half-undone.

"There you are!" he called, buttoning his pants with no great haste. "Hope I didn't keep you waiting, but my pa always said to empty the chutes before takin' folks on a drive."

He smiled as if we should be impressed by his father's acumen. That smile seemed to sum up the man: sunny, casual, and his idea of inspired advance planning was remem-

bering to visit the outhouse before leaving on a trip. Our driver (who introduced himself as Bing: "Fred Binghamton, but
my pa always went as Bing, and that's good enough for
me!") was nearly as dark as Impervia and almost twice as
muscular—he was, after all, a blacksmith—but he had none
of the holy sister's knife-edge aggression. Though he was
young (mid-twenties), Bing's face already had abundant
laugh lines; his eyes showed a permanent twinkle and he
moved with the contented slowness of a well-fed bear.

Bing obviously enjoyed life . . . and if his wits were less
than lightning-fast, his good nature had a contagious quality
we badly needed at that moment. It would be ridiculous to
say the sight of him cheered us up—that was impossible. But
Bing was so pleasantly *normal*, he served as a reminder that
the world contained more than grief. His smiling presence
eased a bit of the tension wrapped around my heart.

I couldn't help noticing his smile grew wider when he
looked Impervia's direction. He obviously liked what he saw,
and didn't mind anyone knowing. I doubt if he even recognized Impervia's tunic and trousers as nun's apparel—Magdalenes weren't often seen in backwaters like Crystal Bay,
and besides, Impervia's clothes were still clinging wet from
getting splashed. I could forgive Bing for ogling a nun; the
question was if *Impervia* could forgive him.

Several long seconds passed: Bing smiling broadly, the
rest of us holding our breaths to see what Impervia would do.
Slowly she lifted her hand . . . then, incredibly, she brushed it
through her snip-clipped hair as if trying to comb it into
some more orderly arrangement. A moment later, she
dropped her gaze; with her jet-dark skin it was impossible to
tell, but I would almost have said she was blushing.

I shook my head in amazement. Any other man on any
other day would have received a sharp-tongued reprimand;
Impervia might even slap his face. But today . . . grief affects
people unpredictably. I could have sworn Impervia was so
angry over Myoko's death, she'd lash out at anyone who
gave her the least excuse. Obviously, I'd been wrong. Maybe
she'd been ready to roar at Bing—to go through her usual

routine of instant hostility toward male attention—when suddenly, she just didn't have the heart. Not enough energy to work herself into a rage: especially not over someone as transparently harmless as Bing. I don't know if that's what actually went through Impervia's mind, but I could see the bottom had dropped out of her fury. Nothing left but that weak almost-feminine gesture of straightening her hair.

Her fire had turned to ashes. She looked exhausted.

Bing was not the sort whose smiles lengthened into leers. After only a moment more, he turned from Impervia and began talking pleasantly with Pelinor: explaining some nicety about the way the horses had been hooked to the coach. ("My pa made that harness; it's got special features.") When Bing bent over to point out some detail about the cinch under one horse's belly, Impervia's gaze flicked over to study him behind his back. As if he was a puzzle and a challenge.

But her eyes still looked tired.

I walked over to her. "How are you doing?" I asked.

She sighed. "Praying for strength."

"Really?"

"Really." She glanced my way, then back at Bing. "Nothing's ever simple, Phil. A few hours ago, I was so . . . *excited* . . . about going on a holy mission. Now Myoko's dead, and we haven't accomplished anything. Not yet, anyway. I, uhh . . . I regret how I felt. Excitement was naïve. Perhaps even a sin. Thinking that I'd *arrived* and would never have another silly little problem."

"What silly little problems do you have?"

Impervia nodded toward Bing. "When I see a man like that, the devil whispers in my ear. It's not lust—not much—but it would be so *uncomplicated* just to . . . you know. Fall into someone's arms right now. To let go. To have someone who would . . . oh, just to have someone. To live like other women. Marry or not, settle down or not, have children or not: I don't know what I'd do, but sometimes I look at a man who's simple and decent, and I think how much *easier* it would be. Just to be someone other than Sister Impervia."

She gave a weak snort. "Impervia. What a stupid name. I

chose it when I took vows at fifteen. Cocky little kid, sure I
was stronger than anything. Why on Earth would anyone let
a fifteen-year-old girl make such an important decision?"

"What's your real name?" I asked.

"It's . . ." She stopped suddenly. "My real name is Sister
Impervia. I'm praying for strength, Phil, remember?" She
stepped away from me, then yelled at the others, "Why are
you all just standing around? There's no time to lose!" She
stormed a few steps forward, then whirled back to glare at
me. "Quit lollygagging, you! Get into the coach. Now!"

Impervia still looked tired; but she also looked strong.

The ride to the Falls took three hours—cramped bumpy
hours, bouncing over OldTech roads whose potholes had
been patched with dirt rather than asphalt or gravel. The dirt
was now mud; the potholes were mudholes. Every time a
wheel hit one, the whole coach jolted.

Pelinor rode beside Bing on the driver's seat. No doubt
they spent the entire journey nattering about horses. I sat in
the carriage next to Annah, with Impervia directly opposite
me and the Caryatid on the other side. Every now and then
we'd hear Bing's booming laugh, roaring about something
Pelinor said . . . and I'd look across to see Impervia listening
keenly to the sound. If she wasn't careful, she might work
herself up into a bosom-heaving crush on the big man; but
then, Impervia was always careful, wasn't she?

Anyway, there were worse things than crushes. I thought
about that as I held Annah's hand. The coach was small
enough that we were pressed in tight on the narrow bench;
and for some reason, we held our hands down low at our
sides, as if trying to hide what we were doing. I'm sure Impervia and the Caryatid knew perfectly well that Annah and I
had covertly linked hands, but they pretended not to notice.
Mostly they were lost in their own thoughts. So was I. So was
Annah. Until some wincing moment when the memory of
some corpse surfaced in my brain (Myoko, Gretchen,
Oberon, Xavier, Rosalind, Hump, Dee-James), and I would
find myself desperately squeezing Annah's hand for reassurance. She would always squeeze back . . . and sometimes she

would fiercely squeeze on her own, as if some similar horror
had silently risen in her mind's eye.

But we didn't speak. None of us. We passed the hours staring out at the late afternoon. Damp fields of muck. Orchards
with bare branches. Less snow here than back in Simka,
more melt-water streaming through the ditches.

Early in the trip, we saw farmers mending fences or hauling the winter's crop of stones off their land; but as time went
on, the men and women we passed all seemed to have
stopped work for the day. They sat silently on rocks or stiles,
perhaps smoking pipes or holding half-empty wineskins in
their hands, perhaps just staring into nothingness as the sun
sank in the sky. Most nodded in our direction as we went
past—some as if they knew Bing, some with an air of vague
courtesy that suggested they would nod to anyone who entered their field of vision.

Shadows lengthened. Soon, the people we saw were more
likely to be walking home than just sitting: finished work,
finished their pipes and their wineskins, turning their backs
to the road and heading toward sturdy farmhouses.

As the sun touched the far horizon, the pavement under
our wheels became smoother—so abruptly that Impervia
stirred from her brooding and lifted her head as if sensing
some threat. The stillness of level asphalt. As Impervia
looked around warily, I said, "We must be getting close to
Niagara. The highway's been paved to impress the tourists."

Impervia relaxed—don't ask me why. I certainly didn't
feel relieved that we'd almost reached the Falls.

In red and gold twilight, we stopped at an inn called The Captured Peacock. Bing told us it lay on the outermost edge of
"Niffles": his name for the city and tourist area around the
Falls. ("Niffles" was spelled "Niagara Falls" but for some reason, Bing made gagging sounds when anyone pronounced the
name in full. I couldn't tell if saying "Niagara Falls" proved
you were an ignorant tourist, or if "Niffles" was a disdainful
nickname by which Crystal Bay folk belittled their big-city
neighbors. Another of those regional rivalry things.)

Bing said he was happy to drive us all the way downtown,

but first he wanted to rest the horses—maybe give them some water and feed. No one objected to the break. After hours in the coach, we were glad to stretch our legs, visit the privy, get some supper. We also realized there was no point proceeding until we'd formulated a plan. Niffles was a huge city: 30,000 permanent residents plus heaven knew how many tourists. Finding Sebastian and Jode wouldn't be easy . . . unless Dreamsinger had already tracked them down, in which case we could just look for the big patch of smoldering rubble.

So while Bing dealt with the horses, the rest of us trooped into The Captured Peacock (ducking under a lurid sign that showed such a bird with golden ropes tied around his neck: teardrops ran from his eyes, but his tail was raised in full display, as if he were weeping bitterly at being snared, yet still boyishly eager to impress any passing pea-hens). I couldn't help recalling I'd entered a similar drinking establishment at almost exactly the same time twenty-four hours earlier: The Pot of Gold in Simka, where we'd joked about quests and faced nothing more serious than drunken fishermen.

Now everything was different. Annah was here. Myoko wasn't. And no one would ever again tease me about Gretchen, or even mention her name in my hearing.

Yesterday. More distant than the farthest star.

The Captured Peacock's interior was slightly bigger, slightly brighter, and slightly less rancid than The Pot of Gold. Actual pictures hung on the wall—watercolor washes over black-ink renderings of the Falls from various angles, probably created by some teenager whom everyone said was "marvelously gifted." But the place was still just a big room with a bar at one end and hard-to-break furniture everywhere else. Without having to speak, we instinctively headed toward a table just past the end of the bar: out of the flow of traffic, but close enough that one could holler drink orders directly to the tapman. We'd sat in the same position at The Pot of Gold . . . and at every other dive we visited.

The tapman nodded amicably as we walked by: a diminutive fellow with a profuse busby of a beard as compensation for his shortfalls in height and weight. "Evening," he said in a surprisingly deep voice. "What can I get ya? Nice chicken stew tonight."

"Then bowls of stew all around," Pelinor said. "And four ales, one tea." Our usual beverage order. Except that we now had Annah instead of Myoko. Pelinor realized this a moment too late; he blustered an apology through his mustache and asked what she wanted.

"Tea is fine," Annah said.

"Three ales, two teas," Pelinor told the tapman. A trivial change, but it started the Caryatid crying. I knew how she felt.

While waiting for food and drink, we talked about finding Sebastian. What he might be up to . . . besides getting wed to an alien shapeshifter. With Myoko gone, I was the only one present who knew the boy in any depth; and I'd obviously missed a lot, because I hadn't known about his psionic powers or his relationship with Rosalind. Still, I'd talked with him many times—at meals and casual "snack-ins" where I'd invite three or four of my boys into my suite to eat cookies, drink apple juice, and chat. No teenager ever confides totally in an adult, especially not a shy and private boy like Sebastian; but I'd got to know him better than most people did, and that would have to suffice.

"What did he intend to do?" Impervia asked. "What was his plan?"

"Plan?" I laughed. "Sebastian wouldn't have a plan; he was just a dreamy-eyed kid. He'd never consider writing ahead for reservations or setting up a wedding in advance—that would have forced him to set an elopement date weeks before it happened, then send out letters, wait for replies . . ." I shook my head. "He'd see that as far too cold-blooded. Sebastian didn't believe anything could be sincere unless it was spontaneous."

"Rosalind was the same," Annah said. "Filled with romantic ideals of how people should behave when they were in love. If she and Sebastian decided to elope, they'd want to do it right away. *Let's go tonight* or *Let's go this weekend*—not

Let's go three weeks from now so we've got time to book a nice room."

"And," I added, "I doubt if Rosalind and Sebastian ever *had* planned ahead. Rosalind's life was run by her mother; the girl couldn't schedule anything in advance, because she never knew when she'd be whisked off to another continent. As for Sebastian, why would he have to think ahead when his powers kept him out of trouble? I didn't know about his powers till Myoko told me, but when I think over things the boy told me about his past . . . well, consider this: how did he get chosen for a full scholarship to Feliss Academy? He's not the energetic go-getter we usually look for in local kids, but Opal immediately signed him up. Was she influenced by his powers? I don't know. But the scholarship was certainly a lucky break for a boy who wouldn't usually have been chosen." I shrugged. "Good things have a way of falling into Sebastian's lap, and he's come to depend on that. He likely had no idea what he'd do when he got to Niagara Falls—he just assumed things would work out. Get married, get a honeymoon suite, no problem."

"And what about the creature he's with?" Pelinor asked. "We're agreed it's a Lucifer, like in Opal's story?"

He was looking at Impervia. She gave a little sniff. "That's the most likely conclusion . . . which means there's no point debating what Sebastian and the real Rosalind would have done. This monster, Jode, won't stick to any preexisting script. It has its own agenda and it will manipulate Sebastian to further its goals."

"Lucky for us," I said, "Jode can't directly force Sebastian to do anything. According to Myoko, the boy's powers kick in automatically when he's threatened . . . so if Jode tries to hurt Sebastian, the result will be baked shapeshifter."

Pelinor sucked on his mustache. "No need for Jode to use violence. The creature looks like Rosalind; surely it can coax the boy into just about anything."

"Yes and no," I said. "Sebastian is a decent kid. He won't commit outright mayhem just because Rosalind asks pretty please. If Jode wants Sebastian to do something extreme, the boy will have to be tricked."

Impervia gave a disdainful sniff. "How hard is it to trick a sixteen-year-old?"

Before anyone could answer, our supper arrived: ale, tea, and five bowls of stew, brought from the kitchen by a tall woman in her twenties whose hair had already gone gray. The gray didn't seem to have come from stress—the woman appeared as relaxed and self-assured as a pampered house-cat. After she'd passed around the bowls, she gave us an easy smile. "Anything else youse wanted?"

"Information," Impervia said. "Has anything unusual happened here in the past day?"

"No, sister, it's been some quiet. You're the first folks who weren't regulars."

"I wasn't asking about your tavern," Impervia said, making an obvious effort not to sound snippish. "Niagara Falls in general. Anything notable? Fires? Fights? Sorcerous explosions?"

"Oh, sister, nothing like that ever happens in Niffles."

Under her breath, the Caryatid said, "The night's still young."

The five of us ate in silence. I can't tell you if the stew was good, bad, or bland—the food made no impression because my mind was elsewhere, trying to reconstruct Sebastian's movements over the past day.

Sebastian and Jode caught a ride on the fishing boat *Hoosegow. Hoosegow* left Dover at 11:05 P.M. It would take at least ten hours to reach Crystal Bay or one of the other harbors on the Niagara frontier . . . possibly longer, since *Hoosegow* wasn't built for speed. Therefore our quarry landed no earlier than nine or ten in the morning—after which, they had to find overland passage from the lakeshore to Niagara Falls. That trip was another three hours.

So Sebastian and Jode reached "Niffles" no earlier than noon . . . and I was inclined to add a few hours onto the calculation, considering their boat was slow and they might have trouble arranging coach transport. No driver would be eager to make a special run into Niagara Falls for two teenagers who were obviously eloping. The kids would need to pay a lot of cash to overcome such reticence. Jode might indeed *have* a lot of cash, either stolen from the real Rosalind or procured some other way—a shapeshifter wouldn't have much trouble filling its pockets at other people's expense. Even so, money didn't guarantee instant service; teenagers with overflowing purses might get hauled in by some town constable who wanted to know how they acquired so much loot.

Many delays possible. Unless Sebastian used his powers.

If the boy wanted, he could ask a trillion nanites to lift him into the sky and fly him wherever he wanted to go. He and Jode-Rosalind could have lofted themselves straight off the school grounds and across the continent. But as far as we knew, they'd traveled by conventional methods, horseback and *Hoosegow*. That suggested Sebastian preferred not to use psionics unless he had to . . . which made sense, considering how much Myoko must have badgered him to keep a low profile. She would have told gruesome stories of psychics who were discovered and enslaved because they took even a tiny liberty with their powers; and Myoko had a knack for putting the scare into teenagers. Sebastian would stringently avoid showing anyone what he could do.

So assume no use of psionics. In that case, the boy's best bet would be telling the truth (as he saw it): "My sweetheart and I are eloping to Niagara Falls and we've scraped together a little money by selling our belongings. Please, Mr. Coach Driver, can't you give us a ride? We'll pay you everything we can afford."

Given a line like that, a lot of drivers would hide a smile and say something on the order of "I've got chores to do first, but I've been meaning to head into Niffles for supplies I can't get here in town . . ."

Suppose Sebastian and Jode could reach Niagara Falls by mid-afternoon. That wasn't unreasonable. Then what?

Sebastian would want to get married . . . and he could do that easily. When I'd visited Niagara on that class field trip, I'd seen a dozen chapels within ten minutes' walk of the Falls—Buddhist, Jewish, Magdalene, New Grace, Marymarch, Taozen, The Hundred, and several more. If those didn't suit Sebastian's taste, there were secular wedding halls too; I remembered one with a sign SINGLES IN, COUPLES OUT, HITCHED IN HALF AN HOUR OR YOUR MONEY BACK!

The boy would have no trouble tying the knot. Nor would he have difficulty finding a honeymoon suite immediately thereafter. Late winter/early spring must be a slow season for hotels—there'd be vacancies all over town, and whatever Sebastian's price range, he'd find plenty of rooms he could afford.

Then what?

Then Jode would let the boy consummate the marriage. I didn't want to dwell on that thought . . . but what else could Jode do? The demon had to play its role as Rosalind, at least in the short term. Eager fiancée; beaming bride; glowingly fulfilled newlywed. Jode had to go along.

After which . . .

Jode would say, "Oh darling, let's go see the sights."

"Oh darling, I've got a surprise for you."

"Oh darling, someone said there's something interesting to visit over here."

Jode would invent an excuse to get Sebastian . . . where? To have him do what?

Whatever it was, it wouldn't be long now. If Sebastian and Jode had arrived in town mid-afternoon, they'd take an hour or two or three to wallow in connubial bliss.

That would get them to nightfall. And whatever skullduggery Jode intended, the Lucifer would probably prefer to do it after dark.

I looked out the tavern's west window and saw the sky washed with red fading into purple. The sun had fully set. Alien Jode would soon make its move.

There was another window to the north, this one looking out on the city. As I watched, a streetlight came on. Then another. Then another and another. Some were mercury blue, others sodium orange.

OldTech electric lights. Powered by the hydro-electric station that tapped energy from thousands of tons of falling water. A station tended by the Holy Lightning, but secretly supported by the Sparks.

The tavern door swung open and Bing entered, shuffling

his feet to scrape mud off his boots. "You folks decided where you want to go?"

"No," said Impervia.

"Not a clue," said Pelinor.

"Not a *fucking* clue," said the Caryatid under her breath.

"I know where they're going," I said.

The others turned to me in surprise.

The target had to be the generating station. Nothing else fit.

If the Sparks supported the station, they didn't do it from blissful generosity; they must be using the power for purposes of their own. And the Falls gave them *prodigious* amounts of power—at one time, Niagara's electrical grid supplied energy to millions of people. Millions of *OldTech* people, with all their refrigerators, stoves, and computers (not to mention factories, office towers, and neon-bright casinos). Now the generators supplied only Niffles itself . . . and the power lines didn't even reach the city's outskirts, as evidenced by The Captured Peacock's kerosene lanterns.

So: enormous generating plant, minuscule public consumption. Where was the rest of the energy going? How was it being used?

I didn't know. But Dreamsinger did. And when she realized Sebastian had the psionic potential to threaten the generators, the Sorcery-Lord took off like a firecracker. Now she'd be guarding the power station; and if Sebastian or Jode got near the place, they'd both end up as sorcerous shish-kebab.

Or would they? Why did I think Dreamsinger would be victorious, given that Sebastian had top-notch psychic abilities and Jode had already killed one Spark? It wasn't at all certain the Sorcery-Lord would win. Then again, Dreamsinger *had* the advantage of twelve hours to prepare a defense, building on whatever fortifications the power station already possessed. (You could bet if the station was truly vital to the Sparks, they'd have done their best to make it impregnable.) Dreamsinger also knew she was dealing with a Lucifer; she wouldn't be taken by surprise like her unlucky brother. And even if the Sorcery-Lord got defeated, it didn't mean Sebastian was safe—Spark Royal would then cry vengeance, and *no one* could win a fight against the entire Spark family (plus the League of Peoples backing them).

So to save Sebastian, we had to reach the power plant ahead of him. Intercept the boy before he came into Dreamsinger's sights. We'd then have to persuade him his bride wasn't the real Rosalind . . . after which we'd thrash the Lucifer, take Sebastian home, and pray the whole thing would blow over.

Sure. Simple.

On the other hand, if I hadn't been in Niffles risking my life, I'd be home in my stifling don's suite, marking geometry tests and bemoaning how little I'd made of my intellectual potential.

Was tedium better than facing death? I honestly couldn't tell. Someone else in my position might suddenly realize geometry tests weren't so bad after all. Others might say, "Compared to being a teacher, I'd rather fight alien shapeshifters any day!"

But I couldn't say which I feared more—which I *hated* more. Quests or tests. Death or monotony.

So it's come to this. And hasn't it been a long way down.

19

THE MUSIC THAT REMAINS

Supper was finished. Darkness had fallen. Outside The Captured Peacock, we waited for Bing to fetch the coach.

Pelinor and the Caryatid huddled together, talking in low voices. Impervia paced back and forth some distance away, surrounding herself with the air of someone who didn't want her solitude interrupted. Annah stood by my elbow, close but not touching.

Silent. Breathing the cool night air.

Stars had begun to appear, plus a few satellites tracking brightly across the blackness at speeds faster than any natural body. Most of the satellites were abandoned and defunct—OldTech derelicts waiting for their orbits to decay—but I wondered if some of those eyes-on-high belonged to Spark Royal: relay stations for ghost-smoke tubes that carried the Lords anywhere on the planet.

Trust the Sparks to have their own private satellites while the rest of Earth couldn't even re-create the Industrial Revolution.

Annah nudged my arm. "What are you looking at?"

"Oh, just the stars."

"Making a wish?"

"One wish isn't enough. We need at least a dozen if we hope to see the dawn."

"Or we could just go home."

I turned toward her, but she'd focused her eyes on the stars

276

and the dark. "Haven't we been through this?" I asked. "Didn't we decide to drink life to the lees?"

"I've been thinking of other ways you and I could do that. Besides dying."

She looked up at me, eyes white in her dark face. I could see she wanted to kiss me; and I wanted to kiss her. Strange that neither of us made a move.

"I've been thinking of such things too," I said. "But if we just ran off and found a honeymoon suite instead of sticking with our friends . . ."

She nodded. *"I could not love thee, dear, so much, lov'd I not honor more."*

"All these years," I said, "and I never knew you liked quoting poetry."

"I don't, really." She laughed. "I suppose it's because we're on a quest. Poetry just springs to the lips."

The word "lips" made me want to kiss her again. But I didn't. "This isn't a quest," I said. "It's real."

"The best quests *are* real. Isn't that the point? Myths are everyday life in disguise. Slaying the Jabberwock means facing your *own* monsters; searching for the Holy Grail means pursuing some goal you've previously shied away from. But it would be sappy to say that in so many words. That's why poets sing about battling gigantic beasts instead of fending off boredom. And why they sing about finding the Holy Grail rather than . . . oh, the things you can get only when you give up the nonsense that holds you back."

"What kind of nonsense?" I asked.

"Habits. Inhibitions. A flawed self-image." Annah's eyes glistened. "You know what I'm talking about, Phil."

"I do indeed." I still didn't kiss her. "When I get rid of those, that's when I find the Holy Grail?"

"When you get rid of those, the Holy Grail finds you." She let out her breath, as if she'd been holding it. "Or so the poets say. Grails can be awfully damned slow in getting the message."

She took my face in her hands and pulled me down to her mouth.

* * *

When Bing arrived with the coach, everyone piled inside without a word—even Pelinor, who'd decided to forego the driver's seat. Supposedly, he was sitting with us so we could talk "strategy" . . . but I couldn't help noticing how close he tucked himself against the Caryatid. Not just due to the narrowness of the bench. Annah had obviously been right about the Caryatid and Pelinor; with danger soon approaching, they didn't want to be apart.

But they didn't indulge in any last-minute whispering. No one did. Nor any talk of strategy. We all gazed wordlessly out the windows into the dark, like soldiers withdrawing into themselves before the call to arms.

Five minutes after we left The Captured Peacock, we reached the first of the city streetlights: a garish silver-blue bulb on an OldTech lamp standard that tilted fifteen degrees to the right. The pole's concrete support had tipped sideways over the past four centuries, and no one had bothered to correct the slippage. As the horses clopped past, I thought the slanted pole was a perfect symbol of our modern age. Some Keeper of Holy Lightning had worked long hours to construct the lightbulb by hand, yet had ignored the less complicated job of straightening the pole. Why? Perhaps because making the bulb seemed important and special, while straightening a pole wouldn't impress anyone. Or perhaps because the Keeper thought making lightbulbs was his job and straightening poles wasn't.

There were other lamp standards on the road into town—all tilted, some badly—but only one in four was actually lit. I wondered if the Keepers couldn't make enough bulbs or if they'd decided our modern eyes didn't need as much illumination as the OldTechs had. We're far more accustomed to darkness than our spoiled ancestors; they were obsessed with expelling shadows. If they had to live by candlelight the way we do, they'd soon fall to pieces: trembling at the dark beyond the door. They'd probably see this roadway as poorly lit and creepy . . . whereas the truth was we had ample illumination to keep our horses on the straight and narrow, so why did we need more?

Even so, we *got* more. Five minutes later, we reached a stretch of road where every *third* streetlamp was lit instead of every fourth. The poles were straighter too. Most houses on the block showed nothing but the flicker of candles or the glow of an open hearth, but one or two displayed a single electric bulb burning with conspicuous wattage: in an uncurtained window or as a bright glow behind a vividly colored blind. I suspected these families owned only one lightbulb which they carried from room to room as needed . . . but at least they *had* the bulb, and they wanted their neighbors to know.

Another five minutes closer to downtown, and the true gaudy-show began. There were bulbs in every streetlamp now . . . and ahead of us, giant hotel towers with artificial light shining from every aperture. A dazzling electrical showcase.

Newlyweds would surely talk about the spectacle for months when they returned to whatever village they called home. Flashing marquees. Bulbs in yellow and crimson. Casinos always bright as the sun, even at midnight. And when a bulb burned out, it was sent to the nearest souvenir shop and sold to some goober who'd take it home to tell his friends, "You should have seen this when it was alive."

At every hotel, music played from electric speakers mounted over the sidewalk—sometimes amplifications of live performances, sometimes recordings from OldTech times. The OldTech music was always unpleasant, discordant noise . . . not because the OldTechs had wretched musical taste, but because the truly *good* selections had disintegrated long ago: tapes and disks and platters got played so often they literally fell apart. The only usable records left were the ones so bad nobody had played them while palatable music still worked—tuneless, rhythmless crap with self-important lyrics, just plain embarrassing four centuries after the fact.

It didn't matter. Hotels had to play the ugly noise to prove they had electricity. And they'd play it long and loud, till the tapes tore, the disks cracked, and the ridges on the platters wore down flat as glass. People congregating on the side-

walks would listen to this garbage as attentively as they once
listened to much better—marveling at these sounds from the
past, and believing they were hearing the heartbeat of
OldTech spirit—when in fact, they were wasting their time
with drab dingy ditties that had survived only because they
were unlikable.

The horses snorted and shuddered as they clopped past.
Animals are always good critics.

The ruckus didn't fade—the clamor of bad music, plus people walking and talking, carriages rattling, the evening more
busy than daylight—but all lesser noises gradually submerged beneath a greater thunder: hundreds of tons of water
plunging every second into a deep echoing gorge. A roaring
rumble that put the pathetic music to shame.

The Falls.

There were two separate cataracts, but the largest by far
was the one coming into sight outside the coach's windows:
Horseshoe Falls, a great pouring arc whose sheets of water
were illuminated by searchlights mounted along the walls of
the gorge. The lights were tinted (green, gold, blue), projecting through the perpetual mist to shine on the Falls themselves. Despite the chill of the evening, dozens of couples
lined the rail along the gorge, gaping at the display as their
clothes grew wet from spray.

I glanced at my companions and was glad to see them staring in wonder too—even Impervia, who tried to remain un-
moved by anything others found impressive. The water, the
light, the roar: it's easy to be cynical from a distance, but not
when you're right there, peering through darkness at one of
the marvels of our planet. There are taller falls in the world
and wider ones, cascades that pour more water per second or
glisten more brightly in the sunlight . . . but there's no other
place where natural grandeur presents such a perfect view.

We passed in silence, craning our necks to keep the
panorama in sight as long as possible—all along the road that
rimmed the gorge, until we finally came level with the edge
of the Falls and lost sight of the cataract at the point of maximum thunder and spray.

When we turned our heads back to the road, the generating station lay in front of us.

The station was *old*: covered with so many snarls of vines the concrete beneath was barely visible, even in leafless winter. Perhaps the vines held the building together; four hundred years of wind and snow had been shut out by tendrils that bulged like varicose veins. The Keepers of Holy Lightning made no effort to cut back the growth—crisscrossing strands of vegetation even covered the stone steps leading up to the front entrance. The only break was a bare patch down the middle. During my last visit to the Falls, I'd been told that the path was worn clear by the feet of the single acolyte who went out daily to deliver lightbulbs and other electrical goods to the citizens of Niagara.

I could see no other entrance . . . which was strange, given that OldTech safety regulations had demanded multiple exits in case of fire. Somewhere under all those vines, there'd be enough emergency doors to evacuate an immense building like this—three stories tall, a hundred meters long—but everything was roped shut by the wiry green strands woven tight through the centuries.

One way in, one way out: like a fortress. Which it was.

The OldTechs had built the station into the side of a hill overlooking the gorge. With its back underground and its front facing the Niagara River, the station could be approached only along the narrow strip of road running between the hill and the edge of the gorge. Even the OldTechs didn't want the plant easy to attack; this was, after all, the power source for millions of people, and it demanded appropriate security. When the Keepers took over, protective measures must have become even more important: the station would be an inviting target for thieves (trying to snatch expensive electric merchandise), extortionists (threatening to wreck the generators unless a ransom was paid), religious fanatics (raging that the last vestiges of OldTech society had to be destroyed or else God would never allow Earth to become a new Eden), and enemy saboteurs (looking to hit Feliss in the pocketbook by disrupting the profitable Niagara tourist trade).

For all these reasons, the Holy Lightning stayed locked behind fortified doors. The Keepers lived inside and seldom came out. I had no idea how they recruited new members; but I'd met numerous antisocial gadget-lovers at university who wouldn't mind a life of seclusion if they got to play with high-tech toys. Even now, as doom hovered over the station, the Keepers were probably fiddling with electric contraptions, following OldTech schematics or perhaps designing devices of their own . . .

Except: there were no lights on inside.

The building had plenty of windows, all partly covered by vines . . . but the tendrils couldn't encroach on slick glass the way they grew across rough concrete walls. If there'd been lights on anywhere within, some glimmer would have worked its way out. Yet the place was completely dark. Behind us, the streetlights still beamed their mercury blue and the garish hotels denied the night; but the power station didn't show so much as a candle.

The coach stopped and Bing leapt down from the driver's seat. "That's the place," he called. "But if you ask me, it's closed till morning."

"Looks that way," the Caryatid agreed. She opened the coach door and accepted Bing's hand for help getting out. "Then again, there may be plenty of people inside—just not on the main floors. Phil, aren't the generators underground?"

I nodded. If I understood the set-up, water was diverted above the Falls and sent through large sluice-pipes, funneled down to rotate turbines in the guts of the station. After the water had given up its energy, it was released back into the river some distance below the Falls. For maximum power generation, the turbines had to sit at the bottom of the drop, where the plunging water had built up the most energy . . . so even though the entrance to the building was level with the top of the gorge, the machine-works were far below us.

Still, there should be *somebody* on watch up here. Even if the majority of the Keepers spent their time in the subterranean generator area, they'd post guards on the door.

Yet the entrance was pitch-dark.

"This has the whiff of an ambush," said Pelinor. "Lights off, nobody home, one door with a single obvious path leading to it . . . if this *isn't* a trap, I'll be disappointed."

"Meanwhile," the Caryatid muttered, "we're standing backlit by streetlamps on a narrow road with the gorge behind us. A golden opportunity for someone to start shooting."

"Shooting?" Bing said. "With guns? But that would scare the horses."

"Then you'd better go," Impervia said immediately. "Thanks for your help, but it's time you went home."

"You don't need a ride back to Crystal Bay?" He looked at Impervia with hurt in his eyes—as if he didn't want to be sent away just yet. "I mean . . . you'll have to head for the bay eventually. Your ship's still there."

Impervia dropped her gaze for an instant, then forced herself to look Bing in the eye. "Getting back to our ship is the least of our worries. Now you'd better leave before things turn dangerous. Otherwise . . ." She paused. "Otherwise, the horses might get hurt."

She'd found the right argument to get Bing to leave. He gave her a regretful look, then swung himself up to the driver's seat.

"I'll be spending the night at the Peacock," he said. "'Tisn't good to drive country roads in the dark this time of year. If you're in need of transport, I'll still be around come morning."

"Let's hope we will be too," Impervia told him. "On your way now."

She reached up, and for a moment I thought she would pat Bing on the thigh . . . but she shifted her hand at the last moment and touched the seat instead: resting her fingertips lightly on the padded bench, letting them linger for a moment before drawing back. "Go," she said. "Thanks again."

"No trouble," Bing answered. "You have a good night."

"You too."

Bing gave the reins a flick and the horses started forward. Impervia stared after the coach until it disappeared around a bend in the road.

* * *

"At least it's quiet," the Caryatid said. "No sign that there's been a battle. I think we've got here before Sebastian."

The Caryatid's voice sounded unnaturally loud—as if she were shouting, though she was only speaking normally. Impervia must have sensed the same odd loudness because she answered in almost a whisper. "It's a pity we don't have Myoko. She could have given the door a telekinetic nudge, just to see what happens."

"We don't *want* to see what happens," I said. My voice sounded loud too. "We don't want anyone to know we're out here," I whispered. "We just intercept Sebastian and leave before Dreamsinger notices us."

"Still," said Pelinor, "it would be interesting to scout their defenses, don't you think? We could throw a stone . . ."

"No!" shouted the rest of us in unison.

The word echoed off the power station's cement walls and drifted into the night. It took a long time to fade. The world had gone silent—uncannily so. Some important sound was missing . . .

"Merciful God," I breathed. Whirling around, I ran to the edge of the road and looked down into the gorge.

Bare rock glistened in the spill from the streetlamps. Water languished in dozens of pools, and a small stream ran through a channel down the middle of the river bed . . . but the roar was gone. The spray had settled. The colored spotlights danced for the tourists across a cliff-face that had never been exposed to open air.

I realized why our voices all seemed so loud—why the world had gone so quiet.

Someone had turned off the Falls.

20

A CATARACT OF SAND

The others joined me at the railing, everyone looking at where the Falls should have been.

"Damn," whispered the Caryatid. "There's something you don't see every day."

Across the gorge, on the Rustland side of the Falls, people were already clambering over the safety barriers and down onto the rocks where the river was supposed to be. Idiotic bravado—I suppose they wanted to be able to tell their friends they'd walked across Niagara Falls. As soon as those people ventured onto the river bed, the natural perversity of the universe should have sent the water sweeping back in a solid wall of crashing froth. But no such torrent appeared . . . even when a teenage boy reached the weak brook trickling down the middle and sloshed about in the current, laughing to his friends.

Pelinor said, "Oh, look. Where did the water go?"

He turned to me for an answer. Pelinor always believed that because I was a scientist, I could explain anything. "Umm," I said. "Uhh. Hmm. The only thing I can think of is that the entire river is being diverted into the power station. There are sluices upstream to take in water and pipe it through the generators. I didn't think they had the capacity to siphon up the whole river, but if Dreamsinger really wants to maximize electrical production—"

"Phil," Annah interrupted, "there's another explanation."

She was peering upstream, shading her eyes from the nearby streetlamps. The river in that direction was mostly dark: a bridge extended from the Rustland side to an island in the middle of the rapids (or where the rapids should have been), but beyond the shine of the bridge-lights, the river disappeared into blackness. *Deep* blackness. "I can't see anything," I said.

"Neither can I," Annah replied. "It's not normal shadow. It looks like a wall."

"A wall?" I squinted again. Utter blackness covered the river beyond the bridge; but when I looked to the sides of the waterway, I could see vague outlines of buildings, streets, trees: normal things in normal darkness, not utterly swallowed by oblivion.

I shifted my gaze back to the river and moved my eyes slowly upward. Black, black, black . . . then suddenly stars. As I watched, a drifting tatter of cloud disappeared out of sight behind the blackness—occluded by that dark impenetrability.

Someone had lowered a curtain of blackness onto the Niagara River. A wall indeed. Or more precisely, a dam.

By now the others had seen it too. "What is it?" Pelinor whispered.

A trillion trillion nanites, I thought. A vast barrier of them, clustered together to clamp off incoming flow. "It's a dam," I said. "Blocking the river. I'll bet you anything it's positioned to cut off the power plant's intake sluices." When Pelinor looked at me blankly, I told him, "The generators need water to make electricity. That dam blocks the water . . . thereby shutting down the generators."

Beside Pelinor, the Caryatid's face had turned grave. "So the Sparks can't produce electricity. Whatever they use it for will stop working." Her hands gripped the guard rail tightly, as if she wanted to crush the metal in her fingers. "For some reason, I keep picturing a thousand shapeshifters like Jode held captive in an electric cage. The Sparks lock Lucifers there whenever they catch one . . . and the Keepers of Holy Lightning maintain the generator turbines to make sure the power never goes out. Is that possible, Phil?"

"An electric cage?" I thought about it . . . and I recalled the violet glow surrounding Dreamsinger's armor: a vicious energy barrier that could melt bullets. The armor's force field kept things out, but the same technology could surely lock captives in. "It's very possible," I said. "Is this just some scary notion that popped into your head? Or is it another sort of a prophecy kind of thing?"

"I don't know." The Caryatid's voice was weak and distant. "It's not my usual kind of premonition . . . but the image won't go away."

Pelinor took her hand and patted it. The rest of us averted our eyes to give them some privacy. Impervia muttered to Annah and me, "Much as I respect the Caryatid's premonitions, I have my doubts about this one. Spark Royal doesn't jail its enemies; it executes them. Keeping Lucifers alive is foolish, no matter how carefully you lock them up."

"But maybe," I said, "Spark Royal needs Lucifers for something. Or maybe the Sparks' alien masters don't want the Lucifers killed. If so, you couldn't keep a shapeshifter in a normal prison—you'd *have* to build some kind of energy confinement field."

"And everything else," murmured Annah, "the lights and music in this city—it's just a cover. The Sparks realized they couldn't keep the power station a secret: local people would know the place was in use. If nothing else, the intake sluices and outflow pipes must need maintenance from time to time; and you can't hide a bunch of workers playing around with giant underground plumbing. The Sparks pump a small ration of power to the public so people think they know what the generators are doing. But the real purpose of this station is to imprison Lucifers."

"Except," I said, "now the river is shut off." I waved toward the nearest streetlamp, still bright and undimmed. "There'll be power until the plant uses up the water in the intake pipes. Beyond that . . . if the Sparks are smart, their electric cage has emergency batteries to deal with a short power outage; but if the cage normally soaks up most of the energy from Niagara, it's going to burn out its batteries fast. Then the Lucifers will escape, and there'll be hell to pay."

"And we know who created that blasted dam," Impervia muttered.

"Sebastian and Jode," Pelinor said.

I thought he was answering Impervia; but when I glanced his way, he was looking down the road that led back to the center of town.

Two figures were walking toward us: a teenage boy and girl.

They walked hand in hand—bare hands, no gloves or mittens. The air around Sebastian must have been warming itself for his comfort. As for Jode, the Lucifer didn't seem bothered by anything so paltry as a late-winter chill.

Jode looked exactly like Rosalind; and I found it disquieting to watch the girl cuddle up to Sebastian when I'd seen her corpse the previous night. Appalling how lively she appeared—more animated than I'd ever seen the real Rosalind. This version was laughing at something Sebastian said, slapping his arm in mock offense, then nuzzling and kissing his ear.

Nothing like the melancholy girl I'd known.

It amazed me Sebastian couldn't sense something wrong. Every gesture this Rosalind made seemed false: the touching, the giggling, the giddy flirtation. Jode was laying it on thick; yet Sebastian returned every kiss and whisper. No matter how strong he might be with psionics—powerful enough to stop Niagara Falls—Sebastian was nothing more than a sixteen-year-old who could be exploited by his hormones. Jode had wedded him, bedded him, then brought the boy to the power station before the post-nuptial euphoria wore off.

They hadn't noticed us yet. Our group looked no different from other tourist parties, staring blankly into the gorge and wondering where the Falls went. We were also bundled up in coats, hats, and scarves, which would make us difficult to recognize in the dark. Jode was watching for trouble—in between attentive pats and snuggles, the faux Rosalind found excuses to turn her head this way and that, keeping a constant lookout—but even the Lucifer couldn't have guessed how many forces had converged on Niagara: Dreamsinger, the

Ring of Knives, and of course, a small but determined band of teachers.

Not that we teachers amounted to much. We'd never even discussed a strategy for dealing with this situation. Violence certainly wouldn't work; if, for example, Impervia attacked Jode, Sebastian would immediately use his powers to protect his "Rosalind."

Our best hope was talking sense to the boy—and not just saying, "She isn't Rosalind." We had to prove Jode was evil.

A good place to start would be pointing out how destructive that big dam was. Whatever story Jode had invented, we could make Sebastian realize that his wall across the river would cause severe flooding. Upstream of the dam, water must be accumulating at a fearsome rate, spilling over the banks, deluging inhabited land. We had to make Sebastian care about the possibility of drowning people, animals, houses, farms; but at the moment, he was too busy kissing his beloved "Rosalind" to picture the consequences of what he'd done.

"I'll talk to Sebastian," I told the others in a low voice. "I know him best." I took a step toward the boy, but Pelinor grabbed my arm.

"Better let me do this," he said. "You're no fighter, Phil, and Jode might try some tricks."

"Then *I* should go," Impervia said.

Pelinor smiled. "Sorry, old girl, but you're not quite the right person for tactful discussion."

"And you *are* the right person?"

"I'm a knight," he said. "Fighting the foe and parlaying honorably. What I was born to do."

Without giving anyone else a chance to speak, he moved out into the roadway.

Pelinor planted himself directly in Sebastian's path. "Fine night, isn't it?" he said in a hearty voice. "Bit quiet all of a sudden."

Sebastian and Jode were ten paces away from the knight: twenty paces from the rest of us. The newlyweds stopped and stared; Sebastian just gaped, astonished that someone from the academy had tracked him down . . . but the Lucifer's eyes filled with hatred. Jode obviously knew who Pelinor was. As I'd suspected, the shapeshifter must have spied on our school, getting to know Sebastian and his teachers.

"We have to talk," Pelinor said. He kept his eyes on the boy, not even glancing at Jode. "Your girlfriend isn't—"

Jode screamed: drowning out the rest of Pelinor's words. The next moment the Lucifer hurtled forward—faster than the real Rosalind ever ran in her life. Metal flickered in the lamplight and I shouted, "Blade!" Jode had whipped out a sword from a sheath at its hip: a rapier, one of the weapons missing from the case in Sebastian's room. The weapon's point came up with inhuman speed, aiming for Pelinor's heart as the alien sprinted to close the gap.

If I'd been in Pelinor's place, I would have been skewered: caught flat-footed, numbly staring at the incoming blade. Even Pelinor didn't have time to draw a weapon of his own—but knight or border-guard, Pelinor was no stranger to sneak attacks. He twisted aside at the last instant, batting away the lethal tip of the rapier with his arm. Cloth ripped as the sword-point slit his coat-sleeve . . . but now he was inside the arc of the blade and relatively safe from being stabbed. The rapier was purely a piercing weapon, with no cutting edge to harm opponents close in.

Unfortunately, Jode *wanted* to be close in. Perhaps that had been Jode's plan—the Lucifer might have known Pelinor would evade the thrust and come within reach. Jode's body blocked Sebastian's view of its face; therefore, the boy didn't see the false Rosalind's features dissolve into a curdled white mess . . . as if the lips, the nose, the eyes, everything, had putrefied into maggots.

Pelinor grimaced with revulsion and retreated a step—still keeping up his arm to prevent a rapier strike, but distancing himself from the ooze of Jode's face. The Lucifer raised its other hand, the one not holding the sword . . . and I could see its fingers had been replaced by another mass of curds, a soft cream of white chunks. The gooey hand darted toward Pelinor's nose with a boxer's punch; but when Pelinor tried to deflect the blow, the alien's entire forearm spurted out of its coat-sleeve, like slime shot out of a hose.

It hit Pelinor full in the face: splashing across his cheeks and mustache, then flattening outward to cover every bit of exposed skin. Pelinor's hands came up, clawing in a frenzy to get the stuff off . . . but the fat moist chunks evaded his efforts, dodging from his grasp.

Beneath the damp white coating, Pelinor bellowed in anger and pain. The sound was muffled. Smothered. Choked.

Jode's puffy curd face quivered and refocused, once more shaping itself into the likeness of Rosalind. For a moment the alien leered at us as if to say, "You people are fools." Then it jumped backward, retreating enough that Sebastian finally got a view of Pelinor's scum-covered face. "I told you!" Jode said in Rosalind's voice. "It's not your teacher, it's a monster made by my mother's sorcerers. Just a bag of skin filled with pus. When I hit it, you see what happened. It went all *gooshy*."

Pelinor tried to object: to tell Sebastian the truth. The only noise that came out of his mouth was a suffocated mumble, broken off quickly . . . as if the curds had poured down his throat as soon as he opened his lips.

"Sebastian," I said, stepping forward, "you know who we are—"

"Don't listen, don't listen!" Jode-Rosalind screamed. "You can see they aren't real; they're just goo!" The Lucifer waved its sword toward Pelinor. It couldn't gesture with its other hand, because that hand was smeared across Pelinor's face—Jode's coat-sleeve dangled empty from the elbow down.

"Sebastian," I said again.

"Shut up!" the boy yelled. "Not another word or you're dead. Rosalind warned me her mother might try something like this . . . but it won't work. It *won't*."

"Yes," said Jode, smirking under Rosalind's face. "We're married now. Completely married." She waved the rapier in our direction. "My husband and I are going straight into Ring of Knives headquarters . . ." She gestured toward the generating station. ". . . and we're not going to let you *monsters* stop us from finding my mother. We're going to make her give us her blessing and promise to leave us alone."

"Ring of Knives headquarters?" Impervia said. "That's not—"

Jode cried, "You're talking. You were told not to talk. Sebastian, make it stop!"

Impervia flew off the ground, slammed back into the guard railing. For a moment, an invisible force threatened to throw her over the rail—propelling her out above the gorge until she plummeted to the rocks below. But the psionic shove ended as quickly as it began. Impervia slumped forward and dropped to her knees gasping. She was lucky she hadn't broken her spine when she hit the railing's metal bars . . . but she'd only had the wind knocked out of her.

"That was a warning," Sebastian said with exaggerated gruffness—a teenage boy, showing off his manliness for his sweetheart. "One more word, and you're gone." He glanced at Pelinor, now making strangled noises in his throat. "I know you aren't people; you're *things*. Stay out of our way and I'll leave you alone . . . but I won't let you keep us from confronting Rosalind's mother."

Jode smirked again, angling away from Sebastian so the boy wouldn't see. "Let's go," Jode said, sheathing its rapier. The Lucifer took Sebastian's arm with its good hand—the other sleeve was still half empty—and led him up the steps of the generating station.

If there were any booby-traps in the area, they didn't go off: Sebastian's nanite friends were on the job, deactivating trip-wires, defusing bombs. As the two reached the darkened entrance, Jode took a moment to look back at us all. The Lucifer's face was silently laughing.

Even before Sebastian and Jode disappeared into the station, the Caryatid was on the move: pulling a match from her pocket; striking it on the rusty metal guard rail; exerting her will to make the flame blossom as she hurried toward poor Pelinor. She could see there was no point just trying to scrape off the curds—Pelinor himself was raking his face with his fingers, but the curds had attached themselves as tight as lampreys. If Pelinor couldn't pluck them off, neither could the Caryatid . . . but fire might succeed where fingers failed.

Better to burn the man to blisters than let him suffocate in front of our eyes.

She reached Pelinor just as he toppled to his knees. Beneath the mask of curds, he was still making throaty noises; but they were growing more feeble and plaintive, no longer bellows but sobs. "Keep your head bent over," she said. "Lean forward so the stuff can't get down your throat."

I wanted to tell her the curds didn't just slide into his mouth by gravity—they crawled like hungry grubs wriggling toward his windpipe. Tilting Pelinor's head forward wouldn't stop them from climbing into his air passages. But this wasn't the time to distract the Caryatid with futile objections; she was concentrating hard on her match-flame, as if planting her entire consciousness into the tiny speck of fire. A moment later, the flame hopped off the match, touched down for an instant on Pelinor's shoulder, then plunged itself into the gelid morass on the man's face.

For a few seconds, I lost sight of the flame; its light dimmed and I heard a wet sizzle. The Caryatid made looping gestures with three fingers and muttered under her breath— one of the few times I'd ever seen her resort to actual abracadabra when commanding flame. The glow on Pelinor's face sputtered, then stabilized. More sizzling and hissing. A few curds fell burning to the roadway, spitting sparks as if they were comets. The choking in Pelinor's throat continued. An ugly gargle, its volume growing weaker.

The flame moved across Pelinor's face like the tip of a hot poker, selectively searing the largest patches of goo. The Caryatid had to crouch on hands and knees so she could see where to move the little fire . . . and even then, her control wasn't perfect. With a gush of smoke, Pelinor's mustache caught fire, blazing bright as it scorched the skin beneath. His lips blackened like charred wood; but neither he nor the Caryatid flinched.

Burned by the ignited mustache, more curds fell to the ground.

I'd been paying such close attention to Pelinor, I hadn't noticed Annah moving toward him. She appeared behind him now, kneeling to match his height and wrapping her arms around his stomach. Her gloved hands locked together at the level of his belt, then pulled in hard, scooping into his stomach: the OldTech maneuver to help choking victims, driving up into the diaphragm to force out air and clear the throat. I felt ashamed I hadn't thought to do it myself—inadequate Phil, still stupid in a crisis.

The push of wind up Pelinor's esophagus forced out a mouthful of maggoty white. I cringed as some of the spill fell on Annah, her arms still around Pelinor's stomach . . . but she was protected by her thick coat and gloves, the curds unable to reach her bare skin. I rushed to sweep the wet chunks away, brushing them off with my own gloves, wiping Pelinor's clothes too, then scraping myself free with a stone from the road. It seemed they couldn't lock onto our clothing— like leeches, they could attach themselves only to flesh.

Meanwhile, the Caryatid continued to singe off curds, raising a hideous stink of wet rot. She was doing her best to minimize damage to Pelinor's skin, but he was still a puckered red. Second-degree burns at least. His mustache was fully incinerated. The hair on his scalp had wizened to a crisp in a dozen places . . . and still the curds weren't gone. Gooey white oozed from Pelinor's nose and gleamed between his blistered lips—just like I'd seen on Rosalind.

Dead Rosalind.

Annah yanked up hard again, driving her joined hands into Pelinor's belly. More curds bulged out of his mouth; but they slithered back inside as soon as Annah released her squeeze. Again and again she went through the prescribed motion, scoop in, relax, scoop in, relax . . . but her very first compression had forced out as much gunk as she was going to get, and subsequent squeezes ejected no more. Pelinor's throat remained clogged—the blockage was too big to dislodge.

When Annah realized that, she let go of Pelinor and gestured at me. "You try." We traded positions and I jammed my hands into Pelinor's gut with every gram of strength I possessed. More curds squirted out of Pelinor's mouth . . . but not a titanic volley, just a coughing dribble. Not nearly enough to clear his windpipe.

I could picture a glistening mass of white clotted all the way down to his bronchial tubes. Each time I squeezed, the mass was pushed and the top part spilled into his mouth; but I couldn't crush in hard enough to push the whole squirming bulk out of his esophagus, and as soon as I let go, everything slid back down again.

"This isn't working," I said. "We have to think of something else."

"Get his mouth open," the Caryatid commanded.

Annah reached in to pull down Pelinor's jaw. Pelinor resisted, probably just out of instinct: by now, he couldn't have been thinking clearly. Beneath the flame-ravaged skin, his face had gone purple with suffocation; when I looked at the whites of his eyes, they were dotted with the same red petechiae pinpricks I'd seen on Rosalind's corpse. Tiny blood vessels burst by the exertion of trying to draw breath. Pelinor was straining so fiercely, I didn't think Annah could possibly get his mouth open—but a few seconds after she started to try, the rigidity slumped out of his body as he fell unconscious. Immediately, she flopped his jaw wide . . .

. . . and the Caryatid plunged the flame into his mouth.

The tiny ball of fire disappeared inside. From where I was kneeling, I couldn't see anything but a yellow-orange light shining out between his lips, the flame so bright it lit his cheeks from within. Smoke wisped out of his mouth and nose; I prayed it was only the ash of charred curds, but I was afraid some of the smoke came from Pelinor himself—his tongue and inner cheeks turning to cinder, maybe even the soft tissues of his throat. The Caryatid would be as cautious as possible, focusing the flame's heat only on the alien chunks that were filling Pelinor's air passages . . . but she was, after all, playing with fire, and it was Pelinor getting burned.

As the Caryatid worked, she talked in a voice I'd heard from time to time as I passed the door of her classroom. A teacher who reflexively explained everything she was doing, the way she'd talk students through a sorcery exercise. "I've started burning chunks of alien material in his mouth. The nuggets want to avoid the flame . . . they're crawling away from the heat . . . but after a few seconds' exposure, they stop moving and drop. Annah, could you sweep out the remains from the bottom of his mouth? Don't burn your glove on the flame. Good. Now"—she took a deep breath—"we'll start on the throat. Phil, I'll need you to squeeze his stomach. As tight as you can and don't let go. Do it."

I dug my grip into Pelinor's diaphragm. In my mind's eye, I imagined wet white nuggets being pushed up his esophagus into the flame. Burn, you bastards . . . every last one. More smoke billowed from Pelinor's mouth—rank-smelling stuff, like swamp rot. Annah swept out the dead debris. We were making progress.

As long as we didn't let ourselves think about what the flame was doing to Pelinor's windpipe.

Eventually, the Caryatid had to propel the fire so deep into Pelinor's throat she lost sight of it. I don't know if she lost control of the flame at that point; I don't know if she ever lost control at all. But even if she could direct the cauterizing heat wherever she wanted, she was operating blindly—as she looked into his mouth, all she could possibly see was a dim gleam shining past the blistered epiglottis. Yet she didn't dare reduce the strength of the flame, for fear it would gutter out amidst the moistness of the alien curds.

The end came quickly: a sudden eruption of blood from Pelinor's mouth, extinguishing the flame, splashing in torrents onto my hands where they were still wrapped around his abdomen. In the light of the streetlamps, the blood was bright red—arterial blood from the carotid. Inside Pelinor's neck, the Caryatid's flame had burned through the esophagus and seared into the major artery carrying blood to the brain. There was nothing we could do to stop the gusher; the rupture was deep down, out of sight, out of reach. Even if we could staunch the bleeding, pinch the artery shut, Pelinor's blood-starved brain would die within minutes.

So we watched the blood spill. Watched it gradually slow down. Watched Pelinor die in a pool of crimson and white.

* * *

By the time it was over, Impervia was kneeling on the roadway with the rest of us. Her breathing was ragged; being
thrown against the guard rail may have broken a few more
ribs. But she still had plenty of breath to say prayers for our
dying friend. Tears slid down her cheeks as she asked God to
have mercy on Pelinor, sword-sworn knight, Christ's
beloved son. A man fallen for a righteous cause, called to this
mission by heaven itself.

Impervia wasn't the only one weeping. Annah and I had
tears in our eyes . . . but the Caryatid's face was as hard as a
gravestone. I longed to tell her it wasn't her fault; if she
hadn't tried to burn away the curds, Pelinor would surely
have choked to death. What she'd done was the only chance
Pelinor had.

But my mouth refused to speak. None of us seemed able
to do more than mumble prayers. The look on the Caryatid's
face said she didn't want to hear anyone say, "You did your
best."

She waited only until Impervia said, "Amen." Then the
Caryatid stood up, wiping her hands (damp with Pelinor's
blood) on her crimson gown.

"We're going in now," she said. "We're going to burn that
demon in the fires of hell."

For a moment, nobody spoke. Then Impervia said again,
"Amen."

Together we headed up the steps of the generating station . . . and if any one of us looked back at Pelinor crumpled
in the roadway, it wasn't the Steel Caryatid.

21

THE SHAFT

The station's front door stood open—left that way by Jode or Sebastian. No bombs went off as we climbed the steps, no spikes shot out as we entered; whatever defenses might have been here, they'd been swept away by nanotech brooms.

The inner lobby was resplendent with carved marble: a massive alabaster reception desk, a wide ascending stairway behind it, doors going off in several directions. I recalled that the station had been built in the 1890s . . . a time when OldTech culture admired stolid geological décor, before tastes mutated to glass and steel and chrome. This room, this whole building, smelled of stone—stone kept damp by the perennial mist blowing off the Falls.

Not so perennial now.

All but one of the doors off the lobby were closed. The exception was immediately to our right, a door left ajar with dirty wet footprints leading up to it. If Jode and Sebastian (or their muddy boots) continued to leave such an obvious trail, we could track them all the way to the generators.

How convenient. Considering how flagrantly Jode had taunted us, did the shapeshifter *want* us to follow? Perhaps into a trap? If the Keepers of Holy Lightning had laid nasty surprises along the route to the subterranean machine room, Jode might persuade Sebastian to deactivate everything as they went through, then reactivate the devices behind them. But that didn't sound like Jode's style; I suspected the Lucifer liked to *see* the mayhem it caused. It wouldn't set a bomb unless it could watch the explosion.

In which case, our group might have clear sailing all the way to the generating room. Jode couldn't waste time tormenting us small fry. The Lucifer had more pressing priorities—perhaps, as the Caryatid suggested, freeing a group of its fellows from an electric cage—and Jode couldn't afford to dally before the mission was accomplished. After the jail break, then . . . then . . .

I had an unpleasant thought. What if Jode was deliberately making it easy for us to follow? What if Jode intended us to make it safely to the electric cage so some newly escaped Lucifers could use us as playthings? Or as lunch? I opened my mouth to suggest this to my companions . . . then changed my mind. The others knew we were walking into a trap—Dreamsinger's trap, Jode's trap, somebody's trap—and my friends weren't running away.

I wasn't running either. Not with Pelinor and Myoko dead. And when Impervia kicked open the door ahead of us, when the Caryatid sent a fist-size fireball flaming forward to light our way (and perhaps scorch the smile off anyone lurking on the other side) . . . I didn't wince at the commotion.

We were going in. All the way.

Down a short corridor to a pair of metal doors: two elevators, side by side. I'd read about elevators but I'd never seen one till the first time I visited Niagara. All the local hotels had them. Many visitors spent hours riding up and down; some people preferred the glassed-in variety that showed the world outside, while others liked the spooky chill of not being able to see, just moving blindly until the doors opened and you found yourself thirty stories higher than where you started.

The elevators before us were the closed-in type, traveling through pitch-dark shafts. I could tell this because one of the doors had been ripped from its frame, leaving nothing but a hole and a very long drop.

I peeped cautiously into the shaft, taking a good look up and down. No threats were immediately visible. Two bundles of cables dangled in front of me, one for each elevator car, side by side in the same shaft; but even with the Caryatid's fireball lighting our view, I couldn't see the cars themselves. I *could* see up to the top of the shafts, the lift mechanisms glowering in the shadows three stories above me . . . so neither car was on an upper floor. Both had to be in the blackness below.

When I thought about it, I decided the cars must be on the bottommost level; it made sense for the Keepers to lock the elevators down there so intruders would have a harder time reaching the generator room. Not that such tactics would slow down Sebastian—he'd ripped the one door open, and for all I knew, he'd summoned his nanite chums to carry him and "Rosalind" down the shaft, like feathers floating on the wind. Too bad our group couldn't do the same; but since none of us could fly, we needed a practical alternative.

On the far side of the elevator shaft, a ladder was embedded in the concrete, running as far as I could see both up and down—no doubt used by workers when the elevators needed maintenance. I didn't relish a climb down umpteen stories, with the very real possibility of running into booby-traps set by the Keepers . . . but what other choice did we have?

Impervia answered that question by jumping into the shaft and catching the nearest bundle of cables. The bundle had four cables side by side, all in a line with a fist's distance between adjacent ones . . . like four strings on a harp, except that the cables were each as thick as my arm. Impervia had no trouble grabbing two of the four with her hands and jamming her feet between adjacent pairs for extra support. The cables were taut but not totally unyielding; they pinched her boots with what looked like a strong (but not painful) squeeze.

"How is it?" the Caryatid called to Impervia. "Can you just slide down?"

Impervia freed her feet, loosened her grip, and tested to

see how far she slid. After only a few centimeters, she stopped and shook her head. "The wires aren't smooth—they're prickly with rust. If you tried to slide far, the friction would rip your gloves, then start on your fingers."

The Caryatid made a face. "Then I'll have to use the ladder. I'm not strong enough to clamber hand over hand down a few dozen stories."

"The ladder might not be safe," I said. "It's such an obvious way down, the Keepers might have booby-trapped it. A loose rung . . . a trip wire . . . there are lots of possibilities. But I don't think they could booby-trap the cables—too much chance of damaging the elevators."

"I can't manage the cables," the Caryatid replied. She held out her arms as if showing off her roly-poly little body. "I know my limitations; by God, I know my limitations. Even the ladder will be a challenge."

"Don't worry," Annah said. "I can climb down the cables ahead of everyone and check that the ladder's safe. I have a good eye for traps."

"You do?" The Caryatid looked dubious. So did Impervia.

"I, uhh . . . my family . . ." She stopped, glancing nervously in my direction.

"Your family is much like the Ring of Knives," I said. "In similar lines of business."

"You knew?"

"I guessed." I'd guessed from the way she'd talked about criminals after we found Rosalind's body. *I wish I didn't believe you—that there aren't people vicious enough to kill an innocent girl just to hurt her mother. But I know all too well* . . . How did she know all too well? And how had she acquired her uncanny knack for blending into darkness? Or her clever little mirror for seeing around corners? "You were a sort of Artful Dodger?" I asked.

Annah nodded. "It runs in the family. My Uncle Howdiri still claims to be the best thief ever to come out of Calcutta. Which is saying a great deal. I was raised in the same tradition and everyone said I was good . . . but I was also good at singing, and my father had ambitions of using me to become respectable. I was supposed to make myself the toast of the upper classes, then introduce my father into their circles. He had the money, he just didn't have the respect."

She gave a bitter laugh. "Like most social-climbers, my father was naïve. About gaining other people's acceptance. Also about the quality of my singing. But by the time it became obvious I didn't have star quality, he'd bought me enough music education to spoil me for a life of crime. Or so I convinced him. Believe it or not, he was thrilled when I became musicmaster at the academy; now I'm rubbing shoulders with dukes and princes, so he thinks there's a chance . . ." She shook her head and gave another humorless laugh. "Anyway. I'm not in Uncle Howdiri's league, but I survived several years of breaking into some very well-protected estates. I can do this."

Annah looked around at the rest of us. Her face was timid, hopeful, defiant. The Caryatid met her gaze with a smile. Impervia didn't go that far, but showed no hostility either—our holy sister wouldn't tolerate present-day faults, but she never held your past or your family against you. I could attest to that. If Annah had once been a thief as a child . . . well, she wasn't a thief now, and that's all Impervia cared about.

I took Annah's hand and squeezed it. "No problem. We're glad you're here."

Annah gave a brilliant smile, then leapt out to join Impervia on the cables. She began to shinny downward as if she did this kind of thing every day.

The Caryatid split her fireball in two: half for herself, half for Annah. We descended slowly, with Annah leaning out from the cables and scanning the ladder rung by rung in search of unwelcome surprises. After only thirty seconds, she called, "Stop!"

Annah gestured for the light to move closer. The fireball complied. Higher on the cables, Impervia let herself dangle near the ladder for a better look. "What is it?"

"A trip wire." Annah pointed to the ladder. "Set a few millimeters above this rung. You wouldn't see it till you stepped on it; then . . . I don't know what would happen, but I'm sure we wouldn't like it."

"Looks like the wire is broken," Impervia said. The Caryatid and I were trying to see, but we were much too high on the ladder to have a good view.

"It's not a break," Annah said. "The wire's melted in the middle, as if it got touched with something hot. Don't ask me how you could do that without setting off the trap."

"Sebastian could do it," I said. "The boy's powers let him do practically anything."

"Would Sebastian have to know the trap was there?" Annah asked. "Or would he just, uhh, ask the world to disarm every threat in the area."

"Probably a general order," I said. "The way his powers work, I don't think he pays a lot of attention to details. He doesn't have to."

"Then we're in luck," the Caryatid said. "Sebastian probably cleared every trap in the shaft with a single command."

"Probably," I agreed. "Let's hope Jode didn't ask him to reactivate a few, just to keep us on our toes."

But as we continued down the shaft, Annah found nothing but severed wires, smashed-in pressure plates, and molten messes which looked as if they'd once been electronic. Sebastian's nanite friends had done a thorough job of eliminating dangers . . . which meant we made our way without incident, descending story after story until we came within sight of the bottom.

As expected, both elevator cars had been locked in place on the lowest level. That might have put us in a quandary—how to get into the cars or past them so we could reach the floor itself—but Sebastian and Jode had solved that problem for us by blowing out the entire shaft wall just above the elevator doors.

It must have been a massive explosion. The wall was poured concrete, reinforced with embedded steel rods. The edges of the concrete were charred black; the ends of the rods were half-melted blobs.

Annah, leading the way, peeked through the wall's ragged hole. She quickly pulled her head back again.

"What do you see?" Impervia whispered.

"Bodies." Annah took a breath to settle herself. "I think they were Keepers; they're wearing brown robes like monks. The Keepers had set up a reception party outside the elevators—plenty of guns, fancy ones, not ordinary firearms—and I suppose they intended to shoot as soon as the elevator doors opened. But the doors didn't open; the wall blew out on top of them like an avalanche. The Keepers didn't have a chance."

"Stupid of them," Impervia said. "They should have positioned themselves farther back. Given themselves plenty of safety range."

Annah shook her head. "They didn't have enough room. When the OldTechs built this place, they didn't think to put in a proper kill-zone."

Impervia tsked her tongue at such lack of foresight. I decided it was pointless to mention this plant had been a commercial installation, not a military one; Impervia wouldn't have understood the distinction.

Instead, I continued down the ladder until I could see the carnage for myself. The room in front of me was lit with electric lights, very bright after the darkness of the elevator shaft. The place looked like a formal reception area, a spot where visiting dignitaries might gather before a tour of the generating machinery: high-ceilinged, with an ample supply of plush chairs and sofas. At one time, the furniture must have been spaced around the room . . . but now it was all drawn up in a barricade near the far wall. The Keepers had hidden behind that line, waiting to open fire. Unfortunately for them, their defenses had been no match for exploding rubble—heavy chunks of masonry had blasted out of the wall, smashing through chairs and couches, crushing the people behind. Male and female Keepers lay bleeding beside the barrier, most with fragments of concrete piercing their skulls.

"Jode must have known they'd be waiting here," the Caryatid said.

"Either that," I said, "or Sebastian just looked through the wall and saw them." I thought about nanites filling the air—

ready to transmit remote images into the boy's brain whenever he requested. "If Jode asked, 'What's ahead of us?' Sebastian could easily find out."

Annah frowned. "If Sebastian knew people were out here, would he really cause an explosion to kill them all?"

"Why not?" Impervia asked. "Jode has convinced the boy this building is headquarters for the Ring of Knives. Filled with vicious criminals, and commanded by Rosalind's evil mother who wants to interfere with true love. Then, what does Sebastian see when he gets here? People with guns, ready to shoot first and ask questions later."

"Don't forget," I added, "Myoko constantly warned Sebastian about groups like the Ring. She believed all such organizations enslaved psychics; she'd have told the boy he mustn't pull his punches if he ever fought them. Be ruthless, show no mercy—you know how Myoko talked. So even without Jode urging him on, Sebastian would be inclined to rip through anyone who stood in his way."

"He wouldn't listen to Pelinor," Impervia pointed out. "And he won't listen to us the next time we meet him. He thinks we're doppelgängers working for Rosalind's mother. Bags of skin filled with pus."

The Caryatid gave a soft sound that might have been a growl. "We'll show him it's Jode who fits that description. Let's get moving."

Annah went first, still on the lookout for traps. She stepped down to the roof of an elevator car and walked to the hole in the wall. Since the hole was more than two meters above the next room's floor, Annah seated herself on the edge of the broken concrete, then turned and lowered herself as far as she could, hanging on to the lip of the hole with her hands. She still had to drop the last half meter: landing without a sound, her black cloak billowing.

That's when the Keeper stirred and lifted his gun.

It was a young man, plump and bald, with blood smearing his face from where his left eye had been pulped by hurtling debris. He must have been knocked out by the initial blast, then left for dead by Jode and Sebastian. When he woke again, his first thought was to fire on the closest target: Annah. Maybe he was so dedicated to the Holy Lightning, he wanted to spend his last breath destroying what he believed was an intruder; maybe he just wanted to make someone pay for his ruined eye; maybe he was so dazed, he didn't know what he was doing. But he hadn't lost his weapon when the wall blew out on top of him. All he had to do was raise the muzzle.

I shouted to Annah, "Down, down, down!" The Keeper fired before I howled the second, "Down!" but I kept yelling, unable to stop myself.

Annah began to drop flat to the floor . . . then all hell broke loose.

The Keeper's weapon was an Element gun—a four-barreled monster of overkill invented by Spark Royal. The guns were rare, but my grandmother had received one as a gift the day she was anointed as governor. She'd let me examine it many years later: a big chunky rifle with four barrels arranged in a diamond, one for each of the classical Greek elements.

Earth: ordinary lead slugs, shot at high-velocity.

Fire: a gout of burning gas like a mini-flamethrower.

Air: a focused hypersonic barrage, causing no serious damage but able to knock out a charging rhino for hours.

Water: a stream of acid, corrosive enough to eat through steel.

Element guns were versatile weapons that could harmlessly subdue a single target or incinerate a mob. The guns had their limitations: they were brutally heavy, they couldn't be reloaded except by the Sparks, and you had only a few shots on any one setting. Still, if you liked a lot of options for wanton destruction, an Element gun fit the bill. You could fire each barrel separately, or mix and match to tailor your attack to your target.

The Keeper fired all four barrels at Annah. Simultaneously. The resulting blast was a pandemonium of light and sound, a blare of pure chaos that lasted only a fraction of a second; but in my mind's eye, it seemed to break into distinct pieces that each lasted forever.

I imagined the bullets reaching her first: an eruption of lead traveling faster than sound. Since she'd been diving forward, facing the shooter, the slugs would hit her in the head, the shoulders, and chest.

The hypersonics would arrive next. It was the same kind of attack Opal had talked about—the pistol she'd been carrying in the tobacco field. It hadn't affected the Lucifer, but I prayed it would work on Annah: frazzling her nervous system, hammering her into merciful unconsciousness so she couldn't feel the horrors to come.

Then fire. A flammable gas, something that blazed bright orange, pouring in a burning jet. Igniting her clothes, her hair, her beautiful skin.

Finally, the acid, its spray traveling slower than bullets, sound, and fire. Acid splashing onto the flames. I couldn't tell whether the acid would burn off harmlessly, or if the heat would make it work that much faster: disintegrating what was left of Annah's corpse.

Annah's *corpse*.

Then it was all over. The Keeper toppled forward across the furniture barricade, smoke pouring off his body. The gun clattered from his hands. Impervia leapt to the floor as if there was something she could do for Annah, but I remained frozen where I was.

The Caryatid slumped beside me. Her face was damp; not tears, but perspiration. "Ugh," she said. "Let's not do that again."

I stared at her, shocked at her lack of feeling for Annah. Before I could speak, something fluttered down in the room: Impervia had just kicked Annah's cloak and a few more pieces of clothing halfway across the floor. "Get down here, Phil!" Impervia snapped. "We need your first aid kit."

We?

I leaned over the edge of the hole. Lying tight against the wall was Annah, stripped to her underwear and blood drenching her left arm, but still very much alive.

She looked at me and smiled. "Keepers might be good with electrical things, but they sure are lousy shots."

                              *   *   *

I held her in my arms as Impervia bandaged Annah's only
wound: a bullet had passed in and out of her left biceps
muscle, missing the bone and all major blood vessels. As
she'd said, the Keeper had been a lousy shot—not too surprising for a man who'd lost one eye and was dazed from
being battered unconscious. All but one of the bullets had
gone wild, and the hypersonic stun-wave was off target too.

Annah would still have been cremated by the
flamethrower if not for quick work by the Caryatid—our
mistress of fire had redirected the blaze back at the shooter
before Annah was hit. (Good-bye, poor misguided Keeper.)
That left only the acid, also badly aimed; Annah's thick winter outfit protected her from the caustic splash, and she'd
managed to peel off her clothes before the corrosive fluids
ate through to her flesh. (Smoke still rose from the discarded
bundle of cloth. Her long parka was pocked through with
holes, as if chewed by huge moths. The black cloak that let
her vanish in the dark had vanished itself—totally consumed
by the ravaging chemicals.)

But Annah was safe. Shot, yes, and trying not to wince as
Impervia wrapped bright white bandages around her dark
arm; but when I considered the alternative . . .

I held her tightly and lowered my face against the top of
her head. I didn't cry; I just breathed in the warm fragrance
of her hair.

"Phil . . . Phil!" The Caryatid was shaking my shoulder. "We
have to get going right now."

"Can't we let Annah rest—"

"No," the Caryatid interrupted. "I heard voices up the elevator shaft. They're whispering, but the shaft carries echoes a
long way."

"Probably the Ring of Knives," Impervia said. "No doubt,
Mother Tzekich has been running around Niagara Falls, asking
at every hotel if they've seen Sebastian and her daughter. She
must have found someone who saw the two heading this way."

Either that, I thought, or Tzekich noticed the Falls had
stopped flowing and came to investigate. She'd have seen

Pelinor's body in the roadway, immediately in front of the power plant. After that, it was just a matter of following our tracks.

Annah put her hand on my cheek. She was bandaged now—looking painfully vulnerable in nothing but underwear, and probably weak from blood loss—but her smile was genuine. "We have to go before they get here. I'm strong enough. Really."

I helped her to her feet. As I did, Impervia slipped off her own winter coat and draped it around Annah's shoulders. "No," I said, "I'll give her *my* coat."

"She's already got mine," Impervia said. "I don't need it—this place is heated. Anyway, a coat will only slow me down if the time comes for . . . punishing the wicked."

Impervia smacked her right fist into her left palm. I stifled a laugh. In the past twenty-four hours, Impervia had been kicked by fishermen, gut-punched by Hump, kicked by Zunctweed, tossed around by Sebastian . . . and *still* she was looking for a fight.

Annah whispered softly in my ear, "That's what happens to some people when they take a vow of celibacy."

When I stifled the laugh this time, I nearly hurt myself.

I kept my arm around Annah as we moved forward; I don't know if she really needed my support, but she didn't push me away.

As we passed the fallen Keepers, Annah suddenly stopped. I thought she just needed to rest—but she bent down and pried an Element gun from its dead owner's grip.

"You want one too?" she asked.

Thinking of Pelinor and Myoko, I nodded. This was not just a quest; this was war.

22

HALF A LEAGUE, HALF A LEAGUE, HALF A LEAGUE ONWARD

A single door led forward. It had once been equipped with a fancy electronic lock connected to a keypad. Half the keypad was missing now, along with a chunk of the door frame. Sebastian hadn't wasted time on delicacy.

Beyond lay a short corridor with a door in each side wall and another at the far end. All three doors had been blown off their hinges.

The side doorways opened into locker rooms where the plant's OldTech personnel had changed from street clothes into whatever work-suits they wore on the job. The lockers had been knocked helter-skelter, some tossed against the walls, others cracked open like eggs. I wondered if Sebastian had smashed around the lockers just to show he could . . . or because he'd begun to *like* pointless mayhem.

Our friend Caryatid had also developed a liking for displays of mystical force. Before this business started, I'd never seen her juggle flames any larger than a big candle—but now she'd built a blaze the size of a cow's head, floating in front of us at chest height and pouring out heat like a furnace. No one dared step within five paces of it . . . no one except the Caryatid, whose face glistened with heat-sweat. She barely seemed to notice; she and her flameball just plowed ahead toward the next smashed-in doorway.

The entrance to the main machine room.

The place was as big as the academy's main building: a single chamber more than four stories high and a hundred meters square, its ceiling supported by dozens of pillars. The walls and floors were painted kelp-green; they tinted the space like a sea-grotto, ripe and weedy. In OldTech times, the place must have been brightly lit—bank upon bank of fluorescent fixtures hung from the roof, with multiple light-tubes in each fixture. But the days were long gone when such tubes could be mass-produced. Three-quarters of the fixtures had no light at all, and the remainder each only held a single long bulb. The result was an oceanic dimness, a full-fathom-five gloom filled with shadows.

Most of the shadows came from huge turbines held down by massive bolts that passed through the plastic floor and down into firmer footings below . . . possibly all the way to bedrock. The turbines were great hulking things with monstrous cooling fans, the actual turbine blades unseen under thick metal hoods. Water from the Falls ran through pipes beneath the false floor, rushing through the turbines and out again to the river. I had the impression this place should be deafeningly loud—roaring water, spinning metal, whirling fans—but the room had gone lethally silent. With the Falls dammed up, the tumult was suspended.

We could see no movement. No one was close to the door we'd just entered, and our view farther in was blocked by the ponderous machinery. A single corpse lay halfway between us and the nearest turbine: a middle-aged woman in brown Keeper's habit, facedown with a spill of moist white nuggets puddled on the floor beneath her. After choking her, the white goo had dribbled out of her mouth. The Caryatid dispatched a fireball to incinerate the alien curds; they burned with a hissing splutter, the only sound in the whole cavernous space.

Impervia turned to the rest of us and mouthed, *Wait; listen*. Annah and I obeyed. The Caryatid didn't. She gave her flames a moment to finish charring the last of the curds (filling the air with the smell of meat as the Keeper's face roasted), then she and her fireball moved forward. We hurried after her, fanning out so we weren't easy fodder for a single burst from an Element gun. Even Annah moved off on her own, wearing Impervia's too-big coat and cradling the Element gun in her arms. When I tried to tag along behind her, she waved me off: all her concentration was focused on the room before us, eyes and ears straining for any sign of trouble.

So we moved forward—like a platoon in enemy territory, walking silently in a line between trees. In our case, the "trees" were giant steel generators, two stories tall, their cooling fans motionless. The sparse lighting proved the station still had power, but it must have been coming from batteries; the turbines had all run dry.

With so many individual turbines and so many pillars holding up the roof, the Keepers would have had plenty of places to hide for an ambush; but apart from the single corpse, there was no one left in the room. After a while, I realized the Keepers must want to avoid a firefight in the midst of their machinery: Element guns could damage the generators, or even bring down the ceiling. That would be disastrous, especially since this equipment was virtually irreplaceable—the turbines were OldTech originals, bearing the names of defunct manufacturers, covered with a hundred coats of paint, jury-rigged with patch-wires, emergency welds, and other obvious repairs to squeeze a few more years from antique rust-heaps. A battle in this room might put the final nail in the coffin of machines that were ready to be junked anyway.

How long before this whole place ground to a halt from its own obsolescence? A few years, no more. If Jode had possessed any patience, the blasted Lucifer could have sat back and waited for this plant to stop on its own.

But that wasn't Jode's way. A passive approach wouldn't produce nearly enough death and suffering.

I tightened my grip on the Element gun and continued forward.

* * *

The far end of the chamber held another doorway . . . or rather a hole knocked into the room's original wall. This wasn't the work of Sebastian—this hole had clean edges painted the same green as the rest of the place. I suspected the hole had been dug when the Sparks took over the power plant, whenever that was.

The opening was three paces wide and the same distance high, hidden from other parts of the room by nearby turbines. I appreciated the concealment. The Ring of Knives were somewhere to our rear; by now, they must have picked up Element guns of their own, plucked from the hands of dead Keepers. Our only protection was staying out of sight: scuttling into the hole in front of us before Elizabeth Tzekich could catch up. I had the strong suspicion we were retreating down a dead-end passage . . . but staying put was certain suicide.

Jode and Sebastian were somewhere ahead. No doubt Dreamsinger was too—since she hadn't joined the ambush at the elevator or taken a stand to prevent Jode from reaching the generator room, she must be farther on, protecting something even more important. An electric cage full of Lucifers? I didn't know . . . but I'd soon find out.

The hole in the wall led to a tunnel dug into Niagara bedrock—limestone, cold and gray. Rubber-coated cables as thick as my arm had been strung down the tunnel: dozens of them lined the walls, spaced a hand's breadth apart and fastened to the rock on ceramic insulator mounts. They obviously fed power from the turbines to whatever lay ahead . . . and when the electricity was actually flowing, this tunnel must have been saturated with an awesome magnetic field induced by the inevitable fluctuations in so much current. I didn't want to think what would happen to a living creature who wandered into the corridor while most of the energy of Niagara Falls coursed through such a small area. Is there such a thing as death by magnetism?

Now, however, the power was dead. Not just because the Falls were shut off: each of the electric cables had been severed cleanly near the mouth of the tunnel . . . thick strands of copper sliced as easily as if they were melted cheese. It had to be Sebastian's work—even if the Falls resumed their flow, the power lines wouldn't be repaired any time soon.

The tunnel had no built-in lights, so we were forced to depend on the Caryatid's fireball—like Moses and the children of Israel guided by flame through the desert night. The fireball's blaze would give us away to anyone watching from farther up the tunnel . . . but I was willing to take that risk. My nerves were too frayed to creep through pitch blackness into the mouth of heaven-knows-what.

Anyway, the people watching from farther up the tunnel turned out to be dead.

The first indication was the barrel of an Element gun dangling limply from a slit in the tunnel wall. A hand was attached to the trigger, but no person attached to the hand. When I peeked through the slit, I saw the remains of the shooter, but couldn't tell whether the corpse was male or female, young or old.

The body had been compressed to a bloody mass the size of a roast turkey. Its top still showed dark curly hair; near the bottom was a recognizable toe; but in between lay nothing except a mangle of flesh and robes, with slivers of bone sticking out at sharp angles. I could only conjecture that the air had closed around the gunner like a giant fist, then pressure had been applied down on the head, up on the feet, until the whole body was crushed into a ball.

Blood had squirted like juice from a squeezed tomato. Death must have been quick and loud. I could almost hear the crunching of bones still echoing through the tunnel.

And the wall had many more slits . . . with many more balled-up corpses. This was the kill-zone Annah had expected earlier: a shooting gallery where Keepers could massacre anyone coming up the tunnel. Gun-slits ran along both walls, offset from each other so there was little chance of the defenders on the left accidentally shooting the ones on the right. The crossfire would have been devastating. Any conventional invader would be stopped right here, bathed in bullets, fire, and acid.

But the people behind the gun-slits had no protection

against psionics. Sebastian talked to his nanite friends . . . and the Keepers' resistance had literally been crushed.

The tunnel extended another hundred meters. Its smell grew foul: blood and feces from the dead. A few more hours and the unventilated tunnel would be a nightmare of putrid gases; an open flame like the Caryatid's fireball would surely set off an explosion. For the moment, though, the bodies were fresh enough that they didn't constitute a danger—just a cloying stink that made my gorge rise.

I was therefore glad when I saw light ahead—even though it meant we were approaching the final hell. One way or another, this would soon be over. Sebastian, Jode, Dreamsinger, and the Ring had all drawn together . . . with us in the middle.

End of the line. End of the quest. I was drained enough to be happy it had finally arrived.

The Caryatid gestured for her fireball to stay back so we could approach the tunnel mouth without attracting attention. Deep breaths all around . . . then we silently padded forward.

The final chamber looked almost as big as the generator room, but lit more dimly: with a faint violet glow like a guttering candle-flame inside tinted glass. The light didn't come from bulbs overhead; it trickled from the middle of the room, barely strong enough to reach the rock-hewn walls.

Hush, hush, moving slowly: the Caryatid and Impervia stuck close to the right hand wall of the tunnel, while Annah and I took the left. We advanced until we could see the source of the light.

The Caryatid's "feeling" had been right. The power plant's secret was a prison: a perfect cube, twenty by twenty by twenty meters, raised slightly off the floor. Its edges were sharp strands of violet light—so straight they had to be OldTech lasers, their beams crisp but with a grainy texture. Where the beams met at each corner, a small box of glass and chrome floated in the air . . . not suspended on wires or poles, but simply hovering as if supported by the light rays themselves. I suspected those boxes were the source of the lasers, each little machine projecting the light in razor-fine lines to the three adjacent corners. The faces of the cube, framed by violet, looked perfectly transparent—nothing there, as if you could simply step over the nearest edge-beam and into the cube's interior. I knew that couldn't be true. A prison is still a prison, even if you can't see the walls.

Inside that prison cage loomed a shapeless black bulk: a mound as big as a house, its surface like coal dust in the lasers' violet glow. As we watched, a ripple went through the heap, like a shiver in a horse's flank. It made a sandy sound . . . as if the mass before us was constructed of small dry grains rasping against each other with the motion. One could almost mistake the thing for a dark lifeless dune, and the ripple we'd seen no more than the drifting effect of an errant breeze; but there *was* no breeze so deep underground, and the mound radiated a brooding intelligence that pressed against my skull.

The thing in the cage was a living creature. And it was watching us.

This was what Jode had come to release. An old-style unmutated Lucifer, of the kind Opal met in the tobacco field: dark and dry "like gunpowder" she'd said. And like gunpowder, this huge mound had dangerous explosive potential. It was a giant of Jode's kind: perhaps a hive mother, a queen that could spawn thousands of shapeshifting young.

But the creature in the cage wasn't only a pile of dark grains. Dozens of incongruous objects protruded from its surface, like animal bones jutting out of desert sand. I saw long glass tubes; lumps of metal; cards of green plastic with wires embedded; and frosted white pustules that resembled lightbulbs.

Lightbulbs. Like the live ones in Niagara's hotels, or the burnt-out rejects in souvenir shops. They bulged profusely from the dusty mass, as if the monster was a garish casino marquee that had just been turned off. Was the caged Lucifer eating the bulbs . . . or was it *extruding* them? *Producing* them.

Could Jode and its alien kind do more than mimic other people and things? Could they actually create such objects for real?

In our journey through the generating station, we'd seen no other facilities for high-tech manufacturing: nowhere the Keepers could make bulbs, appliances, or any of the other electrical goods in use throughout the tourist areas. We hadn't searched the whole plant . . . but looking at the caged alien, I knew we didn't have to. This creature was the source of Niagara's largesse. The Keepers must feed it a diet of metal scraps, hydrocarbons, and whatever other components were needed as raw materials; then the monster's unearthly biochemistry somehow assembled the basic elements into complex electrical devices.

One had to admire Spark Royal's efficiency—why let a prisoner loaf in idleness, when your captive could be put to work?

On the other hand, who'd be crazy enough to enter that cage and retrieve the beast's creations? No one was that desperate for lightbulbs. And at first glance, I couldn't see any way to enter the cube unless you turned off the laser barrier . . . a terrible idea, even if you only shut down the beams for an instant. What kind of fool would risk freeing a gigantic Lucifer, just so hotels could play bad OldTech music?

I was so distracted staring at the thing in the cage that many long seconds passed before I realized there was no one else visible in the room. No Sebastian, no false Rosalind, no Dreamsinger. I leaned my head out of the tunnel mouth to get a better view. There were open entrances on either side of the tunnel, leading into the two recesses where the Keepers had died at their gun-slits; but those were the only side-rooms and they contained nothing but corpses.

Our quarry had to be on the far side of the cage. Anyone over there would be hidden from us by the great pile of gunpowder dust. I glanced at Impervia and the Caryatid; they were looking at Annah and me with grim expressions on their faces. *Ready?* Impervia mouthed.

Annah and I nodded. Together, we four crept into the room.

The creature in the cage took no notice of our presence . . . no more than the occasional shiver across its powdery surface. I assumed it could see us, despite its lack of eyes; it could probably hear us and smell us too. But it showed no sign of caring as we entered the room—it just lay silent, watching.

Waiting till the lasers died from lack of power.

The cables coming out of the tunnel fanned out around the rocky walls of the chamber, circling the perimeter of the room and converging again on the other side of the cage. Because of the alien blocking our view, we couldn't see where the cables rejoined; but I assumed they connected to some machine on the far side, thereby feeding power to the lasers. The lasers were now subsisting on battery power . . . and I dearly hoped the batteries wouldn't fail as we were tiptoeing past the cage.

Impervia led, followed by the Caryatid and her fireball. Annah and I trailed behind; she walked with her finger on her Element gun's trigger, ready to fire at a moment's notice. I had my gun ready too . . . and I'd set the weapon to shoot all four barrels at once. Bullets, fire, acid, sound: tonight there was no such thing as overkill.

As we moved forward, Impervia drew her knife—not a fighting weapon, but just a jack-knife she carried for cutting tough meat and trimming candlewicks. I wondered what good that would do against Jode . . . but I decided she'd pulled out the blade more to bolster her spirits than to use in battle.

Unless she intended to slit her own throat if things got too rough. Magdalenes considered unwarranted suicide a mortal sin . . . but when death was truly inevitable, they approved of flamboyant gestures that robbed their enemies of complete victory.

Better to stab your own heart than allow an infidel to do it.

* * *

At last we reached a point where we could see behind the giant Lucifer. The electric cables from the turbines hooked up to a device that had to be the main controller for the laser cage. It was bigger than I expected: a box of black metal and plastic the size of a privy-shack. The box even had doors— one opening out into the cavern and another into the prison cube. Looking at it, I realized the shack was more than just a machine that controlled the lasers; it served as a sort of air-lock that would let Keepers enter the cage to retrieve the lightbulbs and other things produced by the captive beast.

Again I shuddered at the idea of harvesting electric gad-gets from the monster's dust-body. What prevented the Lu-cifer from devouring any Keeper who entered the cage? Or even worse, from planting black grains in the Keeper's robes, in the lightbulbs, in the toasters, smuggling bits of itself to freedom? But the Sparks would undoubtedly be prepared for such attempts. Anyone passing through that airlock shack must surely be scanned by both science and sorcery. Any nuggets of Lucifer trying to escape would be detected and eliminated.

As long as electricity kept flowing through the cables. Now that the power was cut, the small airlock shack might be a death chamber.

Standing by the door of that shack, his back pressed against it, was Sebastian Shore. We saw him as soon as we came around the edge of the cage—the boy leaned back like a man with nothing to fear, even if the door fell open and dropped him into the prison cube.

In his arms a girl snuggled against his shoulder, her lips nuzzling his neck. But the girl didn't look like Rosalind; it was my lovely cousin Hafsah, harem pants and all.

Dreamsinger.

For a moment I just stared dumbly: had Dreamsinger snared the boy with some love/lust enchantment, despite his psionic protections? No, of course not; this was the work of that irk-some Chameleon spell Dreamsinger still wore. When Sebas-tian looked at the Sorcery-Lord, he saw the most beautiful woman he could imagine—his own dear Rosalind. Somehow Dreamsinger had swapped herself with Jode, replacing one false Rosalind with another.

That raised the question of where Jode was now. If we were lucky, Dreamsinger had vaporized the accursed Lucifer; but I doubted even a Sorcery-Lord could have pulled that off without Sebastian noticing. Whatever she'd done, it would have to be quick and quiet while the boy's attention was elsewhere—perhaps when he was slaughtering the Keepers behind their gun-slits. During those few seconds, Dreamsinger had somehow removed Jode and put herself in the alien's place.

Once again, I remembered our chancellor's story about the Lucifer in the tobacco field. Opal said Vanessa of Spark had tapped the alien's severed parts with a small rod that glittered red and green; the pieces had vanished <BINK>, as if ejected from our plane of existence. If Dreamsinger possessed a similar <BINK>-rod and used it on Jode when Sebastian wasn't looking . . . could it be the alien was gone, gone, gone? Dispatched to a different somewhere, removed from our lives forever?

No. I didn't believe it. Nothing was ever that easy. The alien would return; I could feel it in my bones. For now though, we had only Sebastian and the Sorcery-Lord to worry about . . . which was plenty enough.

The Caryatid and Impervia didn't hesitate after sighting the boy and Dreamsinger. My friends continued boldly forward, striding within five paces of the lovey-dovey couple and planting themselves side-by-side where they couldn't possibly be missed.

"Sebastian," said Impervia.

"Dear sister-in-sorcery," said the Caryatid.

The boy and the Spark Lord turned, their heads almost touching. Dreamsinger's face was dark with warning: her fierce glare suggested she wanted to rip us into component atoms. Lucky for us, the Sorcery-Lord couldn't behave so un-Rosalind-like.

Sebastian's expression was no more friendly than Dream-singer's. "Didn't I tell you to stay away? I know you aren't who you look like."

I sighed with relief: he hadn't murdered us instantly. The boy's conscience allowed him to slay Keepers—people armed to the teeth, shooting at him and his beloved—but he balked at destroying someone who looked like one of his teachers, especially when she offered no threat. Better still, the Rosalind in his arms wasn't Jode . . . who would have been screaming, "Kill them!" to keep us from giving away the truth.

"We *are* who we look like," Impervia said. "We discovered you were missing a few hours after you left. In Dover, we found you'd chartered a boat named *Hoosegow* and sailed in this direction. We realized you were headed to Niagara Falls—to this building here. So we followed."

"I don't believe it," Sebastian said. "Rosalind says you're just doppelgängers created by her mother's sorcerers. Bags of skin filled with pus." He paused as if he was beginning to doubt his own words; then his face cleared. "It's true. That copy of Sir Pelinor was all gucky."

"No," said Impervia. "He was flesh and blood. So am I."

She lifted her hand: the one holding the small knife. I understood now why she'd taken it out. Slowly, deliberately, she pulled back her sleeve and placed the blade to her flesh, halfway between wrist and elbow. She had to press hard; the knife's edge was adequate for cutting T-bone steak, but not for slicing Impervia's hard-toned muscle. When she broke through the skin, blood oozed in a thick trickle.

The dim glow of the laser cage didn't cast enough light to show the blood's harsh scarlet . . . but suddenly a dozen small white suns materialized in the air. They were obviously Sebastian's work—illuminating the room with his psionics so he could see clearly. At last.

"Sister Impervia?" he said with horror in his voice.

"Yes," she answered. "It's me."

"No, it isn't," said a new voice. And Impervia erupted in flames.

23

FIRE IN THE HOLE

Another Rosalind had appeared—Jode, escaped from wherever one went when tapped with a red and green <BINK>-rod. The Lucifer had sneaked around the far side of the laser cage. While the rest of us were watching Impervia cut her arm, Jode had moved into position just beyond the cube's airlock shack. The Lucifer had obtained an Element gun from one of the fallen Keepers; and the gun was set to shoot flames.

Impervia's clothes ignited. Beside her, the Caryatid was also engulfed in fire . . . but the Caryatid waved the blaze away before it could singe a single hair. She turned and grabbed the flames surrounding Impervia as if they were solid matter; then the Caryatid yanked backward, pulling the fire with her, like tugging a crackling red cloak off Impervia's body. A quick flick of the Caryatid's wrists, and the flames winked out in mid-air. Curls of smoke wreathed Impervia from head to foot, but the woman beneath seemed unharmed.

Jode, alas, was a fast learner. The Lucifer must have tried flames to begin with because they'd cause the most agonizing death . . . but when fire proved ineffective, Jode switched immediately to bullets.

A burst of high-velocity slugs rattled toward Impervia and the Caryatid, some rounds striking home while others zinged past to ricochet off the rock walls. Annah threw herself to the ground; I joined her, but in the instant before I dropped, I saw the Caryatid point toward Jode and shout a single incomprehensible word. Her pet fireball shot across the room toward the alien, the ball's blazing heat augmented by fire from Jode's own flamethrower . . . and I prayed the inferno would hit its target with enough energy to incinerate Jode on the spot.

It didn't. Head down, I heard a clatter and a heavy whoof of air. When I looked up, the Element gun had been knocked from Jode's grip and all fires in the room were snuffed . . . including the flameball the Caryatid had sent toward the alien. Sebastian had obviously told his nanite friends to stop the violence until he could sort everything out.

Therefore Jode was still intact. The Caryatid had slumped to the ground, her face ashen; one arm hung limply, while the other hand pressed hard against her opposite shoulder. Blood seeped between her fingers from a deep wound just below her collarbone. There was another mess of blood near her waist where a second bullet had plowed its way through the plump rolls of flesh she called love handles . . . but the Caryatid didn't have a free hand to stop the bleeding down there. Perhaps she didn't even know about the second wound: the shot in her upper chest, piercing ribs and muscles and internal organs, might have eclipsed the pain of a straight in-and-out hole through simple fat.

Besides, the Caryatid wasn't concentrating on her own injuries. Her gaze had turned toward Impervia . . . who'd been knocked off her feet by the gunfire. When she hit the rock floor she landed in an awkward heap, with no attempt to make a graceful breakfall. Blood gushed out of her in a high-pressure fountain, an arc of it streaming into the air. The blood had to be pouring from an artery, but her body was so crumpled, I couldn't tell where she'd been hit. In the leg? The chest? The throat?

Abruptly the red geyser stopped . . . as if the heart supplying the pressure had ceased to pump. Impervia didn't move; nothing moved except the edge of the blood pool, trickling across the uneven ground, flowing toward the lowest point in the chamber.

I thought to myself, *She would have preferred to die in righteous battle*. But battle deaths are often the easy way out for people blind to other possibilities. If Impervia had to die, better that her last act was cutting her own arm. Not stupid fisticuffs, but proving she was human.

"What's going on?" Sebastian roared. At least, I think he wanted it to be a roar. It came out closer to a whine. He'd seen Impervia was flesh and blood; he'd also seen her gunned down by his precious Rosalind. Except that he could see *two* Rosalinds: Jode and Dreamsinger. "Who are you?" he yelled at the Lucifer.

"I'm Rosalind," Jode answered. "The *real* Rosalind."

"You aren't," the boy said . . . but he cast a furtive glance at Dreamsinger.

Jode caught the look. "That's another of my mother's doppelgängers. Created by sorcery. She rolled me aside when you weren't looking, but—"

Sebastian interrupted, "What do you mean, rolled you aside?"

"Pushed me sideways. Out of this world. But I had a magic wand that let me come back."

Jode held up a small rod as wide as my pinkie-finger and twice as long. He pushed a button on one end, and suddenly the rod sparkled with lights, like red and green sequins glittering in the dimness. I bet when the rod touched you, it made a soft <BINK>.

Dreamsinger glared. "Where did you get that?"

"Stole it from one of my mother's sorcerers. A gullible man who always wore orange."

Jode couldn't hide the taunt in those words. The <BINK>-rod had come from the Spark in orange armor—Mind-Lord Priest, killed at the winter anchorage. With such a rod in hand, Jode had apparently avoided the fate of the Lucifer in the tobacco field: when Dreamsinger had "rolled" Jode aside, the alien shapeshifter could use its own <BINK>-rod to return. Apparently, such rods could both send you away and bring you back.

Even wearing Rosalind's face, Jode looked smug. And the

Lucifer wasn't finished. "Do you want to see who's real?" Jode asked Sebastian. "Use your powers to dispel all the sorcery in this room. You'll see the whole truth."

Dreamsinger had time to narrow her eyes—her beautiful Hafsah eyes, so calm and perfect. Then something went thud in my head, like a concussion from the inside out: things rearranged themselves in my brain, making my body as weak as water. If I hadn't been down on the floor already, I think I would have collapsed. But the dizziness passed in seconds; when my vision stopped reeling, the woman in Sebastian's arms had changed.

The first thing I saw was red—full body armor colored sorcerer's crimson, made of plastic and molded in the shape of a chunkily voluptuous female figure. This was no graceful Hafsah in harem pants; the armor wasn't as bulky as plate mail, but it possessed a similar stolidity. The breasts and hips built onto the underlying shell had the crude excess of a Stone Age fertility carving . . . so extreme they were almost a parody. Especially in contrast to the woman beneath.

I could finally see the real Dreamsinger because she wasn't wearing her helmet—she must have decided to remove it when she started kissing Sebastian. Surprisingly, the Sorcery-Lord looked the same age as the girl she portrayed: Dreamsinger was a reedy weedy sixteen-year-old whose tan skin revealed vivid acne pimples. Her facial features would have fit in well on the streets of Seoul, but her hair was dyed an unnatural red, the same bright shade as her armor. She hadn't touched up the hair coloring for quite some time, as evidenced by a deep darkness at the roots.

Behold the all-powerful sorceress: a plain-faced poseur decked out like a femme fatale. But I reminded myself Dreamsinger was still lethal—perhaps more than ever, now that her disguise had been stripped away.

Sebastian cringed back from her, sliding along the wall of the airlock shack. Dreamsinger didn't go after him. One hand twitched, and suddenly a rod appeared in her grip, identical to the one held by Jode. She thumbed the activation button, waking red and green glitters along the rod's length. Meanwhile, her other hand snapped into a sorcerous pose, some

fingers bent, some splayed, aimed at Sebastian in case he
tried a psionic attack; but the boy did nothing except stare
aghast.

"Don't look at me that way," Dreamsinger told him, not
lowering her guard. Her voice had changed from Hafsah's
purring alto into a high and scratchy soprano. "You can see
I'm a Spark Lord—you must recognize the armor. So don't
get ideas about taking me on. I doubt if you'd win . . . and if
you did, my brothers and sisters would come after you. You
wouldn't like that. You wouldn't like that at all."

Sebastian was still staring in horror. "What . . . when . . ."

Dreamsinger laughed—a false laugh I'd heard from
teenagers many times before. Trying to sound amused and
superior when her feelings had just been hurt. "When did I
take over Rosalind's place? Did you sleep with me when you
thought you were sleeping with her? That would have been
just *awful*, wouldn't it? But I'm not the one you have to
worry about, dear brother. I only stepped in a short time
ago . . . while you were killing my Keepers."

Sebastian looked outraged. "They were trying to kill *me*!"

"True. I knew they wouldn't succeed, but at least they distracted you so I could make my substitution. A valuable sacrifice, don't you think?"

"No," Jode said. The Lucifer hadn't moved since Sebastian knocked away the Element gun. "Sacrifices are only valuable if they accomplish their goal. Otherwise, they're just
deaths."

"Rosalind . . ." Sebastian began.

"You're in for a surprise." Dreamsinger laughed again.
This time her laughter sounded more genuine. And mean-
spirited. "Dear brother Sebastian, do you realize you've fulfilled your final purpose?"

The boy glared at her. "What do you mean?"

"You were used to gain access to this station. To shut off
the electricity. To cut the cables feeding this room so nothing
will happen even when the water finally spills around your
dam. On top of that, your lovely wife just tricked you into
dispelling every enchantment in this room. My Chameleon

glamour wasn't the only spell you removed; you also erased thirteen charms of protection to prevent this cage from opening." Dreamsinger made a mock bow toward the Lucifer. "Clever you. But your kind has always been clever."

"More so recently," Jode said.

"So you believe."

"What are you talking about?" Sebastian demanded.

Jode gave a nasty smile. "You'll never know, boy. You've outlived your usefulness."

The Lucifer made a darting motion with its hand. Something went bang, like thunder.

For a moment I was certain the bang meant Sebastian's death: some murderous alien surprise that would beat the boy's psionic defenses. The Lucifer might have planted a booby-trap while consummating the sham marriage—one long deep kiss and a tiny curd of maggoty white could have slid down Sebastian's throat. That curd might lodge itself in the boy's stomach, stealing atoms and molecules from nearby tissues to build an explosive chemical . . . or perhaps the curd could mutate into an explosive all its own. One way or another, Jode must have a trick for blowing people up from the inside: that's how it got the Mind-Lord, blasting him to pieces above the winter anchorage.

But the explosion we'd heard didn't come from Sebastian—the bang erupted back near the exit tunnel. Jode's leer of triumph dissolved to bewilderment . . . and Dreamsinger laughed at the sight.

"I'm not the only one who's predictable," she told Jode. "I knew you'd rig the boy for a fatal finish . . . so I removed your surprise from Sebastian's small intestine. Switched it by sorcery to the corpse of one of my Keepers. As I said, they made a valuable sacrifice—without them, I couldn't save one of the most powerful psychics the world has ever known."

Jode's face twisted with fury. The Lucifer's right hand turned puffy, as if the creature was so enraged it didn't have enough self-control to retain its Rosalind form . . . but the moment passed and the hand resumed human shape. Sebastian seemed to have missed the brief transformation—he was too busy staring at the alien's fierce expression. "I don't understand," he said. "Rosalind, what's this about?"

"She's not Rosalind," said the Caryatid. Her voice was wheezy—the bullet through her shoulder must have pierced a lung. But she struggled to her feet, still pressing her wound with a blood-drenched hand. "The real Rosalind is dead. Murdered by this bag of skin filled with pus." She took a shaky step toward Jode. "We found Rosalind's body last night. Dead in her dorm room. The thing you married was her killer."

"No," Sebastian whispered. "No. The Rosalind I married . . . she was *my* Rosalind. She knew things—secrets only we . . . how could anyone else know?"

"How do you think?" The Caryatid took another step toward Jode. "This thing is called a Lucifer. It's a shapeshifter; it can look like anyone it wants. If it made itself look like you and visited Rosalind in her room . . . secrets would naturally spill out. Amongst other things."

Bile boiled up in my throat. I remembered the position of Rosalind's corpse: lying naked in the bed, arms and legs splayed wide. If Jode had come to her in Sebastian's form soon after supper . . . if Jode had said, "I know we didn't plan to get together till later, but I just couldn't wait . . ."

I could guess what the Lucifer would want. Not just talk. Not just secrets. Jode wanted the perversity of bedding the girl before killing her. Certainly, there were practical reasons for such an atrocity: seeing the girl naked in order to duplicate any moles, birthmarks, etc., hidden by her clothing; learning if there was anything distinctive in how she made love. Fundamentally, though, the Lucifer was just so damnably evil it wanted to be astride Rosalind when it spewed curds into her mouth—filling her with death and horror at the moment the betrayal would be most shattering.

Jode liked to cause pain; it was that simple. The Lucifer reveled in the anguish on a victim's face just before the face went slack. Even now, though the alien hadn't managed to kill Sebastian, Jode must have enjoyed the boy's look of dawning revulsion.

"No," Sebastian whispered. "No."

"Oh yes," Jode said. Then three things happened almost simultaneously.

First: Jode lunged toward Sebastian, slamming a fist toward the boy's face. The blow didn't make contact—Sebastian's nanite friends would never permit that—but the boy reflexively retreated from the attack. Backward. Into the airlock shack that led to the electric cage. At some point when we'd been distracted by other things, Jode must have opened the shack door. Still backing up, Sebastian tripped over the lip of the airlock doorway and fell to the floor inside. He didn't hit the ground hard—his nanite friends cushioned the fall—but Jode shut the door behind the boy and threw a lever on the shack's outer wall. The inner door of the airlock, the one to the prison cube's interior, slid open in response to the button. The mass of dusty black inside the cage, quiescent all this time, lurched instantly toward Sebastian and rolled over him like a midnight avalanche.

Second: the Caryatid cried, "Damn you!" and erupted into flame. Spontaneous human combustion—an age-old legend dismissed by scientists, but if anyone could manage the feat, it was the Steel Caryatid. She lit no match to start the blaze; she simply waved her hands, and suddenly she was burning. Not just *on* fire . . . the Caryatid *was* fire, a woman turned an inferno: advancing on Jode as her legs withered to ash, then continuing forward as flame incarnate, a final conflagration accelerating across the room and roaring into the alien at full speed. Jode was just turning away from shutting Sebastian in the airlock. The fire struck the Lucifer blind-side and ignited its Rosalind clothing. A howl of pain. A wet sizzle. There was nothing left of the Caryatid at all, her flesh and bones incinerated in a flash; but Jode was awash in searing flame.

Third: Dreamsinger turned toward the burning alien. The light of the flames lit her face with orange intensity, but the Spark Lord's expression was blank. She'd been caught by surprise when Jode and the Caryatid acted. I think Dreamsinger had expected someone to attack *her*; she wasn't prepared to be ignored, treated as if she meant nothing compared to more important targets. Now as she approached

Jode-in-flames, I couldn't tell if she intended to put out the fires incinerating the alien or to stoke them higher. Dreamsinger apparently couldn't decide either—she moved slowly, distractedly fingering the <BINK>-rod in her hands, finally coming to a bemused stop in front of the Lucifer ablaze.

Which is how she was standing when the Element gun went off.

She was hit by a volley from all four barrels—bullets, fire, acid, sound. The first three attacks stopped short of their target as the force field around Dreamsinger's armor blazed into violet life. Bullets turned to molten lead as they hit the energy barrier; fire and acid splashed the violet glow but couldn't reach the gawky girl inside. Only the hypersonic waves got through . . . and I assume they would have been stopped as well if Dreamsinger had been wearing her helmet.

Without that helmet, she was vulnerable to simple sound. Amidst the clatter of bullets and the whoosh of flame, she gasped and crumpled to the floor.

A Spark Lord defeated. Unconscious.

Elizabeth Tzekich raced around the corner of the laser cage and ran to what she thought was her daughter. Knife-Hand Liz held an Element gun; its barrels were still smoking.

Tzekich was followed by the same two bully-boys we'd seen in Nanticook House. They'd all come around the far side of the prison cube: moving quietly, hidden by the great alien mound in the cage and by the noise the rest of us had been making.

I didn't know how long Tzekich had been listening, but obviously she hadn't understood that the girl who looked like Rosalind was actually an alien shapeshifter. Or maybe she *had* heard and didn't believe it. We'd told her the previous night that her daughter was dead, replaced by some kind of double . . . but she hadn't believed it then, either. And who knows what goes through a mother's mind when she sees what looks like her daughter enveloped in flame? She only had our word this wasn't the real Rosalind; and she wasn't prepared to trust us.

Not when her daughter was burning.

The moment Tzekich reached the fiery Jode, she tossed her gun aside and whipped off her thick winter coat. She used the coat to swat the flames, muffling Jode's body when the fire had been beaten down enough to be smothered. By then, Jode's face was black and flaky, scraps falling from the creature's cheeks like bits of burnt paper; but the Lucifer still retained some semblance of Rosalind, enough to fool a frantic mother. Tzekich was murmuring teary words in a language I didn't understand—leaning close as if she wanted to kiss the girl but was too afraid of damaging the blistered face.

"You know what's going to happen," I whispered to Annah.

"Yes," she said. "If the Lucifer's still alive . . ."

"It is. Bits of it. Remember, each curd is a separate organism. What Opal called cellules."

"And even if the cellules on the surface got burned, there are plenty alive underneath?"

"Right. So as soon as Knife-Hand Liz gets too close . . ."

Annah shook her head. "Jode won't attack her. Jode will say, 'Oh yes, I'm Rosalind, please save me, Mommy.' Anything to kill time until the cage runs out of power and the thing inside gets loose."

"How can we stop it?"

"We can't. Only Sebastian can. He can start the Falls flowing again. Reconnect the cables he cut."

I looked into the prison cube. There was no sign of the boy under the mass of black that had deluged him. The giant Lucifer had returned to the main part of the cage, hauling the boy with it—like a crocodile dragging a meal back to its lair. "How do we know he's still alive?"

"We don't," Annah said. "But his psionic powers give him a chance. They might have formed a barrier between him and the monster. An air bubble."

"If he's still alive and his powers are working, why hasn't he escaped on his own?"

"I don't know. Maybe he needs our help."

That almost made me laugh. "So we just waltz into the cage and rescue him?"

Annah pointed to the Element gun I was holding. "The flames and acid should drive the monster back. And Sebas-

tian's powers will protect him from the blasts. I hope." She
shrugged. "It's the only chance we've got to beat Jode. What
all the others died for. We have to try."

I hesitated. "What if the Ring tries to stop us?"

She kissed me, soft and sweet. "Leave the Ring to me. You
save Sebastian." Before I could react, she scrambled to her
feet and shouted, "Hey! You! Knife-Hand Liz!"

I don't know if the Ring-folk had realized we were there—
we'd been down on the floor and out of the action, on the opposite side of the cage. Now the two bully-boys whipped up
their guns, so jumpy they might have cremated Annah on the
spot; but she held her hands high and harmless, her own Element gun slung out of sight behind her back.

"Hello," she said, walking slowly toward them. The Ring-
men tracked her with their gun barrels. "We've never met,
but I know you. Do you know me?"

The bully-boys stared without answering. Elizabeth Tzekich, cheeks smeared with tears, looked up from what she
thought was her daughter. "I've watched you from a distance.
The don on Rosalind's floor. What the hell's going on?"

"My friends told you everything last night. A monster
killed your daughter and took her place. That creature is now
at your feet."

Tzekich looked down at the burnt figure wrapped in her
coat. A whisper came from Jode's throat. "Mother . . ."

"It thinks you're gullible," Annah said. "It wants to play
on your sympathies. Then, when you're no longer useful, it'll
kill you as heartlessly as it did Rosalind."

"So you claim."

"Talk to it," Annah said. "In your own language. Ask questions only your daughter could answer."

Tzekich stared piercingly at Annah. Then she turned to the
Lucifer at her feet and said something in her native tongue.
Jode only groaned, "Please, Mother, it's me . . ."

In English.

I nearly laughed. Annah, clever Annah, must have suspected Jode couldn't speak whatever Balkan dialect Knife-
Hand Liz used with her real daughter. Mother Tzekich didn't

give up immediately—she tried several more sentences with short pauses after each: probably questions Rosalind could answer easily . . . but not Jode. The shapeshifter only gasped, "Mother!" repeatedly, trying to fill the word with so much anguish, it would touch a stony heart; but the look on the mother's face had changed to loathing.

She knew the truth: this wasn't Rosalind, it was Rosalind's killer. And a woman who'd earned the name Knife-Hand Liz had no pity for such an enemy.

Her bully-boys felt the same way. Whether or not they spoke Tzekich's language, they could see what was going on; when this "Rosalind" couldn't answer simple questions, the bodyguards shifted their guns toward Jode. They'd realized the Lucifer was a deadly threat, and they wanted the monster in their sights.

The Ring-men were right about Jode being dangerous. But they shouldn't have taken their eyes off Annah . . . who reached behind her back and swung her Element gun to bear on Knife-Hand Liz.

Tzekich either saw Annah's move or had an inborn sense of when a weapon was aimed at her. She looked up, no fear in her eyes, and said, "What is this about?"

"It's about you leaving. Your daughter is dead and I'm sorry . . . but there's nothing left for you here. Just go."

Softly Tzekich asked, "Without revenge?"

Annah waved the gun's muzzle toward Jode. "If you want to incinerate that monster, be my guest."

"And what about the teachers who were supposed to keep my daughter safe? Or the psychic boy who was the cause of everything? This creature, this Lucifer . . . it wanted to use the boy, yes? If not for Sebastian, my Rosalind would still be alive."

"And if not for your own actions, the same!" Annah's voice was sharp. "Rosalind came to our academy because you'd made so many enemies, the girl wasn't safe elsewhere. But do you blame yourself? No. You blame the teachers, you blame Sebastian, you want everyone else's head to roll. But heaven forbid *you* take any responsibility."

Annah gestured her gun once more toward Jode. "There's

the real killer. No one will stop you from doing your worst. Snuffing out that monster might be the noblest deed you'll do in your life—not just revenge, but justice. How many people get such a gift? To vent their grief on a thing of pure evil. To take a vengeance unquestionably right. But you get only the demon; nothing more."

Tzekich looked into Annah's eyes, staring past the muzzle of the gun. Softly she said, "My daughter has been murdered. If I could kill the whole world, it wouldn't be enough. Don't you understand revenge?"

Annah didn't answer right away. I don't know what was going through her mind—what memories of her family, its vendettas, its hatreds. The previous night, she'd talked about people who hungered for revenge, who considered it more important than life itself: "an absolute necessity, a religious imperative."

I wondered what Annah had seen—what atrocities her family had committed, what horrors had been done to them in return.

"I understand revenge," Annah said. "It can't stop itself. Someone else has to put it out of its misery."

She fired her gun into Knife-Hand Liz's face.

An instant after Annah pulled the trigger, she dove forward onto Jode's body. I thought she must be diving for cover . . . as if hitting the floor was any protection.

The Ring-men fired on her at point-blank range.

Gushes of flame lit the chamber. The smell of burning gas mixed with the bitterness of acid. Bullets caromed off the rock walls so fiercely, I buried my face against the floor and covered my head with my arms.

Moments later, a gun blew up. I heard the explosion as shattering metal: a pressurized ammunition chamber filled with flammable gas or acid that was breached by a bullet and burst its deadly payload into the world. I didn't know whose gun it was—Annah's or one of those held by the Ring—but they were all so close together, it didn't make a difference.

Total mutual destruction in the first half-second. Burnt, shot, corroded.

As I lay listening to the roar of weapons, I realized Annah must have known what would happen. What she'd be forced to do. Even if Tzekich hadn't explicitly threatened Sebastian or the school, violent retribution would still have hung in the air. "My daughter has been murdered. If I could kill the whole world, it wouldn't be enough." Sooner or later, Tzekich might lash out against the boy . . . or the academy . . . or someone Annah loved.

Like me.

So Annah made sure that wouldn't happen.

She also granted Elizabeth Tzekich's final wish. The way Knife-Hand Liz looked into Annah's eyes . . . had she been pleading for an end? Her daughter was dead; her heart was broken; and though she spoke of revenge, perhaps Mother Tzekich was actually asking for release.

One can be so crushed with grief, one prays for death so the pain will stop.

Believe me, I know.

24

REVELATIONS 12:9

Some time later, I stood up. My boots scraped against the stone floor, filling the chamber with hollow echoes.

Where Annah and the Ring had been standing, there were now only smoldering lumps. Thin smoke rose from their remains. I considered saying a prayer for the dead, but didn't have the heart for it.

Alone in a world full of corpses, I thought. But that wasn't true—Dreamsinger was still alive, protected from the explosion by her armor. Her breathing was soft and calm, as if sleeping peacefully. I wanted to seize her by the shoulders, shake her roughly, wake her up . . . but the hypersonics from an Element gun knocked victims out for six hours, and nothing I could do would rouse the Sorcery-Lord sooner. Besides, she was still surrounded by that force field, the one that melted bullets; if I tried to touch her, my hands would disintegrate.

I looked down at Dreamsinger once more. The <BINK>-rod she'd been holding lay a short distance away. It must have fallen from her grasp when she'd been shot. I bent, picked it up, then felt foolish at the gesture. Did I think this was some kind of magic wand? A wonderful *deus ex machina* I could wave and abracadabra, bring back all my friends?

There were nothing but blackened lumps where Annah

had been standing . . . and farther off lay Impervia's body, outside the range of the explosion but sprawled deathly still. I couldn't bring myself to take a closer look. What would be the point? Let her rest in peace.

So there I was: last man standing. Pelinor would say that made me the hero of our quest; but I'd done nothing anyone would call heroic. The hard work came from my friends— the protecting, the dying. All I could do was ensure they hadn't died in vain.

Element gun in one hand, <BINK>-rod in the other, I approached the laser cage.

The door of the airlock shack had one simple control—a lever with three positions marked INNER SHUT, BOTH SHUT, OUTER SHUT. It was currently set to the last: outer door closed, inner one open. I moved the switch to the middle and watched as the inner door slid into place. The imprisoned Lucifer had withdrawn into the main area of the cage, taking Sebastian with it. I guessed it didn't want to leave the boy in the airlock shack where he might be easier to rescue.

Deep breath. I moved the lever again.

The outer door opened. I had my gun set to shoot flames, ready to scorch any bits of Lucifer hiding in the airlock. But the shacklike space seemed perfectly clean: white walls, white floor, white ceiling, where the tiniest black grain would show up clearly. No doubt the airlock had cleansing devices that sanitized the place every time the doors cycled. I didn't know how decontamination was possible without killing any humans in the airlock . . . but if the Keepers harvested lightbulbs from the Lucifer's mass, people must go in and out through the shack all the time. One just had to trust that the Sparks could eradicate alien cellules while leaving *Homo sapiens* intact.

I stepped into the airlock. The inside wall had a three-position lever like the one outside. I moved the lever to BOTH SHUT and waited.

A flat plane of green light rose from the floor, like a platform of jade ascending around me. The surface was too glossy to see through, but I could feel a tingle as it climbed my legs: like the brisk scraped sensation after drying oneself with a rough towel. The feeling increased to wrenching pain as it reached my abdomen—an unknown force clawing my intestines, scouring deep in search of alien intruders. Some part of my mind wondered what kind of energy the light was, how it could distinguish between human flesh and alien particles. But I didn't care that much. Like a man plodding the last hundred meters of a marathon, I just wanted to get this over.

The jade surface rose. As it reached my heart, congestion squeezed my chest. I tried to breathe normally; I closed my eyes and waited, feeling the tingle flush up my throat, my face . . . then a burst of jade flared as it swept past my retinas.

When I opened my eyes, the plane of light was vanishing into the airlock roof. I caught my breath, lifted my weapons, and moved the control lever to open the inner door.

The Lucifer didn't attack. It didn't even move. Its black powder mass sat silent. Waiting.

"Release the boy," I said.

No response. As if the creature didn't understand my words. But I was certain it knew what I was saying.

I raised my gun. "Give me the boy or I'll hurt you. Kill you if that's possible. Heaven knows why the Sparks kept you alive at all; but I'm sure they'd rather see you dead than loose in the world. So let the boy go."

Still no motion visible in the black heap, but a rustling sound came from the mound's dusty heart. The Lucifer towered above me, three times my height: like the mountain of coal that was dumped behind the academy at the start of each winter. My Element gun was no more than a pea-shooter compared to the Lucifer's bulk; the gun's supply of fire and acid could only braise the monster's surface. If the beast withstood the immediate pain, I'd soon run out of ammunition. As for the glittering <BINK>-rod, I didn't know how much mass it could "roll aside" at any one time . . . but surely not the entire mound. I might banish a few handfuls of black before I was overwhelmed, but that would just delay the inevitable. Sebastian would remain trapped, the batteries powering the cage would run dry . . .

"Give me the boy!" I shouted. Conserving my more effective attacks, I fired a burst of bullets into the mound. Lightbulbs on the surface shattered into sprays of chipped glass; but the Lucifer itself was unhurt.

Quickly, I switched the gun back to flamethrower. "I'm counting to five. Give me the boy or I'll—"

Something shifted within the mound. My nerves were so jittery, I almost pulled the trigger . . . but I stopped myself on the minuscule chance the monster might be letting Sebastian go.

The heap closest to me bulged with a human-shaped protuberance: head and shoulders coated with gunpowder black, pushing their way out of the pile with a dry rasp. Crusted in midnight grains, a figure struggled to wrench free—pushing, pulling, until it abruptly tugged loose from its surroundings and stumbled forward, trying to catch its balance.

I kept my gun trained on the figure. "Don't come too close." If a thing that *looked* like Sebastian materialized out of that mess, I'd be a fool to believe it must be the real boy. Besides, the thing before me was still just a humanoid clump of black, standing weak and wobbly, head turning back and forth as if trying to get its bearings. Then the outermost layer of powder slumped away to reveal . . .

Rosalind Tzekich. As naked as when I had seen her last, but with life and health shining where there had only been the limpness of death.

The new Rosalind gave me a tranquil smile. Beatific. A much different look from the listless way she'd endured math classes. The distance and loneliness were gone now: she had the look of a prisoner who'd been released.

Reluctantly, I trained the Element gun on her—hoping that wherever the real Rosalind was now, she wore exactly the same kind of smile. "I've seen enough fakes of this girl," I said. "Let her rest in peace."

The Rosalind-thing didn't answer. She held her arms out at her sides, hands open, palms toward me: the pose of someone showing she was no threat, as if I were a dog who had to be mollified. "Stop it," I said. "You're nothing more than shapeshifting sand; a piece of Lucifer, trying to distract me. I want Sebastian and I want him now. One . . . two . . . three. . . ."

She stepped toward me, still smiling. I cursed the Lucifer under my breath, and switched the gun back to bullets. What I had to do next would give me nightmares . . . as if my brain didn't already contain enough horrors for a thousand sleepless nights.

I pulled the trigger. A single bullet at point-blank range, straight into the chest of a teenage girl.

But it wasn't a girl at all. The shot hit the creature dead center, scattering gouts of black sand out the thing's spine; but a shock wave of blowback sent grains spraying forward, splashing onto my feet, my coat—and my face. I reached up blindly with the <BINK>-rod, hoping it would spirit the dark flecks away . . . but by then, my world had vanished.

No sight, no sound; but I could still breathe. The grains hadn't gone down my throat—not yet. I couldn't even feel them on my face. In fact, I felt nothing at all: as if my body had dissolved, leaving only a consciousness divorced from my five senses.

Then a sixth sense dawned: a feeling of connection and dispersion, my mind spread across the universe. A million, billion, trillion places at once. I had no eyes or ears, but I sensed myself standing on a plain covered with lacy blue ice, not frozen water but solidified nitrogen, oxygen, and methane; I was also floating through hot sulfur clouds where fat balloon creatures built cities from cottony fibers that drifted as light as dust; and I was deep undersea, clinging to the ocean floor as a warm soup of my own children clustered about me in the jelly stage of their life cycle. I lurked in the heart of trees. I swam through the bloodstream of an animal as big as the moon, and together we fed off dark energies filling the interstellar vacuum. I sipped on magma at a planet's core; I conversed with red moss in a tumbledown city peopled by senile machines; I clotted in a solid shell around a giant sun as it collapsed into supernova.

None of these scenes reached me as normal vision; I simply comprehended my surroundings, *knowing* instead of sensing. I was a million, billion, trillion shapeshifting grains spread through the galaxy, conjoined in a single mental whole: a hive mind with every cellule in contact with all the others despite being separated by countless light-years. A single unified consciousness distributed over untold star systems.

This was the past—a stunted ghost of memory that didn't come close to the Lucifer's true splendor. I sensed its frustration at not remembering more clearly . . . at not being able to impress me with its full former glory. It had been a creature vastly higher on the evolutionary ladder than *Homo sapiens*: like a god compared to us mere mortals, or at least like an angel.

And like all angels, it eventually fell.

Another memory: this time on Earth. A human doppelgänger similar to Jode, a colony of cellules shaped like a handsome man pretending to sleep beside a beautiful woman. Suddenly, the door burst open. People were there in plastic armor—four Spark Lords. They grabbed the false human and hustled it into the night. The Lucifer didn't protest; its impersonations had been discovered before, had been captured, tortured, and burned. The experience was unpleasant, but not a cause for concern. The death of a few cellules had no effect on the whole . . . and the great Lucifer consciousness had plenty of other representatives on Earth to continue observing our species.

So the Lucifer didn't resist. It even laughed as the Sparks said, "We're doing this for your own protection. Word has come down from the League." The Lucifer kept laughing right up to the moment where it was thrown into a cage made of light . . .

. . . at which point, the world went silent. Communications cut off. Isolation. The cage somehow blocked mental contact with the hive mind gestalt.

For a time, the Lucifer went mad. Not just from the shock of separation—the creature had been part of a single far-flung brain, with psychological functions distributed over all the component parts. Now a tiny chunk of that brain was forced to survive on its own. Almost all its memories vanished, stored as they were in other individuals that had dropped out of touch. Its angelic wisdom dissolved; its knowledge of the galaxy; its personality, whatever that had been: lost, lost, everything lost.

Eventually, the imprisoned creature stabilized—each remaining cellule taking its share of the burden, creating an entity that was far from the original but at least able to function. Still, it was a grossly diminished version of its former self: less memory, less intelligence, less far-reaching perception . . . like a creature that was once a whale now reduced to a gnat.

Even so, the gnat had regained its sanity.

When the Sparks were sure it had found a new balance, they turned down the cage's blocking power an infinitesimal amount . . . and the Lucifer reached out eagerly, trying to reestablish contact with its fellows.

A moment later, it reeled back in horror. The angel outside the cage had become a devil: a shouting shriek of corruption, poisoned with hate and violence. Lusting to conquer and kill—many of its component colonies committing murder at the very instant the Lucifer made contact. During that fleeting touch of communication, the prisoner in the cage got the impression its parent mass now deliberately choreographed its actions so it was *always* in the act of killing sentient creatures somewhere in the galaxy . . . so that it never lacked the taste of blood and death.

The great hive consciousness outside the cage had changed from the archangel Lucifer . . . into a howling Satan.

How could such a thing happen? Had some distant cellule been twisted by mutation, poison, or sabotage? If a single cellule went mad, could the madness spread instantly through the whole, like a disease infecting the entire consciousness? An explosion of evil no cellule could resist, so that in the blink of an eye, a wise and mighty creature was lost to the cancer of malice. Or had the parent mass simply turned vicious as a whole, rejecting its passive observation of lower species and deciding to tyrannize them instead?

The caged Lucifer had no answers. All it knew was that its parent had become a malignant embodiment of hate . . . and if that hate ever broke through the blocking power of the cage, the Lucifer's mind would be washed away in the flood, perverted by the sheer mental force of a billion trillion former siblings.

So the Lucifer remained in its prison, grateful to be protected against its Satanic parent outside. It spent its time wondering how the League had foreseen the coming corruption. Who had enough advance warning to rescue a small part of the whole, when the Lucifer itself never suspected a thing? Wouldn't the Sparks have needed months to build a cage and adapt the generating station to power it? Could the League really look so far into the future? And if so, why hadn't they warned the hive mind itself? But neither the League nor the Spark Lords ever offered to explain.

The Sparks *did* explain why they'd captured the Lucifer. By preserving a piece of the "angelic" Lucifer, the League one day hoped to cure the "demonic" part. Little by little, year by year, Spark Royal would turn down the cage's blocking field . . . and gradually the imprisoned Lucifer would grow stronger, better able to resist the psychic onslaught of its depraved Satanic brethren. In a few more centuries (or millennia, or eons—the League was patient), perhaps the good could win back the evil, just as the evil had forced out the good.

Meanwhile the Lucifer waited. And it grew. Its kind had a complex life cycle and didn't reproduce quickly . . . but with the Keepers providing its needs, the Lucifer expanded from the original human-sized doppelgänger to the great black mound now occupying the cage. For something to do, the cellules had busied themselves as little chemical factories, building lightbulbs and other equipment, molecule by molecule.

The evil outer consciousness had kept busy too. Just as the imprisoned Lucifer could touch its parent Satan's mind, the parent could feel its small uncorrupted child: an aggravating hold-out, a slim incompatibility, an itching flea-bite that couldn't be scratched. Satan raged at the tiny irritation; perhaps it couldn't tolerate any reminder it had once been an angel, or perhaps it feared for its own existence, recognizing that someday its corruption *might* be reversed. Whatever the reason, Satan despised the caged Lucifer. The galactic demon couldn't rest till the prison was bashed down and the independent black mound was bludgeoned back into the venomous whole.

So Satan declared war on Lucifer . . . and on the Spark Lords who guarded the cage. Many times in the past, evil doppelgängers had tried to break into the generating station. On each attempt, the aliens penetrated farther into the Keepers' defenses. On each attempt, the Sparks stopped the intruders and destroyed them. On each attempt, Satan kept a few cellules of itself safe elsewhere on the planet—enough, in time, to build a new body and try, try again.

This was a war of move and countermove: Satan would devise new strategies of attack; the Sparks would respond with new modes of defense. Spark Royal had always maintained the upper hand, thanks (as I'd guessed) to equipment that could detect gunpowderlike cellules at the range of a kilometer. The Niagara region was spanned with hundreds of such detectors, immediately reporting any evil Lucifers that dared to approach.

But Satan was vastly intelligent, a single brain spanning the galaxy. It had learned science tricks from a thousand cultures . . . and whatever was known by the whole could be used by the fragments on Earth. If the Sparks could detect dry black cellules, why not mutate into moist white nuggets?

I don't understand how Satan managed it—I received vague impressions of the demon grains bathing themselves in chemicals, bombarding themselves with radiation—but the specifics were lost on me. Anyway, the details didn't matter; the demon somehow changed itself to a new form Spark Royal couldn't detect. A form that caught Sparks unaware.

Mind-Lord Priest had been first to meet the mutated demon. Priest's detector equipment identified Jode as nonhuman, but the device which should have said THIS IS A LUCIFER was fooled by the mutation into maggots. Result? Priest had no idea what he was dealing with. He'd been taken by sur-

prise and killed. Jode sailed away doubly triumphant: not
only had the Lucifer obtained Priest's <BINK>-rod but Jode
had proved its new curdlike form could fool the Sparks' defenses.

Though I got this information from the Lucifer in the
cage, it had known none of it at the time. Yes, the angel had a
faint mental link with its demon siblings . . . but the connection was patchy, seldom providing more than quick glimpses
of Satan's violent acts around the galaxy. The good Lucifer
hadn't perceived the death of Priest, and it hadn't caught a
whiff of Jode's plans for Rosalind and Sebastian—Satan
concealed what was happening, veiling its thoughts to prevent the caged Lucifer from foreseeing the imminent attack.

So no alarm sounded till Dreamsinger deduced the truth at
Nanticook House. She'd hurried to Niagara and rallied the
Keepers' defenses . . . but I'd seen how it all turned out.
Crushing defeat. Now Satan pounded the still-angelic Lucifer with its thoughts—boasting how clever it had been, like
a villain in a melodrama explaining everything in the last act.
The mutation from black to white. The death of Priest. The
murder of Rosalind. Inside the laser cage, the angel wished it
could shut out the gloating tirade; but the cage's defenses
were weakening and Satan's hideous strength was close to
breaking through.

Yet no matter how much the mental onslaught pained the
good Lucifer, I could sense no fear in its soul. The angel had
embodied itself as Rosalind, wearing a radiant smile; I could
feel the same beatific assurance filling the Lucifer as it
touched my mind. A confidence that everything would work
out for the best.

How can you believe that? I asked. *You're hanging by a
thread, yet you still think you'll be saved?*

The answer didn't come in words. Instead, I had a vision
of the Caryatid in her classroom, watching a dog's tongue
predict she would go on a quest; I heard Rosalind's harp
playing in empty darkness; finally, I was shown again the
moment in our chancellor's suite when Opal said, "It sure is
a bitch living in a universe where so many species are
smarter than you."

What was the Lucifer trying to tell me? That the League of Peoples had anticipated this, the same way they'd foreseen the fall of Satan? That they'd *arranged* to bring me here because I could somehow put things right?

If not for the haunting, we wouldn't have discovered Rosalind's death till many hours later—too late for any of us to reach Niagara Falls in time. If not for the prophecy, I wouldn't have thought to call my friends after finding Rosalind's body. And without my friends, without the haunting and prophecy, I wouldn't have arrived where I was now.

Was that it? The League had manufactured supernatural events to nudge me and my friends in the direction we'd gone?

A wave of agreement came from the Lucifer. It believed I'd been brought here to play the hero. *Me*. As if I could save the world.

Suddenly, my link with the Lucifer broke. A moment of dizziness. Then I was back in my own body, seeing with my own eyes by the dim violet light of the lasers. The <BINK>-rod and my Element gun lay a footstep away. The mound of black grains had pulled back against the walls of the prison cube, leaving me lying in a clear space in the middle. I felt as if I'd woken inside a volcano cone, with heaps of dark ash all around me.

I wasn't alone on the cage's floor. A short distance away, Sebastian lay squeezed into fetal position. He looked dead.

Slowly, carefully, I moved across the floor to Sebastian. When I tried to touch him, my hand was thrown back as if something had shoved it away. Nanites. They'd formed a shell around him, ready to repel anyone who came close . . . like a ring of growling dogs protecting their fallen master. If I tried to touch the boy again, I suspected the nanites would respond with more than a harmless push.

Now that I was closer, I could see Sebastian was still breathing. He didn't look injured: just catatonic. And who could blame him? He'd discovered he'd bedded a monster— the monster who'd killed poor Rosalind. The boy might also have realized he'd butchered dozens of innocent Keepers at the monster's prompting. Then there were the ugly deaths he'd seen: Impervia and the Caryatid. Enough to drive any-one into a stupor . . . especially a sensitive teenage boy whose head had been full of romantic notions.

It's devastating when you finally recognize the world is cruel. But time was running out, and Sebastian was the only one who could put things right.

"This is it, isn't it?" I said to the Lucifer. "Why I was brought here. I'm the boy's don; I'm supposed to get through to him. You think I can wake him before it's too late."

A rustle went through the surrounding black mound: a scratchy sandy hiss.

I nearly gave a bitter laugh. All this way, through bullets, fire, and acid; then it turned out my role was not to slay mon-sters but to talk to a teenager.

Almost as if my destiny was to be a schoolteacher.

"Sebastian," I said, "it's Dr. Dhubhai."

The boy didn't move. Still scrunched into a tight fetal ball.

I tried again. "You've just experienced some horrible things. Worse than you could imagine. And you probably don't understand a bit of what's going on."

The gunpowder mass rustled again. I took that to mean agreement. When the Lucifer covered Sebastian, nanites must have immediately formed a shield around the boy. They'd prevented the mound from establishing a mental link; otherwise, the Lucifer could have melted into Sebastian's thoughts and perhaps eased away the catatonia.

"I could explain everything," I told the boy, "but that would take time and we don't have much to spare."

Once more the black grains rustled in agreement.

"So here's how it is," I said. "You're feeling like the world is broken. Your life is ruined and nothing will ever be the same.

"Well . . . you're partly right. Good people are dead: peo-ple who never deserved what happened to them. And you've done some ghastly things. You were tricked into doing them, but you'll still have to live with the memory. That's going to hurt; perhaps forever.

"But you know what, Sebastian? Everyone's life is a mess. *Everyone's*. We all make mistakes . . . and not just little slip-ups. Major mistakes that hurt us and other people. We all go down wrong paths because we don't know better . . . or because we're too lazy, lonely, and afraid to change.

"I've screwed up my life just like everyone else. I've been a teacher ten years and I've *never* taken it to heart. Isn't that ridiculous? I should either get out or accept where I am. No more acting like the job is beneath me.

"And women! I can't begin to list the ways I've been a fool. Staying with one woman because she was convenient . . . even though she and I knew the affair was a poor substitute for what we should have wanted. And for years I looked down on another woman, even though she was far more than I ever dreamed; not to mention how I was completely blind to a third woman, who must have been hurt every day by my obliviousness.

"Those three women are dead now, Sebastian. I'll never get the chance to make it up to them. I'd like to curl up into a ball and cry until my eyes bleed.

"But crying won't help. Nothing will. I can't fix the past. I can only resolve to do better in future.

"Are you listening, Sebastian? Can you hear what I'm saying? Because I'm going to tell you something important: something everybody knows and everybody forgets. Are you listening? Here it is. You have to confront life. That's all. No matter how tempting avoidance may be, you have to confront life. I know it sounds trite, like the usual nonsense teachers tell their students. But it's true. You have to confront life. If you don't, your problems just fester. Nothing gets cleaned up. The messes you've made just grow worse.

"Believe me, I know. In the past twenty-four hours, I've seen people confront their lives. I've seen them do what had to be done . . . even if it meant they'd die. They faced up to necessity. I don't claim to be a great example myself—but you know what? I'm doing it."

I stood . . . walked back to the Element gun and the <BINK>-rod. Picking them up, I told the boy, "I could leave right now. I could head for the door and this big sand-heap probably wouldn't try to stop me. If it did, I could blast my way free. Out of this cage, out of this building, out of the whole ugly mess. I wouldn't go back to the academy—my purse is full and I can live like a king almost anywhere on Earth. No one would track me down. I'm not important enough for the Sparks or Satan to care about.

"But I'm still here with you, Sebastian. Because you have the power to set things right. You can't bring back Rosalind; you can't resurrect the people who've died. But you can remove your dam; you can reconnect the power cables; you can save the sanity of an innocent creature; and you can foil the plans of a monster who killed the girl you loved. All you have to do is use your power—speak to those little puppies who want to follow your orders. It would be so *easy*. I know you're tired; it must seem impossible to make the tiniest effort. God knows I've felt the same. Paralyzed. You can barely breathe, Sebastian, and I'm just some pompous adult preaching platitudes.

"You wish I'd shut up . . . but I have to say something you might not have considered. About Rosalind. I've been thinking of her ever since last night, and the image that keeps coming to mind was the way she'd gaze out the windows during math class. Just staring, as if she was light-years away. I would have said she was disconnected from life: stuck in a trap of her mother's making; wrapped up in numbness and three-quarters dead. But then she made a decision—to elope with you. Not a decision I'd agree with, and if I caught you two sneaking out, you'd both get homework detentions for the next thirty years . . . but it was a sign of life, Sebastian. Rosalind recognized something had to change, and she *did* something about it.

"So did you, Sebastian. You and Rosalind together. It must have taken courage; and now, after horrible things have happened, maybe you're thinking you never should have done it. But there's no such thing as playing safe. Life might hurt, but it's better than numbness. Rosalind knew that. So did you when you agreed to elope with her. Be brave again, Sebastian. Wake up and do something. It'll get easier once you start. Just talk to your nanite friends and ask them to help."

The light in the room flickered. For a moment, I didn't realize what that meant; I thought Sebastian had come to his senses and done something . . . told the nanites to start repairing everything that needed to be fixed. Then the flicker came again and the truth struck me: the only illumination in the entire chamber was the soft violet glow from the lasers.

The lasers flickered once more, then went out.

Deep blackness—the thick absence of light that happens only underground. One tiny glitter remained: the red and green nuggets on the <BINK>-rod I held in my hand.

The room was utterly silent: nothing but the thud of my pulse. Then all around me, black gunpowder grains whispered against one another.

Uh-oh.

The cage had run out of power. No more mental shield protecting the angel from the demon. I could imagine Satan screaming in triumph as it crushed its good enemy with galaxy-sized willpower.

A million black cellules rustled again.

Quickly turning off the <BINK>-rod and tucking it up one sleeve, I gripped my Element gun in both hands. I pulled the trigger and swung in a fast circle, spraying a bright stream of fire spiraling outward. Dark grains sizzled as the flames swept across them, but the blaze only scorched a thin layer on the outside of the mound. Underneath the blistered surface, the Lucifer rolled itself forward like a dune in a windstorm.

"Sebastian!" I yelled. "Wake up!"

The boy didn't move.

I moved to his comatose body and stood astride him, gun ready to fire again. I'd released the trigger after the first burst, but there was enough light to see by—small patches of the Lucifer were burning, weak orange embers all around me. Those tiny fires must have caused the creature pain, but it showed no sign of being intimidated; the great black mound continued to close in, rasping as sand crept across the floor.

"Sebastian!" I loosed another gout of flame from the gun.

Roaring orange streamed forth, painful to the eyes; it cast the Lucifer's shadow onto the room's stone walls. I made another complete circle with the fire, then quickly switched to acid. It spattered like deadly rain, hissing when it hit hotspots left by the flamethrower. There were more ember patches on the mound now, dozens of them . . . but they just made it easier to see that the bulk of the Lucifer wasn't damaged at all. My gun could only dole out flesh wounds; and it would soon exhaust its ammunition.

Flame. Acid. Flame. Acid. Nothing stopped the Lucifer's steady approach. I was sure the alien mass could move faster—Jode had lashed out like lightning at Pelinor—but this was a creature who toyed with its prey. Before it killed me, Satan wanted to smell my fear.

Flame. Acid. Then I pulled the trigger and nothing happened.

I switched to bullets and emptied the clip. Despite the noise and muzzle flash, my barrage was as useless as firing rounds into a sandbank. When I ran out of lead, I tried hypersonics. No discernible effect; if anything, the rustling around me grew louder with gleeful anticipation.

The battery powering the hypersonics went dead. I dropped the gun and pulled the <BINK>-rod from my sleeve, pressing the activation button immediately. With luck, I'd banish a few more cellules from this plane of existence before a flood of them rushed down my throat.

Embers in all directions. The mound towered above me, twice my height.

"It's okay," I said to Sebastian—not from calm acceptance, but because I didn't want Satan to see me panic. "Your nanites will keep you safe; and I'll join my friends in whatever comes next. Gretchen. Oberon. Myoko. Pelinor. Impervia. The Caryatid. Annah." I took a deep breath. "Rosalind. I'm going to die like Rosalind, Sebastian. Unless you do something."

Glowing embers showed the Lucifer was almost within reach. "In the name of Most Merciful Compassionate God," I said. "Praise be to God, the Lord of all Being; All-Merciful,

All-Compassionate, the Master of the day of judgment. Thee only do we worship and of thee do we beg assistance."

I lifted the <BINK>-rod to swing it at the mound . . . then suddenly, an idea blossomed inside my beleaguered brain. Inspiration. I dropped to my knees and whacked the rod hard on Sebastian.

To be honest, I doubted it would work—the nanites protecting the boy might resist the <BINK>-rod's effects, might even knock the rod from my hands before it made contact. But either the nanites couldn't resist or they were smart enough to recognize I had Sebastian's interests at heart. The <BINK>-rod came down . . . made contact . . . and the boy disappeared.

The gunpowder heap loosed a furious hiss, like a poisonous snake cheated of its prey. It hurtled toward me, no longer teasing out the moment of fear but trying to avalanche across the gap before I too escaped. The leading edge slammed against my legs, knocking me off my feet; but as I fell, I had time to swing the rod, slap my own chest with the tip . . .

. . . and the sandy roar fell silent. The burning embers vanished. I finished my fall and struck dust that billowed up in clouds on my impact.

A weight clinging to my legs sloughed off: gunpowder grains that had traveled with me on this abrupt trip to wherever. They dropped limply from my clothing into the dust, all sign of malice gone.

I looked up. I was inside another laser cage, much bigger than the one I'd just left, but still delineated by thin violet beams outlining a cube. Those beams showed this cage was still working, isolating the captured cellules from the Satanic overmind outside. It made perfect sense; since this was where Spark Lords sent bits of Lucifer, they'd erected a special holding cell to separate the parts from the whole.

Beyond the cell ceiling, stars shone untwinkling in a pure black sky. There was no sun, but amidst the starry waste floated a large cloudy blue moon. I knew it wasn't really a moon at all—I'd seen photographs from OldTech space missions, and I recognized the Earth when I saw it.

My homeworld. My planet. Drifting overhead as I stood in a laser prison on the moon.

"Pretty, isn't it?" said a voice behind me.

I turned. It was Annah.

25
EARTHRISE

For a moment, my heart surged with joy; then the joy was crushed by depression. "I know you're not real," I said. Dull weariness washed over me. "You're just another doppelgänger—a collection of all the cellules sent here over the years. I don't know how you realized that looking like Annah would torment me . . . but frankly I don't care." I still held the <BINK>-rod in my hand; I waved it in warning, like showing a cross to a vampire. "Come any closer, and I'll hit you with this. Unless I miss my guess, that will send you back to Niagara Falls. One tap brings you here. Another returns you to wherever . . ."

My voice trailed off. The Annah in front of me had brought out an identical <BINK>-rod. "This is the one Jode stole from Mind-Lord Priest. I was standing over Jode when I shot Knife-Hand Liz. The rod was right at my feet. I fired my gun, then dived to grab it; I used it on myself a millisecond before the Ring of Knives men tried to shoot me."

I stared at her numbly. Forcing myself not to believe.

"It's true, Phil," she said. "I got out in time. Didn't you notice I was gone?"

"There was an explosion," I mumbled. "Nothing but charred heaps of . . ." I didn't finish the sentence. "Annah?"

"Yes, Phil. It's me." She held open her arms.

I walked forward—knowing full well it might be a Lucifer trick. But I didn't care. If this vision of Annah transformed

into a slurry of maggots that choked me to death, so be it. I
was numb to fear, numb to hope, numb, numb, numb.

She wrapped her arms around me. I laid my head on her
shoulder. She kissed my hair, but said nothing.

For a long time we just stood there, body to body. Her
breath soft beside me; the smell of her skin and hair slowly
working into my consciousness.

At some point, I put my arms around her too. But neither
of us spoke as the Earth slowly drifted overhead.

We might have stood that way forever. What broke the spell
was something bumping hard against my leg. I looked down
and saw an amorphous black blob trying to wrap itself
around my ankle. It was the size of a housecat but made of
gunpowder grains that glinted in the Earthlight; I shook it off
in disgust and it slid away, leaving a haphazard track in the
moondust.

Annah unwrapped her arms from me. "There are lots of
those things here," she said as she watched the blob weave
away. I could see she was right; the cage held more than a
dozen masses of similar size, moving apparently at random
across the lunar surface. They showed no sign of intelligence—deprived of contact with Satan, they seemed as
mindless as worms.

"They're used to being part of a larger consciousness," I
said. "This laser cage cuts that connection; I guess it sends
them into shock."

I told Annah what I'd learned from the good Lucifer . . .
and as I talked, questions rose in my mind. If the good Lucifer had eventually come to its senses after being blocked
off from the whole, why hadn't that happened to the wandering blobs in this cage? Were the blobs perhaps too small to
regain their intelligence—not enough cellules, so not enough
collective brainpower? Did the "angelic" Lucifer have a
stronger self-identity than the Satanic version? Was it just
that the angel had Spark Lords caring for it, and somehow
the Sparks had nursed it back to sanity? Or could this version
of the laser cage be different from the one in Niagara: not just
sealing off the cellules from the hive mind outside, but sup-

pressing their mental capacity so they couldn't collect their thoughts?

No answers, just questions . . . and when I'd finished my explanations, Annah had a question of her own. "If I understand this correctly," she said, "Dreamsinger sent Jode to this prison too. Jode had that rod which let him escape; but while he was here, wouldn't he have lost touch with the main consciousness just like these blobs?"

"You're right. Yet he kept enough intelligence to use the <BINK>-rod for his return." I shrugged. "Maybe the difference was that Jode was ready for the experience. He *expected* to get sent here. Maybe that expectation let him retain intelligence long enough to use the rod." I looked around at the scuttling blobs. "Or maybe every Lucifer retains intelligence for a while. It's only prolonged separation from the hive mind that makes them stupid. Or even . . . look, Jode knew in advance he'd get banished here. He could have prepared some sort of device, a clockwork attachment that swung the <BINK>-rod a few minutes after he'd arrived on the moon. That way it wouldn't matter if he went mindless—the rod would tap him automatically, so he'd return to Earth, and immediately link back with the hive."

"That last sounds most likely," Annah said. "It doesn't leave as much to chance; he could have been hiding the whole contraption right inside his body." She looked up at the bright blue planet in the sky. "By the way, I don't think that's the real Earth . . . and this isn't the real moon. There's no air on the moon, is there?"

"True. And there shouldn't be this much gravity either." I took a tentative jump. It felt like jumping on Earth—nowhere near the big bounce I'd have made under weak lunar gravity. "Both Jode and Dreamsinger talked as if those fancy rods sent you to an alternate dimension. I guess it amused the Sparks to make this prison look like the face of the moon: emphasizing the sense of banishment. But you're right, this isn't the real . . ."

A sizzling noise interrupted me. Annah and I whirled toward the sound.

Three paces away, Sebastian lay in the dust, still hugging himself into a fetal ball. One of the Lucifer blobs had pushed up against him during its mindless wanderings. Now, plumes of smoke billowed between it and the boy, as Sebastian's nanite protectors fought off the alien cellules; but the blob was too stupid to realize it had caught fire. It turned to one side, like a worm that has bumped against a wall and starts to inch along the wall itself—the worst thing the blob could do under the circumstances. It continued sliding along the length of Sebastian's body, burning all the way as the nanites continued to attack . . . but even before the blob reached Sebastian's toes and wobbled away smoldering, the nanite-generated flames had begun to dwindle. They just weren't as strong as when the blob had first stubbed up against the boy.

I wondered: was that because the nanites realized the blob wasn't bothered by fire? Or could there be another explanation?

Carefully, I stepped in and eased the bottom of my boot toward Sebastian's knee. I felt some resistance, like pushing through sand . . . but after a moment it yielded and my foot touched the boy's pant-leg.

"What are you doing?" Annah asked.

"Nanites," I said. She looked at me blankly; she hadn't been there when Myoko explained psionics to me. "It's too complicated to go into details," I told her, "but just as the Lucifer consists of little independent cellules, Sebastian's powers come from the same sort of thing: microscopic entities, sort of like bacteria. They're ubiquitous on Earth . . . but not here. The only nanites in this place are the ones we brought with us—in our bodies, in our clothes, and in Sebastian's protective shell."

Annah wrinkled her forehead. "So these nanites are cut off from the whole, just like the cellules?"

I nodded. "They're used to operating on Earth, where they're always surrounded by trillions of their kind. So think about them burning that blob just now—the nanites probably did it by incinerating themselves. On Earth that would be no problem, since there'd always be plenty of replacements for the ones that went up in flames; but here, where there *are* no replacements . . . every nanite that dies protecting Sebastian means the shell around the boy gets weaker."

"And I'll bet," said Annah, "the nanites left over aren't as smart. These things must be another collective intelligence, right? Just like the Lucifers. And when nanites burn up, it's like losing brain cells. The rest get more stupid."

She had a point. Under normal circumstances, nanites could draw on each other for brainpower—all the nanites in the air, the soil, everywhere. But here on this barren moon, with no fellow nano except themselves . . . it really was like the Lucifer cellules: once part of a huge brain, now fending for themselves. My ability to touch Sebastian proved his nanite protectors were no longer functioning normally.

I dabbed my foot once more against Sebastian's leg. This time there was no resistance at all; the protective shell had dissipated, the nanites too feeble-minded to stick to their pro-gramming. I crouched and hesitantly moved my gloved hand to the boy's arm. No nanites tried to stop me . . . so I gave him a light squeeze. "Sebastian. It's Dr. Dhubhai. Are you all right?"

He whined softly and tried to crunch himself into a tighter ball. Annah knelt beside me. "Give him time, Phil. There's no hurry, is there?"

I thought about the evil Lucifer, unrestrained now that the laser cage in Niagara had lost its power. Surely it would flee from the generating station as fast as possible, splitting itself into human-sized doppelgängers and blending into the local populace. If the creature *didn't* run, more Sparks would eventually show up, at which point . . .

At which point, the Lucifer could have disguised itself as a group of Keepers, wearing robes pulled off the corpses of real Keepers. The aliens might take the Sparks by surprise—might even kill a Lord or two by leading them into a trap. And if the trick didn't work, so what? Satan just lost a few million cellules. The overmind wouldn't care; it lost cellules all the time. Satan would gladly sacrifice a bit of itself for the chance of killing even one Spark.

The first Spark to die would be Dreamsinger. Even now,

she lay unconscious before Satan's malice. The great black heap could simply press down on her until it had exhausted whatever batteries powered her force field; or maybe it could form an airtight dome over her, preventing the inflow of oxygen until Dreamsinger smothered. For that matter, maybe the same biological mechanisms that made lightbulbs and toasters could also manufacture neurotoxins: poisonous gases that the unconscious Sorcery-Lord would helplessly inhale.

All kinds of possibilities.

"I think we might be in a hurry after all," I told Annah. "We should wake Sebastian and get back to Niagara fast. Sebastian can use his powers to cage up the Lucifer . . . or destroy it outright, now that it's turned bad." I paused as another thought struck me. "Even if the Lucifer isn't raising havoc, we have to remove that dam across the river. By now, it's surely causing a flood—in the middle of a big city. People could die."

She met my eyes, then nodded. "Any ideas on how to break through the boy's trauma?"

"No. I tried and got nowhere."

Annah gave me a reproachful look. "You weren't working under the best conditions . . . but if you don't want to talk to him again, I'll see what I can do."

"He's all yours. He might respond better to a female voice."

She held my gaze a moment longer . . . then turned to Sebastian and called his name softly. I stood and walked away—as if my very presence could hamper Annah's progress. Ridiculous to feel self-pity at such a time; but as I stared at the Earth in the big black sky, the only thing on my mind was the leaden weight of failure.

The good Lucifer had believed that some force—the League of Peoples or someone else—recruited me to preserve the angel's soul. I'd been brought to Niagara Falls by the haunting and the prophecy because I supposedly had some strength, some skill, some gift which would let me save the day. Part of me had wanted to believe the myth: that I *was* special, a hero with hidden depths who could turn defeat into victory.

But I hadn't got through to Sebastian. The laser cage had flickered out. The good Lucifer was gone forever, its consciousness swallowed by evil. And if Sebastian eventually came to his senses, the credit would be Annah's—Annah, who'd rescued herself quite handily without any help from me.

I hadn't rescued a single person. Hadn't died in noble sacrifice. Hadn't used my scientific knowledge to conquer the foe. Hadn't used anything except my friends and my money-purse . . . as always.

A surge of disgust swept over me. I reached into my pocket, pulled out the purse, and cocked back my arm—intending to hurl the damned thing away from me, a symbol of my perennial uselessness. But before I completed the throw, I stopped. Something wasn't right. The purse: it was heavier than it should have been. *Much* heavier. And bulging tautly, like a rubbery black soccer ball inflated to maximum pressure.

I opened the purse. A rush of gunpowder grains spilled dryly onto my hands.

For a moment, I stared stupidly at the dark sandy flecks. How could a shovelful of cellules get into my purse? Only one answer: it must have happened while I was mindlinked with the good Lucifer—while I was surrounded by the mound, blind to the outside world. And it couldn't have happened by accident. The purse always sealed hermetically shut, airtight, watertight, impenetrable. The angelic Lucifer must have shaped itself into fingers, opened the purse, deliberately crammed the interior with cellules, then closed it up again . . . all while I was oblivious.

I turned toward Annah, intending to tell her about this strange development; but I never opened my mouth. All around the cage, the blobs that had been blundering blindly were now slithering my way: moving with sudden purpose, converging on my position. Cellules rasped against each other and the moondust beneath them—a hiss like the sound of the great black heap when the lasers had winked out and evil poured in.

Uh-oh. I dropped the purse, then ran to Annah and Sebastian, vowing I'd protect them from whatever happened next.

The closest blob reached the purse and flowed over it, merging with the cellules that had been inside. A ripple went through the dark mass, like a shudder of pleasure. Then another blob arrived and the process repeated: a melding, a ripple, the sounds of grain on grain.

"What now?" Annah asked.

"I had a stowaway. It seems to have given the other cellules a new lease on life."

"Was it a good stowaway or a bad one?"

"That's the question, isn't it?"

More blobs coalesced in the center of the cage—like tumbleweeds blown into a rock niche and massing in a single snarl. When all those cellules finished coming together, they'd create a mound as big as the one in Niagara . . . and judging by the purposeful way the blobs were moving, I was sure the mound would be intelligent.

Intelligent, yes; but good or evil? It had to be evil, didn't it? The good Lucifer's consciousness had been erased as soon as the laser cage lost power.

Unless . . .

Could my purse have kept the angelic Lucifer safe? The angel had stuffed its cellules into my purse before the protective field collapsed. Therefore the little black grains had been angelic when they went in. Could the purse have kept them isolated from the onslaught of Satan?

A normal purse couldn't . . . but this purse was a gift from the Sparks to my grandmother . . . who bequeathed the purse to me . . .

I suddenly found myself laughing. Laughing freely out loud—not with hysteria but truly appreciating the joke.

"What is it?" Annah asked. "What's so funny?"

"My purpose in life," I said. "To carry . . ." I broke up again, unable to speak.

I inherited the purse from my grandmother. She'd received it from the Sparks thirty years ago. The Sparks got it from their mysterious sponsors in the League of Peoples. And the League, with flabbergasting prescience, had pro-

duced this high-tech purse way back when because they'd
foreseen that on this very night they'd need a small container
to protect the sanity of a few million "angelic" cellules.

My purpose in life was to carry the purse. Just that. My
brains, my scientific training, whatever other virtues I
counted as points of pride—they weren't important. I was
merely intended to carry the purse.

Curiosity made me wonder how much the League had
tampered with my life. I didn't believe for an instant they
could actually see thirty years into the future; no, they'd
made this happen by subtle pushes and shoves. Not just the
haunting and prophecy that aimed me in this direction—how
much had they influenced me back in the past? The League
controlled the nanites that pervaded my brain; had those
nanites been the reason I chose to leave Sheba? Why I
crossed the ocean and took a teaching position at Feliss
Academy? And what about my friends? Were they manipulated too, prodded this way and that to satisfy the League's
scheme? Probably. Without the sacrifices of everyone else, I
never would have arrived at the right place and time to save
the Lucifer.

To carry the purse.

"Insh'allah," I said, still laughing.

"What?" Annah asked.

"It shall be however God wills. Or if you prefer *King Lear*,
'As flies to wanton boys, are we to the gods. They kill us for
their sport.'"

"Now you're doing quotations too?"

"Why not?" I smiled . . . but the smile was bitter. "We've
done what we were supposed to, Annah. We've fulfilled the
quest and redeemed Lucifer. We've won."

"How?"

I gestured toward the accumulating heap of cellules. Just
as big as the mound in Niagara. Lucifers had been sent here
over the years and rendered mindless by the suppressing
laser field—turned into blank slates ready to be assimilated
when the good Lucifer arrived. That had been part of the
League's plan too: assembling sufficient mass to be re-
claimed. Now the angel had arrived; now the mindless cel-

lules had become part of a new consciousness. A *good* consciousness . . . or at least one that pleased the League better than the roaringly defiant Satan.

Now we had a saintly mound as big as the demonic one back in Niagara. I didn't have the prophetic powers of the League of Peoples, but I could guess what would happen next.

A humanoid clump of black pulled away from the pile in front of us. It shivered as if it were cold; then the outer crust of gunpowder flaked away to reveal a smiling, radiant Rosalind.

"Hello again," the Lucifer-Rosalind said. Her voice was soft; her eyes shone. "Do you understand what's happened?"

Annah didn't answer. I said, "I understand in general. You might explain a few specifics."

"Such as?"

"How much of this the League made happen. How much they interfered in all our lives."

"I can't answer that," the Rosalind said.

"Can't or won't?"

"Can't." The girl lowered her eyes. "Your purse is roomy for a purse, but it couldn't hold enough to preserve my entire consciousness. I saved the most important parts of my personality—at least I think I did—but I had to sacrifice almost all of my memories. Whatever I knew about the League's plans . . . the knowledge is gone. I'm virtually tabula rasa."

"How convenient for the League."

"Very. I'm as curious as you are about the League's influence. How, for example, did I choose which memories I'd discard and which I'd keep? Did the League do that, or did I choose of my own free will? Does free will exist at all?" The Rosalind shrugged. "I have no answers. Considering that the amount I stuffed into your purse was roughly the size of a human brain, at this point I'm no wiser than you."

"At this point?"

The duplicate Rosalind smiled and gestured to the looming black heap behind her. "I've acquired new brain cells.

With each passing moment, I can feel my mind expanding."

"Lucky you. The laser cage isn't trying to expunge your intelligence?"

"No. The suppression effect turned off as soon as you showed up with the purse. I believe the purse sends out a signal."

"Oh." I shook my head ruefully. "The League thinks of everything, doesn't it?"

"They do plan for contingencies."

"But you don't know what their plan is?"

"No." The Lucifer-Rosalind gave an apologetic look. "Short term, I'm sure you can figure it out for yourself."

I nodded. "We wake Sebastian . . . or rather, *you* wake Sebastian. In your current form, he'll listen to you more than Annah or me."

"That's likely," the Rosalind agreed.

"Then," I continued, "Sebastian uses one of the <BINK>-rods to return to Niagara. He undams the Falls, fixes the wires, and re-activates the laser cage . . . trapping inside any bits of Satan that are waiting to ambush the Spark Lords."

"Correct."

"Then *you* use the other <BINK>-rod to go back to Niagara. After a brief struggle, you assimilate the evil cellules that are still in the cage."

The pseudo-Rosalind smiled. "Let's say I restore them to sanity."

"So you increase your mass significantly and you get practice in bringing evil Lucifers back to the straight and narrow. One step closer to fulfilling the League's plans for you."

"I'm sure they have my best interests at heart."

I couldn't tell if the alien was being sarcastic. An upswell of bitterness made me say, "The League has *everybody's* best interests at heart. They're the good guys, aren't they? Supremely powerful, yet generous enough to let lesser beings take part in their schemes. Like Gretchen. And Myoko. And Oberon and Pelinor and all the others who died in this mess. If the League is so omniscient, they must have foreseen my friends' deaths. But the League let it happen anyway; in fact, they *instigated* everything, because we'd all be safe in Simka if the League hadn't nudged us into getting involved."

"You don't care that I'd have become evil?"

"The League could have prevented it without our help. A voice from the sky might have told Sebastian, 'That thing beside you isn't Rosalind.' Or the League could have gone to the Sparks. If the League had warned Mind-Lord Priest what was waiting for him at the winter anchorage, Jode could have been stopped right there. But instead, they left Priest in ignorance. So Priest died, Rosalind died, my friends died . . ."

I stopped. The Lucifer-Rosalind had her head cocked to one side as if she were listening to something. But the cage seemed very silent—the great black mound had stopped its rustling, leaving only the sounds of Annah's soft breathing and my own heartbeat. At last the Lucifer in Rosalind's form lifted her eyes to meet mine. "That was the League," she whispered.

"Speaking to you?"

She nodded. "They say . . . they don't interfere as much as you think. They can't. They think there's a chance some human will do something—they won't say what—but something that will solve a problem . . . answer a question . . . they think some member of your race may someday provide a bit of knowledge that even the League doesn't have. The creatures of the League are too locked into their own perceptions to see some . . . something . . . they suspect there's something they're not seeing, but they're blinded by their very omniscience. And *Homo sapiens* are at just the right intelligence level: a bit above animals, but not so smart that you genuinely comprehend . . . you haven't developed a truly logical view of the universe, so you're more open to stumbling on . . ."

I waited for her to finish her sentence. When she didn't, I said, "You mean if we were any smarter, we'd see the world in a consistent and rational way . . . which would prevent us from tripping over whatever the League is after."

"That's it," the Lucifer-Rosalind agreed. "And that's why the League hates tampering with your kind. They don't want to push you in any particular direction. They're afraid of imposing their own biases. So they changed Earth into a venue where your species would have ample freedom to do any-thing—*anything*. The only time the League gets involved is when something threatens *Homo sapiens* so severely that it endangers . . . whatever it is you have the potential to do."

"And one such threat is an evil Lucifer being loosed upon the world."

"Exactly. The League *had* to prevent that—but as unob-trusively as possible. Heavy-handed interference like voices from the sky or direct warnings might ruin everything they hope for."

"But not prophecies or hauntings?"

The Lucifer-Rosalind shrugged. "They don't want to tell humans what to do. They don't want to *direct* you. They oc-casionally have to catch your attention; but they never inter-fere with your choices." She laid a hand on my arm. "Everyone who died made a conscious choice. Gretchen chose to leave the prison of her house, pursuing a new life as a sorceress. Myoko chose to abandon her pretense of weak-ness and use her powers at full strength. Oberon chose to throw himself on Xavier. Pelinor chose to be the one who faced Jode. Need I go on?"

"None of them chose to die."

"But they knew they were taking risks. Some risks were more obvious than others . . . but your friends knew the risks were there."

"And Rosalind?" I asked. "Did she know she was taking a risk? How could she possibly realize her boyfriend was a killer in disguise?"

"She knew elopement was a risk. Marriage. Love. Sex. Not to mention the risks of angering her mother, and running off to Niagara where she might run afoul of her mother's en-emies. But Rosalind chose her path willingly—joyously—and if the result wasn't what she expected, that's just the human condition. Your species has a severely limited ability to foresee the consequences of your actions; and if some more advanced species can tell what's going to happen, you invariably think you're being manipulated . . . when really you're just being predictable."

"Thanks so much," I muttered.

"Don't be upset," the Lucifer-Rosalind said. "It's precisely your lack of foresight that makes you valuable to the League. Smarter creatures always pursue their goals in the best way they know how—terribly boring! But you humans are mostly blind to the future, no matter how much you believe you're taking precautions. That's why someday, you might accidentally . . ."

She stopped. "I've said enough. And now it's time for me to whisper in Sebastian's ear."

The creature walked past Annah and me, a placid smile still on her borrowed Rosalind face. She knelt beside the boy; she began to talk softly to him, touching his cheek, caressing his hair. There was no way to tell, but perhaps she was also linking with Sebastian's mind, showing him the same things she showed me. Now that the boy had no nanite shell sealing him off, the Lucifer could touch him directly.

Annah took me aside. "Do you really think she'll get through to him? He's seen so many false Rosalinds; another might send him over the edge."

I shrugged. "If we were on Earth, he'd use his powers to reveal the truth; then he'd probably make the impostor explode. But here, there aren't enough nanites to allow psionic tricks. Sebastian can't send this Rosalind away or make her shut up . . . so in time, I think she'll find the words to bring the boy to his senses." I paused. "After all, this Lucifer is so much smarter than us mere humans, it can say exactly what's required."

Annah didn't answer right away. Finally, she said, "Do you think that was really the truth? All that stuff about the League hoping humans will do something or discover something . . ."

"I don't know," I said. "Maybe it's just a lie to keep us happy—to make us think we're important, and that the League isn't controlling our lives. *Oh no, we aren't using you as puppets, you're too valuable to tamper with.* Or maybe it *is* the truth . . . in which case, we'll find out soon enough."

"How?"

"The Spark Lords will come for us. If the League really told the truth, they can't have us free to tell everyone else what's going on. That would spoil the experiment: ruin the naïve spontaneity that the League claims to value in the human race. So the Sparks, acting on League orders, will either kill us or conscript us . . . like War-Lord Vanessa did with Opal in the tobacco field. We're loose ends now; we have to be tied off."

Annah made a face. "I wish you hadn't said that."

"You'd rather not think about it?"

"No. Now the League *has* to kill us or conscript us; that's the only way to convince us they weren't lying."

"Sorry. Didn't think of that."

She smiled ruefully. "My Uncle Howdiri—the greatest thief in my family—always had a saying. 'Don't be a *little* paranoid; worry about everything, or let it all go.' So shut up, Phil, and let's just enjoy the Earthlight."

Obediently, I shut up.

We held hands.

We drew closer.

We enjoyed the Earthlight.

26

THE END OF THE RAINBOW

A sound caught my attention. Reluctantly, I turned from Annah and saw Sebastian standing a short distance off. He looked shockingly pale, like someone out of bed for the first time after a month-long illness; but the boy was conscious and vertical, his eyes able to focus even if they didn't quite meet my gaze.

The Rosalind look-alike was gone. A girl-sized mass of black slithered back through the dust toward the main heap of cellules. That surprised me a bit—I thought the Lucifer might have remained in Rosalind form to prod Sebastian in case he showed signs of a relapse. But maybe it was wise not to keep reminding the boy of the girl he'd loved and lost: best just to wake him and get out of the way.

Annah released her grip on me. "How are you feeling?" she asked Sebastian.

"Bad," he said. "But I'll live."

"Did the Lucifer explain everything to you?"

The boy nodded.

"You couldn't have known," I said. "There's no reason to feel bad because you were fooled by a monster."

"That's not why I feel bad." He took a quick breath. "Let's get this over with, okay?"

"You know what you're supposed to do?"

"I know what I'm *going* to do," he said. "Back to Niagara.

369

Put things right. Once the cage is working again, we can bring the Lucifer home."

Home. Interesting choice of words.

I'd tucked the <BINK>-rod into my sleeve. Now I pulled it out and held it up. "I'll go with you," I said.

"No." Sebastian gave me a hard look. "I want to do this alone."

"You *will* be doing it alone," I said, "but the first few seconds might be messy. The rod likely takes us back exactly where we started—which means the middle of the cage. If the evil Lucifer is still there . . . well, it'll take your nanite friends a moment to swoop to your rescue. I want to make sure you survive that moment."

"You think I'm just a helpless kid?"

"No," I said, looking into his angry eyes. "After everything you've been through, you aren't a kid. But you aren't a man either—not if you let stupid pride reject a reasonable offer of assistance. A true man knows when he can use help."

"Oh good," Annah said. "Then you'll let me come too. I was afraid you'd want me to stay here until you big strong males made Niagara safe for womenfolk. But if a true man knows when he can use a help . . ."

I glared at her. She returned a look of total innocence.

"Let's just go," Sebastian said. "I'm tired."

Annah put one arm around the boy's shoulders and the other around me. "If we're linked together, will we transport together?"

"Only one way to find out," I said. I raised the rod.

<BINK>

I expected we'd return to blackness—the utter absence of light that had filled the prison cavern once the laser cage stopped working. But now there were oil lamps burning near the entrance to the chamber: lamps held by eight figures in Keeper robes, shedding enough light to see the entire room.

Every last cellule had moved outside the prison cube. They must have wanted to avoid getting trapped if the lasers miraculously reactivated. A mound of them now lay heaped where Dreamsinger had fallen—probably trying to penetrate her armor's force field, or to suffocate her by sealing out fresh air. The mound was much smaller than the original Lucifer heap; the remaining mass had reshaped itself into human figures, those who were now dressed as Keepers. The false Keepers were busy assembling devices near the mouth of the cavern, contraptions of metal and plastic and electronic parts. I assumed the devices were weapons, traps to spring on the first Spark Lords who came to investigate. The components of the devices must have been produced by the evil Lucifer itself, in much the same way it created light-bulbs.

A moment after Annah, Sebastian, and I materialized, every Keeper turned our direction . . . their attention drawn by the distinctive <BINK> noise. The black mound pressing on Dreamsinger hissed sharply as if it too had noticed our arrival. The mound didn't move—if it shifted off, the Sorcery-Lord would be able to breathe again—but the Keepers by the entrance dropped what they were doing and charged at us full speed.

Their eyes were on Sebastian. They obviously realized they had only a tiny window of time to kill the boy before his powers reasserted themselves. Already, nanites in the air must have been processing Sebastian's presence; soon they would recognize him and congregate en masse to do his bidding. But not instantly—I didn't know how fast nanotech could work, but I suspected it would take several seconds to analyze the situation and summon sufficient force to provide adequate protection. Most of Sebastian's life, he'd been surrounded by an attendant nano cloud, immediately ready to do his bidding . . . but he'd left the normal plane of existence, and now that he was back, the nanites needed time to regroup.

Annah and I had to buy the boy that time.

We stepped in front of him, putting ourselves in the path of the charging Keepers. When we'd first arrived, they'd had normal human faces; but in their haste to reach us, they made no effort to control their features. Eyes and skin reverted to masses of granuled black, with here and there a maggot of white from the mutated Jode. All semblance of humanity vanished in a flash . . . and yet their writhing fleck-filled faces conveyed ferocious hatred, a lunatic hunger to splash our blood onto the cold stone.

I raised my fists the way Impervia always did when facing drunken rowdies. Beside me, Annah did the same. Our job was simple: keep the Lucifers away from Sebastian, even if we ourselves got torn apart in the process.

I wanted to tell Annah I loved her but that seemed so trite.

The Lucifers hit us like a battering ram. I managed to throw a punch in the split-second before impact . . . but my fist simply buried itself in yielding grains of sand, and then I was knocked off my feet by the sheer mass of attackers.

Two Keepers went down with me, unable to keep their balance after the tackle. We all hit the stone floor hard. I took the impact on my shoulder, slamming into the uneven rock; fortunately I was still wearing my winter coat, padded with enough eiderdown to soften the blow . . . but shoots of pain still lanced down my arm, leaving my fingers numb. The Lucifers, clad only in light robes, made more of a splash: close to my face, one of their arms literally exploded when it struck the stone, like a sandbag rupturing at the seams. The arm devolved into black grains spurting out the robe's sleeve. The splashing cellules made a raspy sound; but seconds after they burst apart they began skittering together again, trying to recoagulate into the semblance of human flesh.

More robes rushed past me as I sprawled on the floor. I lashed out wildly, hoping to trip someone; my leg caught somebody's foot but I don't know how much effect it had. The world was a chaos of robes, cellules, and pseudo-anatomy. I couldn't see either Sebastian or Annah. The Lucifers seemed as disoriented as I was—if they'd made an effort to hold me down I could have been pinned easily, but they showed no interest in doing so. Even the Keepers who'd tackled me had scrambled off, struggling toward Sebastian. *He* was their target; I was nobody, a mere distraction.

Therefore I had the freedom to claw at the creatures that crawled close beside me, with no answering attacks from the Lucifers. They were simply trying to get disentangled while I was doing everything I could to slow them down.

In the middle of all this confusion, I caught sight of Sebastian: still on his feet, but with three Keepers clutching him, one with its hands on the boy's head. It was trying to snap his neck . . . to give a sharp twist that would crack the cervical vertebrae or even rip the head clean off. Sebastian was fighting back, and perhaps a small number of nanites were helping him—resisting the pressure that torqued on his skull—but thus far, there was no overt sign of nano coming to the boy's aid. Millimeter by millimeter, Sebastian's head was turning too far; and even as I watched, one of the other Keepers sprouted a long bony claw and reached out toward the boy's exposed jugular.

A mass of black fury hurtled into the fray. For an instant, I thought it might be a chunk of the good Lucifer, <BINK>ed in from the moon. Then I saw it was . . .

Impervia.

Blood smeared her hands and the front of her clothes. I thought I could see a bullet hole pierced through her shirt high on the chest; but she was moving too fast for me to be sure.

She slammed a foot hard into the knees of the Keeper who was trying to break Sebastian's spine. Her heel drove straight through the Lucifer's legs, spraying cellules in all directions: instant amputation at the knees. The Keeper, no longer braced and supported, couldn't maintain the pressure on Sebastian's neck . . . and a moment later, the creature had to worry about its own head, as Impervia's elbow smashed into its temple.

The Lucifer's skull burst like a melon struck with a ball-peen hammer. Gunpowder grains flew in a black shower, splashing hard into the faces of the other two Keepers holding Sebastian. Considering that neither had eyes, they couldn't have been blinded by the sandy facefuls . . . but they were distracted long enough for Impervia to sweep one of the attackers off its feet and to hit the other with a palm-heel that dislocated its shoulder. Literally. The arm ripped off the torso and slumped limply, its fingers still gripping Sebastian's jacket.

I don't suppose any of Impervia's blows caused the Lucifers true pain. When you're a galaxy-spanning intelligence, a little wear and tear on your component parts can't hurt very much. But Impervia was striking hard enough to disrupt the intercellule cohesion that kept limbs attached and bodies in one piece. In other words, she was destroying the Lucifers' *effectiveness.* A detached arm has no leverage; a legless torso has no balance or mobility. The pieces were still danger-ous—lethally so if you gave them time to sprout sharp exten-sions or garroting tendrils—but Impervia was systematically eliminating their capacity to fight in human form, and they obviously needed a few seconds to reshape for other modes of combat. One of the legs Impervia had kicked off was start-ing to shove up spikes along its surface, and the other was stretching out into something like a spear. In half a minute, both might be serious threats . . . but I doubted they'd have nearly that long to do what they wanted to do.

A wind had picked up in the cavern: a brisk breeze pour-ing through the tunnel mouth, whipping at loose clothes even as we all struggled to gain the upper hand. Impervia was still on her feet, punching and kicking; Sebastian stood now with a family-built saber in his grip, slashing at the hands that tried to grab him; Annah rolled silently on the ground, wrestling at least two opponents; and on the ground beside her, I lashed at every Lucifer within reach, punching, trip-ping, anything to keep them busy . . . while all around us the wind increased, stiffening into a gale that whistled past our ears.

I tried to inhale and the air was as gritty as smoke. It rasped in my mouth and nose, leaving a bitter taste like the crushed shells of insects. Some other place and time, I might have spat it out in disgust . . . but not now. Now, it filled me with vengeful joy—the nanotech cavalry was charging to our rescue, thickening the air like dust.

Despite Impervia's best efforts, there was still a Lucifer clutching Sebastian. It grappled with the boy, trying to wrest the saber from his hand—twisting the blade around in an attempt to force the weapon's cutting edge against anything that would bleed: Sebastian's arms, his legs, his throat, whatever target was vulnerable. For a moment the Lucifer loomed over the boy, a head taller, physically imposing . . . then the alien was nothing but an exploding sandstorm, a bursting flurry of black that blew apart so fast it shredded the robes containing it. The Lucifer detonated into a smeary ash-cloud, splashing out toward the walls of the cavern.

An instant later, the other Lucifers disintegrated in exactly the same way. Black grains flew past my face and robes ripped to tatters in front of me . . . but every ruptured particle. missed me by a hair's breadth, as if a bacteria-thin barrier had sprung up to shield me from the blast.

Thank you, nanites. Thank you, Sebastian.

No sooner had the enemy been dispersed into individual cellules than they began to be gathered again: piece by piece, grain by grain, the cellules were lifted off the ground and swept toward the center of the laser cage—like errant goats being herded back into a pen. I could picture teams of nanotech goatherds entrapping each fragment, levitating it, fetching each cellule back to its designated prison.

Annah laid her hand on my arm. "Time for us to move."

We were still in the cage ourselves, both of us on the floor; as we got to our feet, Impervia joined us. Sweat beaded her face, but she looked happy—not in her usual grudging way, but with a genuine smile. "I'm not quite sure what's happening," she said, "but I think we won."

"Sebastian won," I told her. "But you helped hold out till he got reinforcements."

"Good enough. Where's the Caryatid?"

Annah was the one to answer. "The Caryatid is dead . . . but she died well. If there *is* such a thing as dying well." She paused. "We thought you were dead too."

"Don't be ridiculous," Impervia said, her face shifting

from that rare smile into a more typical look of disapproval.
"I admit I got shot, but it was just a graze. I blacked out
briefly, but I'm perfectly fine now."

I looked at the shirt of her habit. "Perfectly fine, are you?"
Now that she wasn't a blur of motion, I could see there *was* a
bullet hole straight through the cloth. I pointed it out to her.
"What do you think caused that? Moths?"

She dropped her head to look at the hole. In surprise, she
pulled out her collar and looked down inside her shirt.
"There's a wound," she said slowly, "but it's completely
healed. Nothing but a scar. Bullet-sized." She lifted her eyes
in wonderment . . . then sudden disgust crossed her face.
"It's not a miracle. It must be Sebastian's work."

I thought about that. When Impervia got shot, a geyser of
blood had come fountaining out of her; then it stopped
abruptly, as if cut off. I'd thought the stoppage was due to her
heart giving out . . . but Sebastian had still been awake at the
time, in full command of his powers. He'd also just realized
this was the real Impervia, a flesh-and-blood woman who
bled when she cut her arm.

Sebastian must have told his nanite friends, "Heal her."
Immediately nano-surgeons flocked in to seal her wounds,
repair the damage, set things right—and while she lay there
healing, she'd looked so much like a corpse that neither I nor
the Lucifer had bothered to check whether she was really
dead.

I turned toward Sebastian to ask if that's how it happened;
but the boy was englobed in a dim golden shell, an egg-
shaped container of light that pulsed like a heartbeat. Inside
the shell his eyes were closed with a look of deep concentration. I could imagine him giving telepathic commands to the
nanotech world . . . or perhaps just communing with some
nano overmind, not handing out orders but amiably discussing what should happen next.

Smash the dam. Restart the generators. Mend the cables.
Restore the laser cage.

And was he asking for more? I didn't know. Would Sebastian ask his friends to bring Rosalind back to life? Or create a

being from nano who looked and acted like Rosalind? Could he do the same for the rest of the dead: raise up doppel-gängers of Myoko, Pelinor, the Caryatid? And if that were possible, would I want it? Would I accept artificial stand-ins for my friends, even if the replacements were perfect copies? Would Sebastian accept a replica Rosalind?

Annah nudged me. "We have to get out of the cage; the lasers might start any second." I nodded and let her lead me off . . . but as I did, I couldn't help gazing at her in doubt. Was *she* real? Did the original Annah truly <BINK> to safety in time? Or did the League create a duplicate to smile and greet me once I reached the moon? And what about Imper-via? Did she really survive or was she some League simu-lacrum, sent to buy time for Sebastian?

Ridiculous things to think about. If the League wanted Annah and Impervia to survive, the universe would oblige. Annah *would* have an escape route, and she'd use it with mil-liseconds to spare. Impervia's wounds would heal at exactly the right speed for her to recover and charge in like an aveng-ing angel. There'd be no need for artificial replacements.

And yet . . .

I looked at Annah again. She smiled back, but there was questioning in her eyes, as if she wondered why I was staring at her so oddly. "It's nothing," I said. "It's nothing."

With a crackle and hum, the lasers pulsed on. Sebastian re-mained in the cage, still surrounded by his shell of golden light. Several seconds passed, then <BINK> . . . and suddenly, there were twice as many cellules within the prison cube. The saintly Lucifer had returned from the moon. With no vis-ible hesitation, all the black grains flowed together into a sin-gle heap—the formerly evil cellules instantly converted by the force of the angel's mind.

"And there we go," I said. "Mission accomplished."

"*Quest* accomplished," Impervia corrected. "But there'll be more quests to come."

"Why do you say that?"

She nodded toward the mouth of the cavern. Two figures

had appeared in the entrance, lit by lamps left behind by the Lucifer-Keepers. One of them wore green plastic armor, similar in style to Dreamsinger's but not endowed with female appurtenances; it had to be Science-Lord Rashid, the Spark who'd passed me by in college. The other person was more familiar: Opal Quintelle, Chancellor of Feliss Academy. When she caught sight of us, she whispered to Rashid— probably telling him who we were. Then she hurried forward to greet us.

Rashid stayed behind . . . maybe getting ready to shoot us if we turned out to be Lucifers in teachers' clothing.

"Sorry we didn't get here sooner," Opal said. "The High Lord decreed that Dreamsinger had to handle this mess on her own. I think he was following a request from . . . higher up. Anyway, we had to wait till it was over." She smiled apologetically. "But you're alive. That's wonderful."

"*We're* alive," Impervia answered. "The others weren't so blessed."

Opal dropped her gaze. She had the good sense not to recite that inane phrase of hers about being expendable—Impervia might have punched her. After a moment, Opal lifted her eyes again. "What about Dreamsinger?"

"We haven't checked on her yet," I said. "Last I saw, the evil Lucifer was still trying to smother her. I suppose that's a good sign—if the Lucifer had actually killed Dreamsinger, it would have gone on to other things."

"Where is she?"

I gestured to the rear of the laser cage. From where we were standing near the chamber entrance, I couldn't see the Sorcery-Lord's unconscious form. Opal couldn't see either; she tried for a moment, then waved to Lord Rashid. "Your sister is around at the back. They think she might be alive."

Rashid nodded but didn't move. He was still staring at us; I suspect he was scanning us with devices in his armor, making sure we were actually human.

"What's going to happen now?" Annah asked.

"I discussed that with Rashid on our way here." She glanced at the Science-Lord as if asking permission to speak; he made no sign one way or another, so Opal continued.

"Rashid thinks it might be best if everyone went to Spark Royal for a while."

Impervia's eyes narrowed. "How long a while?"

"That depends." Opal gave a sheepish look. "You're lucky Dreamsinger isn't on her feet—she'd probably just kill you. But Rashid is sane . . . and inclined to be softhearted when there's no need for ruthlessness."

"Can't this Rashid speak for himself?" Impervia asked.

A chuckle came from the green armor. "Of course I can," the Science-Lord said. "But I thought I'd go with the strong silent act. My family thinks I should be more imposing."

He came forward with a light step, removing his helmet as he did. When he'd visited the Collegium Ismaili, Rashid had never taken the helmet off; now I saw why. Judging by his face (with a droopy mustache and Asian features, framed by long black hair), I guessed he was at least five years younger than me . . . which meant he must have been Sebastian's age when I was in university. Wise of him to remain a mysterious armored figure back then—if he'd shown he was just a teenager, he'd have received far less respect from us "sophisticated" twenty-year-olds.

Now a full-grown adult, Rashid gave a placating smile. "I'm not here to drag you off kicking and screaming . . . nor do I make a habit of killing people to keep them quiet. If you promised not to divulge the true purpose of this power plant, I'd be inclined to let you go. But," he said, glancing at Sebastian (who still glowed in an aura of light within the laser cage), "there's the boy to consider. We can't let someone that powerful run loose—not when he's only sixteen. The world is full of unprincipled people and someone's bound to trick or seduce him into things we'd all regret. So Spark Royal wants Sebastian under its wing till he can be trusted not to cause trouble."

"You mean you want to enslave him?" Impervia asked.

"Don't be ridiculous. Why would we antagonize someone so powerful? If we tried to put Sebastian in chains, he'd hate us for it; even if we succeeded in locking him up, we'd have to expend a great deal of effort keeping him quiet, after which he'd probably escape anyway and become a dangerous enemy. So what's the point? I won't pretend that Sparks are too noble to imprison an innocent boy, but why provoke needless hostility? We want Sebastian on our side as a willing ally. That's where you come in."

He looked at us expectantly. Impervia bristled, but Annah only returned the look. "You want us to persuade Sebastian to do what you want?"

"Not quite. I want you to be Sebastian's chaperons. His *teachers*." Rashid smiled. "You'll come to Spark Royal where you'll help the boy gain maturity . . . and of course, my fellow Lords and I will provide any assistance you ask for. You and Sebastian will be respected guests—no bars on your windows, no locks on your doors, no obedience spells, no blackmail. Opal tells me you're talented people. That's good; we always have jobs for talented people."

"In other words," Impervia said, "you intend to use us."

"Exactly," Rashid answered with a grin. "Don't you want to be used? Damned near everyone longs for something meaningful to do—a reason to get out of bed, a justification for living. This is your chance: not just looking after Sebastian but helping Spark Royal keep the planet from falling apart. I admit we Lords aren't saints; we're ruthless bastards and we always play dirty. If you agree to work for us, half the time you won't know the purpose of your duties . . . and when we do explain, we might not be telling the truth. But that's the real world, folks: not quests, but strategic missions. And I promise, you'll always be able to say no."

"How much are your promises worth?" Impervia asked.

Rashid laughed. "I break promises as easily as I break wind, but only when it makes sense. It's seldom sensible to betray a useful colleague . . . and that's what I hope you'll be."

"Impervia," Opal said, "if you work for the Sparks, you'll truly make a difference. And they do let you say no. They won't coerce you into assignments you hate, because they know your heart won't be in it."

"And of course," Rashid added, looking straight at Impervia, "your first assignment will be to look after Sebastian.

Surely a Handmaid of the Magdalene would have no qualms about that. Helping mold the character of a powerful psychic? Teaching him right from wrong? Need I point out that if you don't do it, someone else will?"

Impervia's eyes narrowed . . . but the ghost of a smile played about her lips. "Lord Rashid, you have the serpentine voice of worldly temptation. However, if I were allowed to consult about this with my Mother Superior . . ."

"Do you think your Mother Superior will refuse a chance to win favor with Spark Royal? Not to mention you'll be in a position to obtain useful inside information and to influence Spark decisions for the greater glory of your Holy Magdalene. But if you really think you need to talk to your boss, I'll arrange it." He turned toward Annah and me. "As for you two . . . Opal tells me you're a scientist, Dhubhai. It so happens I need a personal assistant; my last one didn't work out. Would you like the job? You'll learn more in two weeks with me than you would in twenty years at your precious academy."

"Uhh . . ." I looked toward Annah.

"Oh, Ms. Khan can help too." He smiled at Annah. "Opal says you're musical. Do you happen to play violin? I love the violin. In fact, I have an uncanny fondness for male and female assistants who know science and play the violin." He gave a sly look at Opal, then turned back quickly to us. "Ignore me—I'll explain some other time. The question is, are you interested?"

I looked at Annah. She returned the look and shrugged. The shrug turned into a smile—a *lovely* smile.

Impervia gave a loud sniff. "Stop that," she said. "If I have to go to Spark Royal, you both do too. Do you think I want to drink tea alone on Friday nights?"

I whispered to Rashid, "Do you have bar brawls in Spark Royal?"

"Not *in* Spark Royal," he said. "But when you work for the Sparks, you'll get plunged into brawls all over the world. I pretty well guarantee it."

I winked at Impervia. She gave another loud sniff.

Annah put her hand in mine and kissed me on the cheek. "We can do this," she said softly. "What is there for us back at the school?"

"Nothing," I answered. Not Myoko or Pelinor or the Caryatid. Not Gretchen either. I'd cry for them in the days to come; but the past must yield to the future.

The future was Spark Royal, Lord Rashid, and Annah. I smiled at her.

"Oh for heaven's sake," Impervia groaned. "Just kiss each other and be done with it!"

Laughing, Annah and I kissed . . . but I hoped we'd never be done with it, ever.